THE LUCIFER KEY

BOOKS BY THE AUTHOR

PROTEGE

THE LUCIFER KEY

```
I=1 TO. I= 1 TO 48,
J=1 TO J= 1 TO 48,
I,J,1)K=I+J; IF K> 48
X(I,J,1)+I;

TO 48;
TO 48;
RANDOM
=X(K,J,
ND:END:
I=1 TO 48,
J=1 TO 48,
ODE(I,J)=SUBSTR(
(X(I,J,1),
```

THE LUCIFER KEY

A NOVEL

MALCOLM MacPHERSON

E. P. DUTTON • NEW YORK

Published in the United States by Elsevier-Dutton Publishing Co., Inc.,
2 Park Avenue, New York, N.Y. 10016

Library of Congress Cataloging in Publication Data
MacPherson, Malcolm.
    The Lucifer key.
    I. Title.
PS3563.A3254L8   813'.54   80-27914
ISBN: 0-525-14985-6

Published simultaneously in Canada by
Clarke, Irwin & Company Limited, Toronto and Vancouver

Designed by The Etheredges

10 9 8 7 6 5 4 3 2 1

First Edition

For
David Auchincloss
Michael G. Conroy

THE LUCIFER KEY

PROLOGUE

"We weren't remotely close to World War III."

—THOMAS B. ROSS,
*Assistant Secretary of Defense,
after a Systems
Command computer
failure June 3, 1980;
reported in the
New York Times.*

Vasily Domintrin, the Soviet Union's foremost computer scientist and member of the First Directorate of the KGB, stared at the preset lines of digital imagery on the screen. Within that single spread function—Pixel i to Scan i-1—the modified IBS-57 computer would determine his fate and, more importantly, the future of computer science in the Soviet Union.

The underground control center of the Vladimir Komarov Test Range, with its breathless quiet, moderate temperature and clean, well-lit telemetry panels might have been located anywhere. Its yard-thick concrete casing isolated it from the Krasnoselkpusk plain above, a frozen, treeless wasteland broken only by the River Taz. Far to the west rose the bluish Ural foothills and beyond, Moscow, the capital city from which Domintrin had ventured by helicopter late in the morning of the same day. All those years, he thought, all the pure research, the massive effort of his fellow scientists—all that to arrive at this single point in time.

In the background of the control center, the voice of a technician came through the speaker in a monotonous drone, "We will lift off from a hard site."

The SS-18 Mod I ICBM rocket huddled in the sheath of its silo nearby downrange. The heavy, concrete lid rolled back on the immense castors as liquid propellant was forced into the stainless tanks. The umbilicals were disconnected, and the countdown began.

"Thirty seconds. The lid is back; we are topping up. . . ."

The atmosphere inside the room turned electric.

". . . Lift-off," the launch technician announced, his voice a determined flat and impersonal tone. "It looks okay," another faceless voice said over Domintrin's shoulder.

Domintrin's eyes were glued on the digital images on the screen facing the telemetry consoles. Radar antennas from below and satellites from above bounced electronic signals off the metallic skin of the SS-18, charting its trajectory through the ever-thinning air. The preset parabola and the red blip of the digital image signifying the missile's progress met as one on the screen. The red signal remained well within the guidance parameters of Pixel and Scan. The IBS-57 onboard guidance computer had cleared its first hurdle. Good, thought Domintrin, balling his fists.

The digital clock on the wall read −5.71 from launch.

Make it succeed, Domintrin shouted to himself. "Come on," he hissed between clenched teeth.

"Suborbit . . . orbit," the launch controller announced.

The red blip on the screen reached the apogee on the preset parabola. Now the missile was about to enter the critical deceleration-shift phase of the Fractional Orbital Bombardment System (FOBS)—against which the United States' defenses in time of war would be helpless—the phase where the IBS-57 onboard computer would finally prove itself, or fail.

Domintrin hugged himself, almost willing the tons of metal, tubing, wiring, ceramic and plastic to respond to the computer's commands for the shift into FOBS orbit. He watched the blip as the deceleration began.

"Now!" Domintrin yelled.

As though a bubble in a glass tube, the red blip of the SS-18 slowly started to veer off the preset course, separating from the FOBS trajectory at an angle of forty-five degrees, then sixty, then—it was correcting itself!—lower to fifty-five. The IBS-57 was working. The guidance controls had misread the instructions and turned the missile off course, but the computer had read the error and automatically compensated, bringing the missile back on course. It was going to work!

"Get down!" Domintrin hissed.

There was no way now to tell whether the guidance controls or the computer were in error. Domintrin knew that the computer would be blamed, no matter what. The missile now seemed to waver in space. In response to what? Domintrin asked himself. Faulty controls or an error in the programming? Then the missile seemed to make its final decision, and Domintrin knew instantly that the computer had resigned. There was no better way to express it. The computer had stopped thinking.

The SS-18 now flew mindlessly into ultra-atmospheric orbit.

Seventy-five degrees . . .

"ABORT . . . ABORT," the controller commanded, lifting the black safety covers on the detonation switches.

The red blip of the SS-18 disappeared from the screen without a sound. The only noise in the control room was a whimper from the throat of Vasily Domintrin.

Colonel Alexi Borznoi dusted his fingernails on the lapel of his cashmere jacket as the "Fasten Seat Belt" sign lighted on the forward bulkhead of the Eastern Airlines 727 in its final approach to Logan International Airport. A nervous flier, Borznoi cinched the belt around his middle and looked out the window onto the dull gray waters of Boston Harbor, trying to gauge the aircraft's angle of descent. Although essentially a fruitless exercise, it nevertheless gave him the illusion of control. Borznoi was not afraid of death. But he disliked the anonymity of death in an exploding airliner.

Seconds later, the Boeing thumped onto the runway and quickly reversed thrust, then taxied to a gate. Borznoi, among the first passengers to deplane, carried with him his briefcase and a small overnighter with a fresh suit and change of shirt. He strode past the luggage bays on the lower level and outside into the clean spring air to a cab rank, where he gave his destination to the first driver. If this were the Soviet Union, he thought, climbing into the rear seat, he would still be waiting in an endless queue. Borznoi had no objection to stringent regulations for other people, the ones the State watched constantly, like the rebellious Ukrainians, but he detested being counted among the herd himself.

As the cab headed toward the Sumner Tunnel in light traffic, Borznoi reflected on how middle age had brought with it certain dependencies. One was routine, a daily and predictable pattern. He felt unsettled more and more when he traveled from Washington, away from the Soviet Embassy. He made the best of it, though, and didn't complain. He compensated with small things. As another man might carry a photograph of his wife and children, Borznoi brought along one of his Fabergés. He displayed it for an audience of one on the dresser of any hotel he visited. It was a touch of home. On this trip he had packed the cobalt-blue one with the delicate and detailed drawing of a troika of bay horses pulling a sleigh through Moscow's snowy streets. In the sleigh two laughing Czarists were bundled warmly in thick wolf-skin rugs. Borznoi yearned for those simpler, class-ruled years— the years before Scorched Earth entered the code lexicon of the First Directorate, KGB.

The taxi maneuvered past the ziggurat of the City Hall and shot up into Park Street. To their right Boston Common was in full bloom of spring. He looked up toward the State House building. Just below its steps stood the monument to black soldiers who had fought in the American Civil War.

The doorman at the Ritz-Carlton helped Borznoi out, politely informing him that he would settle with the cab driver. Borznoi walked through the revolving doors and across the thick carpet to the reception desk, where a uniformed employee gave him a smile. Borznoi registered under the name of Egon Lymer; profession, art dealer. With brisk efficiency, he was escorted to his room by a bellhop, who unlocked the door, then opened the draw curtains and turned on the air conditioner. After inspecting the bathroom, he gave Borznoi a courteous bow and disappeared. Minutes later, another bellhop delivered his suitcase, setting it on the luggage stand. Then turning to Borznoi, he asked, "May I lay out your suits, sir?"

Borznoi shook his head and tipped the young man. Once he had departed, Borznoi unfastened the latches on the suitcase and tenderly removed the Fabergé, placing it in the middle of the desk blotter. He looked at it once again. No matter how many thousands of times he had examined the egg, its beauty gave him pleasure. He removed his necktie and unbuttoned his shirt, running the tip of his finger along the rose-colored scar in the middle of his chest. It had been carved by a surgeon's scalpel in the Moscow clinic four years ago after the coronary occlusion that had taken him home to Moscow on emergency medical leave. The surgery had been successful, but he would live with the tiny stainless-steel pacemaker embedded in his chest for the rest of his life. He barely thought about it anymore, though he recalled, now looking again at the Fabergé, that he had bought the egg in celebration of renewed life.

Putting on a clean shirt, he checked the time, realizing he must hurry if he was not to miss his appointment. He knotted his necktie and put on his jacket, then went out the door.

A gentle breeze stirred the leaves in the maples in Boston Garden, across the street from the Ritz. Borznoi checked traffic and walked across, his nostrils catching the perfume of flowers arranged neatly in their beds. There were few people in the Garden at this hour, and as he traversed Charles Street into the Common itself, he saw to his satisfaction that the same was true here. He walked along the path that led diagonally up to the State House. Minutes later, he approached the bas-relief Civil War monument.

A group of schoolchildren passed in single file behind their teacher. After their laughter had faded, an attractive woman in her twenties, with auburn hair and green eyes, approached the monument. Borznoi smiled as she set up an easel and produced a palette for oil paints from a wooden box. In different circumstances, he would have talked with her about her art. Instead, he folded his arms and examined the nails on his right hand.

Soon, a lone man limped toward him. Borznoi looked up, then away. The man carried a thistle walking stick, and wore a tam-o'-shanter pulled down to his ears. Without looking, Borznoi could hear the approach of the tapping stick and the scrape of the shoe on the man's lame leg. As the man passed Borznoi on the narrow walk, the man dropped a leather glove, then continued on his way.

"Sir, your glove," Borznoi said in perfectly unaccented English, spoken like an American. He stopped to pick it up in both hands. Examining it carefully, he then reached into his coat pocket.

The man turned with a tired expression. He looked at the glove, then at Borznoi. "You must be mistaken," he said. "It isn't mine."

"But I saw you drop it."

"You're mistaken, sir. I don't wear gloves."

The girl glanced up from the easel and gave them a bemused look. First the Anglophile had dropped the glove, now he was denying it was his. She shook her head. The elaborate exchange sounded to her like some prearranged signal between homosexuals.

Borznoi walked up to the man and handed him the glove. Then, without a word of acknowledgment, they started along the path back in the direction of the hotel. The girl followed them with her eyes. She was right, she thought: a couple of old poofs.

As they walked, Borznoi anxiously assessed his man. The limp was genuine. He was about fifty. His mode of dress—the tam, the Highlander's walking stick, the heavy, ill-cut Harris tweed jacket, the lumpy knot of the wool tie—all fit the description he had been provided with. The man, obviously nervous, was licking his lips. He wheezed when he breathed, and probably suffered from a lung ailment. Every few steps, he coughed and spat on the grass. No, there was no mistaking this ailing academic, thought Borznoi. His code name was Data Code Red; his real name: Dr. Arthur Gellitsen. Borznoi had been given a complete background on this man.

Gellitsen was an embittered mathematics professor from MIT. He had had his moment of glory in the fifties, but since that time the honors—and the most prestigious teaching chairs—had eluded him. The last straw had come only three years earlier, when he was ultimately passed over for the coveted Lionel Professorship. This position had been held open for him for many years—in 1958, as a man of barely thirty, he had been on the verge of receiving it. The appointment board had decided he was too young then, but promised him that sooner or later he would get it. For over two decades they had not filled the chair; then, three years ago, they had given it to a man who was only twenty-two. Discouraged and desperate, Gellitsen had retreated into academic oblivion; somehow, in a fuzzy process of thought, he had salvaged his pride by passing secrets to the Russians stolen from the Labs' data banks.

When they came abreast of a wooden bench Borznoi extended his arm, and they sat down, facing into the warm rays of the early-afternoon sun. For several minutes, they neither spoke nor looked at one other. To all appearances, the two could have been harmless middle-aged men on a coffee break. Gellitsen handed Borznoi a piece of paper. "That contains the name and address," he said, then with a cough, he slowly started to rise.

"One minute, please," Borznoi said tensely.

Wearily, Gellitsen resumed his seat. "That's all I was told to give you."

Borznoi fixed his eyes on the paper. "I'll need more than this," he said.

Gellitsen stared straight ahead, beads of perspiration forming on his lip and forehead. This was the first time in three years that he had had direct contact. To face an agent of the KGB, a flesh-and-blood character, confused his thinking, embarrassed him. He wanted to get away.

"First of all," Borznoi spoke in a tone above a whisper, "how is he to be approached?"

"Directly," Gellitsen replied instantly. "But you are not to mention your affiliation. He has what you need. He'll cooperate, so long as you concede to his ideals and his sense of personal mission. I told him that you will contact him." He turned to Borznoi. "I thought you knew."

The Russian didn't reply immediately. "I was told only to meet with you. Nothing else."

Gellitsen took the paper from Borznoi's hand, and then with a pen he wrote quickly: "You are to identify yourself by this name. Last employed by the National Security Agency. He's been told."

"One last thing," Borznoi said, pausing. "What if I need leverage?"

Gellitsen stared at him, his lips tense. "What are you asking that for?"

"A weakness, a pressure point," Borznoi said, his voice tinged with impatience.

"It's my understanding that you are to move at his pace. If you push him, he'll run. The man is no traitor." He paused, reflecting bitterly on his own status, then said, "Yes, he has a weakness. A woman. He calls her Eagle."

"Eagle?"

"Not a code, but a pet name. We Americans are fond of pet names."

"And her real name?" Of all the amateurishness, thought

Borznoi. What use was a name uttered across a pillow? If the woman was his lover, he might never get to her.

"If I knew, I would have said. I don't play games. You can remind your people, there will be a speech given at the Labs. As a consequence, I expect security to tighten. For the foreseeable future, contact between us will be too dangerous."

Borznoi crossed his legs and looked away, toward Boston Garden. He noticed the swan boats gracefully navigating the pond. "You can go," he said.

Gellitsen stood up. As a means of communicating a dignity he did not truly feel, he put on the left-hand glove, working the soft leather with his fingers. "Thank you," he said, putting on the glove that he had dropped. As he did, his eyes narrowed suddenly, then opened wide in surprise. "Ouch," he yelped, pulling his hand from the glove. He examined his middle finger and sucked at a tiny blossom of blood. There was confusion in his eyes as he abruptly turned and walked away, leaving Borznoi alone on the bench, concealing a grin.

SUNDAY,
JUNE 14, 1987

". . . the espionage connection is a reality. Many senior executives doubt that it is widespread—until they realize that they have been victimized. Sometimes victims never know they have been 'had.' "

LEONARD I. KRAUSS *and*
AILEEN MACGAHAN,
Computer Fraud and
Countermeasures

4:00 P.M., *EDT: Marblehead, Massachusetts*

Below the abandoned lighthouse on a promontory a few hundred yards from the Eastern Yacht Club stood the nursing home, surrounded by manicured lawns and topiary gardens that sloped down to the harbor, which in this spring season was clogged with small sailing boats being outfitted for the summer racing season. Across the busy harbor the town of Marblehead, once the center of America's boatwright trade, appeared as quaint, serene and unchanging as ever.

The Wainwright Home had once been the estate of John Alexander Goodwin, the ship-building magnate who dominated the industry during its heyday in the middle of the nineteenth century. The main dwelling was a large and rambling stone building with mansard roof, somber brown clapboards and ornate window shutters. In the garden by the harbor stood a folly that Goodwin had called his "pride" and that present-day tourists visited for its beautiful wood-carved, whale-hunting scenes.

By architectural standards the house was superb, and by nursing home standards it was equally distinguished. Its sixty-eight exclusive "guests" paid $175 a day for the privilege of rest, quiet and unsurpassed medical attention. No one had ever thought to complain about the cost because the permanent physicians cultivated the bedside manner of Cary Grant, the nurses were solicitous to the degree of saintliness and meals would have rated a star in a gourmet guide. The medical and care facilities, naturally, were as advanced as anywhere in the world.

Nothing at Wainwright was left to chance. Fate ultimately took its toll, but not first without a severe test of wills with Wainwright's staff. Patients with coronary disease often seemed mere extensions of body surveillance equipment, scans, EKG and digital blood-pressure readouts and computer-vigilant sensors. Several patients, who lay in what should have been the final days and weeks of life, were sheltered from the terminal ravages of carcinoma and respiratory ailments by artificial means. At Wainwright the right to life, even if artificial, was sacrosanct.

This afternoon, in one of the private rooms off the central monitoring station, Claudette Louise Rousseau lay on her back, watching the ceiling above her. A spidery, frail woman in her midfifties, she had the dry, ascetic look of a figure in an American gothic painting. The creases of her mouth and at the corners of her eyes drooped in a permanent expression of disapproval. Three years ago Claudette had been paralyzed with a stroke. Although she had retained her faculties of speech and could move her head freely, the remainder of her body was frozen. Despite her condition, she had carried on with her single ambition—her son, who continued to be the reason for her life. Had it not been for him, she might have let death overwhelm her three years before. Now Claudette lived only to watch and guide him through to the success he was assured.

At this moment she was staring at the hairline crack in the ceiling, as she did every day about this hour. When she was first admitted to Wainwright, the tiny fissure had been only a fraction of an inch long. Now it had expanded to more than a foot. The crack had become her calendar, a measure of time more appropriate to her physical predicament than seasons and clocks and dates. Last year when the Home had hired painters to redecorate the rooms in soothing pastels, they asked Mrs. Rousseau what color she wanted. She had replied sharply, "None at all." The room needed painting, insisted the staff. No, she argued, leave the room as it is! They had called her eccentric, but went along: The room remained white, and the exposed crack continued its journey.

Claudette played a game with herself, judging the distance it had yet to travel before joining the wall against the head of her bed. She wondered if she would outlive it; she wanted to, for Stark.

A nurse in a starched uniform walked briskly into the room. Margaret Lindstrom, a powerful young woman with fleshy arms and solid legs, was more efficient than the other day nurses but less courteous. She said a curt good afternoon and placed a tray on the service table. She took a brush and ran it through Claudette's graying, thin hair. "Would you like a bit of makeup, Mrs. Rousseau?" she asked. Claudette shook her head no. "Well, we'd better finish getting ready."

She left the room and returned within minutes pushing a wheelchair, which she positioned and locked beside the bed. Then she pulled down the sheets. Claudette's legs were like yellowed sticks and the patient avoided looking at them, arching her head backward into the pillow. Lindstrom slipped one arm under Claudette's knees, the other behind her shoulders and lifted her gently from the bed, depositing her in the wheelchair. Claudette said nothing while the nurse removed the sleeping smock and replaced it with a cotton shirt, over which she placed a sweater. Last, Lindstrom carefully tucked a blanket around Claudette's abdomen and thighs and put on socks and slippers.

Lindstrom examined a computer punch card on the tray that indicated precise dosages of medications for each patient. She checked that the pills in the small paper cup were what the punch card had prescribed, then placed them one at a time on Claudette's tongue, giving her sips of water from a glass with which to wash them down. "Good girl," Lindstrom purred.

A young man appeared at the door and stood silent as the nurse medicated the older woman. He stared intently at the scene, as though searching for an answer to a question nobody had even thought to pose. He was tall and thin, with a frame that had not filled out even by this, his twenty-fifth year. He had a handsome, boyish face with dark eyebrows, alert brown eyes, a fine nose that was charmingly small against the high cheekbones and a mouth that somehow balanced the sensuous with the severe. His hair was yellow-brown and swept thoughtlessly back from his temples, making him look younger still. At his side on a leash, a black Labrador retriever puppy whipped at the air with his tail.

Nurse Lindstrom turned, nearly bumping into the young man. "Oh . . . !" she exclaimed in a girlish, startled voice. "Mr. *Rousseau* . . . you scared me!" She composed herself with a self-conscious brush of her hand through her blond hair, then turned to Claudette. "We're all ready for your visit, aren't we, Mrs. Rousseau?"

Claudette bristled. Nurse Lindstrom always called him "mister" when she knew that he was a doctor. The annoyance quickly passed, however, as Claudette looked at her son with eagerness. She checked to see that he was well and fit. "You look like you're taking care of yourself," she said, half questioning.

Stark smiled, "How are *you*, Mother?" he asked.

The exchange between them was formal, almost cold, belying their love and emotional dependence. That bond was never expressed. There were no soft touches, no kisses or reassuring embraces. They had nothing against intimacy. Yet physical displays of affection were not part of Claudette's character, not even toward her husband when he was alive.

"I *could* use some fresh air," she replied, darting a glance at Nurse Lindstrom.

Their habit was that in winter Stark would "walk" her through the sheltered enclosures, and, on balmy early summer days like today, he would push her wheelchair along the paths among the greenery in the fresh salt air. Together now with the puppy tagging behind, they went past the folly, onto the promontory. The sun felt warm on their faces, and the breeze ruffled their hair gently. For that moment each was comfortable in private thoughts.

Claudette had given birth to Stark and raised him, but not as a normal mother might. Stark had been her experiment, and she had tested him as a boy again and again to determine his limits. She ignored those qualities that made him like other children. Now, looking at him, she was glad that her parental focus had been singular. Stark was different because he was the only child of Claudette Louise Rousseau. He was her obsession.

She hoped that he knew how much she loved him, that it had all been for his good. He had turned out well beyond her wildest imaginings. He possessed the strength now to achieve mastery on his own. True, she wondered sometimes about his loneliness. He rarely spoke of friends and colleagues and never about women; but those would come, she felt certain. For the moment their absence in his life was an acceptable price to pay for what he had already achieved.

Stark set the parking brake on the chair, then came around with his back to the harbor and adjusted the blanket on her knees. "Are you comfortable, Mother?" he asked.

"It's slightly chilly," she said. "But it'll be all right."

She always complained like that. She inhabited a middle ground where nothing was ever completely right and nothing was ever completely wrong—a reflection, really, of her paralysis. She always found flaws in him that still, even as an adult, spurred him to try harder, do better, accomplish more. He did not think about it often and he harbored no resentment. She was now all that he had. Certainly there had been his father, whose memory he cherished, but he had died when Stark was ten, at about the time when Claudette had started to make her demands felt. From that day forward, he had strived to satisfy her wishes and even more, to please the ghost of his father.

"How is . . . what do you call him?" Claudette asked.

Stark reached down and patted the Labrador's head. "Bart. He's okay—aren't you, pal?" The dog, which he had bought from a pet shop four months ago, jumped against his leg, begging affection. Stark laughed, for he loved the openness of the little creature. Everything was new and wonderful to the pup in this first springtime of his life, from the smell of grass to the wind and the rain. "I tried to teach him the other day about birds," Stark said. "It's supposed to be instinctive with Labs, but not Bart. He took one look at the swans and tucked his tail and ran. Some retriever!"

A breath of wind blew in Claudette's face as she stared across the water. "What *are* they doing over there?" she asked, annoyed.

Across the harbor near the Hood Sail building, a launch towed a yacht with a cherry-red hull toward a pier. A large crowd gathered to see the sleek boat. Cheers and applause drifted across the water. The boat—a twelve-meter model—had been selected to

defend the America's Cup against a British challenger that summer. She had sailed into Marblehead for a week of refitting and
testing.

"It's a racing yacht, Mother, named *Sceptre,*" Stark said.

"Well, they surely make a to-do about it."

He explained about the America's Cup. *"Sceptre* cannot
lose," he concluded.

"You sound pretty certain," she remarked, wondering if he
knew anything about it. Yachts were the playthings of rich and
frivolous people, "the Newport Set," as she called them. She had
not toiled at the Veterans' Administration office all those years in
Shrewsbury to provide Stark with an education to have him now
start frittering his time with that sort of people.

"Oh, I am very certain. The Labs computed the hydrody-
namic equations for *Sceptre's* hull. Against what I've seen of the
British, she's a sure bet."

"And you helped?" Claudette asked anxiously.

Stark laughed just a little. "I wasn't asked," he replied.

Claudette turned her eyes from the pier and stared at him.
"Why on earth not?"

"Because, Mother, I wasn't. Anyway, I've been preparing
for the symposium tomorrow. . . ." His voice trailed off. He had
mentioned the symposium earlier to Claudette, but he had talked
about his research only in broad outline. Not that the symposium
was a secret. Nearly everybody at the Beeman Labs was talking
about it expectantly. At long last computer security was going to
be examined in hard, factual terms, and specific dangers and solutions discussed. Stark had concentrated hard on his assignment,
and it had led him into unusual areas of computer research. Some
of what he was discovering actually frightened him. Given that,
he thought it prudent not to discuss the symposium, with Claudette or with anybody else.

Claudette did not press him to explain. She understood—
she was actually thrilled by the thought—that much of his work
at the Labs was classified. Stark had already accomplished so
much. She knew the research he had completed in satellite design,

guidance systems, artificial intelligence and hybrid programs. Often, she could barely understand the terminology. But that did not matter. She attached a mystical significance to the computers that Stark had mastered. Computer science was an unfathomable religion to her, presided over by high priests like her son, in temples called laboratories. That Stark was the preeminent computer scientist in America was enough for her.

"I brought a tape," he said, changing the subject. He produced a minicassette recorder from his pocket. Together, they shared a deep but different appreciation of music. Stark enjoyed its mathematical precision, while her imagination took flight in operatic stories and romantic crescendos of sound. The cassette tapes were an important part of their weekly ritual, one that Claudette had grown to expect.

"I hope you didn't bring that . . . that electronic foolishness," she said, recalling the horrible sounds of last week's symphony, something, Stark had explained, based on the Tibetan *Book of the Dead.*

"Musique concrète," he said. Pierre Boulez was a favorite composer of his, and he had hoped that she would like it. She had talked all through the long piece and finally, before it ended, asked him to turn it off.

Now he pressed the "play" button on the recorder and adjusted the volume. The long first strains of the prelude sounded deep and rich.

Claudette looked at him, irritated that she did not recognize the piece immediately. She could not put her finger on it.

"Parsifal," he said.

"I know that," she replied sharply.

"Do you remember the story?" he asked, knowing she didn't.

"Of course . . ."

"About a man who searches for the Holy Grail . . ."

"Oh yes."

They listened in silence for nearly a quarter hour. Suddenly she asked, "It *is* important *this* time, isn't it?"

"Yes," he replied earnestly.

Claudette was impressed. She pressed for more information. "What's so special this time?"

"Because, Mother, there have been incidents lately that bother me. They are calling into question the integrity of the computer."

"I haven't heard," she said. "What is it?"

"Oh . . . little things," he said, "but they add up. It began with little incidents of fraud and theft. Stealing money is bad enough, but now they're able to steal information—important, confidential information. Mother, it's come to the point today where one in ten people now has contact with computers. Computer bank robberies, computer stock and bond frauds are becoming commonplace. Then there are thousands of defense secrets, all on disk files."

"Why, that's just horrible," she said, her mouth a small oval.

Stark shook his head. "Not horrible enough to convince people that existing security is inadequate. In light of our vulnerability and the incessant threats, what we have is plain suicide." He shrugged. "People won't look at facts."

"And you're going to show them?"

He gazed into the distance. "I don't know," he said. "Maybe . . ."

Stark caught a glimpse of something, back toward the nursing home. Frowning, he turned off the tape recorder.

"What is it?" Claudette asked.

"The nurse," he replied, glancing at his watch. They had been on the promontory for forty-five minutes.

Nurse Lindstrom took a direct line to them, skirting the folly. Clipboard in hand, she panted for breath as she approached. "Whew," she inhaled. "I'm awfully sorry, Mr. Rousseau," she said, a slight blush coloring her face. "We'll have to bring your mother in."

"I don't understand," Stark said. They always had the whole hour together, uninterrupted.

The nurse stammered and the coloring in her face darkened. "It was my fault," she said, examining the clipboard.

"What was?" he asked impatiently now.

"The head nurse is on my back, and so is the duty doctor. The new computer instruction has your mother scheduled for another treatment at four-thirty. I hope *you* understand." She looked at him, and could sense that he would cooperate. "Can you bring her up in five minutes or so?"

Stark sacrificed to keep Claudette in Wainwright. A sizable chunk of his salary went for her care, and to make ends meet he even had taken on consulting work for the Pentagon. He wanted value for his money, and that meant quality treatment and efficiency. But Stark could not get angry at Lindstrom. The girl had been reprimanded enough without his joining in. After all, the treatment was for Claudette's own good. The computer-dictated radiation treatment was designed to heal, over a period of time, the destroyed nerve fiber that caused her paralysis. The process was experimental and revolutionary and sometimes required unorthodox treatment or erratic scheduling. The computer diagnosed Claudette's vital signs and monitored the drug dosages. It must have detected some alteration in the nervous system and ordered a crash treatment in response. The doctors at Wainwright were enthusiastic about the technology, and they held out hope for Claudette, but only if she followed the computer's orders down to the last detail, whether or not they made apparent sense. In his private thoughts, Stark had resisted the idea of his mother's being used as a guinea pig. Still, there was a *chance,* no matter *how slim,* that it might work a miracle. "Of course," he said now to Nurse Lindstrom, "I'll wheel her right in."

"Land's sake, they're too efficient around here for anybody's good," Claudette remarked once the nurse had gone. "When they make some silly mistake, they go into a tizzy. Especially *her.*"

"She means well, Mother," he soothed, and turned her chair around.

Back inside the Home, they were met by an anxious Nurse

Lindstrom, who took over the wheelchair and briskly pushed it down a long corridor to the treatment wing. It was here, among the monitors and machines, that the Home had made its name. Wainwright was not satisfied to have patients languish until they died. Staff doctors considered any patient who was not discharged a personal failure.

Nurse Lindstrom turned back to Stark and asked, "Would you care to watch?"

"Certainly," replied Stark. He had always liked to look on, and on occasion he had even discussed the program of the dosage computer with the doctor in charge. "While you get her ready," he said to Lindstrom, "I'll put Bart here in the car."

Lindstrom smiled and pushed Claudette into the radiation room, a small space with white walls shielded by lead. As the nurse positioned her patient, Dr. DeAngelis entered the room and settled in at the computer console. He began to calibrate the equipment. Designed by Imperial Industries in Britain, the radiation scanner worked in tandem with an IBM 3033 computer. After its installation, technicians from Imperial and IBM had worked with the home staff to familiarize them with its complexities. Dr. DeAngelis now inserted a computer tape under the hasp. The tape fed the precise instructions for Claudette into the computer, which in turn commanded the scanner.

Lindstrom lifted Claudette from the wheelchair. Gently, the nurse placed the fragile older woman on a Stryker rack, a cot supported by aluminum tubing on a track. At the computer's command, the Stryker would slide along the track into the radiation oval. Lindstrom cinched the straps firmly around Claudette. These held her stable as the Stryker rotated a full 360 degrees. In effect Claudette had been placed on a sort of barbecue spit, where the radiation constituted the "flames." Lindstrom looked into the oval—in some ways it resembled the mandible of a huge insect. She glanced back at her patient. Claudette was staring stoically at the ceiling, not one bit afraid.

"I'm ready when you are," Lindstrom said to the doctor, who finished punching in the instructions. "Comfortable?" Lindstrom asked Claudette, brushing a wisp of gray hair from her patient's forehead.

"Ummmm," she murmured in reply. "Tell my son I want him to wait."

Lindstrom nodded, then followed the doctor from the radiation chamber, carefully closing the heavy, lead-lined door behind them. Stark had already returned from the parking lot and was standing at the observation window.

"How's she doing?" he asked the doctor.

DeAngelis gave a half grin. "It's her age, really," he said to Stark. "The nerves may not regenerate. If she were younger, my guess is she'd be on crutches by now."

"Has there been any progress at all?"

The doctor shook his head. "None, I'm afraid. But we'll keep trying."

All three hushed as the computer ordered the Stryker into the mandible. Then Stark asked, "Does the radiation have any side effects?"

"It may make her cranky," DeAngelis quipped, more at Nurse Lindstrom than at Stark, who remained impassive before the scene.

The Stryker was now inside the ring of the mandible. Lights shone on Claudette's head and she blinked, apparently from boredom. The radiation pulsed from cones fixed like teeth on the mandible's upper jaw. As the Stryker rotated a quarter turn, Claudette looked at Stark through the window and managed a weak, twisted smile. He returned a reassuring wink and raised his thumb in a "go ahead" sign.

"She looks almost as though she likes it," he said.

"It doesn't hurt, you know," the doctor replied. "But I'll wager she'd rather be talking to you out on the promontory."

"Can I take her back out, after?"

Lindstrom looked at the doctor, who smiled. "If she still feels like it," she said solicitously.

Stark gave his full attention to what was happening in the chamber. Claudette was upside down now, her stomach facing the bottom ring of the oval. Suddenly, something moved. Stark blinked hard, then looked over at Dr. DeAngelis. "Did you see that?" Stark asked.

DeAngelis pushed his face against the window. "What?"

"I thought I saw her move," Stark said excitedly.

"That's really not possible at this stage," DeAngelis said. "You were mistaken."

Stark looked back through the window. "I'm certain of it," he said. "Her hand, watch it."

But now DeAngelis gave Stark a patronizing look and raised his eyebrows: " 'I suppose anything is possible,' you'll say."

"I mean it," repeated Stark.

DeAngelis, too, noticed the movement. "This is impossible," he said, removing his glasses and wiping them on his sleeve to clean them. "No person, especially not an older woman, can regain the use of a limb so quickly. Not after full paralysis!"

Lindstrom gasped. "My God, I don't believe it," she said.

But there was no doubt of it now. Dr. DeAngelis could see it as plainly as his fist. Claudette's right hand had moved. She was flapping it in a waving motion—a controlled, willed motion. There was nothing spastic or uncoordinated about it. DeAngelis looked at Stark. "This should not be happening," he said.

Stark smiled broadly. "But it is, Doctor. It really is."

"On numerous occasions, programmers have conducted formal and informal projects aimed at testing the security of operating systems by penetration—by writing programs that obtain access to information without authorization. . . . In each case the result has been total success for the penetrators."

STEVEN B. LIBNER,
Mitre Corrporation

LIEUTENANT COLONEL ROGER R. SCHELL,
Computer Security Specialist
Command and Management Systems Division
United States Air Force

1:27 A.M., *EDT: Yorktown, New York*

The IBM tower was bathed in floodlight. A Jeep moved from the shadows of the building along an asphalt road to a twelve-foot-high hurricane fence on the perimeter of the grounds. The Jeep contained two uniformed security guards, hired by IBM from a private protection agency in nearby Yorktown. Since no one had ever tried to penetrate the grounds, security was lax as a matter of course.

Inside the Jeep Harry Verdeen removed his hand from the wheel, pushed the channel button for a country-and-western station beamed from New York City and sang along with Waylon Jennings. Although he was born and raised in the Bronx, where he lived with his wife, Ruth, and two children, Verdeen was a hillbilly of the mind. He had started developing his rough-country manners about ten years ago, and tentatively at first; by now, however, he was truly a cryptocowboy. Off duty and out of uniform, he wore Tony Lama boots and a flamboyant hat with pheasant feathers in its band. He chewed Skol, drank Wild Turkey, spoke of " 'coon hunts" and "jumpin' mules" and his favorite phrase for the failure, whether of nations, presidents or his family, was, "Boy, he's stepped on his ol' dick this time." Dolly Parton was his vision of the goddess Venus, and he wished she were singing now—except he didn't really mind Waylon Jennings either.

Horace, his partner, a young black man from the Brownsville section of Brooklyn, was reading *Of Time and the River* by the light of the glove compartment. Horace marveled that someone as young as Thomas Wolfe, who had died at the age of thirty-eight, generated such a book. It was as though Thomas Wolfe was *born* old, he thought. Horace read slowly, the way his professor at NYU had taught him, not for the story but for the richness of the words. Absent-mindedly he reached up with his left hand and pushed the channel button for a New York classical music station, WNYC.

Verdeen stopped singing in midsyllable. "Hey, Horace, you know ah don't like that classic shit."

"But I do," Horace replied without turning from his book.

"Man, fuckin' lace underpants, what that is. Beer-lee-oz don't hold no candle to Hoyt Axton. Remember the deal we made."

Horace looked up and grinned. For all Verdeen's bravado and foolishness, he was a good partner. They were friends, and they had helped one another out over the years. Most recently Verdeen had loaned Horace a hundred dollars to buy books for the supplementary syllabus in his American literature course. Because Horace was younger and a bachelor, he had become an added part of Verdeen's family, often spending weekends at their house, baby-sitting sometimes as though he were the older brother to Verdeen's children. Despite the difference in their ages, their relationship was equal, and Horace gave as good as he got. "I remember very well," he replied now. "Fifteen minutes of noise, fifteen minutes of music, but your time gets cut in half when you sing along."

"You didn't say that afore," Verdeen complained. "Train don't switch once she's left the station."

"This one did."

"Man, you're a real cunt, what you are, but I like you all the same. Here," Verdeen said, reaching for the pint of Southern Comfort pressed between his thighs. "Swig?"

Horace usually didn't drink on duty. IBM laid down strict rules against it, and Horace didn't have much taste for hard stuff anyway. Still, it was only a few minutes before the next shift, so he took the bottle and tilted it gently to his lips. It tasted like children's cough syrup, but it warmed his stomach all the same. "Thanks," he said, resuming his reading.

Verdeen turned the Jeep, and the headlights scanned the fence and the woods beyond. "I think I got it figured out," he said cryptically. Horace grunted, and guessed what was coming.

"You know the steampipes they got steamin' up all over the city in winter?"

Horace grunted once again.

"You know, you seen the stacks and chimneys they got all over the streets, shootin' up swirly stuff like somesort o' witches' pot?"

Actually, Horace had to acknowledge to himself, this looked like a pretty interesting theory.

Verdeen was a sort of amateur, back-seat detective. Every time news of a murder or a spectacular jewel heist splashed its way onto the front page of the *New York Post*, Verdeen was off and running with his own calculations and deductions. He gathered background information from other sources, sometimes going so far as calling up crime reporters on the dailies or making inquiries directly with the police. Verdeen's passion for solving crimes intrigued Horace, and it was a way to pass the time. Verdeen spent weeks figuring the angles of a favorite case, until he had solved the crime to his satisfaction. Horace had to admit that Verdeen's conjecture often turned out to be right. In some ways Horace never understood why Verdeen was content to sit out his life as a security guard—he was sure he could have made his mark as a detective, either on his own or joining the police. Horace had suggested as much to his partner, but Verdeen had replied that he was too old now to work his way up from nothing.

The series of murders Verdeen was referring to had stumped the police for years, though it had inspired such catch-phrases as the "singing slayer" and "the musical murders." The first victim had been a violinist in the Metropolitan Opera orchestra, who had been found naked and bound in the bottom of an air shaft at the Met. She had disappeared during an intermission. The second victim, an opera singer, was found dead in her apartment across from Lincoln Center. A few months later, a stage technician was found, strangled to death in a tangle of lighting cords. Although there had been no new victims in over a year, the murders had resulted in a wave of security precautions, and all performers still dreaded the reappearance of the criminal. Horace went into the city to the Met often, and had kept Verdeen posted on the case. The police had lost hope of finding the killer.

"It's those steampipes, I'm tellin' ya. He's livin' in the steampipes under the opera house. I knew I'd find the answer!"

As if to celebrate his solving of the crime, Verdeen took a long swig from his bottle. "Sure is some good shit, Comfort is," he said, coughing. He rolled down the window and spat, put the bottle between his legs and reached up to the dashboard for a pinch of Skol, which he tucked between his gum and cheek. Apparently his crime-solving was over for the night, because he lapsed into silence.

"Horace, ever wonder what them bulb brains do in there?" Verdeen said suddenly sometime later. The building they guarded was the Research and Development Center of IBM, the temple of innovation for the most powerful computer company. Most truly advanced research was done at universities like MIT and Stanford, but within the commercial field, this building housed the outer edge of technical development.

"It's way beyond me," Horace replied. "But like their advertisements say, 'Bringing the Future to You Today—Through Computers.' " He laughed. Neither knew much about computers, but having circled the building night after night brought them to mind, and sometimes they had arguments about them. Horace respected the machines because they were making everybody's life easier. He could no longer imagine life without computers. Verdeen, he knew, thought differently.

"Uh-*huh!*" Verdeen said. "Some fuckin' future when you bitch about a bill being wrong and somebody says, 'It can't be, *sir,* the computer is never wrong.' That just burns my ass, and you know why? People are *nothin'* anymore."

"They'd be less than nothing without them," Horace offered.

Verdeen started to sing in a high-pitched voice, "Give me the simple waaaays. . . . Give me the looong, slow daaaays. . . ."

"They weren't so great. If you ever had to live them, you'd hate it."

"I'd take my chances any day. I mean, shit, what in Hades are we guardin' but a bunch of machines that go whirrrr put together by them pansies that work in there? Man, the way they look at me sometimes, you'd think their shit smelled like ice cream. Who *do* they think they *are?*"

"Brilliant."

"Ah, fuck 'em, brilliant." Verdeen twisted in the seat and put his .38 Smith and Wesson on the floor of the Jeep. The pistol's weight and the stiff leather of the holster made him uncomfortable. "Brilliant gets us hydrogen bombs and death rays and junk like that. Don't do me no good. Hell, no. It makes me scared. A few less brilliant people and we wouldn't be so near extinction!" He stopped talking as their Jeep pulled abreast a white box on a pole between the asphalt perimeter road and the fence. This was one of the fifteen stations on the grounds in which they inserted their security clocks; this system had been set up to provide evidence that the guards did not simply go to sleep all night long. "You gonna punch or me?" Verdeen asked.

"I'll flip you," Horace said.

"That's what you always say, and I always lose. Okay."

Horace pulled a quarter from his pocket, flipped it in the air, caught it in his palm and slapped it on the back of his other hand.

"Heads," Verdeen said.

Horace removed his covering hand. "Damn," he said, "you got lucky for once." He reached for the door handle, then got out, dragging the punch clock across the seat by the leather strap. He walked to the box, and with a key from his belt he turned the lock and opened the door, then inserted the probe.

His routine accomplished, Horace swung the strap over his shoulder and moved to the fence to urinate. While he was zipping up, he thought he heard a noise in the dark on the opposite side of the fence. He bent closer to see, but his eyes were not yet adjusted to the dark. He replayed the sound in his mind. It was not that of an animal scurrying away; more like something heavy being dragged over the ground. "Hey," he said in a normal voice. "Who's out there?" The sound changed to the rustling of underbrush, then stopped. Again Horace stood in complete silence. Cautiously he drew his revolver and pointed it at the shadows. "Verdeen!" he yelled over his shoulder. "Come over here!"

"What the fuck," said Verdeen, lowering the window fully. "Quit dickin' around, Horace, and get on back here."

Horace didn't reply.

"Horace?" Verdeen could not see his partner. "Horace?" he said again. When no answer came the second time, Verdeen sighed and picked up the .38 off the floor. He tumbled out the Jeep door and walked in the direction of the punch box where he had last seen Horace. As Verdeen's eyes focused, he caught Horace's outline against the fence. "There you are. What's wrong?"

Horace turned around. "Something's in there, right over there." He pointed with the barrel of his pistol. "It was a noise."

"Did you bring a flashlight?" asked Verdeen.

"Forgot it."

Verdeen kicked the ground and snorted. What happened on the other side of the fence was none of their business. "For all the books you read, you're sure a dumb bastard. More'n likely a little ol' squirrel."

"It was not," Horace said, wondering now if he wasn't making an issue of nothing but wind in the trees. "I think it was a person."

"Or a ghost, most likely. If I know you—" Verdeen stopped in midbreath.

"Hear it?" Horace asked.

"Yeah," said Verdeen, suddenly interested. Anything to break the boredom, he thought. Even a squirrel. Abruptly he broke the silence: "Hey, motherfucka, come out or I'll shoot your ass off!"

The sound stopped.

"A 'coon," Verdeen announced, then, "Can't you tell a 'coon when you hear one?" But he was not certain. Verdeen leaned toward the fence shoulder to shoulder with Horace. There! He saw a shape move, maybe a figure. He couldn't tell. He started to yell, "A 'coon, a 'coon!" Verdeen laughed excitedly.

"If you're right, that's a man-sized raccoon out there," Horace said. Nervousness tinged his voice.

" 'Coon pie. Man, we gonna have us a 'coon pie!" He exploded the .38 into the shadow.

As the concussion of the shot reverberated in their ears, a reply came from the dark side of the fence. There were two shots. The first tore the padding in Verdeen's coat, grazing his shoulder enough to spin him away from Horace. Almost instantaneously another shot sounded in the night. This one entered Horace's temple and splattered out the opposite side of his head, killing him at once.

11:30 A.M., *EDT: Boston, Massachusetts*

The *idiots.* This was supposed to be a private booking, thought Merrill Thornton Fox with annoyance as she scanned the plush reception room of Seligman and Pearce, the ad agency on the eighteenth floor of the Prudential Center in the Back Bay section of Boston. Twenty or more models sat in chairs, awaiting auditions. The agency had telephoned her that morning and asked if she were free to come in for screen tests, but they had made no mention of open auditions.

Merrill recognized many of the models but acknowledged none of them as she crossed the thick carpet to the receptionist's desk, a fortress model of teak and chrome that was meant to give the impression of stability and wealth. She bent close to the ear of the secretary at the typewriter and in a moderate tone said, "Please tell *whoever* that Merrill Fox is here for an eleven-o'clock appointment."

The secretary looked up, her glazed eyes saying that she had not heard a word, and ran an eraser pencil through her brown hair. "Yes, miss," then, "if you'll take a seat with the others."

Merrill felt the models' eyes bore into her back. While she did not much care what they thought, she told herself that she ought to try to get along with them. Still, she took a seat apart from the others, who continued to look at her, then away, almost furtively. Merrill always laughed at those who called her a prima donna. She was a photographer's model, a professional. She expected others to be just as professional.

The other models viewed her with a mixture of envy and resentment. She did not need to work, they heard, and she was smart and connected; her grandfather, Douglas Thornton, the famous Douglas Thornton, had made millions in computers before he had retired and sold his company. What annoyed them most, however, was the way Merrill flaunted her nonchalance. As usual she was dressed sloppily—faded Levi's, a bright yellow blouse, a cable-knit sweater round her shoulders. Her thick blond hair was tied back with a rubber band, and her face was scrubbed clean of makeup. Why didn't she just marry a handsome North Shore banker and life happily ever after on Beacon Hill?

Merrill had slept fitfully the night before and rubbed the raw edginess from her eyes. Awaking an hour after going to sleep, she had tried to calm herself with a cup of tea. She knew well enough what was disturbing her: It was her job. Modeling, she had had to admit to herself, was a vapid profession, and hardly a road to happiness.

Merrill prided herself on her independence; she had gradùated *cum laude* from Vassar and slipped easily into the modeling business. She had another ten years before the wrinkles set in and the job disappeared, but even now the occupation left her feeling empty. Though it paid well for her body, it paid nothing for her mind. Worse than that, it earned her an image that disheartened her. According to convention, no woman with her looks could possess even a modicum of intelligence. Merrill recognized this attitude in those she met, and it made her self-protective and reserved.

She had every reason to chafe at this inaccurate image. As the granddaughter of one of the country's foremost intellectuals and inventors, she had been raised at the knees of men and women of learning; her grandfather had been the pillar of the computer community. What bothered her most, she supposed, was her feeling that she was in some ways a wastrel. As her grandfather's only descendant, she knew somewhere deep inside that she, too, could have made a contribution to science. If only she had not been sidetracked by the glamor and easy money of modeling. With her entrée at the Beeman Labs and particularly with her grandfather's influence, perhaps it was not too late for her to start anew on her abandoned path: Merrill had studied computer science and had sufficient training in the subject to try for a master's degree. She needed only the final conviction to make the leap, and that was what nagged her. She wondered truly if she had the courage . . .

Merrill heard the door open and looked up expectantly, then away, sooner avoiding the girl who came out. Donna Evans was not to be deterred, however, and she came over with a cheerful "Hi!" Merrill grunted a reply, but Donna did not seem to notice. An obsequious and fawning woman, she had recently turned nasty behind Merrill's back. Merrill resigned herself now to a conversation. "Did you get the job?" she asked.

Donna slouched in the chair. "They want a blonde, they said. But they don't really know what they want, as usual." She frowned. "Not me, anyway."

"Too bad," Merrill said. "I was hoping to escape this cattle call."

"You shouldn't refer to it that way," said Donna testily. "These cattle calls, as you so charmingly describe them, pay for the groceries."

"Sorry," Merrill said, not feeling sorry in the least.

Donna faced Merrill. "You know, there's something I've wanted to tell you, for your own good," she said.

Merrill raised an eyebrow. "And?"

"Well, you should just try a little harder to be like the rest of us. You aren't, and it's getting you the reputation of a snob."

Merrill smiled. "Thanks, you just brightened my day."

Donna was not to be put off. "I mean it, Merrill," she said.

Merrill wondered if she should argue; the words slipped out easily. "Who gets more work?" she asked.

"Why, you do, but I sometimes wonder how. Which is part of what I'm saying. You don't look like the rest of us or talk the same or think the way we do."

"If you agree not to take it personally, Donna, I'll tell you why."

"Please do," Donna said.

"These advertising people are bombarded by ignorance. When they find one of us who can actually talk, they go nuts with delight. That's why."

Donna thought for a moment, then got up. "See you around," she said.

The telephone rang. The receptionist picked it up, listened, then said in a loud voice, "If Merrill Fox is here, you can go in now."

Beneath the models' withering stares, Merrill got up and went down the corridor to be confronted by a man with a round, firm stomach and florid face: Buddy Rice. A year earlier they had filmed a television commercial together in Peru. After the day's work, the crew had sat around in the bar of the hotel in Machu Picchu. Buddy, drunk on thin air and a quantity of *pisco,* had lurched over and invited Merrill to "the best damn fuck of her life." She had slapped him, but playfully. He was harmless, and as a friend, undrunk, she liked him. If she should ever proposition him, she knew, Buddy would run for the hills, protesting a solid, happy marriage.

She smiled at him now fondly. "Drunk any *pisco* lately?" she asked, laughing.

Buddy blushed. "God, what a hangover that was!" Rice took her by the arm and led her toward the agency's art department, explaining, "Come see my latest *oovra.* It's fantastic." He stopped in front of a story board. "Take a look at *that.*"

"What's it about?" Merrill asked, sensing his enthusiasm, but unable to tell where he was heading.

Buddy set his legs. "Alpo," he said. "Lorne Greene."

"I'm with you so far," she said, crossing her arms.

"We have one of those firehouse dogs—"

"Dalmatians."

He nodded. "A puppy, it trots up to Lorne Greene with a can of Alpo in its mouth. Lorne bends down and takes the can, then tucks the puppy under his arm. That's the opening shot. Next Lorne gives his spiel, about how meaty and nutritious the stuff is. Then the final windup. The puppy barks four times on cue. The camera pans to Lorne's face, a tight closeup, like. He says, 'See? *He* knows: A-L-P-O.' "

Merrill burst out laughing even before he finished. "Brilliant!" she exclaimed. "You'll have them eating out of your hand."

"Get it?" Buddy asked. "Woof woof woof woof—A-L-P-O? Fucking *dog* talk."

Merrill gulped for air. "I got it the first time, Buddy. And I tell you, better Lorne Greene than me."

"God, no!" Buddy said, his face turning serious. "You'd be all wrong for dog food. But you're perfect for opium."

Merrill looked at him askance. "Opium?"

"Yeah, the perfume. Real classy stuff, just like you."

Merrill gave him a bewildered look. "Then why the others?" She indicated the reception room with her hand.

Buddy shook his head. "Them? Backups. In case you cancel. Come on, follow me."

Merrill followed him into a studio, the gloom she had felt on entering the agency suddenly lifted by Buddy's foolishness. He handed her a script, which she read over rapidly, while someone from the art department turned on a videotape camera and recorder. Merrill perched on a stool in front of the camera and on cue read the lines of the commercial. She was so familiar with the routine that she needed only one take.

"That's terrific," said Buddy, signaling to the man at the camera to mark and wrap the tape. "I wish I could spend more time with you," he said, excusing himself. "But I've got to finish with that mob out there before lunch." He turned to go. "You'll be ready to travel the day after tomorrow?"

"Where's the shoot?" Merrill asked, checking her schedule mentally.

"Florida," Buddy replied. "One day down there should do it."

"Terrific," Merrill said. "I'll call tomorrow about the travel arrangements." With that, she said good-bye and left the agency. Once down on Boylston Street, she wondered what to do with the rest of the day. Chores beckoned, of course, but they could wait for another day. She looked up at the sky, clear and pale blue, and decided to walk home to her apartment on Harvard Street. It was a good long walk, but it would take her across the river and there were always things to see along Massachusetts Avenue.

Midway across the bridge, she stopped and looked out onto the stilled waters of the Charles River. A sailing class of small sloops played follow-the-leader behind their instructor, white sails gleaming in the sun. The embankment on both sides of the river was a rich green. An eight-oared racing shell of the Harvard crew swept beneath the bridge, as the coxswain rapped the boat with wooden knockers, beating out the rhythm. What a beautiful day, she thought, moving on toward Cambridge.

As she crossed Memorial Drive on the other side, a green Volvo suddenly pulled up to the curb ahead of her, then reversed and scooted back. "Which way you headed, beautiful?" said a male voice from behind the wheel.

Merrill was about to ignore him when she recognized the voice, then looking into the car, the face. It was Jim McKinnon, the husband of one of her best friends and a professor of mathematics at MIT. She smiled and said hello.

"Why don't you join us?" McKinnon offered. "I'm on my way to meet Dorothy for lunch."

Merrill did not have to think long. The McKinnons were good company. In fact, while crossing the bridge she had even thought of calling Dorothy. "What a coincidence!" Merrill exclaimed, hopping into the passenger's seat.

3:00 P.M., *EDT: Cambridge, Massachusetts*

Copious notes in hand, Stark Rousseau walked confidently down the corridor of the Beeman Labs. As he passed the long row of offices, he stopped to lay the notes on a radiator while he fastened the top button of his green-checked flannel shirt, then cinched the necktie. He looked at his reflection in the window and ran both hands through his hair. Now he was ready.

When he reached the elevators he looked back down the corridor. There was none of the usual chatter, the whispered hallway conferences, the hustling from office to office, the *hum* that characterized the Labs. Not this afternoon. Except for a few research assistants who wandered listlessly in search of a professor, the place was quiet and abandoned.

The Labs were Stark's special domain. He had helped make them a temple of pure invention with the highest reputation. Only the Stanford Research Institute in Menlo Park, California, approached the Labs for the quality of its staff, the technical sophistication of its hardware—or for its history of accomplishment. Beeman had designed advanced computer systems for the National Security Agency (the largest computer center in the world), the Central Intelligence Agency and the Pentagon. Beeman's researchers invented or refined software languages now used throughout the Western world—such as ASA FORTRAN, FORTRAN II and IV, COBOL and the algorithmic functions of ALGOL. These were all achievements of the past—which at the Labs meant last week, yesterday or only an hour ago.

Recently the Labs' pure research had concentrated in two quite different but equally provocative areas. The first was artificial intelligence—programs and systems patterned after the human mind. With the discovery of experimental heuristic designs using the LISP language, computers could now complete almost all of the problem-solving, logical processes of man. The second area was communication—in particular, methods of relaying high-speed computer data through geosynchronous satellites containing massive data-feed capacities. This was Stark's specialty.

It was a new direction for the young computer genius. Initially he had been drawn to artificial intelligence, since it seemed to represent the vanguard of computer research; but two years ago he had lost interest in artificial intelligence and decided to focus instead on the nuts and bolts of computer communication. Immediately and single-handedly he had created a new discipline. He had written the theory, and soon after the INTELSAT IVa (X) series—five balls suspended in space—had solved the problem of instantaneous signal relay, and was revolutionizing data transmission. INTELSAT had raised Stark Rousseau's reputation to national prominence: Habitually jealous colleagues now conceded that age alone now stood between him and a Nobel Prize.

For the symposium, Stark had worked as hard as he had on anything in his life, including the INTELSAT series. The results were important, he felt sure. He smiled now, recalling how Professor McKinnon had chided him a week earlier.

"Don't drive yourself so hard," McKinnon had said, peering over Stark's shoulder at the CDC 7600 (proto) on which he had been working. "It's springtime, Stark. The flowers are blooming, the Charles has thawed at long last, the grass is green. Live it up, Stark."

McKinnon's words left a certain sourness. Once again the professor was trying to force him to appreciate something that was not really in his makeup to enjoy. Stark saw no purpose to spring, though he felt he could not say as much to McKinnon. Nature was boring—infinite and therefore beyond mathematics. It could be explained in *twistors* and summarized in ridiculous formulas

$$\sqrt{2} = 1 + \frac{1}{8}\left(\frac{2}{1}\right) + \frac{1}{8^2}\left(\frac{3\times4}{1\times2}\right) + \frac{1}{8^3}\left(\frac{4\times5\times6}{1\times2\times3}\right) + \frac{1}{8^4}\left(\frac{5\times6\times7\times8}{1\times2\times3\times4}\right) + \ldots).$$

But in the end, it meant nothing, except for what poets tried to make of it, and Stark was no poet.

McKinnon had persisted. "Stark, go out and have fun. Hell, go to a party, find a girl and walk with her by the river, gaze at the stars for once, *dream.*"

Stark *did* dream, so that the dreams became his day and

dreams of those dreams his nights, but because they were dreams peopled by numbers, equations, integers, they could not be communicated to people like Jim McKinnon. They were not the dreams of happiness and fulfillment, fame and power and love. Neither florid nor excessive, they were dreams that reduced the poetic and the literary to their bare elements.

Such was Trojan Horse, the symposium's official name, based on the Greek myth that Stark recognized as a systems approach to a military problem. The Greeks invented an input, the wooden horse, and gambled that the Trojans would respond to it with superstition, thus producing an event: the opening of the city's gates. When the Trojans' defensive subsystem failed, the Greeks triumphed.

Stark Rousseau cleared these thoughts from his mind now as he rode the elevator to the basement. A few more confident steps down the corridor and he reached the door to the back of the amphitheater. He felt his heart pound when he heard the loud chatter of the symposium participants, who were in their seats and anxious for the proceedings to begin. Stark swung open the door and watched from the top level. The hum that had been absent upstairs in the Labs had moved to the amphitheater. Seated in semicircular rows of hard-backed chairs, his colleagues from the Labs talked in hushed voices. Stark recognized many of them and felt a certain comfort in their presence. Distantly, they were his friends and coworkers, and he enjoyed an odd relationship with them. They were older, some much older. After he had earned his Ph.D., they had welcomed him warmly to the labs and helped him, never considering that one so young might have posed a threat. They treated him as they might a son, and were proud of him.

Stark's eyes shifted across the amphitheater to several straight-backed men in uniform. They were the military establishment, the Systems Command and Control generals who had encouraged the development of advanced computer networks. Stark had worked with them before, and he knew their minds. They were military first, disciplined, skeptical and conservative. Still, they listened to voices outside their establishment and often acted on the advice offered. Always hesitant at first—in fact, some never did see the advantage of new ways—most soon became fanatical converts to the new technologies. It had been that way with IN-TELSAT.

Stark also noticed the men in neat, tailored suits, the executives who headed the multibillion-dollar computer industry. He knew them too. More adventuresome than their military counterparts, they were toughened by vicious competition.

To the right and left of the podium were two closed-circuit television cameras manned by MIT's technicians. To the left and nearer the podium, a computer terminal and Video Display Tube (VDT) were reminders of the purpose of Trojan Horse.

Last of all, Stark's eye caught a flash of bright yellow in the right-middle of the auditorium. Focusing, he could make out a blond girl of extraordinary beauty who sat with arms folded in self-contained repose. Next to her he saw a familiar face—that of Jim McKinnon. At that moment McKinnon himself caught Stark's glance, and McKinnon waved. It was an encouraging, friendly gesture, and Stark appreciated it.

Dr. Walter Regan, the Nobel Laureate director of the Labs, also noticed Stark as the young professor settled into his back-row seat. Regan glanced down at his wristwatch, then made a circular motion to the television technician in the front row. A stooped man in his seventies with a wild shock of gray hair, Regan was a beloved figure at the Labs for his fairness and his wry sense of humor.

"Gentlemen," he said into the microphone in a husky voice. He waited for the audience to stop talking. When the room was finally quiet he continued, "Welcome to the first session of this three-day symposium, which we have fancifully chosen to name Trojan Horse. I am sure that by the end of the presentation, however, you will agree that the subject is far from fanciful.

"Today," he said, suddenly turning serious, "the computer is endangered by oversight and by omission. And while none of us really knows the extent of the danger, security is a subject that *demands* our immediate attention. In the coming days, some of you here will deliver papers. I will not influence your thinking in advance, but I will preconclude with one thought: I have read most of the papers, yours and those written by my colleagues here at the Labs. When the whole is put together from the sum of its parts, you will see that we are faced with a potentially disastrous situation—to wit, the loss of computers to our society through increased penetration. Penetration—the invasion of computer systems—has become a widespread phenomenon, as you know. Until recently, however, penetration has been contained within acceptable parameters. But as more and more people familiarize themselves with systems, the problem has become greater. As a result, we may in the near future arrive at a juncture where the benefits —the enormous benefits—of the computer are outweighed by the risks. At such a point, the computer will suddenly become useless, and modern society will have lost its slave. Were that to happen, America itself would be reduced from its present dominant position to a *Fifth* World nation—one in which the base of power, the technical sophistication, was suddenly removed, leaving us in a nightmare of confusion, gentlemen, that could be equaled only by an unthinkable thermonuclear war. Yes," he said in a loud, penetrating voice, "that would be the result—a society stripped of its ability to function, to defend itself, to progress and to influence. I say 'nightmare,' and I mean nothing less. It would be as though Lucifer himself turned the key to our destruction."

A murmur of excitement ran through the audience. These men were not easily frightened, but they were aware of the gravity of recent breaks in computer security. And, Dr. Regan knew, nothing motivates people better than fear.

Dr. Regan shifted his feet and looked up the center aisle. "There is one paper I did not read," he said, combining a laugh with a cough, "because its author would not allow me to. I don't know what he will tell you, but"—he pointed a finger to the ceiling—"I doubt if we will be disappointed. As the master of ceremonies at variety shows usually remarks when introducing an act, I think we are going to start Trojan Horse with a bang:

"Dr. Stark Watson Rousseau, our Lionel Professor of Theoretical Mathematics," Dr. Regan said.

The audience rustled, anxious for a glimpse of Rousseau. The cameras panned around but, unable to spot him, they focused on Dr. Regan. Stark walked down the center aisle, and as he came within view, the audience quieted. Except for the Labs' researchers, most of the audience had never seen Dr. Stark Rousseau, but his reputation preceded him. They expected a youngish, unremarkable-looking man with a bent, undeveloped body and a large forehead. Many thought he might be prematurely balding. Stark fit none of those preconceptions; to the contrary, he was quite handsome, almost All-American in his looks.

Merrill Fox watched with curiosity as the young professor mounted the steps to the podium. She had been impressed by the audience's response. That someone who looked so young commanded such . . . such awe, she thought, was almost unbelievable. Only once before had she witnessed something similar, when her grandfather had addressed a group of scientists ten years ago at Harvard.

Stark placed his notes on the lectern, his fingers trembling lightly. He had not thought about a preamble, but now, seeing them focus on him with such bold curiosity, he wanted one. "Good afternoon," he said, then reddened around the neck. That was all he could think to say in greeting. He shrugged inwardly. He was not used to speaking before such a large group, and in any case his purpose was not to make these people think well of him.

He hesitated a second, then said: "There is an invalid combination." His voice acquired a crispness and his nervousness rapidly dissipated, replaced by purposefulness. "It is defined in the terminology of our discipline, and I quote, as 'a breach of security in the system output of an information input by a person with undesirable characteristics.' I assume that all of you have heard of it before." Certain numbers of them nodded. The term was generic and had been around as long as computers.

"I am here today to describe a specific, singular invalid combination. It is a formula, really, of complicated mathematical application. With this one formula, I or anyone else can unlock the world's most valuable vault—the vault meaning that collection of computer systems most critical to the safety, welfare and prosperity of this nation. Not just one, but all systems in quick and disastrous sequence, from the Pentagon's to the National Security Agency's. To invoke this combination means the destruction of the computer, all computers as instruments of total accuracy.

"Accuracy," he continued in a voice pitched high. "The Achilles' heel of the computer is its very accuracy. With the invocation of the combination—the formula—it becomes like a square wheel, useless and ridiculous. Billions of dollars of electronic hardware and millions of man-hours of mathematical genius are reduced to garbage."

Stark needed to convince them, but he also had to guard his thoughts closely. He had thought this through with extreme care, and he knew *exactly* how far he could safely go. He stepped down from the podium and faced the blackboard, on which in chalk he drew the rough contours of the continental United States.

"The combination consists of several parts," he continued, turning now to his audience. "But the central component is a chain of five satellites, the INTELSAT IVa (X) series, stationed in orbit at an altitude of 22,282 miles above the earth." He did not need to indulge them with how he had designed the series' data-feed components. "Their orbit is geosynchronous, and therefore they rotate at exactly the earth's speed. With a total data rate of 200 million bits per second, each INTELSAT can provide every man, woman and child in America and Canada with communication channels. But such is not their task at the present moment.

"What service are they providing? These data channels are used daily, hourly, minute by minute, by intelligence agencies, law enforcement, banks, brokerages, government departments such as Defense, the IRS, Treasury and State, oil companies, manufacturers, the electronic media and communications corporations like Bell Laboratories. They use series INTELSAT. But why INTELSAT alone? Because these are the only geosynchronous satellites above North America with advanced data-feed capacities."

Disregarding the audience, Stark went to a side table and poured himself a glass of water. He gulped it down, lubricating the dryness in his throat.

"For the benefit of the government people here today," he started again, "none of what I am saying is classified under any government department's code. The information is available. In fact, gentlemen, nothing about this is classified."

He looked at the five generals seated side by side and recognized Hedley Frank Church, the general in charge of Systems Command and Management at the Pentagon. It looked to Stark as if Church's eyes were narrowing.

Now Stark turned to the blackboard and jabbed the chalk in the center of the contour he had drawn. "This is INTELSAT's print," he said, drawing a circle that encompassed most of America. "The relay capacity of the five satellites covers this territory at a signal strength of 12/14 Ghz SBS—in other words, all except the northeastern quadrant of Montana and the whole of North Dakota, the tip of Texas and one third of southern Florida.

"Now with that as background I will turn to the combination's specifics."

As he returned to the podium, he heard a voice from the audience say, "Point of order, Dr. Regan. Please, point of order?"

Stark looked at Dr. Regan, who said, "We aren't governed by Robert's Rules here, General Church, but go ahead anyway. Please make your point."

General Hedley Church was a rotund man with a fleshy, rose-colored face, a perfect Christmastime Santa Claus. Behind that exterior, however, Stark knew, was a sharp mind and iron-willed character. Church wanted what was best for the United States; his distinctions were narrow. Inside lurked the aggressive cold warrior who viewed the Pentagon's huge computers as modern field guns with which to destroy the Soviet Union.

"It was my understanding," he began in an easy drawl, "that Trojan Horse was to discuss *prevention.* I know Dr. Rousseau and respect him, but I submit that his approach today is antithetical to our purpose."

Stark looked at Dr. Regan and asked, "May I?" Dr. Regan nodded assent. "Sir," said Stark, "prevention and cause are different sides of the same coin. I have chosen to examine the obverse, that is all. I do this because I am not convinced that anyone in high position currently takes the security question seriously."

"In all respect, Doctor, that assumption is not yours to make."

"Is it not?" Stark asked quietly.

Church heard the comment and reddened. "No, I think not. Furthermore, this *combination* of yours," he said, suggesting that he had not believed a word of it, "gives our enemies just the weapon they may be seeking. I for one would feel more comfortable if you would stop."

Church doubted him, thought Stark. The general did not believe in the combination's existence, but he was smart enough to worry that it might exist. "Have no fear, General," Stark said. "I prepared carefully. As a result, no one on earth can piece together this combination from what I will say here. Should you want, I will hand over the full details to you for safekeeping after my speech. Now may I proceed?"

Hardly mollified, Church held his objection for the moment. "All right," he said.

Merrill Fox had listened with growing interest to their exchange. Wildly unpredictable, the young genius at the podium was playing a dangerous, almost childish game, and he was succeeding. Instinctively she was drawn to his side, took his defense, although she recognized the signs of an immature intelligence. There was more, however—an almost agreeable confusion of emotions: the way he blushed on being introduced, flashed anger on being challenged, and chided the military man. She slid back in her seat, sweeping back her hair in an unconscious, feminine gesture, feeling vaguely foolish.

"As I was about to say," Stark continued, "I use a computer terminal with ground microwave links to an earth station to transmit the formula to INTELSAT. I am not talking about a complex computer hookup. The Labs have computers and an earth station adequate to the task; so do government agencies and many corporations. In the future, individuals also will have the equipment available to them.

"The object, then, is to employ all four elements—the formula, the computer, the earth station and the satellites. The effect is to mix, erase, destroy and change the data that stream through the satellites, I repeat, at a rate of 200 million bits per second, per satellite.

"So we now are ready to insert the formula, and this is where timing is crucial. You see, INTELSAT had two structural flaws. They are unavoidable if the satellites are to operate. The first is propagation delay."

He turned again to the blackboard and wrote:

$$P_r = P_t \cdot Z \frac{4 \pi \, F^2 Ar}{c^2} \cdot \left(\frac{c}{4\pi FD}\right)^2 = \frac{ZAr}{4\pi D^2} P_t$$

"This is part of the formula, where P is uplink, F is frequency, D is distance traveled and C is the velocity of light. These components, along with the remainder of the formula, are shadowed into the computer by dummy bits of data and sent through the earth station to INTELSAT; the formula lodges in the satellites' memory components. The insertion is made during the 270-millisecond propagation delay, the fraction of time for signals to reach the satellite and downlink to another, distant earth station. Once inserted during the delay, the formula can alter data assemblies streaming through the satellite—the FBI's, for instance. Therefore, what the FBI sends up to the satellite is not what comes down. Pure gold goes up, garbage comes down.

"Now the second mode of insertion," he said, again going to the blackboard and writing,

$$a_{mc} = A_c J_o \left(\frac{\Delta Fc}{Fm}\right) \sin 2\pi \, Fc + A_c J_i \left(\frac{\Delta Fc}{Fm}\right) [\sin 2\pi \, (Fc + Fm) + $$
$$- \sin\pi \, (Fc - Fm) +] + \ldots$$

"where a_{mc} is downlink, $\Delta Fc/Fm$ is modulation index, $J_o \, (\Delta Fc/Fm)$ are Bessel functions at a transponder signal of 88 Mhz, using a 4.5-meter antenna equipped with 36-Mhz transponders, angle subtended on quadrants 59.0, 0.00001, 36.5, 2.2, at 0.9 degree.

"The second mode of insertion, using this formula, can take place during periods of eclipse. INTELSAT is unavoidably prone to eclipses. When the moon's shadow passes across the satellites, their solar cells cease their operation. This event follows precise astronomical laws and occurs forty-four nights in the summer and forty-four nights in the winter. The maximum eclipses take place on the days of the solstices and last for sixty-five minutes. When the outage happens, the formula is inserted from an earth station by the computer. The effects are the same as with propagation delay: Gold up, garbage down."

The amphitheater was deathly quiet as Stark stepped down from the podium one last time and stood rigidly in front of his audience. He hesitated several minutes with his head partly bowed to the floor. When finally he spoke, everyone was alert.

"Now, to the central point of this discussion," he said in a cold, impersonal tone. "The combination hits the Achilles' heel of every system that uses INTELSAT. Hidden in the millions of bits of data streaming from the satellite is a signal, a simple signal, gentlemen, that locks into computer memories on earth. It is a trip signal, which acts undetected and at random. And what does it do? It renders the system useless."

Stark's summation was succinct: "Gentlemen, do not doubt that we are vulnerable." He paused, then said, "Thank you for your attention."

The swiftness of Stark's attack was shattering.

Some in the audience realized that their confidence had been the sham of complacence, and for several minutes they sat thinking in stunned silence. Then slowly at first, they turned to their neighbors, until the amphitheater filled with noise.

Stark looked over at Dr. Regan, who gave him a warm smile. "You sure lived up to my introduction," Dr. Regan said above the clamor, then got up and waved his hand for quiet. "We'll take a fifteen-minute recess and then I'm confident Dr. Rousseau will answer your questions."

As the television lights were dimmed and the audience got to its feet, Stark suddenly felt exhausted. He wanted to be alone.

Only Merrill Fox noticed as he walked to the small door and disappeared.

Dr. Regan called the symposium back to order. As members settled in their seats, the television lights were turned on, and Stark stood beside the Labs director on the podium.

"Now, if we're ready, are there any questions for Dr. Rousseau?" Dr. Regan asked.

Nearly every person had the same question on his lips: Is there truth to the combination? But few were willing to risk asking. To assess its validity would have required a full comprehension of Rousseau's presentation and the technical prowess to pose an accurate and flaw-provoking question. They were frustrated because they knew more about computer systems than almost anyone in the country, but they still did not know enough to challenge Rousseau's assertions.

The room was silent.

"Come, come, gentlemen," Dr. Regan chided. "I'm certain that Dr. Rousseau provoked *one* question at least." He looked at Stark and smiled. "Or perhaps he simply left you speechless. Still, if you have questions, ask them now, because you will not have another chance."

At that the Pentagon general seemed almost to explode with his challenge. *"Dr. Rousseau . . ."*

"Ah, there we have one," Dr. Regan said. "General Hedley Church, the Pentagon."

"Dr. Rousseau," he repeated, "what you said sounds very good in theory." He paused to cough. "Let me put that another way. Your so-called combination is theoretical and equally improbable. It is the stuff of thrillers, sir, but its basis in fact is highly questionable, if not outright silly. I do not doubt the theoretical potential of an invalid combination, but its P factor, its probability, is . . . is the one level of occurrence once in four hundred years. All of us here are aware that no computer system is 100 percent safe. If it were it would be unusable. But the destruction of all major systems at once is simply preposterous. Let me explain . . ."

Stark had expected this, but the general's windy defense tired him. He tried to hide his feeling of boredom, but caught himself smiling.

". . . Dr. Rousseau, you may think this amusing," the general scolded, "but some of us are here for serious purposes."

"Excuse me, sir," Stark said. "Please continue."

"I said, 'preposterous,' and I will explain why. First, before I do, I should point out that you failed to identify the objects of your subversion. There is no question that certain systems are quite unprotected. Many businesses have no reason for security, and to lock their computers would be a waste of money. Other systems do have security, mostly internal.

"But if I recall your words correctly," he went on, "you said 'all' computer systems. In that sweeping generalization, can you also mean military computers?"

"Yes, sir," Stark said.

Hedley Church had expected him to recant. When Rousseau did not, Church felt even more confident in his challenge. "I will limit myself to what I know for certain," Church went on. "The Pentagon's computers. They are 98 percent secure, Dr. Rousseau, as you well know. The Department of Defense has thrown its considerable resources into preventing internal or external intrusion. We spent millions in defense appropriations, and I myself guarantee that those millions were not wasted."

"I appreciate your efforts, General," Stark said. "But let me perhaps recall to you a passage from Phenella: 'To be ignorant of many things is expected./ To know you are ignorant of many things is the beginning of wisdom./ To know a category of things of which you are ignorant is to no longer be ignorant.' Like most people, General Church, you fit between the first and second categories."

Church blushed visibly, but held in his outrage. "You'll excuse my ignorance, Doctor, but I do not think you actually do appreciate our efforts," he said, blinking as though a speck of dust had lodged in his eye. "Because computers are integral to the defense of this country, we protect them with encrypted passwords, user identifications, audit trails." He paused for breath. "We routinely use a Vernam system of once-only keys, Geiger-Müller tubes to produce thermal noise and the most advanced devices to encipher and decipher messages. And there are precautions too highly classified to discuss in a recorded presentation." He looked directly into the television camera. "To reiterate, then, your combination in my view is a fiction. Furthermore," he said in tones that were stentorian, "I would challenge you, by any means at your disposal, to penetrate one of my command computers." He finished, and the military officer seated to his right patted him on the sleeve.

Stark had imagined that the combination would stir emotions, but he had not expected such a personal response. After several seconds, Stark remarked, "General, do you challenge me, in fact?"

"Yes, by God," the general replied.

"Of course, I cannot use the combination."

General Church smiled. He had Rousseau on the run. Rousseau's was a trickster's argument: If he tested the combination, it would create a danger; therefore, it would go untested and the idea, unchallenged.

"Using the same theoretical principle as the combination, however, I can still make my point."

Dr. Regan leaned toward Stark and cupped his hand over the microphone. "What do you have in mind?" he asked.

"Is it possible to move the symposium into the computer facility?"

Dr. Regan shook his head. "You'll have to back down, Stark," he said. "We can't get seventy-five people up there. Only a few would be able to see anyway. I'm sorry."

Stark leaned into the microphone. "I withdraw, General Church. Unfortunately, I don't have the hardware. Some other time, though." He felt foolish.

The closed-circuit television producer tentatively raised his hand.

"Yes?" Dr. Regan asked.

"I might have a solution," the producer said. "We have a minicam. It wouldn't take but a few minutes to rig it up. Dr. Rousseau could go wherever he likes, and we could show it to the audience here on the monitors."

"Is that acceptable to you, General Church?" asked Dr. Regan.

"Perfectly acceptable," he replied.

Stark asked, "Perhaps you want to invite one of your aides along, General." He laughed. "Just to guarantee that I have nothing up my sleeve."

Church nodded solemnly. "I trust you, Dr. Rousseau," he said. "But yes, I would like General Colombo here with me."

"Can I do the same?" Stark asked. He did not need anybody, of course, and Stark's colleagues would accuse him, no doubt, of obstreperous behavior, but he was in his element now and if there was any time to take a risk it was at this moment.

"I see no reason why not," Church said.

Stark looked once again into the audience, trying to locate his friend McKinnon. There he was now, Stark smiled nervously, and there was the woman beside him. For a moment Stark hesitated and started to call out his friend's name, Jim, but forced himself to blurt out instead: "The young lady in yellow—there, in the third row—would you mind?"

Nearly everyone in the room looked at Merrill Fox. Blushing, she said, "Yes, I'd love to."

After several minutes the producer returned to the amphitheater with two technicians carrying two minicams and a power pack. Stark left the podium and walked up the center aisle. "If you'll follow me, then," he said to the girl, then turned away from her shyly.

The six walked in silence to the elevators, which they rode to the third floor of the Labs, and then into the computer facility. Here was an environment that inspired no warmth: The colors of the walls and floors were as cold as a hospital's operating room. Precision-built machines hummed and whirred with a life of their own. The lighting was fluorescent, leaving no corner in shadow; everything was spotlessly clean. This place, though, was Stark's sanctum sanctorum. The data banks, terminals, consoles, disk and tape drives, video display tubes and teleprinting machines were the vassals of his domain, and the facility was the castle in which he reigned. Stark understood the systems in that room as God presumably knows His creations. They were his family, his friends, his passion, and they inspired in him affection, understanding, care and concern. He could not help but love them for what they were: logical, baffling, complicated and devoid of emotion and morality.

Stark went to the UNIVAC 1108 and drew up a chair before its typewriterlike console. The generals, flanking the unknown young woman, crowded at his shoulders, while the television men readied their gear.

"Tell me when you're set," Stark said to the minicam man.

"We're rolling now, Doctor," came the reply seconds later.

Stark took a deep breath and slowly exhaled, then closed his eyes for an instant to focus his concentration. When he finally spoke, his voice was determined. "Name the system you want penetrated, General," he said.

General Church rubbed his jowls, choosing the gallows on which Dr. Rousseau would hang himself. He had no wish to make Rousseau's task easy. "IBEX VII," he said. "The Pentagon's strategic defense computer for the target deployment of second-strike missiles." He turned to Merrill condescendingly, saying, "The targets change according to the source of the threat or attack. The computer fixes the target coordinates and relays them to our strategic missile sites."

"Aren't they all aimed at Russia?" she said.

General Church chuckled. "What if China were to attack us? Or France? Odder things have happened. We'd be in a pretty fix then, wouldn't we?"

Stark did not lift his eyes from the keyboard. "General, I'm now going to ask you a series of questions. You are not obliged to answer. In time I could get the answers myself. But for the sake of expediency, perhaps you will cooperate."

If he had to ask for the codes, the demonstration would be a farce. "Ask away," he said cheerfully.

"Is the IBEX hard-wired?" Church's answer would be crucial to Rousseau's hopes, though the young professor did not say as much. If the system were hard-wired, there would be no physical means, save for the invasion of the Pentagon itself, of penetrating. He doubted whether it was, though, because the computer had to communicate with the missile sites.

General Church savored his reply, rolling it in his mind. "You are thinking in absolutes, Dr. Rousseau," he said finally. "Perhaps part of the system is hard-wired and part not. The game is to determine which is and which isn't. But let's assume that it is not."

"Thank you," Stark said. Now his task was easier, and he had to rein in his impatience: "Will you explain hard-wired to the young lady?" he asked.

Church responded, "It is a system designed in a loop, and like any circle, it cannot be broken."

Merrill watched Stark's delicate hands softly touch the white keys. She acknowledged the military man with a nod.

"My victim, then, is the executive system employed to run—" Stark paused, then asked, "What model computer, sir?"

No harm in answering that, Church thought. "An IBM 3081 proto; it's a sixteen megabyte dyadic processor."

Stark raised one hand and lightly applied the fingertips to his temple. The IBM 3081's operating system contained six million assembler-code instructions. That complexity and depth provided the very route to invasion. He had to discover one flaw, one single flaw from six million possible flaws, while the programmers of IBEX VII had to be perfect six million times. It was too much to ask, even of the Pentagon's trained programmers. Nobody was that perfect. "I will assume encryption," Stark said more to himself than to the general. "Also, I will take into account user-identification codes and audit trails, and I will further assume that the system was modified to augment its security."

Church looked at General Colombo and grinned. Rousseau's assumptions were correct. The security existed for one reason: to catch a thief.

Stark's fingers now flew across the keyboard, lighting up the Video Display Tube (VDT) with green LED letters and numbers, as he abbreviated instructions to his UNIVAC.

```
"DO I= 1 TO 48;
DO J= 1 TO 48;
K=I+J; IF K> 48 THEN K=K—48;
X(I,J,1)+I; X(I,J,2)=MOD(I J),48);
END:END:
DO K=1 TO 48;
DO I=1 TO 48;
CALL RANDOM (S2,R); J=CEIL(R*48);
L=X(K,J,*)=X(K,I,*); X(K,I,*=L;
END:END:
DO I=1 TO 48;
DO J=1 TO 48;
ENCODE(I,J)=SUBSTR(KEY,X(I,J,1),1)
    //SUBSTR(KEY,X(I,J,2),1);
DECODE(X(I,J,1),X(I,J,2))=SUBSTR
    (ALPH,I,1)//SUBSTR(ALPH,J,1);
END:END:"
```

Stark created a "piggyback" on the communications lines, by which IBEX VII's data were fed at high speed to the missile sites.

The UNIVAC answered back, "GREPOS," on the VDT. "USE 1170(48−I)."

"Thank you, Bell Telephone Long Lines," Stark said, then to General Church, "Sir, I have telephone access to the Pentagon's facility."

Church's eyes widened as he bent over to inspect the VDT.

Rousseau was telling a truth he found hard to believe. "That's a block-switch system," he said with incredulity. "The lines are outgoing *only.*"

"What goes out can also be used to go *in,* sir," Stark said, trying without success to appear modest.

"Yes, I see." Rousseau's technical brilliance suddenly slammed home.

Now that he was inside the Pentagon, Stark still had to reach the IBM 3081. "I will talk you through the next phase," he said.

The closed-circuit cameraman backed off slightly to give those in the amphitheater a view of the two generals, Merrill and Stark.

"First I will insert a trapdoor in the logic of the system routines. I will call these routines REPs for Re-entrant Processors." Computers could not distinguish, among other things, between good and bad, right and wrong. Thus, Stark knew, a trapdoor subverted the logic system with a rapid series of unexpected requests that would produce the one flaw in six million. Stark's UNIVAC was in effect forcing the IBM 3081 to reveal itself through the exclusions in the answers to UNIVAC's questions.

"I will now introduce a BREAKER," Stark said. "It will prepare an out-of-bounds data receptacle for the victim REP. Are you with me, General?"

Church was no longer on familiar terrain, and as a military man, he knew that he was losing a tactical advantage, so he bluffed. "Certainly I am," he said, guessing that the BREAKER would erase Rousseau's tracks once he had stolen the data. He glanced at his wristwatch. Rousseau had been at work for nearly thirty minutes.

"Now for the STEALER," Stark said, then for Merrill's benefit, "That's an information request that the IBM 3081 will accept as legitimate. If it works, the STEALER will wring compliance, and in we go!"

General Colombo drew in a breath. What Rousseau was doing also was beyond his ken, but he had to acknowledge the power of the genius. Rousseau was inventing an exceedingly complex program. Colombo doubted if there was another person anywhere who could do the same. Fascinated, Colombo felt a chill of apprehension.

Working steadily, Stark was now entranced, focusing at the peak of his concentration on the parameters of the problem. He was transforming himself into pure mind: His breathing slowed, his blood pressure and body temperature lowered. "The BREAKER will change the entry point of the REP," he said. "It moves to a jump at the end of the REP. And because of the IBM 3081's memory management, a number of unused words at the end of the last block allocated to our REP should remain."

The only sound in the facility was the soft hum of the minicam. The amphitheater three floors below was also quiet as Trojan Horse's members kept their eyes glued to the television monitors. Everyone sensed that the moment had arrived. The Lionel Professor of Theoretical Mathematics was stalking his prey and about to pounce.

"The STEALER will determine for me whether there are enough free words to enter a calling sequence," Stark said, leaning into the VDT. "I want to command the BREAKER to erase traces of my call. If there isn't enough memory, I will ask the STEALER to take an error exit."

An image came to General Church of a parasite sucking nourishment from its host, then killing it before the host knew. From what he thought Rousseau was describing, the Pentagon could not detect the penetration. Church did not like it, not at all, and he wanted to stop it.

Rapidly now, Stark continued the sequence. "I have linked with the broken REP," he said. "Control of the system has passed through the calling sequence." He paused to look at the VDT. "Yes," he said with a note of triumph, "there is enough core. The STEALER has added its sequence to the BREAKER." He paused again and blinked twice, as though breaking a trance, then asked General Church, "Sir, what do you want my STEALER to do?"

Church wished desperately that he knew enough to answer. But his thoughts were confused. He guessed that Rousseau, within a time frame of forty-five minutes, had demolished the finest computer defense in America. What the doctor had done was impossible, he thought, but proof could not be ignored, just as the green LED numbers of the VDT could not be erased by force of will. Church had lost.

Stark waited for a reply. Finally, he said, "I will give you six alternatives, sir."

"Please . . ." Church said, as though staving off a physical blow.

Stark misinterpreted him. "I can produce the data on the teleprinters over there," he said, indicating a row of printers against the near wall. "Or if you prefer, I will store it on disk, over there," he said, indicating the far wall.

"That will not be necessary," Church said angrily. A demonstration was one thing, but the readout of the target data was a grave breach of national security.

Stark took no notice of him. "Here are your alternatives, General. One: I can steal the assigned user files—the target data, in other words. Two: I can destroy the assigned user files. Three: I can selectively *rewrite* the target data. Four: I can terminate the user run, which will scramble your IBEX VII. Five, I can control any device assigned to the user. And if you alter your targets, I can alter *them* instantly with predetermined changes. And six—"

Lost in the excitement of Stark's triumph, Merrill Fox let out a yell. In the amphitheater below, the audience applauded and Dr. Regan covered a smile with his hand. But the acclaim was cut short by the reddened, apoplectic expression on General Church's face. He had lost, but he was no loser.

"Your jollity is out of order," he said to the young lady in a bitter, reproachful tone. "What Dr. Rousseau has done is neither commendable nor amusing. Perhaps you do not understand. This is not a football game. He has penetrated to the core of this nation's security. A more appropriate response would be silence and fear. Dr. Rousseau should not be praised. No, he should be censured."

"Oh, come on," Merrill could hear herself say, "you're joking."

"I am *not,*" he said, reacting to her "insubordination." "And by the way, young lady, just who exactly are you?" the general growled at her. "Where is your identification badge?"

"You didn't answer me," Stark said, angered by the general's tone with the woman he had chosen at random from the audience, and anxious to keep the discussion in one direction. "Maybe you want all six alternatives. Okay?" He pressed the "print" button and a teleprinter nearby started to clatter.

Church looked at the teleprinter and suddenly was afraid. He had crawled out on a limb, then watched Dr. Rousseau saw it off. His superiors at the Defense Department would be furious. Had the demonstration been tightly restricted, it might have had a salutory effect. Church understood that major weapons in the arsenal of defense were illusion, bluff, the appearance of strength where little or none existed in fact. The illusion was important to preserve, for without it the world could see that the emperor wore fewer clothes than was conventionally thought. He would report this to the Secretary of Defense. But a report was useless, he thought. In the wake of the penetration, the Pentagon could not shut down its computers. America would be defenseless without them. All strategic missiles were computer-guided; the deployment of troops and aircraft, the collation of tactical battlefield data, supply, materiel—all computer-dependent. In bleak and terrifying terms, Church now saw, the computer was more powerful than all the hydrogen bombs in the U.S. arsenal; without computers, the missiles could not leave their silos. Church reached over Stark's shoulder and slapped his palm against the "Stop Print" button. "That's enough," he said.

"Enough?" Stark asked. "But General, you challenged *me.*"

Church hoped to preserve a shred of dignity, somehow, and he thought only to discredit Rousseau. "My mind is eased by one thought," he said. "You needed a prototype computer to do what you did."

A slogan came to Stark's mind: "Guns don't kill people; people kill people." "The mind is a computer, too," he said.

"I will repeat, a penetrator needs a computer."

"The argument doesn't wash, sir," Stark said. "Thousands of people in America have access to computers."

Church tried another tack. "Tell me honestly, then, how long in advance did you write this program?"

Stark did not grasp him. "What's your point, sir?"

"You needed several thousand man-hours of computer time to write that penetration program."

Stark shook his head mockingly. "I created it as I went, here, right now, before your very eyes, sir."

Church looked at General Colombo and jerked his head toward the door. "Thank you, Dr. Rousseau," he said, and together they left the facility. One thought burned in Church's mind: Rousseau's penetration of IBEX VII meant that the invalid combination was an unalterable reality so dangerous that the highest officials of the American government, including the President himself, could not tolerate its existence; and the palpable form of the unacceptable danger was one person, Dr. Stark Rousseau.

Stark looked at the young woman in the yellow blouse standing beside him and smiled outwardly. "Did I overdo it?" he asked.

She reached down to touch his arm, "Not at all," she said.

TUESDAY, JUNE 16, 1987

"One of the KGB's new assignments is to help close the technology gap between the Soviet Union and more advanced nations. Sometimes this calls for extreme measures."

<u>Newsweek</u>

9:43 A.M., *EDT: Manhattan, New York*

Neddie Vickers' head throbbed and his skin tingled feverishly as he reeled through the members' door on Broad Street in the New York financial district. A squat, solid man of forty, he had self-administered first aid earlier at his apartment on the Upper East Side by downing a Coke. The drink had soothed his stomach, but only time would cure his pounding head. Vickers was known at the New York Stock Exchange as a sour personality who rarely smiled and never had a nice word, and now he scowled at the coat-check woman, who saw the sweat beads on his receding hairline. She contained herself, but inside she was chuckling at his obvious distress.

Vickers entered the floor of the Big Board, thinking back to why he had drunk so much vodka the night before. It had been that sinking feeling about Susie, beginning with dinner and then after, when they went to the disco in the basement of the Sherry Netherland. Susie was not just any date. Susie Kinnard, a lovely, clear-skinned interior decorator with a sleek body and blue eyes that flashed like warning beacons . . . She was his cross to bear, and he hers. They had been a "couple" for so long that nobody remembered when they had first started dating, but their relationship had gone nowhere, except perhaps into a downward spiral of habit and convenience. To Susie, Neddie was her safety net— always there to pick up the pieces when more exciting flirtations failed, such as the affair that had just hit a dead end with the dark-browed, moody artist.

Last night had been a reunion for Susie and Neddie, one of many that had come before. This time Neddie had hoped to *seal it,* ending up for once in bed—it had been such a long time since he and Susie had managed to get that far. But as the evening went on, he had begun to despair. Watching her dance with other men, he had sat, morosely sipping his glass of Stolichnaya.

What galled him most was the fun she exuded when in the arms of others. She appeared coquettish and happy, carefree. Neddie was annoyed. He knew that she was dancing with near-strangers to anger him; perhaps it was not even conscious on her part. Susie rarely did anything consciously, but that had not helped abate his jealousy.

The Sherry Netherland disco catered to bankers and brokers, who considered it among the most select "clubs" in New York. Amid the scarlet walls, cheap furniture and common food, middle-aged men in conservative fifties-style suits pursued their prey: an equally drab collection of fading flowers. The men had less money than they let on: Their talk centered on summers in Southampton and winters in Aspen, vacations they afforded only by painful sacrifice. The atmosphere was strikingly sexless, the business of eating, drinking and dancing between men and women a ritual that would end in cold beds. But last night, Susie, who was nearly a decade younger than most of the women, had awakened the libidos of those with whom she gyrated on the dance floor. Neddie had thought about walking out, but a glimmer of wishful thinking had made him stay.

They were an Upper East Side couple, Neddie and Susie. Neither had married, since choosing a permanent mate from such a large and varied pool of available people seemed impossible. Susie's chamber of desires included a small cottage in the country with a picket fence, children, animals and a husband who came home each evening at six. But this was only one part of her dream, and she was holding out for more. Was it not possible to have quiet security and lavish grandeur at one and the same time? Susie sometimes wished that her country cottage could be as L'Hameau to Marie Antoinette—a playhouse to which she could escape from the grandeur of Versailles. Versailles, in Susie's case, meant a townhouse on Fifth Avenue, a chalet in the Rockies, and a summer home somewhere on Long Island. To give up the dream of any of these was unbearable, so she dated men who owned "Versailles" as well as men with the little country cottage. Neddie's fantasies differed little from Susie's. Eventually, exhaustion and advancing age might bring them together in a permanent union of disappointed dreams.

Last night, when they had finally arrived back at her apartment, the kiss at the door Neddie directed toward her mouth had been somehow detoured to her cheek. With that, she smiled and slithered through the door, as though she were a teen-ager on a first date, with her mother waiting by the fireside for her return.

Neddie should have gone home then, but the frustration ate at him. From his memory he chose a girl named Lora, a model and call girl with a rubber body, an acceptable price tag and an understanding nature. He had arrived at her apartment without calling first; he could tell from the rumpled pillows on the sofa and the unmade bed that he was not Lora's first guest that night. She was wearing a pink kimono, one a Japanese customer had given to her, and because she was tired and wanted to get to sleep sooner than later, she had thrown it open to reveal her large, milky breasts, long, thin legs and flat stomach. Neddie had wanted to talk first, but seeing her standing there, he had dropped his pants. They had screwed standing up, and less than five minutes later Neddie was hitching up his pants. Placing sixty dollars in cash on the coffee table, he took a taxi home.

The evening left him now with a hangover and a mouth that tasted like swamp water. Thinking again of Susie, he thought, persistence. Persistence!

Through the fog in his head he glanced up at the enunciator board. Nothing for him, and he walked to Trading Post Five. This would be a slow day. Nothing in the news, either good or bad, had happened or was anticipated. For once there were no wars, no elections, no disastrous economic reports from Washington, no assassinations or floods. It was business as usual.

Vickers thought about going out for another Coke, or maybe a cup of coffee, when he saw his number appear on the enunciator board. He went to get the order, then walked to Post Nine, where he found the seller. The order was big, very big—the purchase of fifty thousand shares of LTW. He looked at the tape.

The green printout incessantly moved from right to left, and the seller quoted his price. Despite the size of the order, the exchange was routine.

"I'll take it," Vickers announced, satisfied to buy LTW at thirty-eight dollars a share.

"Sold," the man said, sealing the purchase.

Vickers signaled with his arm for a gray-coated clerk, who scurried over and delivered the order to the "ordermats" desk where it was "locked in" to the Exchange's computer, which then handled all subsequent paperwork automatically. Feeling marginally better for the large transaction, Vickers returned to Post Five, thinking that he might call Susie.

An analyst who was standing around bored turned to Neddie and asked, "What was that about?"

Vickers had trouble keeping alert, so it took some time for his neighbor's question to register. He looked at the man. This particular colleague had helped him out on several occasions, so he felt he should give him an answer. "Institutional," Vickers explained. "Clint Hennessy is stirring the brew, that's all. Knowing him, he probably got a tip."

"Do you know anything about it?" the analyst asked, probing for inside information.

"Can't say, but if you want, I'll call him and find out." Though he had offered, Vickers knew that he would not call Clinton Hennessy; his conversations with the West Coast millionaire were infrequent and usually one-way. Hennessy generally did not want to be disturbed—unless the world was nearing an end. That order was specific. Vickers turned away from the analyst, saying, "Excuse me a minute."

The traders' telephones were located under the green quote board. He picked up the receiver and dialed, watching the quotes stream past on the board. After one ring, Susie answered. Vickers tried to sound cheerful, but his heart wasn't in it and he quickly got to the point. "Are you free tonight?" he asked. He waited for the reply, wondering what excuse she would offer *this* time. Susie did not usually lie, or not exactly; she just had her own peculiar truth.

"Yes. Why?"

His voice sounded more hopeful. "I thought we might do something—a movie, maybe a late dinner."

The whine in her voice signaled trouble. "Neddie, I'd love to, you know that. But I don't know. I thought I'd just stay home . . . and read."

"We can make it early if you want."

"It's sweet of you, but I don't think so. Maybe later in the week."

Neddie breathed into the mouthpiece, glancing idly up at the quotation board above his head. The silence persisted between them.

Susie said, "Now you're mad, aren't you? Neddie, I said last night that we can't see one another on a steady basis. Just a *little bit.* Didn't I? And if it works out, then we'll see what happens. You understand, don't you? You said you did."

Neddie wasn't listening. His eyes fixed on the LTW quote as it flashed across the green screen. He thought he must be mistaken. What he had seen simply could not be.

"Neddie?"

"Yeah, right, I heard you," he said, disgustedly, then: "Listen, I have to go."

"You *are* mad." She made the statement cheerily. "If you're going to keep getting mad like this, well, Neddie . . . We don't have any fun together anymore—"

"Susie, I'll call you tomorrow." He hung up, returning at a sprint to Post Five, where the analyst was still leaning against the counter. "What the fuck's going on?" Neddie asked, his voice strained. The analyst looked confused. Neddie did not have time to explain. He turned to the computer terminal on the counter and punched in the code for LTW. The quote came up on the VDT, the same quote he had just seen on the board: 21¼ LTW. "Holy shit," he murmured under his breath. The purchase he had just made for Clinton Hennessy should have *raised* the price of LTW stock, perhaps by half a point. Yet here the price was falling, more than sixteen points in as many minutes. Vickers had just lost a million dollars for his best and most demanding client.

"I don't believe it," he said to nobody in particular. He truly did not believe it. Such a dramatic drop in price of a stock like LTW was unheard of, unless . . . Vickers reached for a telephone, a direct line to his headquarters at Salomon Brothers. From Salomon's defense analyst, he demanded to know what was happening. "Nothing," came the reply.

"Hell there isn't," he shouted. "The stock's gone bananas, and I want to know why, right now."

"Sorry, pal," the analyst replied. "I'll see what I can see and get back to you."

As Vickers hung up, he heard a shout from the other side of the large room, then another. Rather than investigate directly, he ran to the telexes in the center of the room and bent over the Dow Jones terminal. Some major news story must just have broken, he presumed. Had a President been shot or a world war broken out, of course, or had there been a major natural disaster, bells would have sounded on the Dow telex. As it was, the machine offered nothing more exciting than the announcement of a new corporate vice president at General Motors. Vickers could not understand it.

Something more than the disastrous drop in LTW's price was happening on the floor. The level of noise signified it. Trading was becoming chaotic. Vickers turned again to the quote board. Prices—all prices—were off, and yet the trading continued. Three traders rushed up to him and pleaded for the sale of LTW at the quoted price of 21¼. Naturally, Vickers refused. One of them turned to Vickers and said, "Jesus, Fotomat just went from 9 to 125. That stock isn't worth 2."

"Something has really come unstuck," said another. "I mean, wacko." He paused a moment, then announced, "Let's take profit while we can."

Within minutes the floor of the exchange turned into bedlam, as traders shouted to buy and others, whose stocks had fallen, adamantly refused.

Suddenly the tape stopped and the green quote board went

blank. In a voice bordering on hysteria came the announcement from the floor speaker: "Trading is suspended! I repeat: Trading is suspended!"

Vickers went immediately to the traders' telephones and dialed. When a voice answered, he said simply, "Mr. Hennessy, we've got trouble, serious trouble."

12:30 P.M., *EDT: Cambridge, Massachusetts*

Douglas Thornton knew he was right for one indisputable reason: In all his seventy-three years, he had never been wrong.

That awareness now made him laugh inwardly, as he sat on the dais in the middle of the Cambridge Common, with his hands neatly folded. In front of him, out beyond the speaker's lectern, were the several thousand people, young and old, educated and ignorant, professionals, artisans and students, who had come to the pre-Commencement Day rally in the park above Harvard Square to hear his warnings. At the moment he was being introduced in a long and windy paean by the Reverend James Rhodes, the philanthropist and early supporter of the movement. Thornton viewed the assemblage with satisfaction. Ten years ago, when he had begun the International Union for the Sane Use of Computers (IUSUC), fewer than a score had turned out to hear his warnings against the headlong rush to computerize every facet of American society. His message, always the same, had taken years to catch fire, but now it had spread widely throughout the world. The fact that his movement had accomplished little besides raised awareness was not entirely relevant to Thornton. Soon, he thought, there would be dramatic action.

Douglas Thornton's appearance was as thoroughly aristocratic as the man himself. Tall and angular with a leonine head, he conveyed an overwhelming impression of self-composure and inner peace. He had always been considered unfairly handsome— unfairly because he possessed everything else besides, intelli-

gence, success, fame, money and respect. Although he did not care
what others thought about his bearing or demeanor, vanity was
not a stranger to him, particularly so as his years advanced. He
looked patrician, and knew it. He went to London to do his shop-
ping: Blade's on Savile Row cut his suits, such as the gray pin-
striped one he now wore. His shoes, lined up in the large closet
at home and burnished daily by his Irish manservant Michael,
came from Lobbs' in St. James. His shirts and neckties from Turn-
bull and Asser were as crisp and neat as everything about him,
including his mind. No wonder Douglas Thornton was a man who
still turned women's heads. His one affectation, a talisman without
which he would never think to venture from his house on Beacon
Hill, was a silver fob (gold, he believed, was for women) that held
a small silver locket etched with his initials. One end of the fob
fit in his lapel buttonhole, and the locket, which contained a photograph, a snip of blond hair and a four-leaf clover, rested behind
the pressed white, three-corner handkerchief in his breast pocket.
Altogether, Douglas Thornton, the *éminence grise* of the computer
world, looked more like a member of the English peerage than a
blueblood American who lived on Beacon Street, a stone's throw
from Boston Common.

Douglas Thornton's estimate of himself as never having
been wrong might have seemed egotistical, but in fact his accom-
plishments had always had the mark of prescience. In the early
years before the war, he had founded Thornton, Inc., later to
become Thornton Industries. Originally the manufacturers of
business machines, the company had been approached by the War
Department in 1940 to develop a digital "thinking" machine that
could establish trajectory tables for the new range of artillery that
American industry was building for other nations of the Allies,
Britain and the Soviet Union. Thornton himself had worked on the
project, and after many false starts and through trial and error, the
first computer had been born in the basement of his Beacon Hill
house. This computer was a large and cumbersome device, utiliz-
ing vacuum tubes by the hundreds and switches that, by today's
standards, were pre-Cambrian. But they worked, and what was

more, they began an industry that was to change the character of life. Thornton Industries dominated the computer market in the fifties and early sixties, until Thornton retired from the post of chairman and chief executive officer, then sold his shares and invested his resources in gold.

His retirement, brought on by an apocalyptic vision soon after the death of his wife, created the need to complete a full professional circle before he died. A final statement had to be made to preserve his singular invention on a higher, more moral plane, to protect the machines on which the country was now so completely dependent. That decision had led to the formation of IUSUC.

He had invested heavily his time, energy, thought and, not least of all, his money—vast sums for advertising, organization and paid personnel, including lobbyists in Washington, London, Paris and Tokyo. He had also quietly acquired many units of the world's most sophisticated computer and communications hardware, which he had installed in the basement of his Boston house and at his various summer retreats. He had relearned on that new hardware—much of it created since his retirement. He had relearned the gap of invention and scientific discovery. He had learned that he could do amazing, unthinkable things on those machines. He knew that he could scare the daylights out of the entire academic, business and defense communities. Furthermore, he intended to do it.

Thornton listened now with half an ear as James Rhodes, one who knew many of his secrets, continued his introduction of the movement's leader.

". . . We have nothing whatsoever against the *use* of computers," Rhodes was saying. "No one but a fool would charge that they have not improved our lives. Yet, Douglas Thornton and his organization want a *sane* use, the *thoughtful* application of digital machines. We want the computer to have *safeguards,* by law, *to be protected from those who would use them for the purposes of theft and invasions of your privacy."* Rhodes stopped again on hearing Thornton cough. Rhodes laughed nervously into the microphone, then said, "But I am poaching on the subject matter of our founder. I give you Douglas Thornton."

Thornton got up and walked flat-footed to the rostrum, smoothing the lapels of his suit jacket. He cleared his throat into the microphone, signaling the audience to shorten its applause. He began to speak. What he said was short and to the point. As he itemized the dangers involved in the present use of computers, his remarks were greeted by sustained applause. Good, he thought, they were catching on. They were ready to be mobilized. All that was needed was an example, a specific catastrophe that could be tied directly to computers—not to peripheral problems. The press was constantly missing the true cause, the computer-related cause, of so many of the world's disasters. They only saw the effects, such as the Three-Mile Island nuclear power plant disaster (a multiple computer breakdown), the latest New York blackout (another computer failure), the midair collision of two Boeing 747s over the New York Air Traffic Control Center that killed 641 people (nothing but the stoppage of control computers for routine maintenance), the grand theft a few years ago of nearly twenty million dollars from a Los Angeles insurance company (the illegal use of the company's computers).

Thornton's "catastrophe" would, he hoped, harm no one permanently or in any serious way. Money was not an important thing, he believed. People would recover. Then, afterward, they would demand more than a mere symposium on computer protection.

His speech, delivered absent-mindedly, was almost at an end. He asked his audience to petition their congressmen and senators, to force banks and businesses, local and state authorities, to examine the application of their computers. Specific instances of misuse had been identified, specific organizations targeted. This rally marked the kickoff of a week-long series of picketings, rallies, "defensive actions" and sit-downs at locations spread widely throughout the Boston area. Thornton could almost read the headlines now.

An hour later, Thornton emerged from his black Bentley. He unlatched the iron gate and went slowly up the brick walk to the steps of the townhouse, one of the oldest and best preserved on Beacon Hill. Michael, his manservant, who had been watching for him through a side window, opened the door.

Michael deValera O'Shea, a gnarled Irishman in his middle seventies, had attended to Thornton's needs for almost fifty years, ever since he had emigrated from his hometown of Derry. Michael respected Douglas Thornton as a man of greatness. Of course, there were the plaques and testimonial letters on the walls of the study that attested to Thornton's achievements, but the true bases for Michael's reverence were the machines in the basement of the house. In Michael's mind, anyone who could operate such machines had to possess greatness.

"Did the speech go well, sir?" he asked now, taking Thornton's hat.

"Wonderfully," Thornton replied. "We're making good progress," he said.

"That's good," Michael said, uncertain as ever about the organization to which Thornton devoted so much of his time and energy. Personally, Michael thought it was taking a toll on his master, who had become more withdrawn than usual, and had changed the habits of years. Thornton rose earlier now and stayed up later. Except for his daily constitutional and outings, except for speeches, Thornton and his assistant kept to themselves in the basement with the machines. So much hard work could not be healthy for a man Thornton's age. "Can I brew some tea?" Michael asked.

Thornton shook his head. Absently, he removed his coat and laid it on a chair in the hallway. "Is Dr. McColough still here?" he asked.

"He never leaves," Michael replied, wishing that Thornton's new assistant would disappear and leave them in peace. Michael suspected that the assistant's presence spurred the old man beyond the limits of endurance. "It's no good," Michael said now, wanting Thornton to know his feelings. "You and him seem hell bent on killing yourselves."

"Don't worry so, Michael," he admonished. "It'll soon be over." Within days enough "attacks" should have taken place so that the demonstrations and picketings could begin in earnest, and on a national scale. "Make some for yourself, Michael," he said fondly, adding, "and put in a dollop of whiskey, okay?" He smiled broadly and winked at the old Irishman.

"Not without you to join me," Michael said, his face sour and disapproving.

Thornton sighed. "Okay, then, bring me a cup."

Michael hobbled toward the kitchen, a smile crossing his face. Thornton went into the living room, a place that had become unfamiliar to him since his wife's death. As he looked around, seeing the furniture that she had collected with the chintz coverings, the Chinese drapes and the portraits on the wall of his daughter as a young girl and their granddaughter, he remembered fondly the times when the entire family gathered in this room at Christmas and Thanksgiving. The house then was filled with laughter and light, warmth and love. As he passed the fireplace, he glanced at the painting above the mantel. His wife had always hated it, he recalled with wry humor. She complained that a modern picture of a tropical beach was out of character. She had wanted only the children's portraits in the room. Although worth nothing, it was not a bad painting. It was the work of a native of the island, done in a primitive style that Thornton enjoyed. And he had insisted that it remain in the place of honor over the mantel.

"Here we are then," Michael announced, carrying a tray with a steaming pot, two cups and a fifth of Bushmills, which he set out on the table near the window.

Thornton sat down and Michael poured, adding a thimbleful of whiskey. He held the cup in his hand and Thornton said, "Come sit down." After a long silence, as though a forgotten thought had just come to mind, he asked, "Michael, where do you keep your money?"

Michael scratched his head, as surprise turned to mild embarrassment. It was such an odd request, he thought. Mr. Thornton knew that he was of humble means, living on the salary he made. He did not have any money to "keep," at least none to speak of. "What do you mean, sir?" he said.

Thornton was mildly impatient. "Stocks, savings accounts, like that. Do you keep them in a bank?"

Thornton should have known how preposterous the notion was to Michael, who feared the stock market after the lesson people had learned in the Depression. Anyway, stocks were for rich people. Even banks were objects of suspicion. No, Michael hid his nest egg, small though it was, in a metal box that he kept in the back of his closet, near the old shoes. "I most certainly do not, sir," he replied.

"You have *nothing* in banks?"

"No."

Thornton said in a low voice, "That's good, Michael. I wouldn't want to see you hurt."

12:35 P.M., *PDT: San Francisco, California*

Squinting, Clinton Hennessy stared in the far distance. He pumped the brake pedal of the black Ferrari Testa Rossa and geared down to third, then, annoyed by the braying sound, reached up and switched off the radar detector on the dash. Within seconds he reduced speed from a sizzling ninety miles an hour to the legal fifty-five, just as he passed the California State Highway Patrol car on the siding. Hennessy laughed; he enjoyed the cat-and-mouse game, one he played on each commute from his ranch in Los Banos, where he personally oversaw the production of three hundred thousand acres of crops and cattle. So far he had not lost, nor did he ever plan to. Why drive the sleek beauty unless he could let it wail, he thought, accelerating into fifth gear. Limits were set to curb the excesses of other people, but never him.

He reset the radar detector as the car's telephone began its insistent, rasping buzz. He lowered his hand between the bucket seats. "Hennessy," he barked in his gravelly voice into the receiver. As he listened to the voice on the other end, the muscles around his mouth tensed. After a few seconds, he asked, "How soon can you get me a fix?"

"Nobody knows," replied the broker, Neddie Vickers, anxiously.

Nobody knows? he thought with a mixture of anger and alarm. Somebody always knew. On that very fact Hennessy had built his conglomerate—a vast empire that counted communications, oil, shipping, land and finance among its assets. He always knew before the competition did. Jesus, he thought now, couldn't he take off even one weekend without somebody screwing up? He paid Vickers good commissions to keep him ahead of the game, and now the broker was offering lame excuses. In all the years he had dealt with Salomon Brothers, this was the first time he had ever heard that expression, "Nobody knows." He scoffed once again at his broker: "You'd better find out, Vickers, and fast!"

"It can't be explained," replied the broker in New York. "I'm sorry, Mr. Hennessy, but everyone is in the same position."

Hennessy had heard from Vickers earlier in the day that the Big Board had gone berserk. Hennessy had told his man to find out why, and how the breakdown could be turned to their advantage. He had demanded a strategy, and Vickers was providing none. "Vickers?" he said in an accusing tone.

"Sir, as I told you, the Big Board has suspended trading. It's as if somebody threw a bomb in this place. Now the same thing's happened at the American Exchange."

"Has trading been suspended there, too?"

"Not yet, but they'll have to close trading if it's anything there like it is here."

"Where's gold?"

Vickers put him on hold for an instant, then clicked back on, saying, "It's $620 at the London fixing."

Hennessy's mind worked reflexively. He did not want to pull out of the markets, but he did not want to be stuck in, either. By the sound of it, the suspension might well last. "Play with the

Amex stocks as long as you can and use the fluctuations to my advantage before the suspension." His voice was clipped, precise. "Take the overnights—all of them—out of Chase and Manufacturers; dump it in gold." He would not wait for the pack. If *nobody* knew, that could only mean that disaster was around the corner: Gold fed on disaster.

"I think you're overreacting, sir," Vickers said. "If you want my advice—"

Hennessy wanted no such thing. "Damn right I'm overreacting, and I'll pull the flaps in after me."

"You'll start a run on them and, if I might—"

"Who cares?" Hennessy bellowed. "The runners will be in my wake. Now keep me posted. You know where I'll be?"

"No, sir."

"In Mattone's office," he said, slapping the receiver in the cradle, then pressing his foot on the accelerator. He gave no thought to speed traps now. There were larger menaces to avoid this morning. He had to find out what was happening back in New York.

A half hour later, the Ferrari flew down the Embarcadero off ramp into North Beach, then south toward San Francisco's financial district. Hennessy was heading for the executive offices of the nation's largest bank. He had $220 million on account at the Bank of America. Though currently the chaos in New York centered only in the stock markets, Hennessy wanted his money—all of it—safe, and safe meant in his mattress, at least until somebody discovered what was wrong. He stopped the Ferrari in the no-parking zone in front of the towering, fortresslike red-stone Bank of America building and jumped out, slamming the door behind him.

As he rode the elevator to the thirty-eighth floor, he tried to recall if anything similar had ever happened before to the New York exchanges. Suspensions of trade were rare on either of the exchanges, and they were almost never suspended simultaneously. When suspension did occur, there was always a reason; more often than not it was because of excessive volume, or the

SEC suspended trading in *one* stock. In his memory, suspensions had always been announced in advance. Everyone understood what was happening, and order prevailed.

As Hennessy strode the carpeted hall of the executive floor, secretaries looked up from their desks and smiled. Clinton Hennessy might have walked off a movie screen. Tall and slightly too thin, well proportioned, he had a ruggedly handsome, weathered face that was marred only by the broken nose that twisted right. When his friends saw the Marlboro men on television, they instinctively thought of Clint. He wore cowboy boots that were scruffed and worn to comfort. His jeans were the same. Carelessness about his dress had become a trademark. At fifty-five, he was a good fifteen years older than he looked, and proud of it.

Usually Hennessy had a cheerful word for the secretaries on these infrequent visits, but today he went directly to the corner office of Victor Mattone, chairman, Bank of America. Mattone was a small, mousy man with a shiny bald patch in the center of his head. When Hennessy entered, Mattone looked up from a telex report and said, "I expected you sooner."

"What's going on?" Hennessy asked, walking to Mattone's desk. "My man in New York says he doesn't know."

"Sit down, Clint," Mattone said, waving him to the button-backed chair across from his desk. "I'll tell you what *I* know, which isn't much." Hennessy sat on the arm and stared at Mattone, trying to read a reaction. The banker's smooth features betrayed nothing. "I just got off the phone to Chessman, and he says not to worry, not yet, anyway."

Hennessy felt reassured. Robert Chessman, the president of the New York Stock Exchange, was solid and unflappable. "What's that 'not yet, anyway'?"

"That they've got trouble, but chances are it'll be of a temporary nature."

"And if it isn't temporary?"

Mattone did not respond. Hennessy had been known to be impetuous, and at times Mattone had to treat him as he would a sensitive child. "They think they've located the source of the trouble. It's in their computers, but that's all they know now."

Hennessy got to his feet. "In the computers? Of *both exchanges at the same time?*"

Mattone swiveled in his chair and faced the window view of the Bay Bridge. "I have no reason to suspect that the American Exchange is having trouble for the same reason."

"What if it *is* the computers? What does that mean?"

Mattone swiveled back to face Hennessy. "The computers handle the transactions, as you know. Volume on the Board is about forty-five million shares a day. Without computers, such volume cannot be handled. By hand, it is impossible. And since you're asking 'what if,' I'll tell you, Clint. The speed of the markets without those damned machines would revert to somewhere between 1960 and 1970. It would be one hell of a mess."

"It already is, and their computers have been down for less than three hours. Can't they move their on-line operations somewhere? Don't they have redundancies? They *must* have planned for this kind of trouble."

"They think the trouble's in the software. They stripped the machines after trading was suspended. They found nothing."

"If it's the software, we could be talking about days, weeks even, before they find the bug."

"You're right. It's unthinkable. Investors won't be able to trade, won't be able to move their money. Until things start to run smoothly again, it's stuck. Of course, no one's going to steal it from them."

"I wouldn't be so sure. Vickers, my man at Salomon, said the prices were way out of line. Hell, I wasn't going to sit on my fanny. I told him fluctuations or not, work the damn thing, make me some money. Then the lights went out. By God, if the computer's gone mad, someone's behind it. What guarantee is there that the status quo will be maintained when we get back to normal?"

Mattone raised his eyebrows. "Those are questions you'll

have to raise with Chessman, but I'm going on the assumption that no one will lose out. Though no one will win, either."

"I've got questions, Vic. For example, this suspicion about the software. Software! Hell, all that is is a program, a set of instructions for the computer to follow. If that's gone haywire, then some bastard rewrote it to make the machines go haywire. That's not random, that's no mistake. Somebody's out to make a killing, I just know it."

Mattone decided to let Hennessy in on the full content of his telephone discussion with Chessman. "They think it's more particular than the program. If the program bombed out, they could always rewrite another, or reexecute a duplicate. Downtime would be counted in minutes. Chessman said the only reason he *thinks* it's the software is because he *knows* it isn't the hardware. But his technicians can't find a flaw in the program. As far as they can tell, nobody has tampered with it."

Exasperated, Hennessy said, "In other words, nothing's wrong, right?" He did not wait for a reply. "Shit, you'd think with all these anticomputer groups raising hell, you people would find a way to protect the machines. The other day a nut in Dallas unloaded a .45 automatic into a computer. What about him? There're a million oddballs out here who'd jump up and down for the chance at a big casino like the exchanges. Well, it looks to me like somebody finally took it." Hennessy's stomach rumbled loudly. He patted it, then looked at Mattone. "My gut here is my dousing rod, and when it rumbles I run for cover. Right now it's telling me we're in deep."

Mattone hunched his shoulders. "What do you want me to say, Clint? It's their trouble, not mine. I can't help you out."

Hennessy understood that. He had not come up to the thirty-eighth floor to discuss the mess some maniac had made back in New York. He was scared, and his instincts were telling him to duck. "I'm not yelling at you, Vic," he said. "But you've got to understand my position. I've got thirty million dollars in overnight deposits with you. I want them moved today into gold." The balance of his investments on the books at the bank were tied up in the exchanges, and therefore locked up until the trouble ended.

"Clint, Clint," the bank chairman soothed. "You're jumping the gun, believe me." The last thing he wanted was to have Hennessy pull out on such short notice. If other depositors heard, it might start a run on the bank. Mattone knew that Hennessy would eventually listen to reason. Hennessy liked to threaten, but he was likely no more serious about this threat than he had been in the past. "Why don't we sleep on it? If we don't get answers in a couple of days, sure, I'll move you out, gladly. But this thing's only a few hours old. It may mean nothing."

Hennessy saw that Mattone was truly unruffled. "Okay, I'll stay in but only until the close of business tomorrow. If they don't know what's going on in New York by then, you've got a standing order to shift my overnights into gold."

"At your command," Mattone said sardonically. The buzzer on his desk purred softly. It would be his secretary announcing the arrival of Bert Hewes, the bank's vice president for institutional investments. Earlier Mattone had asked him to compile a report on the impact of the exchange's suspension of trading. Mattone depressed a switch on the intercom and waited.

"It's Mr. Miles, sir," the secretary said in a squealing voice. "He has some urgent business. He emphasizes 'urgent.'"

Mattone looked at Hennessy, who had heard the secretary's words. "Are you expecting anything?" Hennessy asked.

Mattone shook his head. "Send him in," he said.

James Miles, the bank's boffin or computer wizard, had designed and now oversaw the operation of the bank's information systems. Running his department smoothly was a point of pride for Miles, who could boast of a nearly uninterrupted flow of operation. At other banks, the atrocious downtimes sometimes lasted half a business day. Nothing but computers mattered to James Miles. He had the efficient and bland personality of one of his machines; he himself was almost without features. For all the years he had known him, Victor Mattone could not have recalled what the man looked like. Now, however, as he came through the door, Miles' face was rose colored. "My computers are down, sir," he exploded. Mattone had never seen a man in such a condition —his lips stretched back against his teeth, his breath coming in gasps and gulps. "And I can't figure out why or how!"

Mattone took the news calmly. Certainly his was no cause for panic. "So?" he asked astringently.

Miles stood near the door, his arms straight at his sides, as if called to attention. His mouth worked, but no words came. When finally he did speak, he stammered. "I . . . we can't . . . this isn't . . . *sir,* we've never experienced anything like this before. *Nobody has."*

Mattone got to his feet and went over to Miles, taking him by the arm. Mattone's solicitousness only exacerbated the EDP vice president. "I'm sorry, sir," he said. "Our hardware is surging balances, bursting transfers, calling up and ordering out where and when it shouldn't. I can't control it. I tried, but it's as if the system went mad."

"Calm yourself," Mattone said sharply, feeling his own blood pressure rise. "Have you shut the system down?"

"Of course. I pulled the plugs the minute I noticed the erratic behavior. We lost a bit, but not much."

"And have you checked it out?" He spoke to Miles in a calm, clear voice, belying his growing anxiety.

"I pored over it before I came up here. *Nothing is detectable! Nothing!* Believe me, sir. Zero."

Hennessy slumped in the corner sofa. "Jesus H. Christ!" he shouted. "Isn't there *any* security in these things?"

Miles did not know who the man on the sofa was, but he presumed that if he was in Mattone's office, he deserved an answer. "I've always taken all the standard cautionary measures— codes and user-identification checks. Yes," he said sharply, "there is security, and if I may say so, it's very good indeed."

"But not good enough," Hennessy said under his breath.

"Miles," Mattone said, "what do you mean there is nothing wrong? Of course there is. I expect you to find out what."

"Sir, I meant what I said. There *is* nothing detectable, and yet the machines are operating as though everything is wrong. I've checked the programs on an independent computer, and they have not been altered in any way. I have gone inside the machines. I have even asked the hardware to inspect itself. Again, nothing. There is nothing in any of the texts to cover this."

Hennessy cut him off as he was gulping for more air. "What does it mean?" he asked.

"That depends on how long we're down," Miles answered.

Hennessy was angry. "Well, let's just suppose it's a *fucking long* while."

Mattone answered, "All our records are on magnetic tapes and disks. We couldn't begin to process orders and transfers without EDP. The Stone Age, Clint. And I mean that."

The Stone Age, thought Hennessy darkly. He was not going to sit around for that. He could play and win in any age, if need be, but he would need access to his liquid capital, and soon.

WEDNESDAY, JUNE 17, 1987

"Can you destroy a person with a computer?" "Not destroy. But you can make that person wish he were dead."

*From an interview,
April 23, 1979,
with a computer
technician, IBM,
New Rochelle, New York*

8:53 A.M., *EDT: Yorktown, New York*

In full western regalia, a mourning band wrapped around his upper arm, security guard Harry Verdeen paced the floor outside his superior's office in the subbasement of IBM's Research and Development headquarters. Two days had passed since the murder of his partner, Horace, and Harry had been caught up inexorably in the aftermath. Horace's mother was an ailing widow, and the oldest of his three brothers was only ten. Much of the funeral organization had fallen on Harry's shoulders, and it was a burden he had taken on gladly with his wife, Ruth. Only last night in the garish brick chapel in Brownsville, where Harry had been setting up last-minute arrangements for the funeral service this morning at eleven o'clock, had the full impact of Horace's death hit him. They had been closer friends than he had realized, and now it was too late. Seeing Horace in the casket had also made him realize how narrowly he had escaped the same fate. Later that night as he rode home, the suddenness and the anonymity of the murder made him choke with anger.

The more Harry reflected on it, the more enraged he had become. The police had discovered not one clue that might lead to the killers. Harry had studied crime statistics enough to know that if a murder suspect was not found within forty-eight hours after the crime was committed, the odds against his ever being found diminished nearly to zero. Racked with exhaustion and frustration, Harry had tossed and turned all night long. A funeral service was not enough, not when the police did not have one lead, one shred of evidence to point toward the murderer, and worse when they did not even seem to care. Their investigation had been routine and cursory. They had taken Harry's statement—the two bullets fired from the dark, one grazing his shoulder, the second hitting Horace in the head; after the explosions, the sound of someone thrashing through the scrub on the opposite side of the fence. Paralyzed with shock, Harry had not returned fire after the shooting, and it had taken him nearly a half hour to gather his wits enough to call headquarters.

The State Police had sent out a forensic team as standard operating procedure, and they had sifted through the brush, finding nothing at all. The murderer was either very lucky, they concluded, or highly professional, a hypothesis they chose to discard, since a professional would have no motive for shooting Horace.

IBM had wanted the matter quickly forgotten. For reasons of its own the company hoped to keep publicity to a minimum, and the corporate executive who had dealt with the State Police had encouraged a swift investigation. The company expressed regrets at the loss of a valued employee, and after considerable prodding from Verdeen they had come up with a generous package for Horace's family. By the second night after the event, it seemed to Harry as though it was being forgotten.

He tried to banish the ugly thought from his mind, but it would not disappear. Horace was black, a little person with no clout who did not mean anything to anybody, except Harry and his family. A murdered black man meant little to IBM or the police —they probably presumed it was some sort of personal vendetta.

But Harry, the amateur detective, could not leave it there. Before falling asleep the night before, Harry had decided to get to work on the case—even before the funeral.

He had been given the week off to recover from the graze wound in his shoulder—nothing more serious, really, than a burn and a cut. Impulsively that morning, he had put on his pegged jeans, snap-button shirt, tooled armadillo boots, silver-buckled belt and his pheasant-banded hat—his official, private-person getup—and driven to headquarters to make his demands.

His boss, Alex Prescott, had once been a sergeant with the Manhattan force, before high blood pressure forced him into retirement and private security work. Harry knew that Prescott felt almost as badly about Horace as Verdeen did, and for that reason, would go along.

The headquarters, like most offices for security operations, had originally been an ad hoc arrangement. Nobody else had wanted the space—it had no view, was dank and was poorly heated. Over the years, a succession of guards had gradually made it more comfortable, bringing in used sofas and chairs, a coffee urn and a couple of posters for the walls. Off the anteroom was one office, Prescott's. A sticker on the door read: "Abandon hope, ye who enter."

The door opened and Prescott appeared in starched khaki shirt and matching pants. The buttons pulled tight against his considerable girth. He looked at Harry and with a small, almost delicate mouth said, "Let's talk."

Harry perched on the arm of the Naugahyde sofa with the sprung cushions and the white tufts of stuffing breaking out of the back. "Alex," he said, "I want a coupla weeks off to check this thing out."

"Aren't you taking this a little too personally?" Prescott looked pained. "I guess I don't blame you. But what the hell more is there to do? The police have covered the field."

"They dragged their asses through the motions, that's all. And you know it. Shit sakes, Al, I don't know what more there is, but I can't leave things like they are. I just can't."

Prescott leaned against the wall and folded his hands across his stomach. Nodding, he said, "I understand. Naturally, you can do what you want; it's your vacation time. But I don't see how I can help."

"You've got some friends on the force, Al, and that's what I want. If this leads me anywhere, I'm going to need a smoothed path."

"Which means?"

"To start with, a private detective's license, and if you can swing it, a license to carry a concealed weapon."

Prescott looked at him. Verdeen's expression didn't change. "You're serious about this, aren't you?"

Verdeen nodded. "Maybe it looks to you, Al, like I'm goofing off, playin' big-shot detective out of fun. But I'm not.

Probably I'll come up with even less than the cops, but I think I owe it to Horace to try."

A few minutes later, Harry was walking out the gate. He said hello to the security guard in the booth, and then followed the hurricane fence to where he and Horace had heard the noise that night. Whoever the murderer was, he had to have been afraid, Harry thought. The noise he made was either the sound of his dragging his own weight across the ground, or of his pulling something very heavy. It made no sense that he would have been crawling in the dark. There was no need for it. Obviously he had heard the Jeep approach, Horace getting out to piss. They could not have surprised the murderer all that much—not enough for him to make a sudden noise, which left Harry with the thought: He must have been dragging something behind him that he did not want Horace to see.

Wild shrubs taller than he grew thickly right up to the fence. Harry walked back through the grounds and, from the point opposite the white punch-box, forced his way through the vegetation. When he had ten yards to go to the fence, he fell to his knees and crawled, taking care not to scrape the shined toes of his boots. There were plenty of shoe marks in the soft dirt from the experts of the State Police's forensic team. Harry gathered that they had bulled their way through the brush in getting to the fence. They had probably not looked closely at the approach, because it was tough going. Those guys liked to spend time in their laboratories, he thought. Field work was to be kept to the minimum necessary to make an appropriate number of plaster impressions of foot and tire marks. They had not helped in this investigation.

Harry now was so lost in the undergrowth he could not tell whether he was still heading toward the fence. He stood up and looked around. He had veered off course, but over there, five yards away, was a small clearing. He got back down on his knees and headed for it. The clearing was no more than ten feet in circumference but, thought Harry with a smile crossing his face, it was enough for a couple of kids, probably, to have a good time. He counted six used rubbers, one hanging limply from a branch, and scattered around were their Sheik wrappers, an empty bottle of gin and a sock.

He plowed back into the brush on his hands and knees, now moving directly toward the fence. This was a regular briar patch, he thought angrily, and that made the murder seem even more senseless: If the killer had only stayed still, nobody could have seen him. In another few minutes he and Horace would have continued their rounds, none the wiser, and the killer could have done whatever he was there to do. Horace would still be alive and kicking. But no, the jackass had to make a noise.

Closer to the fence, Harry dangled his nose as near the ground as possible, sniffing and staring at everything as closely as possible. He began to pick up tracks. The killer had been dragging something heavy: Harry could see the bent-over grass, the light gouges in the soil. Could the killer have been trying to dispose of a body? No, that did not add up, not at all.

As Harry continued crawling, the glint of something shiny caught his eye. It was lodged in the dirt, near the base of a sapling sycamore. Probably the tab from a beer can, he surmised, reaching over to pull it free. He rested on his haunches, inspecting the piece of metal, rubbing off the dirt with his thumb.

He did not know if there was a connection, but his heart beat faster in spite of himself. It was a key, a common key to a lock. It was a beginning.

10:17 A.M., *EDT: Brookline, Massachusetts*

"Stop the tape," John Elliman said.

An Oriental man in a brown pin-striped suit stepped near to the Betamax VCR as the television screen above it darkened. "Do you want it replayed?" he asked in a heavy Japanese accent, the word coming out as "reprayed."

"No," Elliman said, his voice as cool and smooth as the jade stone he rubbed between his thumb and forefinger. Elliman, too, had an accent, although his contained affected flat vowels. In times of stress, Elliman's arch, plummy tones lent his mid-Atlantic speech an unmistakably British ring."Maybe you'll tell me where you got the tape?" The question was offhand; the answer was of no consequence. Dr. Rousseau's speech before the Trojan Horse symposium had become *the* topic for debate overnight in the computer community. Elliman assumed wrongly that pirate videotapes of the closed-circuit broadcast were circulating through the country.

The Japanese man, Mr. Niigata, looked at him with an expression of disdain. How he had acquired the videotape was something he could never tell Elliman. "Does he know what he's saying?" Niigata asked.

Elliman let it pass. "He thinks he does and from what I know about him, if he *thinks,* he knows." Rousseau's ideas about a formula whetted Elliman's imagination. He did not know how he would use it, but he was dead certain that he wanted the combination. Maybe it was the salvation that he so desperately sought.

His Boston-based company, Ling Autonetics, was in trouble. The largest second-line producer of common hardware after giants such as IBM, Control Data, NCR, Honeywell and their brethren, Ling was first in its league but a poor sixth overall. Sixth position galled Elliman and had led him into a cul-de-sac. An Englishman by birth who became a naturalized U.S. citizen at the age of twelve, Elliman had purchased Ling in the early sixties, when the company was a small subcontractor producing peripheral components for IBM. He had used his life savings and borrowed on the reputation he had earned as a tough marketing man and shrewd innovator with a singular command of computer intelligence. Ling had expanded rapidly under his stewardship.

His timing was perfect, for Autonetics was swept up in the computer boom of the late sixties, when hundreds of digital computer companies blossomed. Demand for computer products was insatiable and computer companies from the Silicon Valley south of San Francisco to Brookline profited and expanded. None did better in the wildcat market than Ling Autonetics, which now was a conglomerate with $700 million in annual sales.

Success had spurred John Elliman to make a crucial decision. He had neither the capital nor the resources to compete with the giants in the field of main-frame computers, but neither would Autonetics be content to nibble at the edges of the larger companies with the production of "plug-in" components. He decided to beat the giants at their own game: He would innovate; he would diversify, and not just with new software and accessory components. His idea had been adventurous and, he had thought, right; but his timing was disastrous.

Last year, Elliman poured everything into the development of LA/2000, a minicomputer with broad applications for business and private use. The demand existed, which only Ling could fill —or so Elliman had imagined.

Meanwhile, two unforeseeable catastrophes overwhelmed him. The shakeout, which stock analysts for years had predicted, finally started; boom companies like Autonetics began to fail. A panic occurred. Autonetics' investors were nervous, but the promise of LA/2000's success held them.

Then, four months ago, the hammer blow came with IBM's introduction of its own mini, the 4300 series.

The press praised the IBM arrival, and one newsmagazine wrote, "When IBM sneezes, the rest of the computer industry catches double pneumonia. This year, IBM's maneuvers have left its competitors in intensive care. IBM introduced this week several small and medium-sized computers that provide about four times the calculating power of their predecessors. And rather than pricing its powerful new models above the units they replace, IBM is selling them for less."

Advance orders for Autonetics' LA/2000 were canceled in a stampede to IBM, and the Autonetics' stock plummeted in one week from $37 to $8.75. Those investors who had held onto their stock sold out, and now, unless something was done to renew confidence and put back the orders on the books for the mini, Ling Autonetics was within weeks of folding. A miracle was needed, and a miracle was what Douglas Elliman sought.

The imminent collapse, Elliman knew, would destroy him personally as well as professionally, for it would strike both his home and another integral part of his sizable ego: his wife, Maude Lacey Elliman. A platinum-blond southern belle who had been the reigning Miss Universe when they first met, Maude was twenty years his junior. A strong-willed young woman, she had lobbied Elliman for the purchase of their estate, "Larking Hill" in Welles-ley, a fifty-acre horse farm with a twenty-room manor house, in which she had invested more than three million dollars in antiques and furnishings. "Larking Hill" and all it contained—including Maude, Elliman thought bitterly—was mortgaged in one way or another. With the bankruptcy of Ling Autonetics, all that would vanish from Elliman's life. A divorce was inevitable. He would be left with little more than he had possessed those many years ago when he had landed in Boston as an immigrant boy.

Mr. Niigata was equally interested in Ling's survival. A trouble shooter for Nippon Itubishi, the corporation that had financed Ling's LA/2000 with $500 million cash, Niigata had flown to Boston with a dual purpose: to get details of the combination he had learned about by long-distance telephone, and to save Ling and Itubishi's $500 million.

"Did you talk to Mr. Wessel?" Niigata asked smoothly. Elliman was both ruthless and stupid, he thought. The blundering had failed. Only Occidentals acted with such a startling lack of subtlety.

Elliman laid the jade on the desk. "I did," he replied laconi-cally. Michael Wessel, Ling's chief of security, had given personal assurances of success. It had been a gamble, but so what? Hadn't he always gambled? With the stolen blueprints the LA/2000 would remain competitive. IBM would be forced to share the market, and Ling would survive.

"Did he explain the failure?" Niigata asked.

Elliman looked at Niigata's face; it was the most complete blank he had ever seen. He could study that face for a month and not be able to describe one salient feature. "He took it on himself," Elliman said. "The fault was his, he told me. I told him to forget it. He wasn't equipped to handle it."

The answer wasn't satisfactory. "Can it get back to us?"

"Wessel's nobody's fool," Elliman said.

Niigata thought about that for a while. Americans had such a need for *direct* control. They were all so foolish. They would push here to get an equal reaction there; the relationship was direct and simple and nowadays it hardly ever worked. Niigata pushed here for a desired reaction where nobody ever expected. "You sound as though you've lost hope," he said.

Elliman bristled. "I will never give up," he said, adding, "saving Ling."

"Good, because recovery of your company will benefit us all," Niigata replied, unruffled.

"Then tell me how? Christ, we have already killed a man."

Elliman, Niigata recognized, wanted the easy answer, the simple out. Tell me how? it was like a child's plea for help. Niigata looked at him pitifully.

"We have circled the question," Elliman said. "What do you expect, for me to blow up IBM?"

Mr. Niigata had no capacity for humor. "That would do no good," he replied. "But I suggest an action with equal salutary results."

"You're out of your mind," Elliman said.

"Perhaps not," Niigata said, rising from the chair with feline grace. "May we watch Dr. Rousseau again?"

"Yes," came the reply.

10:45 A.M., *EDT: Washington, D.C.*

General Hedley Church rose from the Queen Anne chair and stood at the window absorbing from across the Potomac the sight of the Marines at Iwo Jima statue, which was now bathed in bluish-green light. He secretly yearned for those days of war, when a battle was either won or lost on the basis of men and munitions, when politics, abstract computer theory and nuclear superkill ratios played

no part in the conduct or outcome of the contest. Today everything seemed destined to be a draw, a compromise, a foggy half
measure. An amateur military historian, Church recently had read
a new account of the Boer War. Now, *there* was a battle, he thought
—naturally enough, in the face of all those Mausers, Maxims and
Creusot "Long Toms." . . . No prevarication there . . .

He turned from the window and faced Stark Rousseau,
who was seated on the sofa. General Church had insisted that he
make this trip to Washington, and Stark knew why without having it explained. It was a high-power conference; the worry was
substantial enough to include the Secretary of Defense, who had
offered his office.

Thank God for Lapham, Stark thought. With General
Church as his prosecutor, Benjamin Lapham, the Pentagon's civilian director of research and development, was his defense counsel.
The Secretary of Defense, presumably, would be the judge. Stark
felt he had done nothing wrong. Perhaps—perhaps it had been less
than judicious to go quite so far with Church, but how was he to
know there would be a nationwide bank computer blowout the
following day, and breakdowns at the stock exchanges as well?
Still, that was no reason for an inquiry into him. Security was the
issue, not Stark Rousseau, and they better face the problem
squarely, and right away.

Stark was certain that he had done the right thing. The
formula was for everybody's good. Lapham, whose opinion he
respected, had told him as much. A diminutive, high-strung man
with a quick tongue and quicker mind, Ben Lapham was not
reluctant to level with Stark. When they had worked together on
the INTELSAT series, Stark had discovered Lapham's cool temper-
ment. Panic was foreign to him, and if the present situation had
involved more than a mild reprimand and a half hour of reasoned
debate, Stark was certain that Lapham would have told him as
much.

General Church was in the mood to attack, and he saw no
logical reason why he should go easy on Rousseau. The young
scientist galled him now even more for what Church perceived as

flippant, insouciant manner. Did Rousseau think the order to fly to Washington was born of whimsy—a field trip to the nation's capital? Church would quickly disabuse him of that notion.

"Are you aware of what's going on in New York and in San Francisco at this very minute?" Church asked, directing his gaze upon Rousseau.

"I read the papers," Stark replied. The suspension at the exchanges and the banks' computer failures had been the front-page item on all the morning papers. Stark had read the latest developments with interest on the shuttle from Boston that morning. "Are you trying to make a connection?"

"Damn right I am," Church said angrily.

"Hold it a minute," Lapham interrupted in a more conciliatory manner. He turned to Stark, "What you read, Stark, is only the tip of the iceberg. We've got real trouble up there. Even the President is involved."

"But it's a simple programming error," Stark protested.

Lapham nodded his head reflectively. "Maybe so . . . We all hope that is the case. But for the moment, here's the reporting we received. The hardware has been checked out thoroughly at the banks and the exchanges—it appears in perfect operating condition. The software has been checked—over and over—and even tried out on other, unaffected computers. The result is always the same. Nothing seems wrong, yet the computers spit out error after error. Nobody can find the problem."

"In other words," the Secretary added, "we are interpreting these 'events' as a direct threat. It is that serious."

"A direct threat from whom?" Stark asked, befuddled. It sounded as though the Secretary was announcing the imminent invasion of the country, or worse.

The Secretary answered, "We don't know. Our suspicions center on certain anticomputer groups." He carefully guarded his answer. They had no real suspects. Something awful was happening to major computer systems, and the answers as to why or how would not come quickly.

"I had thought about that, too," Stark remarked. "But, sir,

the level of competence just isn't there, at least from what I know about those groups."

"What about IUSUC?" General Church asked. "How about their technical competence?"

"I know nothing about them."

Church opened his mouth to repeat the allegation about IUSUC he had received from Army Intelligence, but abruptly, he thought better of it. He knew little yet, and there was no need to expose his real suspicions this early. He scowled at Rousseau and waved aside his implied question. "It's not important that you do," he said. "What you should keep very firmly in mind is the danger. These anticomputer people would love nothing more than to have what you so blithely described yesterday."

Lapham interjected, "The general is saying, Stark, that the people who may have wrecked the computer systems at the exchanges could exploit your formula, too. Apparently they are going about their work piecemeal at the moment. With your formula, if I understand it correctly, they could take out all major systems at once. Needless to say, they will want it, once they know it exists."

"Did you explore ways to neutralize it?" General Church asked, now in a peeved tone of voice.

Stark appealed with his eyes to Lapham, who raised an eyebrow questioningly. He, too, wanted an answer to that one. "As I said at the symposium," Stark answered truthfully, "when I discovered the formula, I also tried to break it. I couldn't. There are no countermeasures, unless you want to bring down the satellites."

Church wagged his head. "Did you *think* about what you were doing? Christ, what foolish bravado."

Stark saw no reason to explain why he had done what he did. The rationale was too personal, and in any case awareness of the combination was now in the public domain. "I was careful in what I said, sir. I gave the symposium only parts of the formula. It's my belief that nobody can create the whole formula from what I gave out."

"That is mere arrogance, young man," the general nearly shouted.

"If you say so. Nevertheless, it is what I believe."

"Our fear, Dr. Rousseau, is simple," the Secretary of Defense repeated for emphasis, expanding his concerns. "Certain ideological and commercial foreign enemies would love to pull our level of computer science down to theirs. Do you see?"

Stark shrugged, the Secretary's reasoning making some sense. Perhaps Stark *had* acted precipitously, and privately he was sorry to cause these men such great concern. But what good were apologies now? "I don't believe that's possible," he repeated, sincerely. "Luck can't play a part."

"It always *does,*" General Church said, then: "Is there nothing you'd advise?"

"Let it die down, I guess," Stark replied offhandedly. "It will, you know."

"I meant specifics, concrete action."

Stark thought for a moment. "To be absolutely safe, those satellites must come down. We all know that. You could send up hunter-killers to destroy all five. That will eliminate any threat. Meanwhile, I will research filters to block the formula's insertion in the future."

"How long will that take?" asked the Secretary of Defense.

Lapham answered, "Days at most. LTW will build us new equipment, and we'll install Stark's innovations. However, I would advise against launching the hunter-killers before the LTW replacements are ready to fly."

"So would I," Church added. The Defense Department's dependence on the INTELSAT chain was critical. The country was vulnerable to attack without the satellites for even a day. The destruction and replacement would have to take place simultaneously. Church was about to make that point, but something else had entered his thinking, throwing him temporarily off track. This was the automatic assumption of Lapham's—made reflexively, Church presumed—that LTW would build the new satellites. Had Lapham already secured the Secretary's approval for LTW to go ahead earlier that morning?

"Do you agree on the timing, Dr. Rousseau?" the Secretary asked, interrupting Church's train of thought.

"Three to four days."

The Secretary turned to Lapham. "When we're finished here, I want the order to get started transmitted."

General Church was still uneasy about Rousseau. He addressed his comment to the Secretary. "I recommend that Dr. Rousseau stay here in Washington, where—"

Lapham interrupted, "If you don't mind, General, I want to discuss Dr. Rousseau in private." He looked at Stark. "Will you wait outside?"

Stark rose from the sofa. "Sure," he said. The jury would hear the final arguments and read the verdict. "One thought, though," he said, approaching the door. "If I'm to work on the filter, I'll get faster results in Cambridge. The equipment's better, I know it more intimately, and most of the papers I'll need are also there." He shrugged. "Just a thought."

"Thank you," Lapham said.

"Wait one minute," the Secretary said, holding Stark at the door. "In the event that we agree, you must promise one thing, and while you're waiting outside, I want you to think about it seriously."

"Yes, sir?" Stark asked.

"Until we have all the answers . . . until we have brought these saboteurs to justice . . . until we have sent up the hunter-killers and the new INTELSAT series, you must maintain absolute secrecy about these events. You must tell no one of our concerns. Because if you do bandy them about, panic will spread faster than anything you can imagine."

Stark wore a serious expression. "I think I'm good for that, don't you, Ben?"

"You've never given me reason to doubt you," Lapham replied.

"Then, please, if you will. Wait outside," the Secretary ordered, and watched Stark quietly go through the door, closing it firmly behind him. Then he turned to General Church and Lapham, "You're both certain about the timing?"

Lapham answered, anxious to recover the initiative from his military colleague, "I believe that in approximately seventy-two hours we can have the hunter-killers ready to fire. At the same time they are being prepared at Cape Canaveral, LTW can fabricate new satellites. It will be the fastest job the aerospace industry has ever done, but they are up to the task."

"They won't have to start from scratch, surely?" the Secretary asked.

"Not at all," Lapham explained. "At any given time, they are fabricating new satellites—not for us anymore as much as for the communications industry. I'm quite certain I can arrange it. We can take the available hardware, and with some adjustments . . . they'll need to jerry-rig some of it—"

"But it *can* be done?" the Secretary interrupted.

"In three or four days."

For several seconds there was a lapse in the discussion. General Church knew that the Secretary would next raise the subject of what should be done about Dr. Rousseau. The General had wanted the scientist to remain in the office to witness their discussing his future; perhaps it would frighten him a bit.

The Secretary cocked his head in the direction of the door. "What do you recommend?" He looked first at General Church.

Church did not need to collect his thoughts. "You can guess my opinion of him," he said. "But I won't leave you with guesses. I want this on the record: Rousseau is a brat with a dangerous brain. He acted impulsively, in the interest of security, he claims. But impulsively nevertheless. Yet consider: If his interest had been national security alone—or even computer security alone—he would have brought his formula to us in secret. Am I right?" When neither man answered, he continued, "Instead, he blabbed it to the symposium, to businessmen with competitive advantages as their foremost concern, to scientists, of whom some might have affiliations with anticomputer groups, and to God knows who else. He may think that they can't put together the entire formula, but we cannot operate on that premise. What does this mean for us? It means the redesign of a new series of satellites, and that alone, Mr.

Secretary, means a pot of money, millions of dollars, simply because of a kid's big mouth. You wonder why I'm angry about this, why I want him controlled here in Washington?" This time he didn't wait for a reply. "I want him taken out of play for his own good, ours and the nation's. I want him held incommunicado here in the Pentagon. He can carry out his research on the filter here, where we can observe him night and day, and where we can keep him safe." He finished, letting out a lungful of air.

It was Lapham's turn. "Do you know anything at all about Rousseau?" he asked.

The Secretary nodded lightly. "Only what you've told me here."

"Then let me give some background." He glanced over at Church. "Some of what the general has said, regrettably, is true. Stark is impulsive; he is a genius; he is immature; he almost never knows where his mind will take him. But his value to us has been enormous. He entered MIT at the age of fourteen, as a sophomore. The dean of students assigned him surrogate parents *in situ;* he was that young. The couple in question are named McKinnon, I believe; he is a professor at the Beeman Labs. Those years were pretty tough on Stark. He was a curiosity—some called him a freak. The Institute saw him as a true prodigy, an experiment, if you will."

The Secretary whistled. "I gathered that he must be intelligent, but—"

"Intelligent doesn't cover it. He's unbelievably brilliant, sir, as in true genius. His Intelligence Quotient leaves the chart at 185, and what he has done with computers is pure power. Needless to say, I've watched him develop over the years, and I know well what he is."

Church made a snuffling, derisive sound. "Prodigy?" he said. "More like an immature brat. What's a prodigy, anyway, but an idiot savant?"

Lapham objected to Church's calling Rousseau an idiot savant but he could see why he might. Some people who were brilliant in one area could barely function in others. That was partly true of Stark, but it wasn't nearly the whole. "That isn't really fair," Lapham said. "In a sense our minds are made up of a series of switches," he explained for the Secretary's benefit. "Each switch controls a different function, like language, physical coordination and so on. The switches are like preprogrammed computers, and some are better than others. Stark's mental computer for mathematics is almost unequaled in the world, but"—he looked over to Church—"his computer for emotion and social interaction, as some sociologists say, is less developed. In other words, to all outward appearances he's like any other young man his age. Because I know him, have worked with him, I know about his extraordinary intensity. At times he can be completely antisocial. Sometimes, when he addresses himself to a mathematical problem, he just doesn't think about other people, barely about himself. Some of the people at the Beeman Labs, just like General Church here, think he's a total jerk, a misfit, a nut." He shook his head and frowned. "They're dead wrong. He is, however, *totally* unpredictable."

Church had his opening. "That's just what I said: unpredictable and dangerous. So you agree that he should be detained in Washington."

Lapham chose his words with care. He understood what Church was saying, and yet it was simply impossible. Not only was it illegal, it would also backfire. The Secretary could not order such an illegal act without causing a major scandal for the Administration. "First, we have laws," Lapham said, addressing his remarks to the Secretary. "We cannot detain him legally, and we can't arrest him without pressing charges. If he doesn't want to stay for his own good, we can't force him. And I think to do that would be to underestimate the man. He is impetuous, that much I admit. But I must remind you, Rousseau possesses the highest security clearances. He has never given anybody any reason to doubt his allegiance. To the contrary, he has helped us, again and again. In his own way, he has contributed beyond compensation by pointing out the weakness in INTELSAT."

"But you—" Church interjected.

"But I, *nothing*, Hedley. Frankly, you are taking this too personally. That he humiliated you before your peers, so to speak, has colored your attitude. You want him smashed—or to use your charming term, 'taken out of play'—to vindicate your bruised ego." Lapham held up his palm, stifling Church's objection. "Yes, your ego. The young man took you down a couple of pegs; he did us all. But that is no reason to arrest him. Further, to your remark about the high cost of another satellite series. It does hurt, I admit. But don't you see? Rousseau pointed out the existence of a computer program that can destroy our systems. It exists. What if the Russians had found it first? What then? In other words, we are now in a position to remedy the design flaw without being hurt. It may cost us, but Rousseau may just have saved our computer systems from destruction."

The Secretary knew the emotional undercurrents between the two men, and tried to steer the discussion away from personal issues. "Please, gentlemen," he said in a conciliatory tone. "Can we stick to what we know?"

"Yes, we can," General Church replied, the veins protruding in his temples. He went to the Queen Anne chair and produced a manila folder from his briefcase. "Facts!" he said.

They waited while he flipped through several pages of the file.

"Facts; what we know," he repeated, reading from the pages of foolscap he had chosen, however selectively, to bolster his argument. "Fact: In 1978 a computer operator in Charlotte, North Carolina, fired a pistol several times into the Liberty Mutual Life Insurance Company's IBM 1401 computer; a similar event occurred two years earlier in Johannesburg, South Africa. During a six-month period in 1979, saboteurs tried four times to destroy the computers at Wright-Patterson Air Force Base. In 1980, the Unita Combattenti Communiste in Rome inflicted $1 million in damage on the terminals of an IBM 2740. And then we have satellites. Last year NASA and the French government launched EOLE, a satellite designed to gather data from 115 balloons carrying instrument packages at an altitude of 38,000 feet. EOLE was to command the balloons to transmit their data through the satellite to ground-station computers that were then to analyze the data. Each balloon had explosive charges commanded by satellite. On the three hundred forty-sixth orbit of EOLE, a computer programmer instructed the computer to destruct the balloons. EOLE destroyed 72 of the 115 balloons. And nobody to this day knows if the programmer was a saboteur or a fool. I selected these random events, Mr. Secretary, to demonstrate the direction of an attitude. All these incidents have led to something much larger. These anticomputer groups are no longer taking random potshots. They are now highly organized and skilled."

"You mean the stock exchanges—"

"And the banks," Church continued, drawing a breath. "Army Intelligence has every reason to suspect these people; so does the FBI. In particular, they suspect this"—he stumbled on the words for an instant—"this IUSUC, the International Union for the Sane Use of Computers. Do you know who's behind that organization?"

Lapham shook his head. Of course he was aware of its founder's identity, but he did not want to have Church think that he took the anticomputer groups that seriously. There had been no reason to, not until now. They had been all rhetoric, placards, demonstrations, noise and clamor. But no deeds. They had yet to prove their point in any public way—at least until the recent events. Lapham had to admit, however, that IUSUC and its allies were pumping the current breakdown for all it was worth.

"Douglas Thornton," General Church continued. "And if anybody, including Rousseau, thinks *he* doesn't have the capacity to develop the unspoken parts of Rousseau's formula, they're fools, outright idiots."

Lapham got to his feet, again in defense. "Thornton has never stated that he wanted computers destroyed. He wanted their use to be temperate and sane. He wants them protected from people who *would* destroy them. Nooo," he said loudly, "Thornton isn't into destruction."

"How do you know?" Church challenged.

"From his record, and from what he's said in public."

"That's not enough, not by a long shot. Not for me. And you, Mr. Secretary?"

The Secretary picked up a pencil from his desk and scratched behind his ear. "I'd need to know more," he said noncommittally.

"And while we're learning, Thornton and people like him continue to destroy individual systems. Now it's the exchanges, the banks; next it's the IRS, the GAO, my God, Defense!"

"I *recognize* the seriousness," the Secretary said, peeved by the general's insinuation.

"But I think he's jumping to very strange conclusions," Lapham remarked.

"Is it a wrong conclusion that some people in this country want to see computers destroyed? They hate the machines for the 'Big Brother' they represent."

"But what do you *recommend?*"

"Their arrest." Now he had said it.

"Preposterous," Lapham replied, half laughing. "First you want Rousseau taken out of play, now you want a witch-hunt. Nonsense."

The Secretary said, astonished, "We just can't round up every member of every anticomputer group."

"And why not?"

The Secretary gave the general an expression of total exasperation. "Because, General, just because."

"And either we or the President would be forced to explain our action. Anyway, the courts would release them in hours."

"Maybe you're right," General Church conceded. It probably would not work, he thought to himself, unless his Intelligence people learned more than they presently knew. "But there's still no question in my mind what should be done about Rousseau."

"And neither is there in mine," Lapham added quickly. "We have laws."

"Laws are intended to protect the public welfare," Church argued.

"Yes, after the crime has been committed, after the fact."

"Gentlemen, please *stop* this squabbling," the Secretary said, aiming his rebuke at Lapham. "I have serious options to consider before I see the President. So please, how do we deal with Dr. Rousseau?"

"A man like Stark will not help his captors," Lapham said.

"Isn't there another option?" the Secretary asked, "beyond simply letting him trot off unprotected?"

"Yes, of course," Lapham said immediately. "And I think I have the answer. I would argue for cyberveillance."

The Secretary leaned back in his chair. "Can you please explain?"

"Surveillance of an individual that uses the techniques of cybernetics. Through a constant computer scan, we can know instantly where Rousseau goes, what he buys, who he calls and who calls him; we can watch telegrams, mail, his bank account and credit transactions. It will profile his activities without his being aware. If someone should pressure him, we'll know the instant he does."

General Church rubbed his chin. "It's still not enough," he said. "There's too much room for maneuver. I'm sorry, Lapham, because I know you disagree, but damnit, I saw him break into IBEX VII. He was doing more than illustrating a point; he enjoyed himself. He is young and impressionable, and if we don't keep him under our thumb, somebody may get to him and convince him to give them the formula."

Lapham threw up his hands. "I don't know what to suggest then," he said to the Secretary.

"I like your cyberveillance; Hedley, you want more than that. Suggest something."

This was the opening that Church had hoped to get. "Does Rousseau have a terminal at his home?"

"I think so," Lapham said. "IBM loaned him one of their new 4331 series for testing. It's a system he uses in the evenings."

"Right. Then I'll agree to your cyberveillance if you agree to our stationing an NSA truck near his house to monitor electromagnetic radiation from his home. However he chooses to use the terminal, we can pick up his single serial data streams. The terminal gives off radiation, sir," he said to the Secretary. "The truck's equipment converts the radiation into data."

Lapham did not like it; the measures were illegal, for one thing. But the Secretary quickly accepted Church's proposal as a compromise and indicated to Lapham that further argument would be useless. He himself was only a civilian, Lapham realized, and he better keep his tongue for the moment. There would be tougher trials ahead.

As Lapham and Church were excusing themselves, the telephone on the Secretary's desk rang. He answered the phone with a scowl. "I thought I told you no calls," he said into the receiver. "It is . . .? Well . . . of course . . . he's right here. Wait one . . ." He cupped the receiver and said to General Church, "It's for you, urgent."

Church went to the extension phone on the table near the Queen Anne, picked up the phone and grunted.

"It's Shimkus, sir," said a voice on the other end. "I wouldn't have bothered you if it weren't important."

"All right," Church said in a tired voice. "What is it?"

"The girl? The one at the symposium you asked me to check out? Sir, her name is Merrill *Thornton* Fox. She's the granddaughter of Douglas Thornton."

3:45 P.M., *EDT: Harlem, New York*

Harry Verdeen almost enjoyed the irony. A clue, he had always thought, was a fingerprint, a piece of hair or clothing, a footprint. But a key? Somehow it was too pat, too much the stuff of an Agatha Christie. It couldn't be real, he thought, handing it to Nicholas Vecchione. Verdeen would have felt much more confident if only he had found one fingerprint, if he had not rubbed the key carelessly when it had been discovered in the dirt. Pelican shit, he thought. All he had was the *conviction,* and not a very strong one at that. He could not admit to himself that the key belonged to the kids who used the clearing as their love nest.

He had been referred to Vecchione by Prescott. Despite his Italian name, Vecchione was a black man, with a weasellike face, crazed, shifting brown eyes, and a nervousness that made his thin fingers tremble. Vecchione ran a check-cashing business on 114th Street in Harlem, ten cents on the dollar cashed. But his sideline was keys. He had started the "reading" while serving time in Attica for burglary. The skeleton he'd used to enter apartments had been the police detective's clue. He had dropped it in one of the apartments as he collected radios and other electronic gear for quick resale. Vecchione used his time in prison to learn about keys, and how the police had been able to sniff his skeleton right home to him. He discovered that keys not only had unique faces, which everybody knew, but also a history and a character. They were mirrors of the people who used them. Anything might be discovered in the zigs and zags of a key's teeth. Unfortunately, after his release from Attica, Vecchione could not use his ability to "read" keys for illegal gains; and he had ended up using his passion to help the cops when they paid a call.

To Vecchione, Verdeen was an anomaly. He had a private detective's license that was newly minted; an uncertainty in his approach, unlike most pushy New York cops; and a simple manner that suggested amateurishness. And that was to say nothing of his clothes.

"It's a long shot, I know," Verdeen said, "but what the hell." Verdeen told him how he had found the key and what he wanted.

"Yeah, a real wild-goose chase," Vecchione cautioned. "What's the case?"

Verdeen told him. "I put him to rest this morning, so it's kinda personal. Anything you can tell me—"

"He was that close, huh?" Vecchione did not wait for a reply. Cases like this always backfired, and when they did, the failed detective always took it hard, one way or another. That was none of his business, however. He lifted the key to the light, then lowered it an instant later, a grin spreading across his face. "Man, you know nothin' about keys," he said. If he had he wouldn't have troubled to come here. A Medeco was the simplest trace. "One call'll head you off."

Verdeen was astounded. "You mean you know who owns it?"

"It's not *that* simple." He wrote down a number from the key, then handed it back to Verdeen. "You see, this here's a Medeco. For every lock the company makes, there are three keys. Each key has a number corresponding to the lock." Verdeen looked closely at the key. Sure enough, the number was stamped on the throat. "Medeco has its headquarters in Salem, Virginia, and they have lists on their computer of where they sold each of their locks." Vecchione pulled a loose-leaf binder from a shelf under the counter. He found the telephone number and dialed. After a few minutes he wrote down an address, and hung up. He pushed the paper through the grate to Verdeen. "They sold the lock to these people," he said. "Unless it was moved around, they can tell you who *they* sold it to."

Anxiously, Verdeen looked at the notepaper. As he read the address, his heart sank. He breathed in deeply and sighed. "Brookline, Massachusetts"—there was scant hope of finding Horace's murderer there. "I guess I was wrong," he said to Vecchione. "Thanks anyway, but this just doesn't add up."

Vecchione replied, "I know. It almost never does."

6:45 P.M., *EDT: Cambridge, Massachusetts*

Jim McKinnon sat crosslegged on the picnic bench watching his wife poke a long-handled fork into the barbecue pit. What a perfect evening for a dinner under the stars, he thought lazily, looking up at the darkening blue sky. The saplings around the border of their back garden were just blooming, and he could smell the hickory from the fire. Strains of a Mozart concerto drifted across the lawn from the house, where Stark Rousseau—who had arrived early—had gone for a bottle of wine. Jim sat comfortably dressed in tattered jeans, loafers and an old checked lumber jacket, but he could not feel so casual as he would have liked. The incident earlier that afternoon still nagged at him. As Dorothy wiped her hands on her apron he said, "They wanted to know why I had Merrill cleared for the symposium."

"What do you mean, 'they'?" she asked, coming over to sit beside him.

"A man from Army Intelligence. It seems a whole crew of them were snooping around the Labs today."

Dorothy and Jim had discussed the symposium with Merrill at their lunch, and Jim had made it sound so intriguing that Merrill had begged to accompany him, sensing, as she had told them, that this might be the very thing to inspire her finally to make the jump out of modeling and back into academe. Jim now wondered if he had made the right decision.

"Were there any problems?" Dorothy asked, concerned.

"I don't think so—there was nothing wrong about it, after all." But he could not be certain, not after the interrogations by Army Intelligence. To allay his own fears, however, he said, "Dr. Regan has met her before, and her grandfather is one of his oldest cronies. Anyway," he said, slightly angry, "the symposium was at the Labs, for God's sake, not the Pentagon or Arlington. Sometimes those paranoids burn me up."

His words had done nothing to relieve Dorothy's concern. "What did they say to you?" she asked, resting her hand on his shoulder.

"Not much. That's the truth. But they kept hanging around, as if they were intent on hassling . . . well, hassling all of us who were there."

"You're worried about Merrill now, aren't you?"

He looked at her with a false grin. "I don't know. They asked what she knew about computers, as if she were a spy or something. I laughed in their faces. As you know, she's conversant about computers, but the subjects were so esoteric, she could have enjoyed it only as theater."

Dorothy asked, "Doesn't the Pentagon check security at the Labs out of routine?"

Jim shook his head. "Not this way they don't. I mean, they come around every couple of years, but it's always cursory stuff, checking to make sure we are following basic security procedures. This time they were hard-assed. The reason is Stark."

"What did he do this time?" asked Dorothy.

"You know him as well as I do," Jim said. "He went overboard, way overboard, and brought up some potentially dangerous stuff. Nobody's ever been able to control him, so I don't know why the Pentagon was surprised this time." He laughed a little at the thought of Stark's dramatic behavior. "Anyway, I'm not supposed to talk to anybody about Army Intelligence's questions. To *no one.*"

Dorothy laughed. "Well, you've just broken that promise."

"I never promised. In fact, I told them off and not very politely, either." As he looked at Dorothy his eyes narrowed. "They have no damn right. Army Intelligence, the CIA, NSA, none of them can just invade the Labs like that. We aren't owned by the government."

"Does Merrill know?"

"Not likely," Jim replied.

"Well, then," Dorothy said, patting his shoulder, "perhaps you should try to forget about it. By the way, they aren't arriving together, are they?"

Jim hunched his shoulders. "How should I know? You arranged this party."

Dorothy got off the bench and fretted with the chicken halves she had placed in the platter to marinate. The dinner had been hastily organized, just that afternoon. She had not been able to get hold of Stark until late in the afternoon, and then he had tried to beg off, saying he had to work. His voice sounded so strained and serious, Dorothy almost relented. But knowing well how overworked he was, she had insisted. "Okay," he had said, "but it has to be early. I mean real early." Indeed, he had arrived a whole hour ahead of time. She hoped Merrill and Byron would arrive soon.

As she carried the platter from the table to the barbecue, the garden gate opened. "Hi," Merrill said, smiling, walking up to Jim and kissing him on the cheek. "I'm sorry about the time," she said. "The old fool doctor of mine still can't decide if I should take the pills."

"The pill?" Dorothy asked.

"Not that kind of pill, Dorothy," Merrill laughed. "The one so I don't have to shoot myself up every day."

"Oh," Dorothy remembered.

"They've developed a new pill, an insulin substitute or something, but he doesn't know if it'll work for me."

"Why shouldn't it?" Jim asked.

Merrill shrugged, as though she didn't care about the outcome. "So far they're only used by light diabetics, and you know me, a needle a day."

The chicken sizzled on the grill. "Will you turn the potatoes?" she asked Merrill.

"I can't find the wine," a voice yelled from inside the house.

Merrill turned around, looking in the direction of the kitchen. "Who's that?" she asked, surprised.

"Stark Rousseau," she said, then to Jim, "Go give him a hand. You men are so helpless sometimes."

When he had gone, Merrill said, "How interesting." She pressed her lips together. "Did you plan this?" she asked Dorothy.

"Of course I did."

Despite their shared friendships, Jim and Dorothy had never introduced Stark. He was Jim's colleague at the Labs; Merrill was Dorothy's friend. In the years they had known each other, the thought of introducing Merrill to Stark had never occurred to Dorothy. Anyway, Stark had become increasingly reclusive, even to the point of turning down dinner invitations at their house time after time. Dorothy was relieved now to see that Merrill did not seem to mind.

Stark looked troubled as he followed Jim out of the kitchen. Stark could not get the morning meeting off his mind, and he felt as if he were playing hooky. There was serious work to be done, important work, and time was crucial. What would Lapham say if he knew he wasn't seated right now in front of a computer terminal? Church would probably put chains on him. Perhaps that was why he had agreed when Dorothy called; he did not like being pushed.

Halfway across the lawn, he noticed Merrill. It jarred him, and his mouth opened awkwardly. "Oh, it's you," he said shyly, avoiding her eyes. An unsettled feeling came over him as he reached out and shook her proffered hand.

Jim looked at them, then at Dorothy, smiling. "I think we should start. Byron probably forgot."

"He's very selective about forgetfulness," Dorothy said, leading them to the table. "A bomb couldn't dislodge Chaucer or Keats from his mind, but a simple dinner party? Impossible!" She laughed, but was irritated. She wanted Byron MacPhail at her party; she had invited him specifically to act as a buffer.

They arranged themselves around the table. Between bites of chicken, Merrill asked Stark, "Who was that military guy yesterday?"

Stark wished she had not brought up the symposium. "Oh, his name is Church," he said guardedly, remembering the Secretary's warning.

Merrill nodded, wiping her mouth with a napkin. "You should have seen him during that intermission. I never knew a man could fume and fuss so." She laughed lightly. "He worked the hallway looking for you. I heard him tell one of his military pals that you were afraid to face them."

Stark nodded awkwardly.

"He looked like a scowling Chinaman when he saw me. I gather he thought the presence of a woman at a gathering like that inappropriate. Did anyone say anything to you about my being there, Jim?"

Jim looked briefly at Dorothy, then said, "Well, actually, yes. Did someone approach you?"

"Not a soul." Her look was a question.

Jim laughed it off. "Well, I think it was just routine. They were asking about everyone."

Merrill looked at Jim quizzically. "Did I get you in trouble? That was supposed to be confidential, wasn't it?"

Jim laughed it off again. "Are you kidding, Merrill? You've practically grown up in the Labs. You're one of the family."

"I hope I didn't upset any applecarts," she said again. She turned directly to Stark: "Do you really think they understood what you were saying?"

"They understood, all right," replied Stark. "Whether or not they believe it is another question. What about you?"

"I . . . I guess so," Merrill answered hesitantly. "But I still really can't see the concern about security. Most people don't know anything about computers."

Stark was speechless, and Jim McKinnon interrupted: "Perhaps I can explain," said McKinnon. "There's a thing called Murphy's Law. It states that if something can go wrong, it will."

"And beyond that"—Stark took up the conversation suddenly—"something else. That even if something *can't* go wrong, it still will."

Merrill laughed. "Now, there's optimism," she said.

"Which is why I theorized the formula."

Dorothy interrupted: "I don't see why people need convincing. Have you read the newspapers?"

Merrill said, "Isn't that amazing? They can't figure it out, can they, Jim?"

"Not yet, but they will. What do you think, Stark? Do you think it's a programming flaw, or somebody doing what we should all be afraid of happening?"

Stark shrugged. "I don't know any more about it than you," he lied.

"But isn't it *slightly* coincidental that *both* exchanges and the three largest banks had their computers malfunction?" Dorothy asked.

Stark shook his head. "They all have similar systems. No, it really isn't that strange. A flaw in one could mean a flaw in the others."

"Then you don't think it's sabotage?"

"I wouldn't think so," Stark replied.

"It sure confirms what you were saying before," Merrill remarked. "Those banks have closed their doors. From what I read this evening, the stock exchanges are in a real mess. No trading and everybody shouting."

Stark wished he could tell his friends what the Secretary of Defense had told him that very morning; to talk about it might dampen his own growing anxiety. He had to change the subject. He looked Merrill directly in the eyes, and with a smile asked, "Do you know anything about pain?"

What an odd question, Merrill thought. She glanced at the McKinnons, who didn't know how to respond either. Merrill looked back at Stark and saw embarrassment on his face. "What about it?" she asked, quickly.

"Nothing, really," he replied, sensing that he had put his foot in his mouth. He could not stop now. "But nothing is why it interests me. Nobody knows anything about it, not at all." His mind raced as he tried to make sense out of his opening comment. Maybe General Church had had a point, after all: He was impulsive, did not think things through before acting.

"Well, we know it hurts," Merrill said and laughed, breaking the tension.

Stark was shaking his head. "We don't even know that," he said, seriously.

"How do you mean?" Dorothy asked.

"Injury means pain and pain *implies* injury," he answered. "In the womb we develop paired nerve fibers near our spinal cord; one fiber detects pressure and heat and injury, the other signals the brain. The fibers detect and register both pleasure and pain."

"So we do feel pain, then," Jim said, slightly exasperated.

"Like I was saying, not always. Of course, there is a state of pure pain. Few people know it, thank God. What most of us feel, though, and *interpret* as pain is often confused with emotions like fear and anxiety."

"And some lucky people never hurt?" Merrill asked. "Maybe I should tell my doctor."

"Your what?" Stark asked, thrown off his train of thought.

"I'm diabetic; injections hurt."

Stark suddenly felt a twinge of sympathy. "I'm sorry," he said. "But if nothing ever hurt, you'd be in worse shape," he said.

That was easy enough to say, thought Merrill, and the people who said it were those who usually had never been hurt. She wondered whether she had read him wrong, and she narrowed her eyes in question.

"Suppose you broke your ankle and couldn't feel pain," he said. "You would continue to walk until your ankle was destroyed forever. Some people are like that."

Now she understood. "How awful," she said, making a face. "Is the opposite also true?"

"Some amputees feel pain in a limb that is missing. They call it 'phantom pain.' . . ."

Jim and Dorothy looked over Stark's shoulder in a smile of recognition.

A falsetto voice boomed out behind Stark, "The pain in Spain lies mainly in the brain." Byron had apparently overheard a slice of their conversation as he approached, singing. "Pardon my entrance," he said, nearly bowing to the group, "But what on earth are you people talking about?" Before anyone could answer, he said, "Sitting there carving up a poor chicken and discussing *pain?* I didn't arrive a minute too soon."

They all laughed. Byron MacPhail, assistant professor of English literature at Harvard, was known and loved for his flamboyance as well as respected for his knowledge of literature. Byron was one of Merrill's friends and he had met the McKinnons through her. Byron had a consuming but brotherly love for Merrill. Jim and Dorothy had never quite figured out their relationship. Byron did not appear to be homosexual; nobody knew or much cared in that regard. Byron was something else—he was interested in everything and everybody, so much so that he could never concentrate on one thing long enough to see it to fruition. He absorbed everything with tremendous energy. When friends were out of sight, they were generally also out of mind, to be substituted by almost anyone—students, other professors, waitresses, policemen, even the Italian janitor at Dunster House, where Byron lived. The reason for Byron's late arrival, as he explained to the group, was that he had been talking about Dante to the janitor for upward of an hour.

Byron whisked a bouquet of flowers from behind his back and gave the bouquet to Dorothy with a kiss, then he turned to Merrill and said, "Who's your friend?"

Introductions made, Byron turned to Stark. "I *heard* about you," he said. "Didn't you cause a rumpus yesterday at MIT?"

"Not really," Stark said, warmed by the flattery but wondering how a literature professor at Harvard would have learned about the symposium. News traveled fast in the small academic community, Stark knew, and it wasn't always good news. Dorothy saved him from answering any more questions by handing Byron a plate of food.

Byron was rail thin. Among all the other things he tended to forget, one was food. It gave his face a hawkish, ascetic look beneath the mane of brownish-blond hair.

"What plans for *this* summer?" Jim asked.

Byron swallowed a chunk of meat. "India," he said. "It fascinates me, and I think I'll get a grant to plow into the roots of Kipling. Not that I'm much interested in old Rudyard, but it's a chance to see the country."

"I've always wanted to go there," Merrill said.

"Then you should," Byron said, earnestly. "If you want to do something, get to it. All it takes is a plane ticket and a guidebook; everything else will take care of itself. Always does. Like everything else—I mean, like everything you do. It's even true of love." He winked at Merrill.

"Byron's also an expert on love," Merrill chided for Stark's benefit. "He's read all about it."

Between forkfuls of salad, Byron continued his banter. Stark, preoccupied with filter designs and mathematical equations, tuned in with only half an ear.

"I decided it was something to do," Byron was saying. "I flew to Cicero, just south of Chicago, where Al Capone used to have his headquarters. There's a big freight yard owned by Burlington Northern, and I walked into the yard and asked the first engineer for a train West. He told me it was illegal, but I charmed him. Next morning I was on a mail freight to Seattle, riding the flatcar under the axle of a piggyback truck. I got kicked off by a yardbull in Cutbank—that's in Montana. I went to the head of the train and told the engineer I'd been riding with him since Cicero, and he told me to walk out of town about a mile and he'd pick me up. And he did. I rode the rest of the way in the cab, up front; we tooted and highballed our way through some extraordinary country. When it got dark we chugged through five solid miles of lightning bugs."

"If you don't mind telling, what does your father do?" Stark asked, curious about Byron's background.

Byron seemed to blush. "I don't think even he knows what he does," he remarked. "But he does it well, at least by the standards of income. He's a professional millionaire, I guess."

"And you ride the rails?" Stark asked.

"Hell, yes. Anybody can buy a ticket. But what fun is that?"

"I guess so," Stark said, then repeated, "I guess so."

"Don't get me wrong," Byron said when no one changed the subject. "I'm no danger freak. I'm about as cowardly as they come. I wouldn't climb a mountain for anything, and violence scares hell out of me. My little adventures are pretty harmless in the scheme of things, but they are fun."

Merrill laughed, remembering a story he had related one evening long ago. "Tell Stark about your Congo thing."

"Oh *that*. Merrill, I was drunk."

"Then have more wine," Jim said. He knew that Byron had gone to Africa two years ago.

Byron smiled broadly. It was a ridiculous story, a disaster really. They were all looking at him now, so he began. "If you have my temperament and you've ever read Conrad," he said directly to Stark, "then you'd do what I did and hop an airplane to Zaïre. I didn't know anything beyond my fascination for *Heart of Darkness,* which I took with me. I took an internal flight from Kinshasa to the old Stanleyville, a town they now call Kisangani." He gulped from the refilled glass. "Must I go on?"

"You can't stop now," Jim said.

"Well, I boarded a barge and off we headed down that monster river—a lot of Africans and me. It was like a floating company store. The natives would paddle up in their pirogues and throw aboard things like skinned monkeys, crocodiles with their jaws tied shut, big crates of vegetables and God knows what else. In return, they'd get paid in the river currency, which meant in bottles of a beer they call Simba. It was very exciting until the captain took a dislike to me. I was playing with a baby chimpanzee in the bow, and the captain came down from the bridge stinking like hell of Simba and ordered me to my cabin. Then that night, he must have been drunker still—we were near Lisala—he ran the mother aground on a sandbank in the middle of the river. We were stuck there in the middle of the Congo for two days. That was exhilarating too, until the beer ran out, and the food. And the heat began to make inroads on us. I lost about five pounds from sweat. Then a totally illiterate Zaïre Army colonel threatened to *shoot me* unless I gave him money to buy a pirogue to take him off. To this day I don't know if he was serious. But I'll never forget his words: *'Je vais vous tuer, à moins . . .'* Well, like somebody said once, nothing concentrates the mind so well as knowing you're going to be hanged in the morning. I didn't have any money, but I convinced the fellow that I'd give him anything he wanted if he got us both off. The rich American and all. And we did just that, floated in this dinky canoe for five or six miles downriver to a Catholic mission station." He stopped and held up his arms. "That's about it."

"Tell how you repaid the guy," Merrill said.

"Oh yeah, that. Well, I sent him a lifetime subscription to the *New York Review of Books.*"

When they stopped laughing, Byron said, "Merrill always promises to come with me, but she never does. Stark, maybe you can convince her. Maybe all three of us should go to India."

After coffee, Jim invited them into his study for a brandy, but Stark held back. Merrill watched him with a half smile. He seemed so vulnerable and fresh to her. There was a quality in him that she could not identify—perhaps a mixture of his shyness and his authority when he talked about subjects he knew. There was an innocence about him that she guessed Byron had never known. Stark had been sheltered, cloistered even in the academic community since an early age, Dorothy had told her, and maybe that was why. The one thing Merrill did know for certain: She liked it.

"Umm, Dorothy," Stark said, "I've still got a full night's work ahead."

Dorothy looked at her watch, then at Stark. "You're not going to work at this hour, are you?"

"I do my clearest thinking in the early hours."

Merrill said, "I think I should be going, too."

"I might as well tag along," Byron added. "I'll walk you home, Merrill."

"We can all go together," she said, then to Dorothy, "I hope you don't think we're running out on you."

"Of course not."

They said their good-byes, then left. Merrill lived farthest from the McKinnons, Stark the closest. They said very little as they walked down the sidewalk, gliding through the shadows. The evening was just warm enough for comfort, a perfect early-summer night.

"That was fun," Stark commented, making conversation.

"It was," Merrill agreed. "They're wonderful people. Sometimes I wonder what my social life would be without them. I must be there at dinner once a week."

As they turned onto Massachusetts Avenue, Byron stopped. "I'm heading right. What about you, Merrill?"

Before she could answer, Stark was asking. "Would you like to come up for a coffee?" Stark blushed. Coffee sounded so square, he thought. Probably most people asked her up for a drink or a snort of cocaine. He rarely invited guests in, and he did not even keep alcohol in his apartment.

"I'd love to," Merrill said instantly.

"Why not?" added Byron.

Stark nodded. There was no backing down now. He wondered what these new "friends" would think of where he lived. His apartment was crowded with books, printouts, files and the IBM 4331 minicomputer. It was not exactly uncomfortable, but it was a mess. There was a sofa and an overstuffed chair. He had not thought to hang prints or posters on the walls. Thinking about it now, he wished he had not been so spontaneous with his invitation.

As they approached the two-story house, Stark steered them up the path to the private side entrance. He took out his keys and unlocked the door leading to the stairway. They climbed the landing with Byron chattering about the high price of rents. Stark stopped in front of the apartment door and inserted the key. "That's strange," he said, turning to Merrill. "I forgot to lock up before I went out." He shrugged, not wanting to make a point of the fact. He never forgot. He withdrew the key and turned the handle.

"Hey, Bart!" he yelled, leading the way in. "We've got company."

A blur of motion in the dark caught his eye. Before he could draw a breath, he was slammed violently against the wall. As he spun around, he could see other shapes pulling down Merrill and Byron. The person who had ahold of Stark was heavy and incredibly strong; Stark could feel the hot breath on his neck. Stark sank to the floor beneath the weight.

Merrill was screaming, and Stark tried to wiggle across the floor, but he was stopped by a pain so excruciating, his head swam. Something hard was being pressed into the soft nerve center under his jawbone, and as the pressure steadily increased, Stark grunted and lost consciousness. As he felt himself go, he wanted to yell out, but his voice failed.

Minutes later, Stark opened his eyes to discover Merrill's face looking into his. "Stark?" she was saying. "Please, Stark, are you all right?"

He turned his head. The intruders had fled through the open door; Byron was on the sofa rubbing the side of his head in bewilderment. As Stark rolled on his side, a wave of nausea overcame him, and he fell back, panting. What had they wanted? To rob him? Slowly he got to his feet and slumped into the chair. Merrill, who appeared to be less hurt than either of the men, came out of the bathroom holding a water-soaked towel, which she pressed on Stark's forehead.

In their collective shock, nobody talked. Stark climbed unsteadily to his feet and went into the adjoining study, where he checked the drawers and desktop. After a few minutes, he returned to the living room. "What were they after?" he asked.

Merrill looked bewildered.

"Did they get anything?"

Merrill looked around her, and Byron probed his pockets. Suddenly it dawned on Merrill. "My purse. They must have taken it."

Byron was regaining his equilibrium. "They got my wallet," he said. "What about—"

"Mine, too," Stark said, checking his pants pocket. "Did either of you see their faces?"

"It happened too fast," Merrill said.

"Yeah, and the dark," Byron said.

"Should we call the police?" Merrill asked.

Of course they should, Stark thought. Housebreakers could be caught. There were fingerprints, or something left behind. But he remembered the warning he had received at the Pentagon from the Secretary of Defense. "Don't get into any trouble now," he remembered Lapham saying to him as he left. Lapham had told him to maintain a low profile. Going to the police would make that impossible; they would want to know what kind of work he did, what the printouts were for. It would get in the newspapers. Church would have a perfect argument for keeping him in Washington.

"I'll do it later," Stark announced to the others. "Byron, why don't you take Merrill home?" Stark wanted to be alone. He would have to inspect thoroughly the printout that contained his initial research on the new filter, and he could not do that with company. He suspected this had not been a simple robbery.

Byron got to his feet. "Are you okay?" he asked Merrill.

"Sure, just a bit shaken." She saw that Stark wanted them to leave. There were hasty good-byes and arrangements to meet at noon the following day.

Once they had gone, Stark went to his desk and checked each item carefully. His working papers and the few preliminary printouts on the INTELSAT filter were untouched. The IBM 4331 checked out perfectly. In his bedroom, nothing was out of place: He guessed that they had not even entered it. As he returned to the living room, he suddenly realized what was missing: Bart. Usually the puppy bounded through the hinged port on the kitchen door from his bed on the back porch seconds after Stark entered the apartment. "Bart," he yelled. "Come here, Bart." He opened the window in the study and repeated the call, thinking the puppy might have fallen asleep in the backyard.

He went into the dark kitchen. There was a scratching sound, like a fingernail being rubbed weakly across plaster. He opened the side door and checked the dog's basket. Not there. Then he turned on the light.

The sound quickened and he saw it: The puppy had been nailed through the neck to the wall by a screwdriver. Stark moaned, "Bart, little Bart."

A blood-soaked note had been speared on the shaft of the screwdriver. "Follow our instructions," it read, "or we will continue to destroy the things around you." What instructions? he wondered, fear and revulsion gripping him.

THURSDAY, JUNE 18, 1987

"Satellites, like other technologies, are vulnerable to certain types of harm. It would not be prudent for a society to depend exclusively on satellite links. There should be alternative facilities. Survivability in an immensely complex technological society depends on diversity."

JAMES MARTIN,
Communications Satellite
Systems

7:30 A.M., *PDT: Los Banos, California*

"It's a *treat* to talk with you, *Mister* Hennessy," Susie Kinnard remarked, kicking her horse to stop it from making unattractive noises. The damn animal was embarrassing her: "Neddie says so many nice things about you. . . ." She tried to blush when Clint Hennessy turned in his saddle to look at her. Instead, she stuttered. ". . . And they . . . they're all true. *I* find, anyway."

Shortly after she and Neddie arrived in Los Banos the night before, Susie, searching for something in common with Clint Hennessy, had billed herself as a horsewoman of distinction. Now, as they finished the early-morning ride, Susie Kinnard had failed. The horse she was riding seemed to sense deception, which was why it insisted on breaking wind.

Galloping ahead toward the stables, Hennessy said, "I told you last night, young lady, the name's Clint."

Encouraging her horse to follow, Susie smiled, thinking that she might be getting somewhere with the handsome millionaire after all. That was her end purpose, and she was paying for it, first by having to sleep with Neddie and now by suffering the discomfort of the saddle. When Neddie had called to say that Clint had ordered him West to his ranch in the San Joachin Valley, she had warmed instantly on the phone, asking him to come up for a drink. It was the first invitation on her part in months. She was working too hard and needed a few days' rest, she had told Vickers. Wangling the invitation to accompany Vickers had been simple. Landing Clint Hennessy was going to be another proposition altogether. When she flirted with him at dinner the night before, using Neddie as a foil, Hennessy had not responded. Hennessy, she knew, had divorced his wife three years ago after a celebrated alimony fight, and since that time, according to the gossip columnists, he had entertained several women, but no one steadily. Despite that, he hadn't seemed interested in Susie. He had treated her with polite reserve, as a guest and the girlfriend of his broker, and nothing more, not even when she had stayed up with him after Neddie had gone to bed. She had talked about issues that she hoped would interest Hennessy, including horses, which had led to this sunrise ride across the ranch.

The ranch itself, she thought, was magnificent. She hadn't taken in much of Hennessy's talk about crop yields, but the land itself was vast and beautiful. The ranch amounted to a private satrapy in the heart of California, and the house itself was a palace. Hennessy seemed to have everything: a black Ferrari, an airstrip where he could park his Beech Baron, a large swimming pool, tennis courts and sauna. More than this, she knew that his wealth made the appurtenances of the ranch—even the ranch itself—trifles by comparison. To be a guest at the ranch was every girl's dream, and Susie was not planning to waste her opportunity by having fun. If only Clint wouldn't be so damned polite, she thought finally as she dismounted and gave the reins to a stable-hand.

"I hope that didn't take too much out of you," Hennessy said, leading her toward the house. "Maybe you should have started a little easier."

So he had noticed her poor horsemanship. "It was perfect," she replied. "I hope we can do it again tomorrow. Takes a couple of days to get used to the saddle, again."

When they came into the air-conditioned kitchen from the hot morning sun, Neddie was sitting at the long table in the breakfast room reading the paper. He looked foolish, Susie thought, in that dude's outfit. He even had on a neckerchief of the Tom Mix vintage, cinched with a turquoise and hammered silver ring.

Clint had read the paper, but asked anyway, "Anything of interest?"

"Nothing we don't know already," replied Vickers. "They are making a whole lot of excuses why they don't know anything, but the bottom line's the same. The computers are down."

Clint put his arm around Susie's shoulder. "You run along

now," he told her. "We'll meet you out by the pool when we've finished."

It was an order, not a request, and she could not object, no matter how much she wanted to stay and listen. She did not want Clint to think of her as an empty-headed bimbo like the ones she had read about his dating in gossip columns. Still, there would be other opportunities to prove her intelligence, and her mind turned to the red bikini she would wear by the pool. Without a word, she disappeared through the door.

After a minute, Hennessy said, "That's a nice young woman you have there." He pulled out a chair and sat across from Vickers.

Vickers lowered the newspaper and shrugged. "She's available to the highest bidder," he said matter-of-factly.

"Just trying to be friendly," Hennessy remarked awkwardly.

"So is she. If you want in the game, she's willing to play."

Hennessy did not want to get involved in his broker's problems. Hennessy puttered around getting himself a cup of coffee.

They had yet to broach the subject that had brought them together. Vickers had been delighted by the sudden invitation to fly West and had come prepared with intelligence on the corporation that interested Hennessy. A diversified aerospace firm, LTW had prospered from its defense contracts, though in recent years it had branched into the consumer area, creating subsidiaries that manufactured solid-state electronic equipment from pocket calculators to LED wristwatches and computer components.

Hennessy initiated the discussion. "You know why I bought those LTW shares the other day?"

"You didn't have a position, and it's a growth stock, particularly now that LTW will probably get the MX contract."

"That's true," Hennessy said. "But the reason I want you here is, we are going to do some trading before the exchanges go back in business."

"The SEC might have something to say about that," Vickers continued. With trading suspended on the exchanges, the SEC had prohibited stock movement on an outside, extra-exchange basis.

Hennessy smiled. "I stand corrected," he said without apology. "I meant to say *promissory* trading."

"Of LTW?"

"To acquire LTW."

Vickers' eyes widened. Such a huge acquisition, of a financially healthy company, was nearly impossible. Stockholders would not sell except at hugely inflated prices, and no single person or consortium had the kind of money to make a plausible offer.

Hennessy enjoyed Vickers' reaction. "I've wanted that property for several years. It's a gamble, I know. A big gamble. But when the exchanges closed, I got an idea. It'll take perfect timing."

Vickers spluttered, "But the stockholders won't sell for what you can offer."

"We'll see. How much weight would you say the MX contract has on the value of the stock?"

"Clint," Vickers objected, "the Pentagon has not even awarded that contract yet. It's only a rumor that LTW will get it. There are three other bidders in the running."

"And the odds-on favorite is LTW."

"Really, yes. They're the only ones anyone takes seriously."

"Then please, answer my question. How important is that MX contract?"

"It means around forty billion over nine years. Sustaining stuff."

"That's how I figure it. You said 'rumor.' What if we turn that rumor around, and play it the other way—say they are not getting the contract and for reasons no one's willing to define."

"That could hurt their credibility."

"Especially if they're perceived as having almost got the contract. That would mean something that had gone wrong. And stockholders . . ."

"That's easy enough. Stockholders would be more willing to sell, and probably at a cheaper price than is quoted now."

"Precisely. I'm only asking for those two things. The majority stock will be within my price range, and it will be available. You know Harvey Streeter, of course?"

"He does some trading for you," Vickers said, suppressing his own chagrin at hearing that name. For months he had hoped Hennessy would shift his major portfolio from Streeter's hands to his. By comparison with Harvey Streeter—a senior partner at Morgan Stanley and one of the country's fifteen most powerful traders—Neddie Vickers was small beer.

"You bought LTW for me the other day. Now Streeter is going to sell it." He looked at Vickers' querulous expression, then added, "Yes, when the exchanges open. You see, I am going to float a rumor of my own, when you and I have decided on the timing. The rumor can't hold for more than, say, twenty-four hours. As narrowly as possible, we have to estimate when the exchanges will go back in business."

"Did you know the computers would go down?" Vickers asked.

Hennessy shook his head. "Me? I had nothing to do with it."

"And the rumor? That LTW has lost the MX contract?"

"That's exactly right. I asked you to buy those LTW shares because I wanted a better position, nothing more. But once the exchanges went down, I saw how I can use those shares to buttress a rumor of my own making."

"By selling them?"

Hennessy sipped his coffee, then set down the cup. "Streeter trusts me implicitly. I've always played straight with him and I never deal in rumors. I'm going to ask him to find me a buyer for my LTW shares. He'll ask why, naturally. I'll tell him what I've heard. He knows I don't trade in fantasy. He will assume I know more than I'm saying—MX has fallen out of bed at LTW."

"Jesus," Vickers almost howled. "He'll spin through his best clients like a dervish, and they'll sell, too."

Hennessy held up his hand. "Not so. Streeter has his reputation on the line, so he'll need independent confirmation." He
looked Vickers in the eye. "Do you know who my mole is in the
Pentagon?"

Vickers shook his head.

"General Hedley Church, head of Worldwide Systems
Command. General Church is fifty-five years old. In two years, he
plans to retire. For some years he has entertained the notion of
joining the LTW Board. I will put him there."

"But he has nothing to do with procurement."

"He has tremendous influence, Neddie. One word from
him goes a long way, and besides, I'm talking about rumor. One
of Church's closest confidants in the Pentagon is a General
Colombo. Guess what?"

"I don't see it."

"Streeter's mole. General Church will put out the word to
General Colombo, and Colombo will pass it along to Streeter when
he calls. *Then* Streeter will move."

"It's brilliant," Vickers remarked in a whisper. "And you
will buy—"

"—through you, Neddie. Once the rumor is firmly im-
planted, you get in touch with Streeter. Tell him you have a secret
buyer for any and all LTW stock he wants to move. He won't ask
who you represent; he'll assume your client is buying out of ignorance. You will be my invisible buyer. It wants to run, and it has
a place to go—at bargain-basement rates!"

"And all of this in promissory contracts . . ."

"With the exchanges down and all the confusion, it won't
be hard to start a panic. But it won't last—the market's reopening
will be a powerful stabilizer. We have to have everything ready
for that first hour of real trading, before things sort themselves
out."

Vickers nodded thoughtfully. "For the moment, before you
contact Streeter, we need the best intelligence we can get on the
exchanges. I'll get to work. Can I use your office?"

"Certainly," replied Hennessy absent-mindedly. His attention had shifted to the pool scene outside the window behind Vickers' head, where Susie Kinnard was bouncing on the end of the diving board, her breasts bulging out of the skimpy red bikini top.

3:00 P.M. (8:00 A.M., EDT): Moscow, U.S.S.R.

Within the hierarchy of the KGB, three men controlled the First Directorate, the arm responsible for overall policy. Theirs was the delicate task of planning the secret needs of the Soviet Union. Each week on Thursday afternoon, the three men conferred, their agenda depending entirely on external events. Normally they limited their discussions to overall strategy, the balancing of needs against strengths in broad areas of concern such as defense, expansion and geopolitical goals set down by the Central Committee of the Politburo, then relegating assignments to the Second and Third Directorates. But on this Thursday, as they took their places in the high-backed velvet chairs around the marble-topped conference table in the KGB's headquarters on Dzerzhinsky Street, they were to examine not a broad policy issue, but a single question of personnel.

The executive director and chairman who led the discussions was a man whose gauntness placed in relief—some thought comically—his most salient features. His nose was a virtual beak, his ears resembled waxen butterfly wings, and he used his chin—a craggy, pointed thing that stuck out like an exclamation point—to punctuate his verbal thrusts. No matter what people thought personally about Uri Dolowsky, they rarely spoke disparagingly; he was not a man to be ridiculed, either behind his back or to his face.

Dolowsky opened a folder. "I find it expedient," he told the others, "to release Colonel Domintrin from prison and to return him to favor."

The group was stunned. Three weeks earlier, they had

agreed to strip Domintrin of all rank and exile him to the North because of the last "tests" of his FOBS program—tests that had failed utterly. A reversal of that decision, thought Nikolai Zimyatov, was dangerous. To reinstate Domintrin would suggest indecision to the leaders of the Central Committee and to the directors of the Second and Third Directorates. Vacillation like this was a weakness. Zimyatov, however, said nothing, awaiting explanation from Dolowsky.

"The reason for this proposal is simple," Dolowsky continued. "We have no other person in the State who can serve us as well."

Vasily Bazhukov, the third member of the committee, objected. "Serve us, comrade?" he asked sardonically. "The man has had nothing but repeated failures. Less than a month ago he destroyed another valuable SS-18 missile on the Komarov testing range. These failures are expensive, comrades—and pointless. He will never succeed with his wild plans."

"I recognize the validity of your argument, Comrade Bazhukov. It was on that basis that, some months ago, we downgraded Domintrin's 'positive development' approach and agreed to set into motion alternative courses of action. What I want to tell you today is that one of those courses has borne fruit. Our opportunity has suddenly expanded. Luck has now favored us. However, to take advantage of our good fortune, we must, I am afraid, turn to the very person we have all hoped to disgrace—Comrade Domintrin."

Zimyatov and Bazhukov awaited details, but few were to be forthcoming.

"As you know," proceeded Dolowsky, "each of us has set up and been pursuing—as part of our overall program of 'staggered' or 'alternate' development—a Scorched Earth objective. We did this because, and only because, we have been forced to concede defeat in the technological race—at least where computers are concerned. This is a defeat we cannot afford; Soviet government and research centers, though acquainted with computers only relatively recently, have already become too dependent on these machines for us to forgo them. However, since the stoppage of technology transfers, practically all of our Western-built computers have become inoperative. We have had only one choice—to bring American technology down to our level. We have agreed to that tactic. Now I am pleased to report the near success of one of our Scorched Earth operatives. Operating procedures prevent me from revealing to you any details. Let me say, however, the following—that he has had confirmation of, and believes he may be able to track down, a mathematical formula by which all computer systems in America using a certain chain of satellites can be rendered useless at one stroke."

Zimyatov sucked in his breath. "At one stroke, comrade?" he asked, disbelieving.

"I cannot elaborate."

"And the banks and stock exchanges are the first targets!" exclaimed Zimyatov. He had read of the American troubles in secret memos, and today in this morning's *Pravda.* Naturally the symbols of capitalism would be the first to be destroyed.

Dolowsky pursed his lips. "I repeat: I cannot elaborate, except to insist that Domintrin be reinstated. His expertise is vital. The formula, should we succeed in locating it, is extremely complex. Understanding is one thing. Implementing it will be another. Domintrin is crucial to both."

"How will he be used?" asked Vasily Bazhukov.

"He must go to America."

Zimyatov reacted with a sour expression. "Too dangerous," he said. "He will defect the instant he lands. I have studied his dossier. I infer that his first love is neither for State nor for the Chairman. It is for the advancement of computer science. I therefore doubt seriously whether he will assist. He is no patriot."

"That, too, has been considered," Dolowsky said.

Zimyatov objected. "Why can't we process the formula here? Domintrin can work in our own laboratories and we eliminate any risk."

"A good question," Dolowsky replied. "Unfortunately, you do not understand. Computer science is an area in which you and I are abysmally ignorant. We are also fundamentally deficient in computer hardware. There is the possibility that the formula can be used only in North America, in which case we will have to have Domintrin on station, once he has evaluated the material." He slapped the table. The cracking sound reverberated off the concrete walls. "Are we agreed, then?" he asked heartily, as though disagreement were possible.

The other two nodded, Zimyatov more solemnly than Bazhukov.

"Then Domintrin is on his way to America," Dolowsky concluded.

12:05 P.M., *EDT: Boston, Massachusetts*

What the frig is wrong with this country, anyhow? mused Harry Verdeen, hefting the duffle bag to his shoulder. Before boarding, the idea of riding *The Patriot* had conjured up images of good food, clean seats and patient, polite conductors. What he had found instead was a clammy passenger car crammed with college kids smelling of patchouli and hemp, overpriced soggy hamburgers and warm beer, and a ride that arrived an hour behind schedule and had bounced and jostled him so much that his bones ached. Amtrak, he thought disgustedly, am *some* track. He wished he'd taken the hound.

Verdeen had needed a ride without hassles. Prescott had called to ask him to fill in on guard duty for two sick employees, and had made the request sound like repayment for getting Verdeen his detective's license. Verdeen had refused point blank, and the arguing had begun. Finally he had hung up on his boss. To play detective was all right in theory, but if it interfered with something they wanted, it wasn't. What if he had been on a *real* vacation? Verdeen wondered. Would they have called him back then?

Almost immediately after he had hung up the phone, Ruth, his wife, had hounded him again for just that, a real vacation. It wasn't fair not to get away when they had time off, she'd complained. Verdeen understood her feelings, but then the bullet fired that took Horace's life really wasn't fair either. Ruth's complaining, though, had served a purpose: It had made Verdeen decide to take his pursuit one step farther.

Maybe four miserable hours in a train to Boston was idiotic. Idiotic or not, he owed this much to Horace. He walked down the platform toward the South Station ticket office. According to the Amtrak timetable, he should be able to catch a four-o'clock train home, which meant he could spend the money now on a taxi instead of blowing it on a hotel room. If he had to stay overnight, he wouldn't have enough for the return fare. Oh well, he thought, he'd hitched before.

On the drive out to Brookline Verdeen tried to strike up a conversation about Boston but the driver, a squat fellow who was all stomach and no legs, pulled the snap-brimmed cap down on his head and said he did not get paid for guided tours. Verdeen wondered why most taxi drivers were creeps, whether in New York or here.

Beacon Street here was an endless thoroughfare, and Verdeen presumed they had arrived several times before the cab pulled up to a halt in front of a busy commercial block boasting a Woolworth's, Filene's, and McCann's. Verdeen searched for No. 1038. "There, over there!" said Verdeen, finally spotting the small, rusty sign over a painted metal door, "Grunwald's Commercial Hardware Company." He paid the driver, pulled himself and his duffle from the cab and walked up to the unprepossessing entranceway and pushed open the door.

Grunwald's was no lightweight house—and hardware store. Like a massive, chambered storeroom, the room stretched before him: row after row of shelving and cabinets. Every item was classified, filed and put away until the proper professional requested it. The place smelled of rubber and preservative grease. No sales help was in sight, but as Verdeen moved toward the back, a skinny black kid appeared and looked at him curiously.

Verdeen said he wanted to speak with Mr. Grunwald.

"Dead," the black kid replied, cryptically.

"The owner, then."

The kid shrugged and disappeared. A moment later a big man with a hatchet face, thick arms and a bull neck came up. He wore greasy coveralls, and looked displeased with the interruption. Verdeen said he needed a favor, and showed him his detective's license. That perked up the owner, who identified himself as Jim Bilkays. Bilkays explained that he had been in the middle of "As the World Turns" when Verdeen interrupted.

Verdeen produced the Medeco key and explained why he had traveled to Boston. "Do you keep records?" he asked.

Bilkays scratched his balding head, leaving a grease mark. "Sure we got records, all kinds of records, thousands of them. We never throw anything out. Follow me," he said abruptly, leading Verdeen into the back office. Strips of aluminum foil were stuck to the aerial of a run-down television. In front of it stood a dumpy chair with broken springs. A long-haired mutt slept in the corner.

"Help yourself," said Bilkays, pointing with a stubby finger to the wall farthest from the television.

Verdeen groaned, Bilkays wasn't kidding. There were literally thousands of invoices, catalogues, order slips, newspapers and God only knew what else. "But this could take days," he said, wondering if he shouldn't just give up.

Bilkays sank into the chair, laughing with great bubbling sounds. "If you want that I should say we're on computer, fine, we're on computer. Mr. Verdeen, you're the computer."

Verdeen waded in.

12:45 P.M., *EDT: Cambridge, Massachusetts*

Depressed and sore from the bruising he had taken the night before, Stark Rousseau shuffled into the kitchen and took a carton of orange juice from the Frigidaire. He poured a glass, dripping some of it down his pajama tops as he drank, then went into the bathroom. As he stood under the warm, fine spray of the shower, he wondered again about last night. After burying Bart, he had gone back to work on the filter, but his thoughts had not stopped roaming. Unable to concentrate, he had tried to sleep but his mind raced too fast. Finally getting up, he had forced himself back on mathematics, and was well absorbed in his equations when the sun finally rose. The research had gone well, and he was almost to the point of sending some data through to the mainframes at the Labs. He had wandered into the bedroom for a few minutes' nap, but had fallen fast asleep. When he awoke, he discovered to his surprise that it was nearly noon.

He soaped himself, then let the lather run off down the drain. He reached down to the tub's edge for a bottle of Prell and lathered his hair while thinking about his assailants. It simply did not add up. They had killed Bart painfully and cruelly, beaten up him and his guests, and taken their wallets. And left that note. Who were they and what did they want? Perhaps it was a matter for the police; certainly Stark did not feel confident dealing with it alone. But the police were prohibited: He could not submit to their inquiries and keep his promise to Lapham and the Secretary of Defense. Stark also ruled out going directly to Lapham for the time being—there was no surer way of having himself locked away in some rabbit's warren in the Pentagon. Stark knew that his most important job was to get the filters redesigned, and at once. He was almost there already, but moving him to unfamiliar surroundings would only break his creative rhythm and delay his solution that much longer.

He stepped from the shower, toweled off, shaved and combed his hair, discovering as he did that his depression was rapidly being replaced by determination. The intruders wanted to frighten him; they had succeeded. They had made good their threat in advance and, given their viciousness, he was consoled that they had not gone farther. If they contacted him again, as promised, he would examine their demands and go to the police, or Lapham, as necessary. In the meantime, he would not give them the satisfaction of knowing how scared he really was.

In the bedroom he pulled on a pair of cords and a clean shirt, the one with the French cuffs that Claudette had given to him. He inserted the collar stays with some difficulty and fixed the cuff links, remembering that he planned to give Merrill a present at lunch, something small that would tell her, without his actually trying to say it, what he was beginning to feel. When he'd finally gone to bed, his thoughts had turned to her. How could he communicate that, without seeming silly? He considered flowers. Too common, he thought, wandering into the study. Jewelry? No, too extravagant. Then he struck on an idea. He sat at the IBM 4331 terminal and referred to a thick telephonelike directory. Flipping up the activator switch on the 4331, he typed "ECHO V." Telephone lines carried the request to the Beeman Labs' central computer. An instant later, a qualifier appeared on the VDT above the terminal where Stark sat.

"SUBJECT AND QUALITY?" it asked.

Stark typed the answer, "SUBJECT—AMERICAN POET. QUALITY—SUCCINCT." Then he waited for ECHO to respond. Suddenly in green letters on the VDT, he had a poem, of sorts—"ALL GOD'S CHILLUN GOT ALGO-RITHM." Stark chuckled at the nonsense. Still, it was better than anything he could write. He instructed again, "SUBJECT— BEAUTIFUL MERRILL. QUALITY—EXTENDED."

The computer digested the references and drew rhymes from its memory.

"YOU SAY MERRILL IS BELLE
BUT HOW CAN I TELL
LOCKED HERE
IN A MECHANICAL SPHERE
WITHOUT EYES.

"YOU BE THE JUDGE
AND IF ECHO DID NOT A
SMUDGE
ON ALGOR INK

```
THEN THIS WILL SAY
FOR YOU
WHAT YOU THINK
WITHOUT LIES."
```

`. . . . . . LINE LIMIT EXCEEDED . . . . . .`

Smiling and inwardly pleased with the result, Stark shut off the 4331. As he was rereading the poem, the telephone rang. He reached across a mound of printouts on the desk. "Yes?" he asked in a tentative voice.

The caller identified himself as James MacDonald, the manager of Stark's branch of the Shawmut National Bank. In a crisp, businesslike voice, MacDonald asked him to come immediately to the bank. "There's a serious irregularity," he said. "Your account indicates a deficit of major proportions, sir."

As the manager talked, Stark became alarmed. This was not another coincidence, another bit of bad luck, an error that had gone against him by mistake. Somebody connected with the break-in was working on him, wearing him down. Somehow it had to be connected—the dog, the robbery, roughing them up and now this fake business with the Shawmut. It had to be fake. He maintained a minumum balance of $500. A check had never bounced on him. Conscientiousness in financial affairs was a matter of pride to him, and even more, a responsibility he could not ignore because of Claudette—when she needed money for treatment, it had to be on hand. "I'll be right down," Stark said.

MacDonald would not be placated. "I must emphasize the seriousness of this irregularity," he said.

"Sir," Stark said, "I heard you the first time."

He hung up, nearly throwing the phone in the cradle. MacDonald's accusations made him angry. To satisfy himself, Stark sifted through the papers on his desk, at last finding the most recent bank statement. The balance was $1,521.

Five minutes later, he copied the ECHO poem from the VDT, put the slip of paper in his pocket and prepared to leave. He took a windbreaker from the closet, glanced once around the apartment and then went down the stairs and into the street.

Despite his concern, he could not help but notice the beauty of the day. It was warm with the fragrance of flowers and new foliage. The sky was a faded blue without a cloud in sight. He was glad he was going to meet Merrill and Byron for lunch— he knew he should get back to his research, but this business with the bank had rattled him.

He pushed open the glass door of the Shawmut National Bank at Central Square and looked past long lines of customers to the platform, a regimental row of desks facing him. He found the placard he wanted. "Mr. MacDonald?"

The man seemed cordial enough, thought Stark, taking a seat and introducing himself.

"Let's see if we can't straighten this out, Dr. Rousseau," he said, then, "Your last check was for $500, drawn last Friday. Is that correct?" He referred to a printout.

"That's right," Stark replied.

"And you're certain about that being the last check you wrote?"

"Absolutely."

MacDonald took a long look at the printout, then said, "According to this, you are now overdrawn to the sum of $4,000."

Stark looked astonished. "That's impossible," he said. "I never maintain that sort of balance. Therefore, I wouldn't withdraw that much at any time."

MacDonald, whose red hair and fair complexion made him look younger than he was, turned the printout around for Stark to see. "It's there in black and white," MacDonald said, pointing to the appropriate column.

Stark did not bother to look. "Clearly the computer has made a mistake," he said. "Have you checked the run?"

"Of course, twice," MacDonald replied. "I made doubly certain because until now, your record with us has been flawless."

"No doubt you know about the troubles at Bank of America and Citibank," Stark said. "Maybe the same thing's happened here."

MacDonald smiled. "Not a chance," he said.

"You shut down your computers?"

"We tightened our security. The computer is checked for accuracy on an hourly basis. If something does go wrong, we would know instantaneously. So far"—and he rapped the desktop —"knock on wood, everything is working just as it should."

"Could there have been a forgery?" Stark asked.

MacDonald produced the check. "This is the last one processed. Is that your signature?"

Stark looked, agreeing it was. "Until you get this straightened out," he said, "transfer the $10,000 from my savings account."

"I already examined that account," MacDonald said, because I was planning to suggest the same. There is no $10,000 in your savings. There isn't $1.00."

For the second time, Stark thought about the computer. "That's also impossible," he said. He never withdrew from his savings, in case Claudette needed extra money.

"I'm sorry, Dr. Rousseau, but I'm going to demand that you cover the overdraft as soon as possible."

"And where do you suggest I get the money?" he asked sardonically.

"Unfortunately I cannot help you there."

Stark nodded. People like MacDonald always believed computers before they believed people. If the computer said he was overdrawn, he was overdrawn, no matter what the truth. "Would it satisfy you, sir, if I got an affidavit from the police to the effect that my house was robbed last night? There is a good possibility that the robbers stole checks."

"An affidavit, unfortunately, is no substitute for the money."

"Don't you see, sir, I'm being set up? Someone has penetrated your computers and is robbing me—robbing *you*," Stark explained.

Replied MacDonald wearily, "Our security systems are highly sophisticated, and we check them daily. We have already inspected them today, after this matter came to our attention. There is no problem in the security system, thank you, Dr. Rousseau. The problem is with your account."

How could they have done this to him? thought Stark to himself. In his mind he ran through all the banking procedures he knew—how deposits and withdrawals were routed through the bank's computers. There was an obvious flaw, and somehow his tormentors had found it. They were sinking their teeth into him, going for the jugular. Well, he knew how to play with computers as well. If there was a flaw in the bank's system, he could find it. He would have to, if he was going to defend himself. A germ of an idea formed in his mind.

"All right, give me until Monday, and I'll have the money for you," Stark said. "I promise."

"Good luck then, sir," MacDonald said, standing up at his desk.

With a curt good-bye, Stark crossed the bank lobby and walked out onto the sidewalk. He was tempted to stride right back in and implement his plan on the spot, at the Shawmut, but thought better of it. Anonymity was a necessity. He looked up and down Massachusetts Avenue. Any other bank would do, he thought, spying the sign "Coolidge Bank" across the street. He dodged through traffic, bounded over the curb and into the revolving doors. The bank was crowded, which suited his purpose, and most of the bank officers were on lunch hour. He looked over the officers' platform, choosing the officer he would approach.

Charles G. Fulton II, the branch's second assistant manager for new accounts, had thinning, sandy hair, a weak chin, frail shoulders and, from the volume of Kleenex in his wastebasket and the redness of his nose, a terrible cold. Stark had a last-minute hesitation—but reassured himself that he was only doing what was necessary. He needed the cash now, and he would never be able to get money out of the credit union in time—and even if he did, there was no bank account in which it would be safe, nor any mattress. He would simply have to "borrow"—unofficially. Stark went up to his desk and clearing his throat said, "Excuse me, but I'd like to open a new account."

Fulton looked up with watery, red-rimmed eyes. "Right you are," he said with a forced cheeriness. He indicated the chair beside the desk with his hand, opened a manila folder and pulled out a form. "Student, are you, Mr. . . . ?"

". . . Owens, Robert G. Owens." Stark replied. "Harvard." He embellished, "Law School."

The manager eyed him.

"I'm a teaching assistant at the summer school."

"The sum of the initial deposit?"

"Will twenty-five dollars do?"

"Coolidge has no minimum," Fulton replied, taking a tissue from a box on the corner of his desk. "Check or cash?"

Stark took several bills from his pocket and laid them in front of the banker, who scooped them up, counted them and tapped them into a neat pile. "Are you from Massachusetts?" he asked.

"Yes, Springfield," Stark replied.

When Fulton asked for his address, income, age and marital status, Stark amplified his alias. He altered his own signature by bending the letters sharply to the left. Fulton looked at the cards and grunted satisfaction, then assigned Stark an account number and gave him temporary checks and deposit slips. "Well," he said finally, "That's about it. You'll get your printed checks in around ten days."

Stark shook his hand and got up to leave. Then, in an apparent afterthought, turned to Fulton and said, "I should tell you, I expect to make a substantial deposit in the next day or so . . . probably in excess of eighty thousand dollars. Is there anything you should know about it?"

Fulton's eyes widened. "That sort of deposit makes little sense, I don't have to tell you, unless you plan to draw against it immediately. Otherwise you might as well earn interest."

"A lot of private accounts are going to be due at once. It

won't be *my* money," he said. "And yes, I'll pull it out just as soon as it comes in."

"If any questions arise, I'll handle them myself," Fulton answered.

"You've been most helpful," Stark said, turning to leave.

On the way out of the bank, he stopped to pick up a thick stack of blank deposit slips from one of the slots at the customer counter. Ten minutes later, he was running up the steps of his apartment. In the coat closet near the door, behind the boxes of books, he found what he was looking for: the IBM typewriter. He drew the deposit slips one after another from the stack he had taken and typed his own account number at the bottom in magnetic, scanner-readable numbers. For all their efficiency, he thought, banks relied too heavily on EDP.

A half hour later, after stealthily returning the deposit slips to the pigeonhole under the counter at the Coolidge Bank, he hailed a cab for Boston. It was only a matter of time, he thought, until his account began to fatten, as the bank robbed itself.

The cab deposited Stark in Crab Alley, from where he could see the bright-colored Cinzano umbrellas of the cafe on India Dock. One of the oldest sections of Boston, and one of the newest, now that the revitalization plan was nearly completed, the Dock attracted tourists and residents alike, who visited it for a slice of history and for the pleasure of boutiques, cafes and shops that lined the wharves. Stark had never heard of the Oyster Cafe, but that was not surprising, since he rarely went out. Apparently it was near where Merrill was working that morning, which is why Byron had suggested it.

Stark checked his watch as he came abreast of the cafe, selecting a table with a clean gingham cloth. He was early, as usual. While he waited for Merrill and Byron to arrive, he observed the other patrons hungrily downing platters of oysters and clams, and gazing across the harbor.

"What can I get you?" asked a waiter in a long blue apron, moving toward Stark's table.

Stark picked up the menu, then set it down again. "I'm waiting for friends," he explained. "A coffee, I guess, till they come."

"Filter, espresso, cappuccino?"

Stark hesitated. "American, please, with cream and sugar."

The waiter disappeared and Stark re-examined the menu. He always thought oysters were oysters, and clams, clams, but here there were a score of varieties. Food was a mystery to Stark. He had always eaten whatever was close at hand without giving it a thought. Drink was the same. He thought, for all the praise he received for his work, what did he *really* know? Mathematics, of course; computers, definitely. But what made life rich and full?

He glanced down the alley where the cab had left him off and spotted Merrill and Byron beside a battered Volkswagen. As Byron locked the door, Merrill waved in Stark's direction. A few minutes later, they joined him at the table.

Byron wore a suit and tie, and grumbled as he pulled up a chair about never getting wound up till evening. Early afternoons were as bad as the morning, he said, burying his face in the menu. Merrill grinned at him and made a face, then asked Stark, "What did the police say?"

"I didn't call," Stark said matter-of-factly.

"You didn't call?" she asked.

"I thought I'd stop and see them this afternoon," he lied. Looking at her, he wished he could explain about the threatening note, but held his tongue instead. He could not tell her his reasons for avoiding the police, and if he mentioned the note, she would only get worried and want to know more. He would have liked to tell her everything, but did not want to involve her further. Whoever had written that note wanted what he alone could provide. Merrill and Byron were accidental victims, and it was unlikely the intruders would bother them further.

"What do you guess they wanted?" Merrill asked.

Stark shrugged. "Like I said last night, I don't know. They were probably after things like cameras and radios, you know. Bart must have frightened them, and then when we came in, they were like trapped rats." Stark did not mention his puppy's murder.

What purpose could that serve? "They had to fight their way out." He sighed. "Anyway, it seems like they might have taken some of my checks." He explained about the call from MacDonald.

Frowning, Merrill asked, "What are you going to do about it?"

"For money? Well, I thought about robbing a bank."

Both Byron and Merrill laughed.

The waiter appeared with the cup of coffee for Stark. "Would you like to order?" he asked, giving Merrill an admiring glance.

"Sure," said Byron, then to Stark, "Try the oysters. They can almost make you feel like facing the day." Then back to the waiter, "A dozen belons for me and a St. Pauli beer."

Once the waiter had taken their orders, Merrill said, "They were busy this morning. Your checks, my credit cards."

"They used them?" Stark asked, more concerned than he let on.

"I called American Express first thing. They said somebody using the card had gone on a real binge. My charge limit was exceeded by two thousand dollars in one morning. I'm not liable, but they asked me to call the police anyway."

"Did you?" Stark asked.

Merrill nodded. "They took down the card number and asked how it happened. They didn't seem very interested. But at least I'm covered."

"Every day Cambridge gets more like New York," Byron said. "They must be pretty hard up if they have to rob poor students and professors." He looked enraged, and turned to look at the waiter. Merrill and Stark sat speechless for a spell. Then Byron looked up: "Finally!" he exclaimed at the sight of the waiter, who carried a tray with their drinks and food. As the waiter put the dishes in front of them, slightly spilling the beer, Byron remarked, "If this place is going to make it, you'd better improve the service."

"Byron!" Merrill scolded. There was no call for such an outburst. "We're in no hurry."

"Maybe you and Stark aren't."

"But you wanted to join us."

"I *did*. Suddenly I just don't feel like it."

"They why don't you leave?"

Byron got to his feet. "Yeah, I think I will." He turned and headed off.

"Byron, come back here," Merrill yelled after him. He did not stop or turn around. "I didn't mean it." Looking at Stark, she shrugged her shoulders.

"What's his problem?" Stark asked, finally.

"It's complicated. *He's* complicated. It all amounts to the fact that he's jealous of you."

Stark began to laugh. "Jealous of *me*. What on earth for?"

"He'd be afraid to admit it to himself, but he's in love with me in a strange way. He's never said anything, or laid a hand on me. But it's there."

"And I'm the competition?"

"He thinks so." She stopped, feeling edgy herself. Stark's comment irritated her. "And why wouldn't *you* think so?"

"I don't know."

She looked him straight in the eyes. "Would you have called me if we hadn't met at the McKinnons?"

He laughed nervously, then said, "I doubt it."

"Why not? I wanted you to."

"Probably what I don't understand is, why me?"

The question annoyed her for a fleeting instant. She raised the napkin to her mouth. The curse of beauty! Was it impossible for a beautiful woman to like a man for himself? Men saw the attraction as bravado, glibness, glamor, money and success, anything but themselves. Beauty put men off, really; she had seen enough men to know. "You're different," she said defensively. "That's the answer to 'why.'"

"I suppose you mean I'm weird. Everybody else seems to think that."

"Maybe," she replied. "And why not? Most men hate the thought of being different. You do what you want and, believe me, that's refreshing." She paused and waited for him to respond.

When he didn't, she continued, "You probably have no idea how *boring* most men are, at least to me. And predictable. God, they have the whole world figured out."

He never looked at himself like that. She wasn't flattering him, that much he could tell. She wanted him to understand his own worth. The words seemed strange. Claudette had never talked to him about what he was as a person. Her praise had been for his achievements.

Merrill said, "Also, will you let *me* decide who I want to spend *my* time with?" She smiled. "In case you haven't caught on, it's you."

Later, as they walked across the Common toward Cambridge, Stark struggled with himself, trying to decide whether to give Merrill the ECHO V poem. He wanted her to have it, but somehow the words seemed ridiculous. She sensed what he felt about her, and that was almost enough for now. Yet the poem seemed to burn in his pocket. It reproached him for fear of showing his emotions, his fear of being ridiculed. Several times he reached into his pocket and touched the sheet of paper, but each time he withdrew his hand.

As they neared the Public Garden, Merrill suddenly stopped short, staring in the distance. "Look who's over there!" she exclaimed. Taking his hand, she led him running down the sidewalk until they came abreast of an old man, whom Merrill promptly hugged. "Granddad!" she said, wrapping her arms around and kissing him. "What a surprise!"

Stark stood several steps away. "Granddad" had a handsome, distinguished face, white, downy hair and penetrating eyes. Despite the differences, he could see Merrill in the old man's prominent cheekbones and small nose.

Merrill turned to Stark. "This is my grandfather, Douglas Thornton." Then to Thornton, "Granddad, this is Stark Rousseau." The two men shook hands formally and exchanged a look of recognition. They had not met before, but each knew the other by reputation. Douglas Thornton had always been something of a hero to Stark. Thornton was considered a peer of Babbage in the field of computer innovation. Douglas Thornton, who had built ENIAC, the first modern computer, and made a fortune from it, had just as suddenly become the proponent of limiting computer application. Stark imagined Thornton as an avuncular, benevolent and kindly old sage. The man in person did not fit that preconception.

"I'm honored, sir," Stark said, and he meant it.

"It's *I* who am honored," Thornton replied.

"Where are you going?" Merrill asked, then to Stark, "Granddad lives on Beacon Hill."

"A friend is ill."

Merrill looked to see that he was well. Usually they dined together once a week, but when she had called recently, he had begged off, claiming that he was too busy. Merrill had wondered if he was courting a woman; it was by no means impossible. "When am I going to see you?" she asked.

"Not for a while, Eagle," he said. "I'm in the midst of something right now." He looked at Stark, then back at Merrill. "Maybe when I'm finished, you'll bring this young man around." He smiled at her, seeing how she looked at Rousseau.

"That'd be fun," she said.

"Well, I must be going." He kissed her, nodded to Stark and slowly started down the Common path.

When he was out of earshot, Stark asked, "Why didn't you tell me?"

She put her arm through his. "I can't believe it," she said proudly. "He's never been *honored* to meet anybody, including Presidents."

"He was being nice."

"He's never *nice* to strangers. The old curmudgeon, he usually snubs them. And he knew you!"

"Yeah . . . well." Stark was embarrassed. Changing the subject to Thornton, "Tell me, why did he get into this anticomputer crusade? It doesn't make much sense."

"He doesn't talk about it. But my mother," she said, mentioning her parents for the first time, "has an idea why. Even she isn't certain, though."

"And?"

"She thinks he's like Robert Oppenheimer, you know, the man who headed the Los Alamos project. He applied his genius to creating destructiveness. It was for everyone's good, back in the forties, and I guess it won the war. But once the war was over, the bomb stayed. Oppenheimer was horrified because his genius was subverted. 'I am become Death, the destroyer of worlds,' he said. He became a crusader against the bomb. And he died a broken man."

"But you can't compare the bomb to—"

"*He* does, according to Mom. He pretty much invented the computer, then late in life, at least in his mind, discovered its potential for harm. That's when he started his organization—"

"The International Union for the Sane Use of Computers."

She nodded. "He once told Mom that he didn't want to die a broken man. I hope he gets what he wants."

"He always has," Stark said. "Always. What did he call you?"

"Eagle."

"Like the bird?"

Merrill unfastened the second button of her blouse, revealing a heavy gold chain with a gold double eagle in a pendant. "Beautiful," Stark said.

"He gave it to me when I was ten. We even went together to Tiffany's and had it mounted. It was his, his lucky coin. He's called me Eagle ever since."

Stark had planned to let her off and go back immediately to his apartment to work on the filter. But when they stopped in front of the house, she asked him up and he readily agreed. "I promise we won't get mugged," she said, then, "I hope."

The hominess of her apartment struck him. He wondered why a woman could make an apartment into a home, while a man considered it nothing more than a place to sleep. There were dainty framed drawings of zebras, two magnificent Chinese ancestor paintings, one of a dour-looking woman and the other of a sage mandarin; there were magazines and art books set just so on the cocktail table, candles, lacquered boxes and mirrors behind a fluffy down-cushioned sofa. He wandered into the kitchen and had the same sense: pots and pans, jars of spices, electric machines and the small breakfast table was set with a feminine yellow chintz. Even a mint plant grew in the window.

The contrast, he thought: He had an IBM 4331, shelves of books, stacks of printouts and a bed!

Merrill came up behind him and touched him lightly on the shoulder. "Snooping?" she asked.

He grinned. "You've made this very comfortable," he said. "I like it."

She went over to the stove. "Would you like a cup of tea?"

"It doesn't matter," he said, clearing his throat. "I should probably go soon."

She turned from the stove, her arms at her sides, a serene expression on her face. She didn't want him to leave. It was as though she were on the end of a diving board, her weight forward and beyond that point when she could recover her balance, though her feet were still in contact with the board. At its best, falling in love was like that. There came a moment when two people almost literally *fell,* and when they reflected later on the plunge, they could not explain why. Of course, Stark had received the approval of her grandfather. That was important, but more than that, Stark was interesting, and he made no demands.

Stark came over to her, reluctant to move. She reached up and touched his face as their eyes met. He put his arms around her then and she responded by leaning into him, dependent on his strength. He brought his face close and kissed her tenderly, feeling the excitement of her body.

Neither of them later could have said how long they stood in that unbroken embrace, but they would remember it forever, because it was their beginning.

3:40 P.M., EDT: Manhattan, New York

Harvey Streeter worked strictly on New York Stock Market time: The day ended for him with the sounding of the four-o'clock bell —even now, when the bell had been silent for the longest period in its history. Despite the closedown, Streeter, a meticulous, middle-aged man of strict habits and ascetic tastes, maintained his usual routine: home early and early to bed—usually alone in his Fifth Avenue apartment overlooking the Children's Zoo—and early to rise. Streeter got up before dawn and breakfasted with the news of what had transpired that day in the international financial markets—Tokyo, Hong Kong, then Singapore and Europe.

Streeter yawned now, picking through the papers on his desk as a sated eater might pick through a second helping. Although the exchanges continued their suspensions—a fact that worried Streeter far less than his institutional clients—he worked as hard as ever, in promissory contracts. Rubbing his cheeks to beef up his circulation, he thought to himself that the exchanges' closings were a mixed blessing. Undeniably, there was no real motion. Losses and gains were paper. But the negotiating of promissories was both real and interesting. Already that day, Streeter had moved several hundred thousand shares on the assumption that buyers and sellers would make good once the exchanges began operating again. Without the boards, Streeter had become an exchange of his own. The prestige of that was all he could have hoped for. Clients trusted him implicitly because he was scrupulous.

Earlier that same afternoon, Streeter had received a telephone call from the West Coast. Clint Hennessy wanted him to dump fifty thousand shares of LTW, expecting, he had explained, that the exchanges would be back in business by Monday. Hennessy had been reluctant at first to explain this unusual, and, to Streeter's mind, unwise, trade. Finally Hennessy had relented: LTW had lost out on the MX contract, according to the millionaire's sources. There was also allusion to vague but serious financial difficulties that had been hidden for years.

Streeter scratched his head, then raised the analyst's report on LTW to his eyes. Nothing in the report hinted at the rumor. It was fresh information—and solid, too, since it emanated from Hennessy. Streeter lowered the report, then turned the Rolodex, reminding himself of which clients were heavily invested in the company. Before he advised any of his clients, however, he would have to place a phone call.

"General Mark Colombo," he said into the telephone. "Hello, Mark," he greeted the general, whose favor he had curried over the years by handling his small portfolio personally, incidentally making him piles of money. In return, Streeter received occasional bits of information.

A trade-off, the understanding had never been discussed, nor would it be. "Mark," Streeter now asked, after Colombo had provided him with the opening, "what's this I hear about LTW?"

"LTW?" replied Colombo.

"The contract . . ."

"Look, Harvey, I can't really talk about that," Colombo said. "No final decision has been made, as you know. Procurement won't have its decision for a few weeks yet."

"I heard—"

"But I can see why it's in jeopardy."

"Oh?"

"I just heard that LTW bombed out on the INTELSAT series they built for us a couple of years ago. The satellites are being replaced. We are in the process of preparing the hunter-killers to destroy them in space."

"Those are important satellites, no?" asked Streeter.

"They certainly are. The decision has taken us all by surprise."

"And the malfunction is LTW's fault?"

"That's what *I* gather," Colombo replied. Church had told him only that there was a design flaw in the satellites, and bitched about LTW's negligence. "I can't see how this can help LTW's case for the MX. I tell you one thing: There's at least one general here who's already screaming bloody murder. They've wasted us millions, and the new series will cost like hell."

"I see," Streeter said softly. "Thanks, Mark." Hanging up, he turned to his Rolodex in earnest.

4:00 P.M., *EDT: Brookline, Massachusetts*

So engrossed was Jim Bilkays in John Wayne's heroics on the afternoon movie that Bilkays had all but forgotten his visitor, the investigator, Harry Verdeen, who continued to root through the pile of paper rubble in Bilkays' TV room-office like a frustrated truffle pig. Verdeen had come up for air only once, to visit the john. Bilkays at first respected Verdeen's persistence, but as the hours wore on, he thought the man crazy. Bilkays found a comfortable new position in the chair as a commercial interrupted the movie. "Damn ads," he mumbled.

"What'd you say?" Verdeen's voice asked. He had decided to take a breather, and was surprised that Bilkays was awake—Bilkays hadn't looked it.

" 'Ads,' I said." He looked over at Verdeen. "Most I can watch. But nowadays they tell me more'n I ever wanted to know about Kotex and Maxi-pads. Next thing'll be marital aids."

"Yeah," Verdeen said, then asked, "Why don't you watch at home?"

"When I'm hungry I do. Otherwise I stay here. The wife's a complainer."

"You wouldn't consider giving me a hand, would you?" Verdeen asked hopefully.

Bilkays didn't move. "I can't understand. What's so important about that key? I'd've given up hours ago."

"I told you, if I find the records, they could lead to a murderer."

"A key's no proof," Bilkays said, mildly intrigued. "Whoever owns it'll say it was stolen, then lost. Not very strong evidence."

"It might lead me in the right direction."

"What if you had to confront the killer?" Bilkays asked.

"If I have to I will."

"Do you have a gun?"

"In my duffle. And a license, too."

Bilkays, feeling a twinge of sympathy for Verdeen, levered himself out of the Barcolounger and joined Verdeen on his knees in the midst of the debris. Bilkays swept his hands through the papers. "Medeco, huh?" he asked. "Before my time. But it'll be in here somewhere." A few minutes passed, Bilkays breathing heavily on all fours. "Here we go, Med-dee-coh," Bilkays said, examining a stapled folder with its cover missing.

Verdeen hobbled over, not knowing whether to believe Bilkays. Verdeen took the folder and turned the pages. This was it, he thought with relief. The key numbers all had purchaser addresses. "Jesus," he said to Bilkays, who was en route to the Barcolounger, "I don't believe it. I just don't believe it."

"Hell, should've asked me first thing."

Verdeen smiled broadly. He had not asked Bilkays, it was true. But the guy *could* have volunteered. "Do you know them?" he asked Bilkays, pointing to the name and address of the company that had bought the Medeco.

"Sure thing. They're practically around the corner from here. There's a guy from there that's always buyin' stuff here— locks, gates, guns even. . . ."

"You sell guns?"

"Shh. Not officially. Let's say I'm an intermediary. It's a sort of sideline. You know, with all that security stuff . . ."

"Anyway, what's the guy's name now?"

"Whistle, Weasel, something like that. Begins with a 'W.' You can use my phone to call him if you want."

"Listen, can I ask one more favor?"

"Fire away."

"I'd planned to return home this afternoon. I still might, but if I need to stay, can I bunk here?" He lowered his voice a little. "I'm a bit short on cash."

Bilkays turned around in the Barcolounger. "You really

move right in, don't you?" He made a grunting laugh. "I guess it's okay. Yeah, why not?"

"I appreciate it," Verdeen said, going to the phone.

4:13 P.M., *EDT: Brookline, Massachusetts*

Jean Crane, the plump, bespectacled company librarian for Ling Autonetics, answered the phone on her desk.

"Library, Miss Crane," she said.

"I'm looking for Mr. Wessel," said Harry Verdeen on the other end of the phone. "His office said he was in the library. May I speak with him, please?"

"Why, no. Mr. Wessel is *not* here," answered Miss Crane.

"That's odd," said Verdeen on the phone. "His office was sure he had gone there. It's very urgent, miss."

"I'm afraid he's simply *not* here, Mr.—what did you say your name was?"

"Verdeen, Harry Verdeen."

"Well, Mr. Verdigreen, I had better transfer you back to Mr. Wessel's office. I'm afraid I have not seen him today in the library."

"But ma'am, won't you take a look at least—"

"I'm afraid Mr. Wessel is not here now. Whether he was here earlier or not, you will have to call back *his* office. I'm afraid, Mr. Verdigris—"

"Verdeen, ma'am."

"Mr. Vertigo. Thank you, and good afternoon."

Jean Crane plunked down the phone, slightly upset. She did not like Frank Wessel—never had—and he was hardly the sort who spent his days in the data storage vault, which was the official name for the library. Besides which, a vague sense of guilt was taking hold of her. She had taken a very long lunch with one of her closest woman friends, having returned only a few minutes before, and she had not yet had a chance to look around. In her absence, no one was supposed to use the premises. But then, she had been gone nearly 3½ hours.

Miss Crane removed her jacket, hanging it on the peg behind the door. It would take a while longer before the air conditioner cooled off the room to a decent temperature. She combed her graying hair in the mirror and put on fresh lipstick. She was beginning to feel better. She never did like phone calls from strangers, especially about people she didn't like, such as Frank Wessel. She tried to brush it from her mind. Humming the theme from *Love Story,* she decided to inspect her domain. She stepped around the counter that separated the long rows of disk-storage racks from her desk.

Odd, she thought, glancing back at the countertop. A disk had been left lying on the counter. Someone with a key must have come into the library and put it there. It was against the rules to use the library without her assistance, because the disks might get out of order. Seeing the disk on the countertop made her angry once again. She checked the logbook to find who had broken the rules. That was odd, too, she thought, running her fingers down the column. According to the log, no disks had been used since yesterday.

Jean recognized the disk program. She had used DOCTOR herself once or twice. Written a few years ago, DOCTOR was based on Rogerian psychotherapy. It now contained a hybrid of the original named ELIZA IX, after the character in *Pygmalion,* that employed artificial intelligence and incorporated thousands of interviews between psychiatrists and patients. ELIZA could reason and solve problems. What's more, ELIZA IX could search for specific data applicable to the user.

Jean was curious. First that odd phone call, now this. She decided to check one step farther. She put the disk in a drive and punched it to life on the terminal beside her desk. Seconds later, a dialogue appeared in LED print on the VDT.

"Men are all alike."

A *female* employee, Jean guessed, had made the statement.

"IN WHAT WAY??" ELIZA asked on the VDT. ELIZA was starting her probe.

"They're always bugging us about something."

"CAN YOU THINK OF A SPECIFIC EXAMPLE?"

"Well, my boyfriend made me come here."

"YOUR BOYFRIEND MADE YOU COME HERE?"

"He says I'm depressed much of the time."

"I'M SORRY TO HEAR YOU ARE DEPRESSED."

"It's true. I am unhappy."

"DO YOU THINK COMING HERE WILL HELP YOU NOT BE UNHAPPY?"

"I need some help, that much seems certain."

"WHAT WOULD IT MEAN TO YOU IF YOU GOT SOME HELP?"

"Perhaps I could learn to get along with my mother."

Then the screen went blank. Some user, Jean guessed, had erased the rest of the dialogue. Jean was about to stop the tape when new data appeared on the VDT.

"THE AREA OF A CIRCLE IS PI TIMES THE RADIUS OF THE CIRCLE SQUARED; THE AREA OF A SQUARE IS THE SIDE OF THE SQUARE SQUARED; THE DIAMETER OF AN OBJECT IS TWICE THE RADIUS OF THE OBJECT; THE RADIUS OF A BALL IS 10. WHAT IS THE AREA OF THE BALL?"

Jean furrowed her brow. Somebody had erased the first dialogue and had tested ELIZA's evaluator by posing a problem. Jean looked again at the VDT. ELIZA was responding.

"THE ASSUMPTION THAT BALL IS SPHERE AND OBJECT CONSISTENT—SHALL I GO ON?"

"Yes," the user had printed.

"IT'S 1256.6359."

Then, Jean saw, the users had instructed ELIZA to make a search of a person whose name Jean did not recognize. But the person was a woman; her address appeared on the VDT, along with Social Security, credit card, and driver's license numbers. ELIZA had taken the data and begun her search, then reported:

```
"MASSGENMED:    PROCEDURE:    APPENDECTOMY:
12.8.80;
SYM: RIGIDITY RIGHT ILIAC FOSSA, FURRED
TONGUE,
NAUSEA;
PREOP: TEMP 37.5 C.: HEART RATE, 97;
ANES: SPINAL CINCHOCAINE;
PROCED: STANDARD GRIDIRON, 7 CENT; ABOVE
ANTERIOR
SUPERIOR ILIAC SPINE:
NOTE: CONGENITAL DIABETIC, 5-15 CC. SUB-
CUT. INSULIN;
PHYS: L. M. CONRAD;;;"
```

ELIZA was trying to tell the user something about the girl's mind, although the program revealed only physical data.

The user had typed, "FEAR."

ELIZA had replied, "CAN YOU BE MORE SPECIFIC?"

The user typed, "ANESTHESIA; FEAR."

"POSSIBLE BUT UNLIKELY."

"SURGICAL PROCEDURE; SCALPEL; FEAR," the user suggested.

"ANESTHESIA OBVIATES THIS POSSIBILITY; ANXIETY MAY BE PRESENT BEFORE AND AFTER PROCEDURE BUT WILL BE MINIMAL," ELIZA reported.

"DIABETES; FEAR." The user.

"IN EVERY DIABETIC; CONGENITAL;

FEAR EXISTS OF PREMATURE HEART FAILURE;
ANXIETY OF OVERBEARING NATURE EXISTS,
RESULTING FROM DEPENDENCE ON INSULIN FOR
LIFE;"

"INSULIN; FEAR." The user.

"COMA."

"COMA; FEAR."

"WITHOUT INSULIN PRESENT, DEHYDRATION:
COMA; FEAR OF DEATH IN LIFE EXCESSIVE AND
PRIMORDIAL; BASIC TO CHARACTER CREATION OF
SUBJECT."

"THANK YOU." The user.

Jean Crane stopped the tape. The data made no sense, although the general drift of it frightened her. Hastily, she removed the disk from the drive and returned it to the correct storage rack. She really ought to report the violation, she thought, and returned to her desk to write out a memo to the head of security. She had done no more than type the date when she realized: The head of security was none other than Frank Wessel.

5:30 P.M., *EDT: Cambridge, Massachusetts*

Merrill wandered into the bathroom, a cup of tea in her hand. If she and Stark were to join up late that evening, she should pack now, she thought, looking at her watch. Stark had been gone only thirty minutes and already she missed him. As she filled the tub and undressed, she thought how close they had come to making love. Certainly the desire was there, but the moment was wrong for them both.

Merrill's needs were as great as those of any other woman her age. That presented a dilemma. If she were to become promiscuous, she thought, stepping into the tub, she could have maintained her independence more easily. But she wasn't; she had already formed long-term relationships. First there had been

David, a Harvard Law student when she was at Vassar. Then Callum Semple, a stockbroker in Boston when she began to model. He had been generous, but he had treated her like a China doll. Her last boyfriend, Parker, was a lawyer with political ambitions who had begun to think of her as part of his image—the candidate with the beautiful wife.

It struck her now how delicate the balance of love really was. The men she had known interpreted love as dominance. But the slave always escaped, or the master grew bored.

Humming contentedly, she got out of the bathtub and dried herself. After dressing, she went to the kitchen and opened the refrigerator. Searching behind the yogurt cartons, she found the box of disposable syringes. Damn, she thought. She'd forgotten again.

She did not want to go out, but there was no choice. She had to stop at the corner drugstore before it closed. Absently she looked out the window, and as she did, she noticed a late-model Chrysler parked by the curb with two long-haired workmen in the front seat, laughing. A young woman sat glumly in the back, isolated from the men's humor.

Resigned to run the errand now, Merrill picked up the keys from the table, took twenty dollars in cash from the cookie jar and started out the door, humming a tune. That moment the telephone rang and she ran back inside to get it. It was Grandfather Thornton.

"Eagle," he said, "I'm sorry we didn't have more time to talk. I liked your young man."

"He's awfully nice, isn't he?"

"I'm calling to see if you two can come by this evening for dinner."

The suddenness of the invitation surprised her. Usually they made plans a week in advance. Damn, she thought, again. This was her night with Stark and nothing would ruin it. "I'd love to," she said, "and I'm sure Stark would, too, but Granddad, I'm just now going out the door. I have a flight in an hour to Florida, another modeling assignment. And I won't be back for three days." That much, at least, was true. "Can we take a rain check?"

He sounded disappointed, which wasn't like him at all. "Sure you can, but promise to bring that young man with you?"

"Granddad, once I get back, I don't plan to go anywhere without him."

Thornton laughed. "All right, then. Have a safe trip," he said and they hung up.

Merrill went out the door. How odd for him suddenly to be so gracious toward a stranger. He had made a point of mentioning Stark, as though he wanted to see him more than her. Oh well, she thought, it was probably the allure of genius. She skipped down the steps. Once on the sidewalk, she headed toward the drugstore. As she passed the blue Chrysler, she noticed that the men inside had stopped talking. She looked at them quickly. They stared back at her with interested expressions.

What a beautiful day this had been, she thought, walking with a happy bounce in her step. Summer to her always meant freedom. Each summer during college her father had insisted that she try new experiences. Once she had traveled through Europe on a bicycle, another time she had worked on a dude ranch in Idaho, and for the third vacation, she had been a girl Friday at her father's brokerage house in New York City. This summer, she thought, she was going to work at love.

She heard a car motor start behind her and glanced over her shoulder. The blue Chrysler followed on the opposite side of the street. She quickened her step and heard a man's voice through the open car window say, "Identification." The girl in the back seat mumbled. Merrill sensed that they were talking about her, and she was suddenly afraid, remembering the robbery. She looked straight ahead, feeling better now that the drugstore was in sight only fifty yards away.

Suddenly three doors slammed. The sounds of running feet hammered in her ears. She turned around, then tried to run. But before she could take three or four strides, a powerful hand grabbed her arm and spun her around.

"What do you want?" she screamed.

He tightened the grip on her arm. "Miss Fox, Merrill Fox?" he asked.

"Yes, but what—"

The woman took her other arm and she was led to a tree. "Put your hands out and spread your legs," she ordered.

Barely conscious of the order, Merrill did what she was told and leaned into the tree trunk with her arms in front of her. She felt the woman's hands run swiftly down her rib cage, then up her legs. "She's clean," the woman said.

Dully, Merrill heard the second man saying, "You have the right to remain silent. . . ."

The woman turned around, while the man reached under his windbreaker and brought out a pair of handcuffs. He locked them on Merrill's wrists behind her back.

"We're police officers," the woman said.

"You have no right."

The first man held a wallet in front of her eyes. He flipped it open: the chrome badge of the Boston Police Department. "You are charged with the felonious use of and trafficking in heroin," he said, then to the policewoman, "Get her in the car."

"But that's insane," Merrill yelled, straining against the chain between the cuffs. "You can't do this to me."

They replied by pulling her by the arms toward the car. The policewoman opened the back door, and the first man pushed Merrill's head down as she climbed in. She looked pleadingly at the policewoman, who got in beside her. "You've made a mistake," she said.

The policewoman stared straight ahead.

"Did you *hear* me? You've made a mistake," Merrill repeated. "Now please *let me go!*"

The car accelerated and Merrill pushed against the seat-back cushion, sliding toward the edge of the seat. The policewoman pressed Merrill's shoulders, and the cuffs dug into the small of her back. "Please, you're hurting me," Merrill screamed.

"Take it easy," the woman said. "We'll be there in a minute."

"Where?" Merrill yelled.

The policewoman did not answer.

The car sped through the back streets of Cambridge and across the Charles River. When they slowed for the heavy evening traffic on the Boston side, the driver put a red light on the roof and activated a siren. Cars pulled aside for them, through the Combat Zone and past the Statler Hotel. They braked hard and turned off the siren as they entered an underground garage. The car tires screeched against the slick concrete; the lot was filled with police vehicles. They had arrived at the Central Police Station.

Merrill wanted to cry out, to scream. Everything was turned upside down. Minutes ago she had been thinking about her date with Stark, and now she had entered a world that was frightening and unknown. She had tried to calm herself, breathing deeply several times. What had they said, "trafficking in heroin"? It was crazy, *but they had known her name. They had identified her!*

The driver came around and opened the door. "Please get out," he said. The policewoman gave her a shove and Merrill stepped onto the pavement. The policewoman took her arm as all four walked through a steel door opened by a uniformed police guard. The long gray corridor smelled of disinfectant. At the end, they approached another door, this one made of steel bars. Another guard slid it back. Merrill darted glances left and right. Women in green shifts looked at her from the cells with expressions of mild curiosity. Finally, they stopped at a door marked 20W, and Merrill was pushed in. The door slammed shut after her.

"Turn around and put your wrists against the bars," the first man said.

Merrill felt the metal against her skin as her left wrist was freed, then her right. She spun around. "Will you please explain this?" she said, trying to sound confident.

The policewoman nodded to the men, who left the corridor. Then she said, "This is a holding tank, miss. You'll be brought upstairs later."

Then she, too, disappeared.

Merrill inspected the cell, feeling cold and frightened. It had a small bed with a thin mattress, a wash basin with a cold tap only, a lidless toilet and a bare wood stool. There were neither sheets nor blankets, she noticed, almost hopefully. If they planned to keep her overnight, they would have given her a green shift, like the others wore, and issued her bedding.

She listened to the sounds, the low murmurs of the other inmates, the scraping of feet on the outside corridor, an occasional laugh from a guard.

She sat on the edge of the bed, and she wept.

6:30 P.M., *EDT: Brookline, Massachusetts*

"It could be one of ours, but I couldn't say for sure."

"That's not what I asked," Harry Verdeen replied. There was no doubt in his mind that the security chief of Ling Autonetics was being evasive. Either that or he was just plain stupid. "It *is* your key, Mr. Wessel. What I asked is whether your company had a robbery lately. That might explain why the key was found all the way down in Yorktown, New York."

Verdeen knew he sounded pushy, but he did not have the time to dance the Virginia reel with Wessel. Verdeen wanted to make the train back home with his suspicions confirmed—then he would not have to spend a night he knew would be miserable in Bilkays' back room. Reaching Wessel had been tough enough. Harry had thought the company was giving him the runaround; his call had been transferred from the security office, to the library, back to the security office. Finally Wessel had come on the line.

When Verdeen outlined his problem, Wessel had agreed to help only if Harry abided by certain rules. First Wessel had insisted on their meeting off company premises, and after office hours. Harry had wanted to see Ling Autonetics, and perhaps talk with some of its employees, but Wessel had not relented on that point. So they had agreed on the Skylark Bar and Grill, where they were now seated in a corner booth. The second point laid down by Wessel struck Harry as ludicrous—that he, Wessel, could answer only questions directly related to security at Ling; no general questions about the company.

Wessel's name fit him perfectly, thought Verdeen as he stared across the table. Wessel had the pinched features of a weasel, a sharp nose, narrow eyes covered by thin brows, and a sliver of a mouth. His turkey neck boasted a bobbing Adam's apple and his bony arms were covered with thin, black hair. Most corporate security chiefs Verdeen had known were easygoing slobs, but Wessel was sharp and nervous.

Wessel pushed the glass to the end of the Formica table and signaled for the waitress. "Want another beer?"

Verdeen shook his head. "Well? Have you?" he asked.

"Ling's security is an internal matter, one we sometimes share with the Boston police. Nobody else. What proof is there that you're on the level? For all I know, you could be working for the competition."

This guy *is* dumb, thought Verdeen. "I told you I work for IBM," Verdeen repeated. "That's no secret. My partner worked for IBM. He's dead. He was murdered, I think, by the person who lost a key to a lock owned by your company. I showed you my license. I told you how I traced the key. Now, will you please answer the question?"

"First, I have questions of my own. You're an amateur, right?" Wessel asked. "You've never investigated a case before this one, right? You're looking into this on vacation time as a means of doing right by a dead friend. And you probably believe that somebody connected with Ling killed him, right? So a Ling employee has to burn before you'll go away and leave us alone, right?" He paused, looking up at Verdeen and not liking what he saw.

"Right," Verdeen replied, mocking.

"Okay, then I'll let you in on a little secret that should make you happy. A week ago we were robbed. They came in a window at night and blocked the alarm. My fault, and I got my ass chewed out for it. They found the security office, *my* office, and they used that key"—he pointed with a bony finger at the Medeco in Verdeen's hand—"from my desk drawer to open a cabinet. I got reamed for that, too. From the cabinet they took two handguns, Smith and Wesson .38s, an M-16, a Remington pump-action shotgun and a few cartons of shells. Nothing else."

Horace had been hit by .38s, Verdeen thought.

"The Boston police were informed immediately. They came on the scene, asked questions and dusted. They found nothing; they have no leads. As a result, we are willing and *they* are willing to let this die a natural death. Nobody was hurt, nobody killed. Only a few weapons taken."

"My partner was hurt; he was killed."

"Until those guns are found, there is no proof of connection. If you'll leave it with me, I'll tell the case officer downtown. How about it?"

"Only if you promise that you'll tell him." Wessel wanted this swept under the rug, that was apparent. But who could blame him? The whole situation made him look bad.

"It was a murder, Mr. Verdeen. I take that seriously. Yes, of course I'll keep the promise, but only if *you* promise to get out from under foot. We'll handle this in our own way, and if the police downtown hear anything, I'll personally get in touch."

"Tell them the New York State Police already have begun an investigation, lousy though it may be. The Boston end should coordinate with them." Verdeen looked at his watch. If he hustled, he could catch the 7:20 P.M. train for New York.

"Then we are agreed?"

Verdeen shook his hand. "Agreed."

9:00 P.M., *EDT: Cambridge, Massachusetts*

Stark swiveled in his chair, his eyes fixed on the computer terminal, as he cleared instructions to put his run through the IBM 4331 into the Labs' mainframe computers. He wanted to be ready, even though it would still take hours to complete the programmed instructions. That and considerable theorizing had to come first.

He started by renewing the process of the formula's creation. In the INTELSAT chain's original design, weight was a severe restriction, preventing development of an independent power source. In the end, Lapham had decided that they could tolerate the eclipse outages. But in the new satellite series, Stark resolved there had to be allowances for batteries, continuously charged by the solar sails. Stark wanted maneuverability, too. And he considered a three-dimensional control using onboard momentum wheels, allowing the satellites to realign their antennas. The new filter itself would correct for propagation delay—the 270 milliseconds—by acting as an arbiter mechanism. Any uplink data that were entered without authentication would be instantly rejected.

So far the equation fit the logical principle, and it, too, could be written in a program and inserted into the Labs' mainframes. As he began to calculate free-space loss, however, he hit a snag with the *directionality* of the antennas. He let out a deep breath, a sigh. The original INTELSAT series had been designed almost three years ago; he wondered how soon this new series would be out of date. What new developments would make the series vulnerable, as well? The technology was advancing so rapidly that obsolescence was guaranteed even as the new satellites were stationed in orbit.

To get around the *directionality* snag, Stark went to his bookshelf and retrieved the working papers on the first INTELSAT series. As he flipped through the pages, his eyes fell on some underlined notations. Surprised at how dated these seemed, he looked at the bound cover—it was the correct binder. He had not read it in more than two years. Even the ink of the underlining was beginning to fade.

On the pages were listed and explained the schematics and formulas for the data feeds used in the satellites. "Domestic and International Safe Communication," Stark read in the index. "NORAD," "DEW," "Interbase Relays."

As he turned the pages, his eye was caught by three paragraphs that had been inked out. The deletion surprised him, and he wondered why that section was missing. Eyes-only data? Function deletions in the final design? Once the design was under way, the Pentagon, he knew, had abandoned several desired functions in the INTELSAT series as impractical or too costly, or in a score of instances, because existing procedures served the military's needs better than the satellites could. Yet, despite the rationale, Stark wanted to be certain about the black blotches.

He shrugged, and his mind wandered. He reached for the telephone. No matter how hard he tried he could not get Merrill out of his head. Unless he talked with her, thoughts of her would continue to distract him. He dialed her number and waited as the phone rang; it went on ringing ten, twenty times before he hung up. He tried to recall whether she had said anything about going out before their planned rendezvous later that night, but he could not recall. He tried again. It rang for several minutes until finally, pursing his lips, he hung up. Perhaps, he decided, she was visiting her grandfather . . . or had it something to do with her trip to Florida?

As his hand left the telephone, he looked again at the black blotches on the page, then deciding that he owed Lapham a call anyway, he lifted the phone again and dialed the 202 area code and the number. The call went directly to Lapham's office. As it rang, Stark checked his watch. Lapham's secretary would be gone by now, and if he remembered right, Lapham would by now be tasting his first martini of the day. Stark was about to hang up when a voice suddenly answered. Yes, it was Lapham.

"I hope you're working as hard there as we are here," Lapham said after they exchanged greetings. "Church has been trying to bully us out of using LTW. He blames you *and* them for this. What's up?"

The sound of Lapham's voice cheered Stark. "I should have something for you, Ben, by tomorrow or the day after. I'm making good progress here, and the mainframes will put it all together. When will you be ready to go?"

"Tough to say, exactly. If Church cools off about LTW, we should launch the hunter-killers in a couple of days. Are we coordinated on that?"

"Positively." Then, "Can you clear up a question, Ben?"

"Shoot."

"Remember the working papers on INTELSAT?"

"Of course. Most of them are right here collecting dust."

"Check out page 357 in binder I-19."

Lapham put the telephone down. A few minutes later, he came back on the line. Stark heard him breathing as he found the correct page. "All right, I've got it."

"Is your copy blacked out? Censored?"

Lapham chuckled. "If I'm censored, we are all in trouble. It's right here. Why?"

"What do the middle three paragraphs describe?"

"The ICBMs, our Minutemen."

"What does it say about them, Ben?" Stark swallowed his apprehension.

Lapham read to himself, then summarized, "The missiles are on tertiary fire control through INTELSAT. It's probably Church—Mr. Redundancy."

"The *fire* control? Which means the missiles can be *launched* through INTELSAT?" Stark tried to control his voice.

"No big deal," Lapham replied. "The first and second launch systems are by locked landlines. INTELSAT is just extra insurance. Why?"

Stark removed the telephone from his ear as he sucked in his breath. He found himself asking, "Why wasn't I told, Ben? The reports I have here make no mention of that capability?"

"I guess it was Church. He handled the security, you remember. Maybe he didn't trust you, even back then. I repeat, though, why do you want to know this?"

"Nothing," Stark replied quickly. "As I said, it was blanked out in my notes. I was curious was all."

"Anything else?"

"No," he replied, and hung up.

He put his head in his hands. The ICBM strike force was on tertiary fire control through INTELSAT, the same vulnerable satellites that were sailing overhead at that moment. All 1,054 intercontinental ballistic missiles were linked to his INTELSAT! The overload, he thought. The operative key to the formula was the overload of the satellites' potential to receive and transmit data streams. What resulted was a spillover, like water out of a pail. As Stark had formulated, the spillover data would be lost. But would they? Pure conjecture, of course, but what if the data were not lost? Stark could only guess at the unthinkable result.

The tertiary fire control could override the primary systems. If that happened, INTELSAT would issue *erratic* commands to the Minutemen. Every fail-safe and security system would trigger out. The computer would be acting on its own at that point, once the INTELSAT signals reached the hard sites. Then computers in the silos would function as they had been programmed—to launch and guide the missiles: The ICBMs would lift off in directionless flight, impacting ten thousand or just ten miles away. Nobody could tell, and nobody could control them.

Stark sat back in the chair, trying to reassure himself. It was a very long shot. The probability of such a disaster actually happening was one in several hundred million. And the new series would replace those satellites in a matter of days. A long shot. It would not happen.

All the same, he reached for the telephone to warn Lapham, but as he dialed, he told himself that it *was* a long shot, too long to panic the Pentagon any more than he already had. Right now the sensible thing Stark could do was finish the program for the filter design at the Labs, then get the satellites in the air fast.

Swiftly he turned off the IBM 4331 and got up to stretch his legs. As he did, he heard a strange sound that he would have missed if it had not been so illogical. He looked over his shoulder and stared at the 4331 mini. The green activator light was on.

But he had turned it off!

He went to the mini, hearing it hum, and stared at the VDT. A message flashed on the VDT.

"IF YOU WANT TO SEE YOUR FRIENDS ALIVE AGAIN ____ HOLD ____"

Stark typed on the keyboard, "IDENTIFY YOUR-SELF. . . ."

"____ END HOLD ____ 123456789 ____ WE INSTRUCT YOU TO INSERT COMPLETE FORMULA CODED INVALID COMBINATION INTO COMPUTER SYSTEM DESIGNATED CALL 55 01 0552 07/28. DEADLINE 0200 HOURS 19/5/."

Seconds later, the screen went blank and the 4331 turned itself off. From memory Stark scribbled the computer call number, then rubbed his eyes, hoping against hope that he had been seeing things. "If you want to see your friends *alive* . . ." He picked up the phone and dialed. The number rang. "Friends *alive* . . ." The image of Bart nailed to the wall went through his mind; the bank deficit; the robbery and Merrill's purse, her credit cards. Somebody had been whispering to him, softening him up, closing down his options, and now they were ready to move.

His fingers trembled as the number on the other end rang —ten, twelve times. Finally, the switchboard at Wainwright answered.

"Dr. DeAngelis, please. It's an emergency."

A few minutes later, the doctor was on the line with a pleasant but professional greeting.

"Is my mother all right?" Stark asked, his voice bursting with tension.

DeAngelis laughed. "Better than that, Dr. Rousseau," he said. "She's responding beautifully."

Stark sighed in relief. "The computer treatments," he said, "I think you should take her off them for a while."

"Funny you should suggest that," DeAngelis remarked. "We already have, out of necessity. But it'll be temporary, rest assured. She'll be back in harness in a couple of days."

"Did anything happen?" Stark tensed again.

"I think you know we're on time sharing here. The main computer has had trouble. Nothing serious. They assure me we'll be back on line in a day or so."

Probably not, thought Stark, if what he suspected was true. "Dr. DeAngelis, do me a favor. I don't want her to receive any further treatment until I say. Furthermore, I want her dosages—the quantities and types of medication, that profile that is usually put together by your computers—please use standard dosages, and administer them only by hand—and only by Nurse Lindstrom or yourself. I know this is unorthodox, but believe me, it's of utmost importance."

DeAngelis cleared his throat. "Well . . . I don't know. This is most irregular."

"There is a reason for what I'm asking, believe me. Only a few days. I will explain."

Reluctantly DeAngelis agreed, and with a curt "Thank you," Stark hung up. Unless they actually invaded the hospital and harmed her, Claudette would be protected. Perhaps he should drive up that evening to Marblehead anyway. DeAngelis could set up a bed for him in her room, he thought.

Suddenly, though, he was reminded of the warning: "Friends . . ."

The chair clattered to the floor as he ran from his apartment. He could reach Merrill's apartment in five minutes, he thought, sprinting down the sidewalk. He crossed the street behind a parked Chevrolet van, grasping the base of its whip antenna for balance. His lungs burned with every stride. He had to find her before they did.

Stark cut through a vacant lot at the corner of Ellsworth Street. As he ran, he watched and listened for trouble, any evidence that something in her neighborhood was wrong. Out of breath, he reached the apartment house. Yelling her name, he pushed against the downstairs door. Its hinges gave with a snapping sound and the lock tore loose from the wood frame. He bolted up the stairs, and panting hard, slammed his fists against the door.

"Merrill!" he yelled.

There was no reply.

"What's wrong?" a woman's voice called from the bottom of the stairs. She sounded tentative and slightly frightened.

Stark turned to see who it was. "Do you live here?" he asked.

"I *own* the building," she said, starting to mount the stairs. "I'm the landlady."

"Please let me in," Stark said.

"That's Miss Fox's apartment."

"I know, I *know,*" he replied. "Something's happened to her. She may be in there injured."

The woman looked concerned; she was fond of Merrill. Such a nice girl, she always said; quiet and reserved, and she always paid her rent on time. When the woman reached the landing, she saw the worry in his eyes and reached into her apron for a set of keys. "Miss Fox gave me permission," she said, explaining the keys.

"Merrill!" Stark yelled again.

Again, there was no reply.

Swiftly, he searched the rooms.

The landlady said, "I'll have to ask you to leave now. She's probably gone out for the evening. If you leave your name, I'll tell her."

Stark went to the kitchen telephone and called McKinnon. He hadn't seen Merrill since their dinner. Was anything wrong?

"No," Stark replied. Everything was fine. Then he saw the telephone book by the chair. He looked up the number and dialed.

"May I speak with Mr. Thornton, please?" Stark asked.

He was put on hold. Seconds passed. The old man's voice answered. "Yes," he said, "this is Douglas Thornton."

Stark identified himself. "Is Merrill with you?" he asked.

"No," the old man said. "Why?"

Stark didn't hesitate. "She's missing, sir," he said.

"What are you talking about?"

Stark didn't want to explain on the telephone. "I have to talk with you, sir," he said.

Thornton said calmly, "Why, yes, of course, come by anytime, as soon as you can. I'll be up."

11:00 P.M., EDT: Boston, Massachusetts

"We lifted her, Bill," Sergeant Barbara Fitzsimmons said matter-of-factly to the head of the Narcotics Squad who was leaning back lazily in his chair, his hands folded behind his head. "Anything yet from Walter?"

Captain William Klein caught the note of triumph, and he tried to remember how many years had passed since he last felt anything about an arrest. One more addict in the lockup meant nothing. The battle was too uphill, and in the scheme of things, it didn't matter who they caught anymore. With every arrest of an addict, four more were on the streets. He did his job, but it did not give him any satisfaction. "He's over there now," he said. Then, "What's she like?"

Fitzsimmons pulled up a chair. "That's what sort of bothers me," she said, her brow furrowed. "She doesn't look the type, you know? Pretty, classy, denies everything, and she seemed genuinely surprised. You know, most of them try to fake it. But she wasn't faking. Could she have been set up?"

"Possibly, but I doubt it. Washington doesn't often make mistakes, and they are positive about her. What do you mean, 'classy'?"

"Elegant, you know? Society pages, debutante parties, that sort."

Klein resented the type. A hophead who fed her habit with rich parents' money. When Klein had first started in narcotics, hard drugs were lower-class. Now they were fashionable. Marijuana gave way to cocaine, and the rich kids poured in. Some who snorted coke graduated to an occasional fix, then addiction and the circle was completed. He resented the wealthy ones because they started with everything and ended with the scum. They had a chance and they blew it. "Don't let appearances fool you," he said.

"She even looks clean," Fitzsimmons said.

Klein looked up, surprised. "Did you check her out?"

Fitzsimmons shook her head. "I wanted to wait for Walter. My point, though, is that she looks healthy. I'd expect to see her with a tennis racquet in her hand."

"And a needle in her pocket," Klein said.

"What do we know about her background?" Fitzsimmons asked, interested in the girl.

Klein shuffled the papers on his desk and found Merrill's makeup sheet. "Not very much," he said. "Remember, Barbara, *we* don't want her. Washington does. They asked us to bring her in. She's their problem from here on in."

"So we can assume that they have more."

"I'd hope they do."

Fitzsimmons went to the coffee urn and poured a cup. She sipped the liquid looking through the glass partition. A month ago she had been assigned to the drug squad, and already she hated it. The squad went after kids—the symptom; it never caught the dealers and moneymen.

She saw the elevator doors open and she put down the cup. Sergeant Walter Franzini emerged, sloppy as usual in a filthy Army jacket, jeans and a knit cap. He stopped at the Coca-Cola machine and shoved coins into the slot. The machine regurgitated a can, which he flipped open. He walked into Klein's office, guzzling the Coke.

"What did you get?" Klein asked him.

Walter barely acknowledged Fitzsimmons and Klein as he unzipped his jacket. He gulped from the can again, then threw it into the wastepaper basket. He smiled. "Enough to put her away."

"Are you going to tell us, or do we have to guess?" Klein asked, annoyed.

"I couldn't find any stuff. Not even traces. But the prosecutor will love the look of these." He reached into his pocket and brought out fifteen finger-length tubes.

Klein looked at them and said, "Circumstantial."

"Bullshit, 'circumstantial.' We got a warrant, and we find this paraphernalia? Why else does a junkie keep syringes?"

"Maybe we should ask her," Fitzsimmons suggested. The evidence was damning, but Klein was right; it wasn't conclusive.

"Yeah, let's get her up here." Klein called the cells and asked the sergeant in charge to bring Merrill to his office. He replaced the receiver, then asked, "You found *nothing* else?"

Franzini shook his head. "I thought these would be good enough," he said, touching the syringes.

"Franzini, you are dumb, you know that? Unless Washington has the goods on her already, we'll have to let her go."

Franzini sulked. "What did you expect me to do, plant some stuff?"

"It might have helped," Klein said.

"I can always go back."

"Let's hear what she says."

A guard opened the cubicle door and led Merrill in. "Do you want that I should wait?" the guard asked Klein, who waved him out the door. "I'll call you."

Franzini turned in his chair. He had not risen for a woman in his adult life, but something about Merrill registered in the recesses of his mind, and he got to his feet, offering her his chair.

Fitzsimmons had missed the description by miles, thought Klein. The girl was a bombshell.

Merrill searched their eyes for sympathy and found none. She was scared, but she repeated over and over in her mind, "I have done *nothing* wrong." Then she heard herself saying, "I want to call a lawyer."

"Sit down, Miss Fox," Klein said, eyeing the vacant chair. "If you wish, it's your right to call a lawyer, after you've been arraigned. First, I thought we might have a talk."

"There's nothing to discuss," Merrill said. "You made a mistake, and the sooner you let me go, the less embarrassment for you."

"I want to show you something," Klein said, pushing the syringes toward her.

Merrill looked but didn't think anything about them. "So?"

"We found these in your refrigerator," Klein said. "Are they yours?"

Merrill made the connection, and her mind reeled. She felt dehydrated, and her tongue was starting to thicken. "Of course you did," she said. "I'm diabetic."

Klein made a sound like the growl of a muzzled dog. He had heard all the excuses, even this one. "And I'm Peter Pan," he mocked.

Merrill's face reddened. "I'm *not* lying to you," she said, her voice uneven.

Klein eyed the ceiling, then he looked at Fitzsimmons. "Sergeant, check her, will you please?"

Fitzsimmons really did not want to know, but she obeyed the order and rolled up Merrill's sleeves. She stretched the skin in the crook of her arm, then looked at Klein and nodded.

"What are those, then, bramble punctures?" Klein asked.

Merrill looked at him. The sight now disgusted her. The small marks had been with her so long, she no longer noticed. "I'll repeat what I said: I'm diabetic." She tried a pedantic tone. "The syringes are mine. I use them for insulin injections. The puncture marks are made by the syringes. What more can I say?"

"If that's the case," Klein replied, "maybe you can tell me why the Federal Drug Enforcement people want you, why they asked us to arrest you?"

"I wouldn't know," Merrill said. "That, it seems, is your problem."

"It's yours, too," Klein said. "Why don't you make it easy and tell us?"

"I've already told you," she said, about to cry from frustration. They weren't even listening. "Call my doctor," she said, challenging Klein. She reached for a pencil. "There's his name and phone number."

"Yeah," he replied, putting it in his desk drawer. He made a mental note to place the call later.

"Do it now!" Merrill yelled, suddenly feeling sick to her stomach.

Her tone reminded him unpleasantly of the girls in crisp white tennis shorts he envied when he was a kid. He was always on the other side of the fence. He resented them then, and he resented her now. But he did not close the desk drawer. Beautiful girls in white tennis shorts had powerful relatives, who could make a world of trouble for captains like Klein.

"Go ahead, call!" Merrill commanded.

Klein compressed his lips. "Okay," he said and dialed the number. He listened for a minute and then he hung up. "Recording says he's out." He looked at Merrill. "Any other suggestions, bright eyes?"

She tried hard to think, but was impeded by a growing feeling of nausea. They would not believe her parents, or her grandfather, or Stark, or the McKinnons. They needed conclusive, objective evidence. Then the thought came to her. "The Massachusetts General Hospital knows," she said. The words tumbled out. "I had an appendectomy last year. Diabetes is on my records."

Klein eyed her warily. Her persistence was convincing. He reached for the telephone book. Once he found the number, he dialed and asked for Records. He identified himself and told the hospital's archivist what he wanted.

He lowered the receiver. A minute later, he asked, "What does it say?" . . . "Is there any history of diabetes?" He waited again. "Thank you, miss," he said.

He gave Sergeant Fitzsimmons a weary, world-wise look. "Take her downstairs," he said, then to Merrill, "Good try. You almost had me convinced."

"But I—"

Klein cut her off. "Get her out of here," he shouted.

They didn't believe her, Merrill thought, the nausea sweeping over her now in waves. Her body was showing them the truth, but they were blind. "Please," she pleaded with Sergeant Fitzsimmons when they entered the basement cells. "Will you call a doctor? I need insulin." She paused, seeing that Fitzsimmons barely listened. "This isn't just a mixup," she said. "My life depends on it."

Sergeant Fitzsimmons touched the cold, clammy skin of Merrill's arm and noticed the thin sheen of perspiration on her forehead. She knew the touch: The same thing happened in the cells a score of times. Junkies were picked up and remanded and within hours they went cold turkey. She glanced at her wristwatch. Right on schedule. After four hours, the girl needed a fix. What a filthy shame, Fitzsimmons thought, locking the cell door. A nice-looking girl with beautiful hair and fine, sparkling teeth. A beauty. And she had to ruin herself on junk. Fox might be stunning, but Fitzsimmons would rather have her own plain face and stern resolution any day.

"Please . . ." Merrill begged, hearing the policewoman's footsteps fade into silence. There was no reply, and she slumped onto the bed, burying her face in the pillow. She cried hot, fearful tears.

Then the nausea began.

There was nothing in her stomach but tea, which dribbled from her mouth onto the mattress. Convulsions shook her body and knotted her stomach. When she wiped her mouth, she breathed onto her hand. Acetone!

Merrill knew. She was going to die.

FRIDAY, JUNE 19, 1987

"More practicable and less expensive would be the jamming of the (satellite's) uplink with large antennas. Here the element of surprise could be achieved."

JAMES MARTIN,
Communications Satellite Systems

12:30 A.M., *EDT: Boston, Massachusetts*

Stark lifted the brass knocker as a man in a white jacket opened the heavy oak door. Without asking his name, he showed Stark in, taking his windbreaker. "Mr. Thornton is waiting," he said softly. "If you'll follow me . . ."

From the interior, the house resembled a private museum. Sturdy antiques inlaid with mother-of-pearl and ivory, Chinese vases, jade figurines and bronze sculpture filled the quiet, dimly lit rooms, and the house smelled of furniture wax and leather. They walked across rich green and maroon Oriental rugs. Flemish and Italian masterpieces depicting religious scenes covered the walls—none later than the fifteenth century, Stark guessed. Over the mantel in the large living room, though, hung a single incongruity among the medieval paintings—an oil of a modern house on a tropical beach.

In the library, books lined all four walls from floor to ceiling. There was a Chippendale partners' desk by the French windows, and a button-backed leather sofa near the fireplace. Douglas Thornton, in smoking jacket and slippers, was waiting for him.

"Dr. Rousseau," the butler announced formally.

Thornton shook Stark's hand, then dismissing pleasantries, went right to the point. "You are concerned about my granddaughter?" he asked.

"Somebody is trying to blackmail me, and they've taken Merrill," he replied. "At least I think so—"

"Come, come, young man," Thornton said. "I talked with Eagle not more than a couple of hours ago. Perhaps you'll share with me what you really want."

"You *talked* with her?" Stark was momentarily thrown off balance.

Oh dear, Thornton thought, looking at Stark's expression. Dr. Rousseau was enamored of Eagle, and she had given him the slip. "She was going out the door, in fact," he said. There was no way to break the news gently. "A modeling assignment in Florida, she said."

"But we were . . ." his voice trailed off. Merrill wasn't to leave until the morning. She wouldn't lie to him; he was certain that she wouldn't. "I don't know what she told you. But I received an extortion message on my VDT. I have until two o'clock this morning to give them the formula."

Something in Rousseau's voice told Thornton to take him at least half seriously. But his evidence was unconvincing. A message on the VDT was no conclusive proof. He knew Rousseau only by reputation in a professional manner and had no idea of his personal characteristics—whether he was hysterical, given to flights of fancy and imagination, whether, in fact, he might be slightly mad. But his voice suggested that for whatever the reason he believed in this kidnap story. Thornton played along. "How are you going to contact these people?" he asked.

"Through a designated call of a computer system." Stark handed him the number.

Thornton pushed a button on the side table near the sofa. "I assume you alerted the police?" he said in half question.

Stark shook his head. "They'll list her as a missing person and take their time."

According to Rousseau's story, Eagle was missing, but he had not informed the police. That did not make sense to him, and it further eroded his confidence in what the young man was saying. He was about to ask further questions when Dr. McColough came into the library. Thornton did not introduce his technical assistant. "Dr. McColough, will you please find out where this system is located?" He handed him the number.

McColough nodded. For a long instant he stared at Thornton, then, averting his eyes, left the room.

"That should only take a minute," Thornton said.

Stark knew already what McColough would find. "It's a neutral system," he said. "Once I've put in the formula, they'll remove it electronically. The exchange will be completely anonymous. Nobody can trace it."

"Very clever, but can it be done?"

"Of course. It's the dual piracy of an unprotected system."

"If what you claim is true, Dr. Rousseau, do you have any idea why these people might want your formula?"

"The Pentagon thinks that everybody does." He shook his head. "Specifically, I don't know. Whoever it is, though, they erased my bank account this morning, I guess as a warning."

"Maybe to restrict your movement." Thornton reached to the side table for an ivory-bowled pipe, which he rubbed in his palm but did not light.

"Excuse me, sir," Stark said, breaking the silence, "but you don't seem worried."

"Put yourself in my position. You've done little to convince me."

"There isn't time. I have less than one hour."

"Then you really do take the threat at face value?"

Stark could not believe the old man's lack of concern. "Of course I do."

"And you will give it to them?"

Stark answered slowly. "First and last I care about Merrill. I won't lose her, not for something I've done or failed to do. These people have shown that they are capable of anything."

Thornton saw his sincerity. He looked around as Dr. McColough returned. "Ah, Wallace," he said. "What did you find?"

"It's for a system owned by the Household Finance Company, here in Boston," Dr. McColough said and remained standing.

This conversation was heading nowhere, Stark thought, and only minutes remained before the deadline. Frustrated, he got up to leave. "Thank you, sir," he said—though he could for the life of him think of nothing the old man had done. "I'll have to figure this out on my own."

Thornton waved him back into the chair. "Sit down, sit

down. You take my skepticism wrong. This may be a problem for all of us, especially for me, you understand. So we'll try to do this together."

"I appreciate that," Stark said, walking toward the hallway. "But I have an hour to put the formula into a terminal."

"There's no need to leave, then," Thornton said, again waving him to the chair. "We have a terminal here, in the basement. Whatever we decide, we can use it or not."

Stark felt relieved. He wanted to stay because he needed to talk with someone. Thornton would help him reach the correct decision. The old man was beyond reproach, and their backgrounds were similar; in addition, they shared a mutual concern for Merrill. He sat down and folded his hands.

"That's better," Thornton said. "Now, you know the consequences. Of course, if Eagle was taken, I want her back. But frankly, I find it hard to believe. I hope you understand."

Stark shook his head. The image of Bart came to mind. He *did* understand the consequences: The blackmailer would do what he threatened to do.

Thornton turned to Dr. McColough. "Go downstairs, will you, please?" he asked, indicating the computer room in the basement. "Intercept the telephone lines leading into this . . . this Household Finance's computers, and stay on-line. Once we've decided what to do, we'll have to act fast."

"And you want me to sign on to their system?"

"Precisely," he said, explaining, "It seems that someone has discovered a new twist to the transfer of ransom. It's quite brilliant, really." He looked at Rousseau. "I admire their ingenuity."

"Can you say what we'll be communicating?" McColough asked.

"A program, Dr. McColough, the formula that Dr. Rousseau designed for the symposium."

McColough looked at Stark piercingly. "If I may," he said, apologizing in advance, "I've heard about your invalid combination, Doctor; I have a great respect for your theory."

"I wish it were only a theory," Stark replied.

"Then it does work in fact?"

"I'm afraid so."

Annoyed by McColough's interruption, Thornton said, "Please, if you'll begin. . . ." Then he turned to Stark. "I agree with him. Your research was truly magnificent. Its use would make the country realize the truth of what I have been preaching for so many years."

"But you wouldn't use it, surely," Stark said, reminded of Thornton's organization.

Thornton pondered an answer for several minutes. Finally, he shook his head. "No, it would be too severe a jolt. You see, young man, I may be many things, but I am not a fanatic. Foremost, I am a patriot. I want computers used in perspective for the *good* of the country. But I would never lift a hand to hurt our nation. Never. Frighten the people in charge, yes. But inflict permanent damage? No, not for anything."

Reassured, Stark said, "It's just as well you think that way."

"It's a conviction I hold dear."

Stark said, "Don't you see, that's why I had to talk with you. Perhaps now you understand. I'm telling the truth. Merrill has been taken. And they will kill her." He explained about the new satellites, the hunter-killers that would destroy the existing series on Saturday morning. "We only need about thirty hours, don't you see?" Stark pleaded. "By then the threat will be obviated. But we need the time now to find her."

"It's a dangerous game you suggest," Thornton said, then he thought how foolish his statement sounded. *He* had been playing an equally dangerous game. Indeed, he had wanted IUSUC only to frighten the public and the government into action. The banks and the stock exchanges; maybe as he jammed their systems, there was an aspect that had not been examined, comparable to the devastating and irreversible impact of Dr. Rousseau's formula. He decided he would have to release the electronic grip he and IUSUC had on the three banks and the stock exchanges.

Thornton now believed Rousseau fully. The young man's thought that nothing could happen in thirty hours was dangerously naïve, however. If something went wrong, the country would have lost, and all for one life, his Eagle's life. Thornton did not moralize. No matter how personal a tragedy, if she had to be sacrificed, she would. One person for the safety of millions. Stark Rousseau could see that, too. All he was pleading for was a hedge, thirty, forty hours of time. Still, Thornton thought, there was a better way, a way in which Merrill could be recovered safely *and* the formula withheld from the blackmailers. "Come with me," he said, rushing toward the basement, explaining his idea as they went.

Reaching the facility seconds later, Stark was overwhelmed by the sight of three terminals and a UNIVAC mainframe with a multiplicity of disk-storage cabinets, drives and printouts. This was a pared-down version of the Labs' own facility, he thought in amazement. He looked at Thornton and asked, "Why . . . why all this?"

"An old man's eccentricity," then quickly he asked Dr. McColough, "Have you got the intercept?"

"I'm on their system, sir," answered McColough. "Ready when you are."

The clock on the wall read a quarter to two.

At the terminal, Stark recalled the formula from memory. Concentrating, he started to depress the terminal keys. Writing out the real formula took five minutes. Seeing now where the errors might best be hidden, he started to rewrite the formula. First, he inserted an error in the relay quadrants so that the subtended angles of the INTELSAT series would not align with the signals sent from an earth station. The uplink would miss the satellites altogether. But just to make doubly sure, he omitted a piece of the downlink function. The formula would be garbled in transmission from the satellite.

The time was two minutes to two. "I've got it," Stark said, leaning back in the chair.

"Okay, Dr. McColough, load it," Thornton said.

They waited in silence until they had confirmation that the formula was inside the data banks of Household Finance. Thornton then activated the terminal on Stark's right. "How do you want this worded?" he asked.

"As a demand," Stark replied.

As Thornton typed, the words appeared on the VDT above his head.

"IN RETURN FOR FORMULA, DEMAND IMMEDIATE RELEASE OF THE GIRL. IF NOT IN OUR CARE WITHIN TWELVE HOURS, WILL OBSTRUCT WITH ALL AVAILABLE MEANS."

"That's it," Thornton said. "Now we wait."

Stark got up to leave. "I'm going home. While I'm waiting, I'll try a line trace of Household Finance."

"Yes, absolutely," Thornton said. A good idea. "Let me know the instant they contact you."

Stark stopped and turned. "And if they don't?"

Thornton replied by shaking his head. "Let's assume that this will work."

When Stark had gone, Thornton turned to Dr. McColough and said, "I want you to clear *everything* from memory here—the formula and the errored formula. Do it now."

3:30 A.M., *EDT: Cambridge, Massachusetts*

"What goes out can also be used to go in." Stark remembered using those words with General Church when Stark had penetrated the IBEX VII. At the 4331 terminal in his apartment, he realized now that it was next to impossible, like catching the sound of an echo hours later. He examined the designated call number: 55 01 0552 07/28. Then he switched on the 4331.

"He's burning again," said the man with the ginger beard, continuing to stare at the radiation oscilloscope.

The man to whom he spoke rubbed his eyes and sat up on the small cot an arm's distance away. He yawned loudly and flexed his shoulders. How he hated the cramped quarters. The NSA had designed their surveillance vans for machines, not for humans. He hoped that they would be relieved soon, and then he could get a solid night's sleep. "Incoming or outgoing?" he asked, his tongue thick with sleep.

"He's trying to reach the designated number. Should we tell Washington?"

"In time," said the other man, peering at the oscilloscope. He sat down beside his partner before a bank of microcircuitry electronics. It was his responsibility to translate the bursts of radiation appearing on Rousseau's VDT into actual data. "Let's wait and see what he's doing," he said.

They had been on station for forty-eight hours, alternating sleep with monitoring. Cyberveillance was almost always deadly dull, but each of them, as GS-12s with the National Security Agency, endured the boredom with a sense of purpose, as submariners do for weeks beneath the sea. Crammed within the interior of the truck was a quarter million dollars' worth of electronic equipment. It was their job to tune and calibrate it to catch the signals emanating from wherever the NSA assigned them. In their careers as a team they had cyberveilled embassies and corporations, but this was the first time for either on a private dwelling, and that, they agreed, presented its own challenge.

They knew nothing about the nature of their surveillance —it was none of their business, really. But they had watched the scenes of the drama unfold on the oscilloscope and through the smoked windows of the van. The extortion message had excited them; then they had watched the young man race from the house. Washington had told them they had done well. The message they had intercepted was important, and so, too, was their subject.

"What's he doing?" the second man, Howard Barkley, asked.

"He's interfaced with the Labs' computer, I think, and searching," replied the man with the beard, Ike Jameson, who read an oscilloscope as others did a book. He mused, "This kid is unbelievable, Howie; he really is. I mean, he works that thing like magic."

"Save the flattery," Barkley said. "We don't know yet where he stands."

"He's tapping a line," Jameson announced. The oscilloscope pulsed with horizontal waving lines, which began on the left of the screen in spikes, them smoothed out to curves near the right border of the screen. "What do you get?" he asked.

"Yeah, you're right; he's tapping." Too bad, he thought, they'd have to wait for Washington to tell them, and only on a need-to-know basis. Barkley checked the recorder. The spools rotated slowly, documenting each electronic impulse emanating from the VDT. "He seems to be working backward, tracking, from the 55 01 0552 07/28."

"I don't get it," Jameson said, confused. Both men were expert with computers, and yet they were witnessing something neither had seen before.

"What the hell; don't ask me," Barkley said. "He's either playing with us, which I doubt, or he's sneaking back along a line. I'm going to key Washington."

Jameson looked at him strangely.

Barkley answered the unspoken question. "They may want a running assessment." The telephone patch had been their first task after parking the truck near Rousseau's house. The line was constantly open and manned at the other end. Picking up the receiver, he said, "We're sending on-line, starting now." He punched up a series of keys on the communications console, permitting the data to flow along a separate telephone link to the Pentagon. "You'd better warn your honchos," he told the man in Washington when the remote connection was made. "I think we're getting data they'll want to read as soon as it's received."

"Will do," the technician in Washington replied.

Jameson hunched over the oscilloscope, his admiration for the young man growing. Neither man spoke now that Washington was monitoring. Fascinated, they were only partly aware of what was happening. They could see and they couldn't see. Like a wounded animal circling back on the hunter, the young man at the 4331 inside the apartment was moving along digital lines; when he sighted *his* prey, he would hang back; he would not pounce. He would bide his time until the prey was most defenseless, then strike. The oscilloscope was a flurry of patterns, some of which Jameson had not seen before. The young man was using the systems, Jameson guessed, in completely new ways. "He's approaching a terminus," Jameson said. Nearly an hour passed.

They both heard the sound at the same instant, but since they were concentrating, they reacted slowly.

A second, more insistent knock came on the rear panel door.

"What the—" Barkley exclaimed. Sometimes they were interrupted, but not often. Students mistook the cherry-red van for a "fuck truck." Barkley had wanted the color changed to dull green, but NSA denied the request, claiming that green looked too official. "See to it, will you, Ike?" he asked.

Ike turned in his seat and duck-walked the few feet to the rear door. He looked out through the smoked glass. A man stood there with his arms folded.

"What do you want?" Jameson yelled; he did not intend to be helpful.

The man did not answer, as though he hadn't heard.

Barkley's voice was excited. "I think he's found the terminus," he exclaimed, then into the telephone receiver: "Did you receive that?"

Jameson opened the door a crack. "I said, 'What do you want?' "

Suddenly, the door was pulled wide open from the outside. Jameson, seeing the stranger, held out both arms. He stumbled back into the van's interior. "No—" he yelled.

"Jesus Christ," Barkley said, angry, looking up from the console. "Watch yoursel—" And he, too, dove for the van's floor.

The stranger perched athletically on the bumper, one leg stretched in front for balance. In his hands he carried an M-16 with a thick tubular fitting on its barrel. A silencer. He raised it to his shoulder and pressed the trigger, releasing the entire clip in a continuous burst. The banks of electronics erupted on impact, sending out electric sparks, which set fire to the plastic wiring. The carpet was lacerated, as were the chairs, the front seats, the windshield.

The shooting stopped. The stranger laid the rifle on the floor and crouched beside the bodies of Jameson and Barkley, pressing the tips of his fingers against their jugulars. Jameson was dead, his stomach and chest torn out and oozing blood. Barkley, the stranger realized, was still alive, his breathing shallow. The stranger reached behind his back and withdrew a long-bladed knife from a sheath, then with a powerful slashing movement, he severed the wounded man's throat.

The heat and smoke were now intolerable. The stranger jumped from the van, his lungs about to burst. Coughing, he drove off at normal speed. In his rear-view mirror, he could see the van burst into flames.

5:30 A.M., *EDT: Boston, Massachusetts*

Douglas Thornton put on his chesterfield, hat and gray kid gloves. That he had to go out so early was unpleasant, but he had no choice. Mrs. Gellitsen had called at five, hysterical and crying, and Dr. Gellitsen was, after all, his friend. Thornton took a silver-tipped walking stick from the porcelain umbrella stand near the door, then turned, almost as an afterthought, to Dr. McColough, who had apparently been awakened by the phone call as well. "I'll be gone a short time," Thornton said. "Stay near the telephone, and tell Dr. Rousseau, if he calls, I will be in touch the minute I return. Do you have all that?"

Dr. McColough nodded. "Maybe you should give me the number," he said.

"Not necessary," Thornton replied.

At the end of the brick walk waited his chauffeured Bentley. The driver got out and came around to the passenger side, opening the door with the slightest bow, and Thornton slid onto the seat.

Minutes later, across the Charles in the Shady Hill section of Cambridge, the Bentley came to a stop in front of a two-story house set back from the street and set off by two large maples. Thornton got from the car unassisted and walked to the door, which was opened before he got there.

Mrs. Arthur Gellitsen looked haggard. Wisps of gray hair fell into her face; the lines around her eyes were drawn from lack of sleep and worry, and her shoulders sank heavily, as though she were already grieving. "It's nice of you to come, Douglas." Her voice was leadened with despair. "He wants to see you; you're the only one he wants to see."

Thornton gave her hand a reassuring squeeze. "What does the doctor say?"

She looked at the floor. "He just left," she said. "An ambulance will be here any minute." She started to sob.

"It's not so bad," Thornton said, trying to console. "It's a simple blood infection."

"The doctor thinks otherwise. He doesn't know. Why would they take him to the hospital if it weren't serious? Arthur never has had a sick day in his life."

"There, there—let's have a look at him."

Thornton went down the narrow hallway. He had visited the Gellitsen house twice before, once just yesterday afternoon. The house smelled of sausage fat and dust, and the cheap, boxy furnishings offended him.

The lamp in the corner of the bedroom threw a dim light on Gellitsen. He lay beneath a white sheet and was staring into space; his thoughts were filled with self-pity. He did not know why they wanted him dead. After all, he had served the cause well, he had not shrunk from duty.

"Arthur, old man," Thornton announced himself cheerfully, and stood at his bedside.

Gellitsen shifted his eyes downward. When he spoke his voice was weak and dry. "I'm going to die," he said with an effort.

"Oh, come now—don't be so dramatic. It isn't like you at all." Thornton winced, though, when he noticed the inflamed and swollen bluish-red area that ran from the base of Gellitsen's neck above the sheet to his ear. It was a blistering infection and, he guessed, horribly painful.

"Look," Gellitsen said, again, each new breath a struggle.

Thornton pulled down the sheet and recoiled at the sight and smell of the wound. Gellitsen's hand and lower arm were black and ulcerated, and swollen to the size of a man's thigh. The breaks in the skin ran liquid with a greenish-white pus. The putrid smell of the wound was horrid. He replaced the sheet, then asked. "What are they doing about it?"

Gellitsen shook his head feebly against the pillow. "They don't know," he said.

"What do you mean, 'They don't know'?"

"They don't know what it is," Gellitsen sighed.

"You mean they can't *identify* it?" Thornton's voice was incredulous. Infections, common or not, had long ago been typed.

Gellitsen did not reply. If his guess was right, the doctors would probably never be able to identify the bacillus. "Come closer," he whispered.

Thornton drew a chair from beside the window, then bent his ear to Gellitsen's face, wondering what could be so important that Gellitsen would waste his strength saying it.

"I took my belief too far, Douglas," he said with an effort. His thoughts were confused by pain, and he swooned between lucidity and hallucination. "Please forgive me."

"Now, listen here," Thornton replied, trying to sound stern. "You did no such thing. We intended to convince the people of this nation, and that's just what we have done. It's over now. So if your ideals are wrong, as you say, then so are mine, and I can't ever admit that to myself, because it just isn't true."

Thornton did not understand, Gellitsen thought. Obviously Thornton had not discovered the truth. Gellitsen was still angry at the Lab directors for giving the Lionel professorship to Dr. Rousseau. But that was not the reason he had helped Thornton's Union, or why, frustrated by the Union's lack of progress, he had helped the others. Ideals! That was the real answer. What a paltry thing ideals turned out to be!

Gellitsen wanted to warn Douglas Thornton of the immediate danger. It was only fair of him to tell the Union's founder. But if he did, Thornton would be appalled, and he would tell the authorities. Gellitsen would be called a traitor, not only to his profession, but more, to his country, and would negate his own contribution to a cause in which he believed.

"Douglas, you must forgive me," Gellitsen said, his voice even weaker than before.

Thornton heard the lonely wail of an ambulance siren in the distance. "You'll be all right," he said softly. "They're nearly here."

Gellitsen seemed to have fallen asleep. As Thornton pulled the sheet over his shoulder, there was a long, wheezing expulsion of breath from Gellitsen's lungs. Alarmed, Thornton touched his wrist, then lifted the lid of Gellitsen's eye.

Gellitsen was dead.

8:30 A.M., *EDT: Cambridge, Massachusetts*

Stark raised his head from the pillow of his elbow, his mouth furry and his eyes sore. He glanced at his wristwatch. He had been asleep for nearly five hours. Looking up expectantly, the blank VDT gave him a momentary shock—he wondered whether he had slept through the contact that would tell him where Merrill was. The same feeling of panic had nagged at him the night before when he heard the sound of sirens. As they came closer and closer he had thought that they were returning her to him. The sirens stopped in front of his apartment. He had run outside expecting to see her walking up the steps. Red lights flashed against the trees, making the night eerie. He had taken in the scene at one glance. There were police cars *and* fire trucks; the street was blocked off; white foam covered a van parked nearby. As he watched, a fireman in black boots and a Dayglo slicker lifted the charred remains of two men from the van. Police photographers snapped flash pictures, and detectives fanned out, asking residents what they had seen. One detective, a thick-set Irishman with cherry cheeks, said that the men had been murdered, their bodies mutilated, and the van set aflame. He knew nothing more. After giving him his name, Stark rushed back inside, careful to lock the door. A murder so near *his house,* he feared, was not another coincidence. Yet there was nothing to do but wait for the blackmailer's answer. Stark stared at the VDT, willing it to produce the message, the signal that Merrill was safe and being returned. Finally, he had not been able to keep his eyes open any longer. . . .

Now in the bathroom, splashing cold water on his face and neck, he made a decision. If nothing else, he was methodical. His world formed a perfect order that was now shattered. To restore that order, he had to follow a logical sequence, just as he had done when he invaded the IBEX VII, created the formula and last night "walked" back along circuits to find the blackmailer's terminal. Yet it was hard for Stark to turn method into physical action, as he now must. In his mind, there were ultimate truths; facts did not lie, just as mathematical truth could not. But with people there were emotions, devious motivations and thickets of lies. It was shaky ground and frightening.

An hour later, Stark Rousseau pulled the McKinnons' borrowed Ford Fairlane into a parking bay designed for "guests." He faced a building of steel and glass with a Henry Moore sculpture in the front. As he got out of the car, he looked again and thought that for such an imposing structure, the owner had been modest about the name. In discreet letters over the door were the words "Ling Autonetics."

His search with the IBM 4331 had led him here; the trail

from Household Finance had been faint, but there were traces, at times almost invisible traces. The search ended at a computer terminal with a designated call sign registered to this company. Some person here, inside this fortress structure, knew where Merrill was.

A guard at the door looked at him with only mild interest. "What can I do for you?"

"I'd like to speak with the president of the company."

The guard eyed him suspiciously. "Do you have an appointment?"

Stark shook his head. "Tell him Dr. Stark Rousseau wants him."

The guard noted Stark's title. "He's a very busy man. I don't even know if he's in today," he lied. He had tipped his hat to Elliman fifteen minutes earlier.

"Just call him, please."

The guard did not want to take further responsibility and lifted the telephone on his stand, relaying the information. Sixty seconds passed while the request went through the secretary. Finally, surprised by the response, he hung up.

He asked Stark to sign the register and gave him a numbered "visitors" badge, which he asked him to clip to his sweater. Then very politely, he directed Stark to the private elevator. "His secretary will meet you, sir," he said.

Stark did not flatter himself. The president of this computer company—or any other, for that matter—would see him unannounced. Although his reputation rarely intruded, he knew of its existence and to a lesser degree, what it meant to others. The president, of course, would wonder why he was there; that same curiosity gave him instant access. As he rode up, Stark tried to understand the pattern. A successful corporation like Ling Autonetics wanted the formula enough to break laws and hurt people. Perhaps the company was not to blame. Ling's computer terminal had been used to notify him. Perhaps it was a mad employee; Stark did not know. Whoever the person was, he had kidnaped Merrill.

The elevator doors opened and a pleasant-looking woman

with her hair tied neatly in a bun greeted him with a smile. "Dr. Rousseau," she said simply. "This is quite an unexpected honor."

Stark did not know the president's name. "Thank you," he said.

"Mr. Elliman's in a meeting, but he'll be with you as soon as he's finished." She led him to an anteroom, and he sat on the sofa, paging through a copy of *Newsweek*.

Minutes later, he heard a buzz on the secretary's intercom and a muffled request.

She stood up. "Please, you can go in now."

Elliman was standing; another man, an Oriental, remained seated. Stark shook Elliman's hand and was introduced to the Oriental, a "business associate," Elliman said, then: "To what do we owe the honor of this visit?"

Stark watched Elliman closely for a sign of nervousness, but there was none. He began abruptly: "Did you attend a symposium last week at the Beeman Labs?"

"Trojan Horse?" Elliman asked affably. "I regrettably couldn't. But I wish I had. I was telling Mr. Niigata here just yesterday what a stir it caused. Is there really truth to your formula?"

Stark was not here to *answer* questions. "Someone in your corporation is blackmailing me," he said, directing his eyes upon Elliman.

Elliman laughed, seemingly embarrassed. "That's quite a charge, really." His plummy, faint British tone was defensive but friendly. "Can you substantiate it?"

Stark related the events of the last twenty-four hours, ending with, "The computer trail leads to this building, and within this building to a specific terminal. I have the designated call." He drew a piece of paper from his back pocket and gave it to Elliman.

"Yes . . . that is one of ours."

"May I see the log?" Stark said.

"I'm afraid not." Now he was defensive. "They're confidential. Company employees *only* are allowed access."

"But you will make an exception."

Elliman looked at Niigata. "I *will* make an exception," Elliman said, trying to sound helpful. "But if I might suggest, this really is a matter for the police. Have you informed them of this . . . this extortion?"

"I have no evidence, at least none they will believe," Stark said truthfully.

Elliman said offhandedly, "I hope you didn't give the formula away to these people . . . these blackmailers."

"Nothing they'll be able to use, no," Stark said.

"Oh really," Elliman sounded intrigued. "I don't understand. You did not give them the *real* formula?"

Stark, suddenly suspicious, deferred the question with one of his own. "What kind of facilities do you have here?"

Elliman turned around. "We are a mainframe computer company, Dr. Rousseau. That should tell you the equipment we use."

"I was thinking about telecommunications in particular," Stark said. "Do you transmit data from here?"

"We have that capacity, yes. Perhaps you saw the parabolic dish on the roof." He paused, then: "Satellite communication, as you know better than most, is the wave of the future for data. We hope to play a part in that market."

"Then am I correct in the thought," Stark said, "that some person connected with Ling Autonetics might be able to transmit the formula from here?"

"I couldn't say," Elliman said. "First I would need an idea of the formula's communications requirements."

"A perpetrator needs only an earth station like the one on your roof, and a mainframe computer. The other hardware required is common in the business marketplace."

"Then they could," Elliman said. "But I would suggest that your suspicions are misplaced. I would venture a guess that none of my employees has the expertise to understand such a complex formula."

"What about yourself?"

"What? That I have that expertise?" Elliman threw back his

head and laughed. "My background, in case you don't know, is in sales. That's how I worked my way up, and it was on that basis that I started Ling. I buy brains, Dr. Rousseau."

"You know nothing about the actual function of computers?"

"Of course I know about the electronic components. I have an engineering degree and have studied advanced mathematics. That much you will discover in *Who's Who*. My point is this: Your formula is not to be understood by the common mind. I doubt if my background would even serve me to read and understand it."

"And Mr.—" he hesitated, looking at the Japanese.

"Niigata," Elliman said helpfully. "He is not an employee of Ling. In fact, his company is based in Tokyo."

"Have you ever heard of a young woman named Merrill Fox?" Stark asked suddenly, hoping to catch them off-guard.

Elliman looked at Niigata, then slowly shook his head. "No, I don't think I have."

Stark put his hands in his pockets. There was nothing left to ask. Elliman, he thought, had answered all the questions smoothly. Yet Stark could not help feeling that Elliman was hiding something.

Elliman said, "These questions are somewhat moot, anyway, aren't they? You said that you deceived the extortionist, and I would gather that you haven't given the formula to anyone else. So there is nothing to fear. The girl will be returned to you when the extortionist discovers that the formula is too complex."

Stark thought now that Elliman was trying to force an answer. Stark looked at the Japanese, who had been oddly silent throughout. Why, Stark asked himself, was Niigata looking at Elliman with that steady stare? What did it mean?

The silence broke as the secretary entered. The logs would show him nothing, Stark knew. He took the book from her and looked at the entries for last night. The log was blank. The terminal had been shut down. He had no more proof now than when he had entered the building, and yet he knew. Elliman—and perhaps Niigata—were his men.

"Thanks for your cooperation," Stark said. "You've been most helpful."

"Wait a minute," Elliman said, his voice pitched slightly higher than it had been.

Stark turned, almost anticipating a blow.

Elliman glanced at Niigata, then waved his hand, grinning just a little. "Nothing," he said. "Nothing at all."

9:15 A.M., *EDT: Boston, Massachusetts*

Butting out the cigarette, Vasily Domintrin rubbed his tongue against the roof of his mouth, trying to wipe away the bitter taste. American tobacco was bland by comparison to the Sobranies and their taste disgusting, but he had barely had time to pack clothes, let alone luxuries.

He felt a dull heaviness, probably from jet lag, he guessed, or maybe just worry. He had thought obsessively about his wife and daughter during his long Aeroflot flight: what they were doing at that very moment, what they were thinking, whether they were being treated humanely, what they had been told by the First Directorate. His worry solidified his resolve: He would do exactly what he had been sent to accomplish, without stinting. Nothing mattered to him but the safety of his family. And it could not be all that bad—the U.S.S.R. was still run by sober, serious men. Upon arriving at the Ritz, he had tried to sleep, unsuccessfully. Indeed, he had showered and shaved and put on a clean shirt. Now there was nothing to do but wait.

He got up from the end of the bed and poured himself American coffee from the room-service trolley. He carried the cup to the window. The small park, which Americans called the Common, looked like the pretty one with oaks off the square where Katya, his wife, Sasha and he had lived so happily.

At first he had considered ways of deceiving the First Directorate, of pretending to carry out their plans. But he could not see how. Domintrin had never been a devious person; a scientist, he knew that reality could not be manipulated. He prayed that the First Directorate would see that eventually and come to its senses.

He turned from the window and lay down the cup. His suitcase was on the bed and from it he selected a necktie, knotting it carefully in the mirror. Katya, Sasha, he thought for the thousandth time.

A knock on the door made him check his watch. He had forgotten to change to local time, seven hours behind Moscow, which made it . . . yes, a little after nine in the morning. He went to the door. Standing there in a neat suit was the man who held the power over his family—Katya, Sasha. The man was small and thin with narrow, hawkish eyes that penetrated. Domintrin remembered what he had been ordered to say: "We are scorching the earth."

Alexi Borznoi repeated, "We are scorching the earth."

"Come in, please."

Domintrin hated the man on sight, of course, for what he represented, but now even more so for his coolness: Borznoi moved across the hotel room with a confidence that astounded Domintrin, who wondered how anyone with such power of death could seem so benign, so small and mere and mortal. One word from Borznoi to the First Directorate . . .

"I have stumbled into good fortune," Borznoi said. Except for carrying out what Moscow ordered, he had no interest in this man Domintrin. He felt no comradeship with him and, now, because the time was short, he could not even learn to trust him—which is why he had asked Moscow to ensure Domintrin's cooperation *without question.* Borznoi knew of this scientist's repeated failures . . . and neither Borznoi nor anyone else in the KGB could ever be certain that those failures were not premeditated. Borznoi assumed that they were; if given the latitude, Domintrin would turn traitor.

Borznoi withdrew a folded computer printout from his inside pocket. "What does this suggest to you?"

Domintrin examined the long sheet: A formula he did not understand, not at first glance. "This will take time," he said.

"It's the program that Dolowsky described to you," Borznoi said smoothly. Borznoi stopped himself, deciding to let Domintrin digest it.

Domintrin stared at him for a long minute, then back at the printout.

"It's much bigger than the Directorate hoped," Borznoi continued. "Their vision was incredibly limited compared to this."

"Where did you find this . . .?" Domintrin continued to read the program.

"A mathematician gave it to me," he replied as vaguely as possible. Then, "In a few minutes, another agent will join us here. When he arrives, we will go for a short walk, then I'll explain everything."

Domintrin wanted answers now. "But who could be such a traitor?"

Borznoi smiled grimly. "A patriot," he said. "A little patriot who is both confused and misguided, someone easy for me to manipulate. Perhaps you forget, dear Domintrin, which side you work for. A traitor to one cause is a patriot to another. When the priority of Scorched Earth is invoked by the Politburo, sides are chosen quickly. I assume you have made your decision?"

Domintrin did not reply. He knew that Borznoi was a watchdog, and if he wavered, Borznoi would kill him.

Borznoi spoke. "If you'll look at that printout again."

Domintrin lifted the paper to his eyes. The program required intense study: He read superficially the high and low parts of the equation as a geographer plots glacial formations by reading the land. An earth station was needed, as were multiplexers, modems and analog communications lines, full and half simplexes, modulators and demodulators, disk drives and the like. The equipment was of great complexity. "It's very convincing," Domintrin said finally.

Borznoi was impatient. "I know that," he said. "What I don't know is: Can you, Domintrin, implement the formula by yourself?"

Domintrin took his time in answering. Ultimately, a lie would be discovered and he would suffer the consequences. "Yes," he said, "with the proper equipment."

"And by 'proper equipment,' you mean?"

Domintrin explained what was needed, then said, "I don't know all of it. Our technology is years behind theirs."

"That's *precisely* why we're here, comrade."

Domintrin pretended to ignore the remark. Moscow's great leveler, he thought. If you could not beat the opposition, you found the means to tear it down. "This formula is on the outer limit of our science," he said. "We might conceive of it, but it would surely take ten years before we could actually write and use it." He looked again at the program, the total brilliance of its conception dawning. He then asked with hope in his voice, "Where will you get the equipment?" He looked sideways into Borznoi's face.

Borznoi stepped around the service trolley and went to the window. "I have access," he said after a pause. Standing there, he looked at his hands, and the memory of a recurring dream returned. In the dream, he knelt before a complicated machine, which he guessed to be a short-wave transceiver. For a reason that was not clear to him, he had to turn it off, and when he tried, he moved the wrong dials, flipped the wrong switches. The more desperate he became, the larger his hands grew, until finally they could not grasp the sensitive machinery. His hands became weighty cabbages with which he could do nothing; he could only rest on his knees.

The dream was the single reason for his request to the First Directorate. He needed expert assistance, and now it had arrived, but oh, how reluctantly, he thought, turning to Domintrin. He had no choice but to rely completely on him. Without the full range of his cooperation, Scorched Earth would fail, and he, Alexi Borznoi, would die. He sighed, thinking how many Russian scientists had turned traitor over the years. He could only speculate why they had turned against their country. Maybe they were more intelligent than the *apparatchiks* who maintained the system. Maybe they saw more clearly. But that made them no less traitorous. Domintrin was one of them, or at least he had the potential; his allegiance was to science, and that had to be qualified. Domintrin needed a jolt, a shock to wipe from his mind any thought of deceit. "Domintrin," he asked, turning away from the window, "You have a young daughter named Sasha?" His expression was calm, but his eyes were obsidian.

Domintrin jerked toward Borznoi, then stopped abruptly. He lowered his head and sank in the chair near the window, his mind as blank now as Borznoi's expression. Domintrin stiffened in the chair, an unconscious mark of dignity and said, "Yes, my daughter's name is Sasha. She is eight years old."

Borznoi paced across to the telephone on the nightstand and dialed many numbers. Once he had reached his connection he handed the receiver to Domintrin. "Listen," he said.

Domintrin pressed the phone to his ear, watching Borznoi as he turned his back. There was a click, then a hissing sound. Finally, he heard the familiar voice.

"Hello, Daddy. This is Sasha. They told us we couldn't go home, Daddy, until you returned. . . . When will you come back? Daddy, please come home to us. It's strange here and we don't have a room to ourselves. They wouldn't even turn out the lights when Mommy asked them. I don't like it here, Daddy. Please come back to us and take us home. . . ."

"Sasha, darling," Domintrin yelled. "Can you hear me?"

The hissing sound came back. He had been listening to a tape recording. As he drew in a weary breath, a knock at the door made him turn.

"Get it, will you?" Borznoi asked.

Domintrin opened the door.

Standing there was a small man of Japanese descent.

"I am Mr. Niigata," he said.

9:45 A.M., EDT: Washington, D.C.

Entering his office, General Hedley Church spun his hat at the sofa, began wriggling out of his tunic and used his free hand to riffle through the stack of newspapers on his desk: the *Times, Post* and *Star,* the *Daily News,* the *Sun-Times, Los Angeles Times.* He removed his other arm and hung the jacket over the back of the chair, then unloosening his necktie, he went to the intercom and said to his aide, a first lieutenant who was drinking coffee outside at his desk, "Get me the *Journal."* Church turned to his appointment book. This was going to be a hectic one: A contingent from LTW was flying up from Houston to meet with him that afternoon and then there was the morning meeting with—

"Oh, there you are," muttered Church. The lieutenant made loud apologies for the oversight and handed him the newspaper, which Church spread over the desk. Good, he thought when he failed to spot any mention of the LTW rumor. The traders had guarded the secret well. A leak now, he knew, could be dangerous. The Secretary would suspect it had come from the Pentagon, and he was not fond of leaks. Word was out in the investment community among those who had a reason to know. That would be enough.

Clinton Hennessy had given him repeated assurances, and if Hennessy did not know the market, then who did? Church understood the strategy only in the broad outline. He knew his reward most of all. A bold stroke, Hennessy had said, but what was bold for him was extremely subtle to Church. Leaning back in his chair, he hoped that nothing had gone wrong. Hennessy had called unexpectedly the night before this morning's appointment.

Church rubbed his chin pensively, then looked up to see Clint Hennessy in the doorway. Church smiled and offered greetings. Looking at his visitor, Church thought, even if Hennessy were meeting the President himself, he would wear that outfit.

"How're things on that ranch of yours?" Church asked, getting up to shake his hand.

"Real fine. To tell you the truth, I hate to leave the place." Hennessy pulled out a chair and sat facing him across the desk. "Is it all right for us to talk here, Hedley?"

Church swept the office with his eyes. "Unless you feel uncomfortable, yes."

"Fine by me."

Church said, "Colombo reported that your trader . . . Streeter, got in touch."

"As I had hoped. Streeter reported back to Vickers, who is buying promissory stock now. Streeter has the sellers. Good move, Hedley."

"And the price?"

Hennessy waved the question aside. "We're getting it for what we're asking. I think we'll come in just under the wire. If the rumor holds through the weekend, we're home free."

Something in the tone of Hennessy's last sentence put Church on edge. "If the rumor holds . . ." It should, at least over the weekend. But what about the stock exchange? "What guarantee do you have that the exchange will open Monday, Clint?"

"I don't. We can only cross our fingers. It's a gamble only that they will straighten things out over the weekend."

"I'm glad I could be of help," said Church.

Hennessy crossed his leg, resting his hand on his boot. "There seems to be a lot of rumors going around these days, Hedley," he said. "Maybe you can check one out for me?"

Church waved his hand through the air magnanimously. "Anything."

"Vickers heard that LTW has received a quickie contract. Any truth to it?"

Church saw no reason to explain the new INTELSAT series, but he nodded his head slowly. "The Secretary himself gave the orders. We need five birds fast. Since LTW built the last series, they are in a position to give us the best results. In other words, yes, the rumor is true."

Hennessy looked at him piercingly. "How far along are they?"

"Nearly ready for delivery to the Cape, from what I heard last night."

"Can you stop it?"

"Why should I?"

"Hedley, don't you see?"

"See what? I did exactly as you asked. The new satellites don't have any effect on the MX rumor." He hesitated. "Do they?"

"It could change everything. If Streeter gets wind of this development, he'll start to ask questions. The new satellites make LTW look good. Real good. At the very least, the contract could make Streeter and his clients think there has been a change of heart around here toward LTW. Maybe . . . they might think that the MX deal is being reconsidered." Hennessy did not want to spook Church, but the issue was crucial to his takeover bid, and to his own reputation. If Streeter discovered that he had been manipulated, Hennessy would be dead.

Church slowly made the connection. Almost before his eyes, he was seeing his reward, the seat on the Board of LTW, vanish from his grasp. "Well, what can I do now?" he asked.

Hennessy leaned across the desk and told him.

10:45 A.M., *EDT: Boston, Massachusetts*

Stark looked for assistance as he surveyed the reception hall on the ground floor of the Boston Police Headquarters. People, some in uniform, some not, strode purposefully across the floor. One desk, to his right and in the middle, along the wall, was surrounded by civilians. The desk was manned by a young, pretty cadet police-woman. He waited his turn. Finally, she looked up at him.

"I want to report a missing person."

"Third floor; you'll see it marked on the door. Stairs are over there," she said automatically, pointing to a staircase.

Instead, Stark rode one of the elevators beside a silent cop with a dagger tattooed on his forearm. On the third floor Stark found the missing-persons cubicle without difficulty. The officer in charge looked at him inquiringly. "What can I do for you?"

"I'm reporting a kidnaping," Stark said.

The young man looked serious, not like one of the many fretful relatives and parents who assumed kidnaping when in fact their children, girlfriends, or wives had simply decided to escape their overly solicitous guardian. "That's a serious charge," the officer said.

"A girl I know is missing. I received a ransom note of sorts. They said she would be returned only if I gave them what they want."

"And what is that?" he asked skeptically.

"A formula, sir, a mathematical formula for computers."

"I see. When did she disappear?"

"Yesterday."

"And the ransom note, do you have it?"

"It was put on a computer video display tube," Stark said, frustrated. "It was erased immediately."

Formulas, ransoms, computers, thought the policeman, nodding solemnly. A paranoid kook.

"You must believe me," Stark pleaded now. "At least . . ." He didn't know what he could ask of the policeman. "At least, can you see whether she has turned up . . .?" His voice trailed off. Elliman had her, he thought; but marshaling the police behind that fact was going to be impossible. He started to wonder why he had come.

The policeman abruptly got to his feet and they descended two floors by the staircase and went to the headquarters' communications room. The dispatchers' radios squawked loudly and incessantly. Stark caught sight of several VDTs, the ubiquitous displays off which the police read computer-held license numbers, wanted descriptions, warrants and records. Without computers, Stark thought, law enforcement would be as inefficient as the Keystone Cops.

"Do you know anything about these?" the policeman asked, evidently proud of the modernized equipment.

Stark glanced at the VDT. "A bit," he said.

The policeman decided the young man deserved more than a simple brushoff. "Let's see what we have," he said, bending over the keyboard. "Spell her name, please?"

Stark slowly spelled it out. He didn't know her middle name, or if she had one. The green letters flickered across the tube and held, then automatically erased as the computer digested the data.

"Right!" the policeman exclaimed.

Stark looked at the VDT.

"REF CODE 4 SEC 13, ARRESTED AND CHARGED, HELD PEND ARRAIGN, NEG BAIL, CAPT KLEIN . . . ."

"Drug bust," the policeman said tersely.

"But that's impossible."

"This thing doesn't lie. Trafficking and use, Code Four. She isn't missing; she's downstairs in the cells."

"I want to see her," he said, his heart beating rapidly. Merrill was safe; she was alive and well! He wanted to shout with joy.

The policeman was confused and suspicious. "We have to ask the arresting officer," he said.

Stark let out a long breath. "Hurry, please," he said.

A few minutes later, they stood outside the Drug Squad's small cubicle. Captain Klein, cradling the telephone receiver against his shoulder, looked up and signaled them to enter. Klein mumbled something into the phone and hung up. Without asking, Klein was treated to a brief recap. He rubbed his forehead.

Once the policeman had finished, Stark blurted out, "Please let me see her."

Klein eyed Stark, nervously licking his lips. It was just one of those unfortunate things that sometimes happened, and he wanted to sweep it under the rug as quickly as possible. The force wasn't perfect, after all. At least, he thought, the young man did not have a lawyer in tow. For his own protection, he decided to say as little as possible. "That won't be possible at the present time," he said. "I'm afraid we cannot help you."

"You don't understand," Stark demanded. "I'm not asking to see her, I'm demanding."

Klein shook his head. "I can't help you." He shifted his eyes to the door, hoping that the policeman would catch the hint and escort the man out.

Stark's anger made his voice crack. "I won't . . . threaten you. But unless you allow me to see her, which is my right, I will bring a lawyer down here in thirty minutes."

The bluff did not work. "She's not here," Klein whispered.

"Excuse me?"

"I *said:* 'She's not here.' "

"Your computer lists her as arraigned and in the cells."

"I know, I know," Klein said impatiently. "But it isn't true."

"Then where is she?"

Klein wiped his forehead. He had no choice but to admit the truth. "Have you ever heard of NCIC?"

"What does that have to do with . . .?"

"Everything, I'm afraid. The National Crime Information Center is run out of Washington by the FBI. It's a computer link with every major police department. It works like this: Warrants are issued, say, for suspect X by department Y. We're department Z; when the data come up on our computer through the NCIC, we arrest the suspect and send him or her in custody to the department that issued the warrant. . . ."

"I don't see what that has to do with Merrill." Stark wanted only one thing: to see her, safe.

"The National Drug Enforcement Bureau, no less, listed her on the NCIC computer. We read it and picked her up."

Stark now understood what they must have done to her. Just as they had altered his bank records, Merrill's name had been inserted into the NCIC's data banks.

"We don't question the data," Klein was saying. "Here it is in black and white." He handed Stark a printout with Merrill's name underlined in red.

"And when you went back to the computer?"

Klein sighed. "Nothing. We asked Washington to double-check. They never had a record of her. She was clean."

"Where is she?" Stark again demanded.

Klein talked as though he hadn't heard. "We thought she was a high-class junkie." He explained about the syringes, needle marks and withdrawal.

"She's diabetic. My God, she's diabetic."

"We know that now." Klein looked at him sorrowfully. "She went into shock. Bad, real bad. She got dehydrated—a lot of medical things I don't understand. Her heart stopped."

Dear God, thought Stark. To have found her . . . to have found her dead . . . He started to tremble.

Klein saw his grief and it hurt him. "If it's what you think, she's not in the morgue." He did not know her condition, however. "We called in a cardiac team. They resuscitated her; she was taken to Mass. General. . . ."

Stark looked up, startled. "Then she's *alive?*"

"I don't know, damnit; I don't know!"

11:30 A.M., *EDT: Washington, D.C.*

Files and reports littered the long conference table. As Benjamin Lapham knew better than anyone there, including the President of the United States, the reports meant nothing. What they finally resolved here in the Executive Office Building would result from blind guesses. All they really had available were options and hope, and not many or much of either.

Lapham smoothed his sideburn in an unconscious move-ment with his forefinger as he listened. His initial argument not to detain Stark had, in light of the NSA murders last night, been proved a mistake. He should have probably agreed to detain Stark for his own safety. But how was Lapham to know?

The Secretary was asking Lapham a question now. "About the trace, Ben. Did it go through?"

Lapham nodded. "The men in the van had communications on direct before they were gunned down. Otherwise it would have burned with everything else."

The President asked, "And the terminal you mentioned, Ben—you're absolutely certain it was Ling Autonetics?" The President had received the news with outward equanimity, but inwardly he was angry and hurt. John Elliman was a longtime supporter from Massachusetts who had stood by him in his Senate races and later in the primaries and final campaign. Elliman had donated money and actively campaigned for him, rallying pivotal business forces behind his candidacy. The two men were not close friends, but as an ally, the President had always viewed Elliman as a model citizen.

Lapham was aware of the political connection between them, and it pained him to say what he did. "I'm afraid so, sir."

The President asked sadly, "Why would Elliman do it?"

"If I may, sir—" began Church. "Elliman's in trouble, sir. Very big trouble. That could be his motive." Church went on to relate details of Ling Autonetics' imminent bankruptcy, details he'd picked up from Defense Intelligence in Boston that morning. "When I reviewed these facts," he said, "I learned something else: Ling is about to be named in a $40 million lawsuit. It's been brought by a group of European insurance dealers. They are charging that Ling misrepresented a reinsurance contract underwritten by the plaintiffs. Further—and far more disastrous—there are about $100 million in claims against Lloyd's of London, which underwrote Ling to insure against losses from cancelations of long-term contracts. Ling's mini failed because of IBM's new entry; the orders are being canceled. Anyway, the point is this: Lloyd's has paid out $30 million and is balking at paying more, which leaves Ling $110 million in debt *before* they start computing the losses from development and lost sales."

"How did it happen?" the President asked, surprised and dismayed.

"Elliman got too ambitious; he tried to beat IBM, and quite unintentionally, they crushed him. It's about that simple."

The President asked, "Can anyone answer why Elliman wants the formula?"

When nobody spoke up, Lapham filled the void. "I can only speculate."

"Then please do," the President said, anxious to know the answers.

"Rousseau's formula renders hardware useless. Elliman gets the formula and employs it against the computer systems manufactured by his competitors, including, of course, IBM. He lets the formula work for a period of time, while he introduces his own mainframes into the market. Naturally, Ling's new computers are immune to the formula's effect, either through the development of a coding system, or more likely because Elliman leaves them alone. The country will clamor for Ling computers, guaranteeing Elliman a virtual monopoly."

"A monopoly that wrecks our economy," the President said in a hushed voice.

"He started his campaign at the stock exchanges and banks," Church announced matter-of-factly. "The timing is slightly off, as you can see from the chronology in the report before you, Mr. President. My theory is that Elliman—"

"But you appraised that the anticomputer groups were involved," the President remarked, looking at Church.

"We were obviously wrong," Church replied. "The proof is in front of our faces. Elliman used force. The girl, we know, was abducted by him—at least this is what the NSA intercept from the van tells us."

"Let's go back a minute," the President said, nervously twirling a pencil. "Hedley, you were saying?"

"A theory, really. Elliman started his attack on individual systems, the banks, the exchanges. If the formula had not come along, he would have continued piecemeal. Rousseau gave him additional ammunition that he needed. His timing is crucial. Piece-meal, the strategy might take weeks, even months, and by then he would run the real risk of getting caught. The formula canceled that risk. He had to have it, but the method of applying pressure had to be subtle. So he broke into Rousseau's house first, then he went after his bank account, and last of all—a tactic that seems to have worked—he took the girl."

"What evidence do we have that Rousseau gave him the formula?"

"Intercepts," Church said. "As part of the agreed-on cyber-veillance of Rousseau, I insisted all along that the National Security Agency monitor data communications lines on a random basis in the Boston area—after all, Rousseau has access to any one of a number of terminals—at the Labs, for example, perhaps even at Harvard. If Rousseau was going to transmit the formula, I felt certain he would not use his own terminal at home. Early this morning the NSA intercepted a land-line transmission of what their technicians believe to be part, at least, of the formula out-lined by Rousseau at the symposium."

"God!" the President exclaimed. "Then it's in the *open*."

Quickly Church added, "We have not yet traced the source of the formula's data transmission or the terminal to which it was sent. Again, though, it had to be Elliman. He applied the pressure successfully."

The Secretary of Defense understood the importance of time. The details of the methods used by Elliman were not impor-tant, not now. "What's before us, Mr. President, are two . . . maybe three decisions. First, Elliman."

Lapham said, "My people pored over the van, and the Boston cops talked to nearly everybody in the neighborhood. No evidence was found linking the fire and the murders to Elliman, or anyone else. The neighbors saw nothing."

"But the intercepts—"

"The formula intercept, sir, will take time, and there is no guarantee that the NSA can find the source or the destination. The first radiation intercept from Rousseau's VDT, the one linking the extortion message through Household Finance to Ling Autonetics? Again, was Rousseau's procedure accurate? We may never know." Lapham sighed. "Nevertheless, I am forced to agree with General Church's theories." Lapham did not enjoy where his reasoning took him: Elliman was the perpetrator, and Rousseau—though Lapham hated to admit it—had compromised national security for the benefit of a girl.

"We're running against the clock, gentlemen," the Secretary reminded them.

The President asked, "Could we talk to him? Scare him off?"

"He'd deny everything," Church said. "And after this blows over, he may try again with a greater measure of caution."

"What's to be done, then?" He knew that the question was for him alone to answer. He looked around the table. They had said all that was necessary. The stakes were too high for Elliman to stay on the loose, even if laws were compromised. If Elliman started to use the formula, laws would no longer have an effect in the country. There would be more chaos, or worse. Finally, the President opened his mouth. "He'll have to be arrested," he said, then to Church: "Hedley, I'm going to ask you to handle it. Have your people use discretion and care. If necessary, have them explain to him that I gave the order."

Church nodded. "May I ask, sir," he said, "what we do about Rousseau?" Before anyone had a chance to reply, Church answered his own question. "I see no earthly reason why he should remain free."

"That point may be moot," Lapham said.

Church did not understand, but continued, "Moot or not," he said, "he should be picked up with Elliman." He stopped, then added, "They're probably together at this moment anyway."

"I do not believe that, the thought's preposterous," Lapham said, yet inside even his confidence in Stark's motivations was waning. "I said 'moot' because Stark seems to have disappeared." He glanced at the President. "I have tried several times to reach him by telephone. He has gone, and, sir, I fear the worst." Anticipating the President's question, Lapham said, "Army Intelligence's regional office in Boston checked the nursing home where his mother stays. He has not been there. They have also searched his apartment and are staking it out now in the event of his return. Sir, we just don't know where he's gone." His tone, plaintive and deeply worried, reflected a basic trust in Stark's innocence. He could not have . . . he would not have yielded to Elliman's pressure.

"As long as the formula remains in his head, Rousseau poses a direct threat," Church said.

"Mostly to himself, I agree," Lapham said. "Somehow we must find him."

The President placed the flat of his hands on the desk. "Then it's decided," he said, turning to Church. "Hedley, you're to instruct Army Intelligence and whatever other agencies you might need to find Rousseau and detain him, as well. But quietly." Already, the President envisaged problems. Elliman was a straightforward matter. But Rousseau's detention constituted a breach of his civil rights. Eventually they had to set him free. The young scientist would complain officially, and the powerful scientific community would close ranks around him. A vocal group, they defended all forms of freedom, from academic expression to Soviet Jewry. They could spell more trouble for a President already with a crisis on his hands. He looked at the faces in the room, then said, "I suggest we convene again this evening. We'll know more then and hopefully"—he stared at Church—"Elliman and Rousseau will be in our control. In the meantime, I want each of you to stay on top of this; report directly to me the instant you know."

Minutes later, out in the anteroom, General Church accosted Peter Shimkus, the Army Intelligence agent who had silently watched the meeting throughout with a disapproving expression. A sadist with a pugilist's face and a simple mind, his one guiding principle—if that was what it could be called—was the efficient execution of any order he received from his superiors. Church had invited him to attend the meeting as an aide of sorts because Shimkus would carry out the President's orders.

Church whispered to him, "What do you think?"

Shimkus grimaced; it was not his job to think. "A frigging mess."

Church glanced at the door through which the others had disappeared. "All they want is to sit on it, detain Elliman and Rousseau."

"But you argued for their detention," Shimkus reminded him.

"The President does not dirty his hands," he said. "He would not have agreed to a stronger suggestion."

"Detention doesn't satisfy you?" He saw Church's expression and said, "Me, neither."

"With Elliman, we have no choice. He's too close to the President, no matter what he's done. Rousseau, however, is different."

"I believe he transmitted the formula," Shimkus said, knowing such agreement would please Church.

"And he's cozying up to Elliman right now," Church said, recalling the order he had sent to Cape Canaveral that same morning immediately following his conference with Clint Hennessy. The country would not really be safe with Elliman and Rousseau in custody. The future—and his seat on the Board of Directors—would depend on Rousseau being silenced.

"What do you suggest?" Shimkus asked, already sensing the answer.

"Find him. Get up there by jet right away and find him."

"And then?"

Church wore an exasperated expression. "I don't know," he said with a sigh. "Do whatever you think is necessary."

11:45 A.M., EDT: Boston, Massachusetts

"It was bad, real bad." The words of Captain Klein echoed in Stark's ears as he ran up the wheelchair ramp and through the revolving doors. He would not lose Merrill; and if he did, some-body would pay, he thought.

"Excuse me," he yelled at a nurse behind a desk examining an index card.

She turned. "One minute, please."

He didn't have one minute; maybe Merrill didn't either. "I want the status of a patient named Merrill Fox." The edge in his voice made the nurse turn again.

"When was she admitted?"

"Early this morning, by the police."

"You're sure? To Mass. General?"

"Positive. Hurry, please."

The nurse looked through the card index, then smiled. "Here she is."

For the second time that morning a feeling of relief washed over Stark. At last he had found her! "Is she all right?"

She laid the card on the countertop. "Hmmmmm," she muttered. Whoever had filled out the card had done a sloppy job. There were blank spaces and some information had been crossed out in ink. "There are irregularities here," she said, more to herself than to Stark.

"You said she is here," Stark said, impatiently.

"Well . . . indeed, she *was,* anyway. Miss Fox was admitted to the emergency room at 11:47 P.M. yesterday—not this morning, as you suggest. She was released approximately five hours later."

Stark gripped the edge of the counter and leaned forward. "Released to whom?" he asked.

"I'm only trying to help," she said. "The card indicates patient status only."

"Where can I find out, then?"

"Let me see," she replied primly, reading again from the card. "The attending surgeon in the emergency room was Dr. Stefan Allen. He can help you, if he's still on duty."

"Where can I find him?"

"If you'll take a seat," she said, pointing with her chin to the wooden benches in the lobby. "I'll page him," she said.

Stark paced the gleaming waxed floor, seized by the hope that the hospital's accounting system was wrong. He heard Dr. Allen's name on the intercom, and Stark prayed that the doctor was still on duty. The blackmailer, Stark thought, then stopped himself. *Elliman!* He might as well name him. Elliman had listed Merrill on the NCIC's data banks in Washington by penetrating their system. Once he'd achieved the desired effect, he had erased the name. If the hospital used EDP, there was no reason why he couldn't have done the same here. Wary now, Stark guarded his faint hope.

If Merrill was not at the hospital, he knew exactly where to start looking. He checked the clock on the wall. Time was essential. He thought of Byron. Byron was Merrill's friend, too, and he would be a help in this situation.

Stark went to the telephone booth in the gift and flower shop near the front doors and looked up Byron's number, then called. Byron answered cheerfully, profusely apologetic for his rudeness at lunch. "I was simply jealous to see how much Merrill likes you—"

"Never mind that, Byron," Stark interrupted. "This is important. Merrill's in trouble."

Byron's voice sobered. "What do you mean?"

"There isn't time now. Maybe it's nothing, but I'm not going to pussyfoot around anymore. Can I meet you, say, in about half an hour?"

"No problem. But I wish you'd tell me what it's about."

Stark asked, "Where are you exactly?"

"Dunster House, room L-13. You know, the first old one on Mem. Drive as you come up the river."

"Next to that redstone monstrosity?"

"Mather House. Right."

"Okay, I'll call when I've finished here. . . ."

Stark hung up feeling more in control. He glanced over at the nurse, who shrugged her shoulders. Pacing the floor once more, Stark heard the doctor paged again. Stark was about to give up when a middle-aged man in a white jacket and with slumped shoulders approached the desk. "I understand you're inquiring after a Miss Fox," he said in a comforting voice.

"Yes," Stark replied. "Did you treat her last night?"

Dr. Allen smiled. "A pretty girl. Are you related?"

"I'm . . . I'm her friend."

"You're very lucky, then. She arrived by police ambulance in critical shape. They—the police, I understand—deprived her of insulin." The description included no judgment. "At the terminal stages of shock, her heart gave out. The paramedics did an excellent job at the police station. They got her heart pumping again, and by the time she reached me, her respiration was regular. She didn't suffer any permanent damage, thank God." Dr. Allen saw the young man's deep concern and gripped his arm. "She came around when we administered small, progressive doses of insulin. She was an exhausted and confused young woman. I don't blame her." Suddenly his eyes lighted up. "What did you say your name was?" Stark told him. "Yes, that's right. When she was in the coma she mentioned your name—something about having to be home to meet you. I couldn't figure it out." He waved aside the riddle. "Anyway, I sedated her. She was transferred to the wards."

"Do you know anything about her being released?"

"Not possible," Dr. Allen said, emphatically shaking his head. "She needed observation. Anyway, I'd have been informed." He turned on his heel and went to the desk. "Miss Fox's card, please," he said to the nurse. As he read the card, he pursed his lips. "Unusual," he mused. "Will you follow me?"

They went down the main corridor and through a door marked "Head Nurse—Duty." The head nurse, an older woman with graying hair and a suspicious face, asked Dr. Allen, "A problem?"

"A mixup, I guess, Millie," he said. "Who was on duty this morning on Ward Three North?"

"I filled in," she said, guardedly.

"*You* did?" The head nurse was an administrator.

"Three nurses were out sick; and as *you* know, last night was damned hectic."

"Was a patient named Fox released?"

She nodded. "I had no choice."

Stark blurted out, "Who took her?"

The nurse did not like the implication in Stark's voice. "Sir, no law requires a patient to remain here," she said. "If a member of their family wants them removed, we comply, even if we think it's wrong."

"She was sedated," Dr. Allen said. "Did she leave here under her own power?"

"Of course not. Her father went with her."

"You must be mistaken," Stark said. He had not met Merrill's father; she had barely mentioned him, but he remembered her saying that he lived in upstate New York.

"I'm afraid *you're* mistaken," the nurse retorted. "A pleasant man, he came in around two this morning. Very worried. Is he very wealthy?"

Stark did not know. "I guess so."

"Well, it makes sense. He had a private ambulance waiting near emergency."

"You should have called me," Dr. Allen said.

"*I tried.* You were up to your elbows, they said."

It was true, Dr. Allen thought. At around two, he was struggling to keep three accident victims alive. He had worked on them for four hours. Saved two, lost one.

"Did you ask for identification?" Stark asked. He didn't believe that Merrill's father had heard so soon and acted. Anyway, he would have kept her in the hospital.

"Oh, he had complete identification. He must have known we would ask."

"Where was he taking her?" Stark asked.

"He . . . he didn't say. No such information is required."

"Can you remember what he looked like?" Stark asked.

"Very handsome," she replied. "About fifty-five, medium height, gray hair at the temples, distinguished, the slightest accent, European—perhaps English."

Elliman!

12:15 P.M., *EDT: Boston, Massachusetts*

Douglas Thornton waited anxiously at the terminal in his basement facility, hoping that Stark would telephone. Meanwhile, the time had come for Thornton to pull back. He could not wait for the other leaders of IUSUC to assemble—and his calls to them early that morning indicated they would not go along without debate. He would have to act alone.

The procedure for blocking the exchanges' computers was extremely complex, but incorporated in the program was a simple jamming mechanism, connected to the target computers by land lines. A flip of the switch would return control of their EDP to those institutions; as though nothing had happened, the computers would again go on-line with their drone work, accurately and without mishap.

Thornton wearily pressed several keys on the terminal, then glanced at the VDT. Finally he reached over and released the decontrol mechanism.

Instantly, the VDT reported:

```
"DIMENSION X (1000), Y(1001),
           Z (1002)
READ (9,5)N
UNLOCK: UNLOCK."
```

He looked up. "Ah, Dr. McColough," he said without interest. McColough stood there quietly. Behind him another man smoked a cigarette; Thornton wondered who he was and why he had been let in. Thornton rested his arm on the side of the chair. "I won't be needing you today," he said to McColough, shaking off his curiosity. He wanted to be alone with his thoughts. He looked again at McColough. Strange. The man just stood there, watching him. Tartly he repeated, "I won't need you, please take the day off." McColough blinked and a grin formed on his mouth. He stood where he was. Finally angry, Thornton said, "Please, leave me alone."

Dr. McColough came closer and Thornton got to his feet. "What's wrong with you, Doctor?" he asked, now bewildered by his assistant's behavior. He had not known McColough long. Thornton hoped that poor Gellitsen had not made a mistake in recommending him. In the brief time they had worked together, McColough had been quietly efficient, always doing what was asked with a thoroughness that pleased Thornton.

McColough uttered a sentence over his shoulder to the man with the cigarette, and the foreign language he spoke registered with Thornton as *Russian.* "What is this?" he asked.

Dr. McColough spoke clearly and softly, this time in English. "My name is Alexi Borznoi. My rank, colonel. My affiliation, KGB." He was not disappointed by the effect on Thornton. The old man seemed to collapse in on himself, staring at Borznoi as if at an apparition. Borznoi continued, "My colleague is Vasily Domintrin."

Thornton glanced back and forth between the two men, finally settling his eyes on Domintrin. The name was familiar, but he couldn't remember how. Domintrin worked with computers, that much he recalled. Then slowly it dawned on him: Domintrin was the *Soviet* computer scientist, Thornton's counterpart by reputation in his country. They had met, he remembered, in Berlin.

Thornton's mind was flooded with sudden, dire realizations. Dr. McColough—this Colonel Borznoi—had deceived him. Gellitsen had deceived him. Feeling faint, he slumped back in the chair, eyeing them with disbelief. "Get out of my house," he demanded.

Borznoi laughed. "It's time for us to have a talk, Mr. Thornton," he said, his voice cold.

"You'll get nothing from me," Thornton said.

Borznoi laughed louder. "I already have most of what I want. I only need a little more."

The formula, Thornton thought, his mind racing. This KGB colonel, Dr. McColough, *his* assistant, possessed Stark's program —McColough had not erased it, as ordered, from the disks.

"I understand," he said, exhaling softly. "You poisoned Gellitsen, didn't you?"

Borznoi swept aside the question. "You told me when I started working for you that I should be succinct. So I will. We have your granddaughter. Eagle, I believe you call her."

At the sound of her name, Thornton seemed to age. He tried to order his priorities, but the single thought of Eagle filled his mind.

"She has not been harmed," Borznoi said. "And she will not be harmed if you do what I ask."

"Never," Thornton shouted, spitting the word at Borznoi.

"She will die then, unless you agree to our last simple request."

As Borznoi was speaking, another man, an Oriental, entered the room, reporting, "The house is clear. An old butler is upstairs, but he will not trouble us."

Borznoi extended an arm in Niigata's direction. "Let me introduce you," he said, turning to Thornton. "This is Mr. Niigata, a valued member of the Third Directorate of the KGB who is based in Tokyo, where they are also doing interesting work with computers. My Directorate, the First, ordered him to Boston after the symposium. We thought he might be of assistance. Mr. Niigata has been engaged in an interesting blocking maneuver since his arrival. Is that accurate, Mr. Niigata?"

Niigata came closer. "Essentially, yes." He shrugged his shoulders a little.

"Please continue," Borznoi said. "I promised dear Domintrin here a full explanation, too."

Niigata looked at Domintrin. "I used a computer manufacturer to put pressure on the creator of the formula, a scientist whom you know by reputation named Rousseau."

Borznoi added, "You see, I had no desire to stand in the front line of this battle. It was too dangerous, too important to win, and, I believe, it would have been ineffective. We are dealing with subtle machines. My idea is simple. . . ."

Thornton refused to follow the trail being outlined by

Borznoi. "Mr. Domintrin," Thornton said, appealing to the scientist, "you must stop them."

Domintrin said nothing in reply. He had recognized Thornton on sight. He had no need for an introduction from Borznoi. Thornton had been an idol, a symbol of what he might accomplish for the Soviet Union. They had met fifteen years ago at a technical conference in Berlin. How cordial Thornton had been toward him. They were scientists, not Russians and Americans, and they reveled in the freedom of discussing pure research. Thornton had spoken at the conference, and everybody there had remarked on his humility. Domintrin said sadly, "There is nothing I can do."

"There is much you can both do," Borznoi corrected him. "But before I get to that, Mr. Niigata, weren't you concerned about Mr. Elliman? You should take him and the girl out of harm's way before the young man interferes."

Niigata nodded. "Yes, of course." On silent feet he turned and disappeared from the facility.

"An able man," Borznoi said after him. "And well schooled in the subtle arts."

"Does he have Eagle?" Thornton asked.

"Perhaps. Don't worry about her, she is quite well. And, Niigata tells me, a beautiful woman."

IUSUC and all it stood for had been subverted. The enemies of the country—the country Thornton wanted to protect—had infiltrated his house and gained his confidence. They owned the formula, and now they had the means within their grasp—the means that *he* could give them—to use it. "I will *not* help you," he repeated.

Borznoi laughed at his stubbornness. "But I have not yet told you what I want."

"It doesn't matter. I will not be like Gellitsen. I will not betray my country."

"Now, now," Borznoi soothed. "It is only a small request." He took Thornton menacingly by the arm and led him toward the door. "There is a painting above the mantel in the living room. I have examined it many times. All I want is for you to tell Mr.

Domintrin here a bit about it. And perhaps you would have a key?"

He knew exactly what they wanted. "You must give me time to think," he said.

"Remember your granddaughter," Borznoi said almost *sotto voce*. "Do you feel nothing for her?"

Merrill meant everything to him, and Borznoi knew that. To help them now, he thought, might cost thousands of lives. In the face of that reality, one life was of little consequence. But Eagle was his own flesh and blood.

"You have exactly three minutes," Borznoi said, and he pulled back his sleeve to count the seconds.

12:35 P.M., *EDT: Brookline, Massachusetts*

Harry Verdeen was having a great time. The juices of his imagination flowed as he wheeled the car up Cypress Street toward Brookline Hills, the vision of a high-speed chase dancing in his head. Wessel's distinctive, gunmetal-gray BMW, two cars ahead of Harry, rolled briskly through light afternoon traffic. Wessel had not spotted him, not even at the danger point when Harry had pulled out after him from the Ling Autonetics parking lot.

Twisting the radio dial, trying to find a country-and-western station, Harry laughed to himself gleefully when he cut halfway into the Hank Williams tune, "Your Cheating Heart," and began to sing along.

Wessel had taken Harry for a sucker, a rank amateur. Yesterday, after he struck the bargain with Wessel at the Skylark, Harry had rushed back in a cab to South Station in time to catch the 7:20 P.M. train. At the Amtrak ticket window he had dug deep into his pocket for the fare. To his surprise, he discovered the Medeco. Somehow he had failed to hand the evidence over to Wessel. While he sat watching the students and bums milling in the station, he had thought again about the key, and slowly he had started to burn. Wessel had lied. He had no intention of telling the police; the key was proof of his betrayal.

Harry had thought—if Wessel lied about the police, maybe he also lied about the robbery. If there had been no robbery, Wessel could not go to the police. And that meant one thing: Wessel was connected to the key—and to Horace's murder.

Harry had glanced at the big clock on the station's wall: Only minutes remained before the train for New York would leave. He ran to a telephone and dialed. After a number of questions were answered, he finally reached a police officer named Lyall in the Public Affairs Office. "Is the Department investigating a robbery at Ling Autonetics?" Harry had asked.

"We can't discuss investigations on the phone," Officer Lyall had said.

Harry explained his predicament and gave his private detective's license number. "I don't need details," he had said, pleadingly.

"Hold on."

Harry had been tapping his boot nervously when Lyall came back on the line. "Nothing, Verdeen," he had remarked in a conspiratorial tone. "That's all I can tell you."

So that was it, Harry had thought, suddenly changing his plans for the night. The train had left without him; he had called home for money that was sent by Western Union, then rented a Honda Civic and driven back to Bilkays', where he spent the night on the Barcolounger.

Harry could still feel the stiffness in his back. The chair, he thought as the Williams ballad finished, was molded to fit Bilkays alone. But with Harry's adrenalin now pumping, he felt alert and alive.

He kept his eyes on the BMW. He had never tailed a car before. To his delight, he was finding it easy. It was so routine, he wished for some action—a quick turn, a diversion, a chase. He clenched the steering wheel, then ran his hand along the dash. If he was still in the mood after this, he thought, he might even drive it back to New York. Beside the gas and tolls, the rental was nearly five dollars cheaper than Amtrak.

Wessel had taken off early from work, Harry guessed, or maybe Wessel worked irregular hours. Harry planned to remain as flexible as possible, a decision that had already served him well. Waiting it out the whole morning in the Ling parking lot had finally paid off. If what he suspected about Wessel was true, the Ling security chief would incriminate himself, or at least lead Harry to evidence. All Harry need do was bide his time.

Suddenly the BMW turned into the curb and stopped. Harry tapped the brake and passed by, turning his head away from Wessel. At the next corner Harry turned right, made a U-turn and returned to the intersection with Cypress Street. From there he watched Wessel get out. Harry scanned the sidewalk. There were too few people out to take the risk of being identified by Wessel, so Harry stayed in the Honda, which he put in gear and edged into the pedestrian lane. Cautiously, he looked down the street. Wessel had entered a drugstore.

Harry moaned. He hated errands. The next stop would probably be the dry cleaner's, then the supermarket, the bakery, the liquor store, then maybe Wessel would visit his ailing aunt. The thought tried Harry's enthusiasm. They always said police work was a boring routine, and now he believed them.

Minutes later, Wessel came out of the drugstore carrying a small white paper bag. When he returned to the BMW, he did not look around. So far so good, thought Harry. When the BMW swept past, Verdeen made the right turn directly behind. He allowed himself to fall back fifty yards, watching for the taillights to blink on.

After two miles, Wessel turned right on Walnut Street, then made a sharp right into Oakland Road. When Harry made the first right, he panicked, thinking he had lost Wessel and more, that he was trying to shake him off. Harry looked right, then braked hard and reversed, finally turning into Oakland Road at the sight of the BMW.

No more errands, Harry thought, watching the BMW slide into a parking space. Tree-lined and serene, the residential street boasted well-painted wood-frame houses, front lawns and sidewalks. At this hour of the afternoon, a few schoolkids were returning home for lunch, a couple on bicycles, and one kid on a skateboard. Harry parked on the opposite side of the street and slid down in the seat, peering over the ledge of the door.

Wessel walked up the front path. At the door he took a key from his pocket and entered. The house looked like all the others on the street—two stories, brown paint, a screened-in front porch. Harry checked the neighboring houses, then looked back at Wessel's. There was one significant difference: Downstairs and up-stairs, Wessel's windows were blanked out by blinds. On a sunny afternoon like today, the house's interior must be as dark and stuffy as a tomb.

Harry settled into the seat, realizing he would have a long wait till dark. His stomach growled, and he thought of a juicy hamburger and a tall, cool beer. He had put nothing in his stomach all day except coffee. A quarter hour passed when Verdeen, play-ing with the radio knob, heard the door slam. Wessel walked down the path carrying a heavy bag that Harry guessed contained laun-dry. More errands, he thought grimly. Throwing the duffle in the back seat, Wessel got into the BMW and started the engine. Harry raised himself in the seat, then thought, Why bother? Wessel was giving him a perfect chance.

As Wessel's BMW swept down Oakland Road, Harry reached for the door handle.

Walking with a purposeful stride, as though he really knew exactly where he was heading, Harry Verdeen skirted the side of Wessel's house, brushing against the shrubbery. Sometimes peo-ple in neighborhoods like this one, he thought, had nothing better to do with their time than stare out of their windows. It was true of the street where he lived in the Bronx, so why not here? If anyone across the street happened to see him now, he hoped he seemed positive enough to pass muster. Otherwise, he'd have a neighborhood vigilante committee on his heels.

He unlatched a picket gate and entered the backyard. It was neat and trim, like Wessel himself, and well-maintained flower beds lined the fence. Harry went to the back porch and tried the handle. Locked, but it wasn't meant to prevent burglaries. He twisted it hard but it still did not give. He slipped the .38 from his waistband and wrapped the butt end in his handkerchief, then tapped the window pane. Crude, he thought, but effective. He reached his hand into the space and found the knob.

The falling glass had made a tinkling sound; nothing, Harry assured himself, that could be heard. He stepped over the glass and went into the kitchen. For several seconds he stood on the tiled floor, wondering where he should go next.

Listening for alien sounds and hearing none, he walked down the hallway off the kitchen, through a small dining room in which there was a plain maple table and four chrome chairs and into the living room. Verdeen concentrated on everything he saw: the magazines neatly arranged on the cocktail table; the silver cigarette box inscribed with the name Ling Autonetics; the empty cut-glass vase; the cheap landscape oil over the sofa. He opened the drawer of the sideboard: old silver.

Verdeen wondered about the furnishings. It was a bachelor's house with none of the touches of a woman. But there was a faint feminine touch, no stronger than the faded paper on the walls. A woman had lived there, but, he guessed, not for many years.

To the left of the dining room, a foyer led to a staircase. Verdeen pulled the blinds an inch from the front window and peered out. The street was empty. He turned and looked up the stairs. Climbing on the toes of his Tony Lama boots to dampen the sound, he reached the landing, then turned right. Three doors opened on the corridor. He quietly opened the first. The room smelled musty. The bed was made, but no one had slept there for a long time. Again in the hallway, he stopped at the next door, pressing his ear against the wood, then turning the handle. A bathroom that had been used recently, he saw. A box of cotton wads and a bottle of alcohol were arranged on the toilet tank. Shaving equipment, toiletries, toothbrush and paste. Everything a bachelor needed for his ablutions.

Verdeen made a mental note to return to the bathroom once

he had checked out the entire house. Again in the hall, he approached the third door and listened. He thought he heard a rustling sound, like dry leaves blown together by the wind, or the brush of cloth against cloth, faint but discernible. Verdeen grasped the door handle. Sucking in a lungful of air, he rushed in.

A girl—a beautiful girl—was on the bed, covered by a sheet and sleeping. Her head was framed by the edges of the pillowcase, and her hair fanned out over it. She looked absolutely normal. Suddenly Verdeen felt embarrassed. As he went to look closer, he again heard the rustling sound; louder this time, from behind him. He swiveled and saw an old woman in white rushing him. In her fist, like a dagger, she held a syringe aimed at his neck. The woman grunted as Verdeen stepped aside and lowered his shoulder. The old woman screamed as she lost her balance and tripped. She sank to the floor, plunging the syringe deeply into the edge of the mattress.

Verdeen grabbed her wrist, so thin and frail that he pulled his own hand back. He stared at her ugly, birdlike face. Round, wrinkled cheeks squeezed against a sharp nose. Her mouth was a small oval, her eyes milky white with hard, black pupils. Verdeen turned his head away, glancing at the girl, who was groggy but seemingly awake now.

She said to Harry in a frail, pleading, sleep-thickened voice, "Please help me."

The situation took him so much by surprise that Harry scarcely knew how to react. Instinctively he wanted to protect the girl on the bed. Positioning his body between her and the "nurse," he drew his pistol—needlessly he noticed, for now she had neither the strength nor the will to resist. Harry demanded, waving the gun in her face, "Where has Wessel gone?"

Trembling, her shoulders slumped in a posture of utter submissiveness, the spidery woman answered, "To Elliman's house. I was to stay here and keep her sedated until he returned. He did not say when." She saw the anger in Harry's face, and continued, "Honest. Elliman called to say that they all had to leave as soon as Wessel arrived. I don't know anything else."

"And the satchel Wessel was lugging?" Harry asked.

"A rifle and ammunition."

Suddenly Harry realized how alone and unprepared he was. He needed to get away. He did not want Wessel returning here armed. "Who is she?" he asked the nurse, without looking in Merrill's direction.

The nurse folded her hands. "I had nothing to do with that," she said.

Oh sure, sister, thought Harry. "Come on," he demanded.

"She was brought here last night from the hospital," she said. "Wessel said she should stay here till Elliman made plans. Believe me, that's all I know."

Harry did believe her. "Can she be moved?"

The nurse nodded.

Harry reached down for the hypodermic and snapped the needle off into the mattress. Tucking the pistol in his belt, he lifted the girl from the bed, wrapping the top sheet carefully around her. She was light in his arms. Peering at her half-sleeping face, he felt a powerful empathy. She looked lost and helpless—much as Harry himself felt.

Ordering the nurse to remain where she was, Harry carried the girl downstairs and out the front door. Moving quickly but carefully, he placed her across the Honda's back seat, then got behind the wheel. He started up the engine, put the car in gear and pulled out. Instinctively he headed in the direction of Grunwald's Hardware. A half mile later, deciding that he needed time to think, he pulled to the curb and leaned over the seatback. He touched the girl's cheek softly. Her eyes opened. "Can you talk, young lady?" he asked. She gave him a weak smile and nodded. "Where do you want me to take you?"

Merrill's mind had been numbed by the trauma and by the heavy sedatives administered by the nurse. She had been asleep almost the full time since she had gone into shock at the police station, and had been only dimly aware of what had happened. During lucid moments, she had surveyed her surroundings at the house and knew them to be alien. She remembered overhearing the nurse talking to a man in the strange room where they had put her, and she knew she was in danger. In dreams and wakefulness, though, her thoughts had returned again and again to Stark. What had happened to her was connected to him, so he too must be in trouble, she thought.

"Please, young lady," Verdeen was saying, "we have to help each other. Where can I take you?"

Panicked that she might fade again into sleep before speaking, she raised her head weakly: "Stark," she said, "Stark Rousseau. He will know what to do." With that, she fell back onto the seat into a drugged sleep.

"Damn," muttered Verdeen, trying to shake the girl back into consciousness. After a few seconds he gave up, and sat back to think. He noticed a dingy bar across the road, and he thought of the telephone booth. Wessel, he thought, could be found later. Horace was dead, but this young woman would live. He opened the door to the Honda.

Nearly an hour later, Harry pulled up in front of Rousseau's house. He'd had a hard time with the directory—who would have thought "Russo" could be spelled like that?—but here he was at last. He parked the Honda in front and bent around to open the door on the curb side. He pulled the seat forward and carefully lifted the girl out. Filled with the expectation of finding someone inside who could finally answer his questions, he carried her up the front walk.

As he was about to reach the door, a sound behind him made him turn.

"Hold it!" a man in uniform shouted, running in his direction.

Seeing the gun in the man's hand, Harry stood his ground.

1:15 P.M., *EDT: Boston, Massachusetts*

"I read about this one," Byron said with a muffled laugh as he inserted the blade of a silver pocket knife in the lock. "You're sure it's okay?"

Standing behind him, Stark replied, "He didn't answer the doorbell, so what choice do we have?"

"There," Byron said with a grunt of surprise and triumph as the knob turned. With a gentle push, the door opened. "Now will you tell me what this is about?"

They entered the house. "When we find Mr. Thornton, I'll explain everything," Stark replied. On the way to Byron's suite in Dunster House, he had reached a decision. He could not conduct his search for Merrill—and pursuit of Douglas Elliman—alone. He needed allies now. Thornton had to be told, despite the Secretary's stern warnings, and so did Byron. *Everything,* including the revelations about the fire-control systems. Together, the three might be able to come up with a concerted and practical plan of action. Stark was concerned that Thornton did not answer the doorbell—he had promised to remain close to the telephone until Stark received a response from their own ultimatum. Stark worried now that the old man might have acted on his own.

"Let's hope he's asleep," Stark said. He yelled upstairs three times, each time more loudly.

"What makes you think he expected you?" Byron asked, walking through the hall to the kitchen in back.

Stark followed him. "He knows Merrill is in trouble. He wouldn't just leave without a reason." Stark feared suddenly that Thornton had informed the police or even the government in Washington. Lapham and Church would be furious if they knew that he had told Thornton anything at all.

The kitchen was orderly. Dishes were put away on shelves, the counters were clean, the waste container was empty. Nothing to indicate that Thornton or the butler had gone out unexpectedly. "Let's try in there," Stark suggested, motioning with his chin.

Byron turned on a light. The living room was empty also,

the drapes drawn over the floor-to-ceiling windows in front. Stark walked over to Merrill's portrait, touching the frame almost tenderly. "Jesus, we have to get her back, Byron," he said under his breath.

"What?" Byron asked, bending on his knee in front of the fireplace, which was set neatly with kindling and logs. A white object caught his eye. Picking it up and examining it closely he asked Stark, "Does Thornton smoke cigarettes?"

"Let's see," Stark said, taking the butt from his fingers. "I think . . . he smokes a pipe. Maybe his butler smokes these." The filter had been torn off, leaving a ragged end of frayed tobacco dried with spittle. He did not see anything unusual in that, so he threw the butt back in the fireplace. "Let's go downstairs," he said, and as they passed through the hall, he yelled for Thornton again.

"I can't believe he just took off like that," Stark said, turning back to Byron as they descended the stairs to the cellar.

"You said Merrill is in trouble. Maybe Thornton's in the same trouble. What *has* happened to her, anyway?"

Stark opened the facility door and turned on the lights. He could not hide the facts from Byron any longer. "Get me those disks from the cabinet over there," he said. He had not marked the disk that contained the true formula and the errored copy, and he would not be certain of an erasure unless he put all the disks in the facility onto drives. No matter how much valuable data developed by Thornton would be lost, erasing all the tapes was the only means of insuring an erasure of the formula. Byron handed him four disks, which he threaded to the drives and began to erase. As they spun in their drives, silently cleaning off the data, Stark told Byron how he had traced Merrill's kidnaping to John Elliman.

Byron listened, nodding solemnly as Stark described his trace of Elliman, the police and the hospital. Byron could not blame Stark for what had happened. Nobody was at fault. In fact, Byron thought, Stark's blunder in creating the formula was the same as if one of Byron's academic papers had backfired. Research was research, whether literary or mathematical. What other people did with it was not the concern of the academic, who could not be expected to understand all the consequences. If that were the case, research would not exist. Without the freedom to create ideas —even potentially dangerous ideas—academic and scientific progress would not be made.

Byron could not allow himself seriously to believe that Merrill was really in danger, despite what Stark described. To Byron's way of thinking, presidents of major corporations did not kill in cold blood. Perhaps they shaved at the law, certainly they grabbed every competitive advantage. But surely not this! When Stark had finished his summary, Byron asked, "Well, what do you plan to do about him?"

"That's what I hoped Mr. Thornton would help me decide." He went to the drives and pulled out the erased disks. "Get me more of these, will you?"

"If you want my advice," Byron said, "You'll go to your friends in Washington."

"Once I have an idea where she's being held, I will. Don't you see, Byron, Washington is suspicious of *me.*"

"Not about Merrill, for sure."

"They don't even know about her. No, a general in the Pentagon is convinced I created the formula to wreck systems. If I come to him with a request for help, he'll hold me. This stuff about Merrill gives him grounds. And while I'm being held, we don't get any closer to Merrill—unless we first find out where she is. Maybe then I can go to Lapham."

"And how do we do that?"

Stark reached for the telephone. "Tell you in a minute," he said, dialing. Dr. Regan, the Beeman Labs' director, came on the line immediately.

"What can I do for you?" he asked cheerfully.

"Sir, I understand that John Elliman was invited to the symposium?" Stark left the question hanging.

"Why . . . yes, I think he was. Why do you ask? He declined the invitation; his loss, I'm afraid."

"Yes," Stark said. "Do you have an address for him?"

"At Ling?"

"At home, sir."

"Hold on."

Stark turned to Byron. "Can you take those disks off? I think we've erased them all."

Byron looked around the facility. A stack of twelve erased disks stood by the desk. "Yeah," he confirmed, "that's the lot."

Stark held up his hand. "Yes . . . Wellesley," he said, writing down an address, ". . . also Hyannis . . . Squaw Island? . . . a summer place. Fine, I've got it, Dr. Regan. And thanks. . . . No, nothing's wrong. I was just curious. . . . I'll explain later. Bye."

Stark hung up and stared at the notepad. Two addresses. They could not afford the time to search together. They would split the assignment. He would cover the farther address. He showed his scribblings to Byron, "Would you mind?"

"Which one?" Byron asked.

"You take Wellesley." He wrote down a telephone number. "If you get in trouble, call this number. It's for Ben Lapham."

"I don't mind Hyannis. It's your choice."

"You take Wellesley." Then: "We'll drive over to Cambridge for your car, and I have a stop to make on the way."

"A stop?"

"The bank," Stark replied. Then after a pause: "We've finished here." He looked around again to make certain.

"Perhaps we should check out the upstairs?" asked Byron. "In case he is sleeping, as you said?"

Stark grunted assent, and followed Byron up the stairs, where they split to look in the various rooms.

Byron was peering into the bathroom when he heard the sound of retching. It was coming from the upstairs landing. He turned around and retraced his steps down a narrow hallway. On the landing Stark, bent onto his knees, was throwing up, his face drained of color, his body convulsed. "What's wrong with you?" Byron demanded. Stark looked at him desperately.

"What's wrong?" Byron demanded more insistently.

Stark, still gasping, pointed at the doorway nearest him. Byron followed his gesture. Inside the bedroom, the door to the closet was swung wide open. The naked bodies of Douglas Thornton and his aged manservant hung from electrical cords that garroted their necks. There was no blood, just ghastly eyes bulging from the sockets, tongues blue-black and horribly swollen, distended necks stretched by the weight of their bodies. Their spinal columns had been severed at the base of their necks.

Byron covered his mouth and gagged, stifling a cry of horror.

2:30 P.M., *EDT: Cambridge, Massachusetts*

"All right, *all right,*" Byron yelled, shaking Stark hard by the arm as they waited for the light to change at the intersection on Massachusetts Avenue. "They're dead! We can't do anything about it!" Now more than ever, knowing that they had to keep their wits about them, Byron had to make Stark think. And Stark had not spoken since Byron dragged him from the house. The light turned green. Byron put the car in gear. "Do you want to go through with this or not?" He looked over at Stark. The color was returning to Stark's face. "Come on, Stark. Answer. You can't give up on Merrill now. Jesus—we can't just run and hide. She's alive. I just know it. And she needs our help—fast, or they'll do to her what they did . . ."

Stark stared ahead through the windshield. He did not want to think about the implications of what they had discovered in the closet. Instead he thought over the events of the last two days: How had they built to include brutal, needless murder? He was in over his head now: There could be no reversing, no rectifying the fatal mistakes he had made innocently, the train of little errors that had placed all of them in such danger. Lapham, he thought finally. Only Ben could help him now. From the corner of his eye, he spotted a telephone booth near a pedestrian crossing. "Stop there," he ordered Byron in a lifeless voice. As the car pulled to a halt, Stark jumped out, waving Byron to stay in the car. Stark

slid a dime into the slot and dialed, telling the long-distance operator to reverse charges.

"Mr. Lapham's been trying *desperately* to reach you," Lapham's secretary announced.

For an instant Stark felt relief. So Lapham had been trying
to find him. Of course, he thought: He had been gone from his
apartment most of the day, and part of the night before.

"I'll put you through," the secretary said, then in explanation: "He's still at the White House, but I was given specific
instructions to transfer the call. Wait, please," she said, clicking
the apparatus on hold.

Stark kept the receiver pressed to his ear while the connection was made. Someone in the White House was answering, Stark
guessed, another secretary . . . or? He could not tell. He heard the
sound of men's voices. Someone had lifted the telephone from its
cradle there and held it out without speaking into it. Impatiently,
Stark said, "Ben; let me speak with Ben Lapham." The answering
party seemed not to hear the instructions. Instead, Stark heard a
voice say, "Take it, General, will you, please?"

Another voice came on the line. "General Hedley Church
here."

Stark said, "I want Lapham."

"Rousseau . . . is that you? Rousseau? Where are you?
Where's Elliman?" Church demanded. Then, dramatically, "We
know you gave him the formula, Rousseau."

Quickly, Stark replaced the receiver. Until he had talked
with Lapham, he wanted nothing to do with General Church.
Stark went from the booth to the car and got in, indicating with
a grunt for Byron to continue toward Harvard Square. Stark would
try Lapham until Stark had him alone on the line.

A few minutes later Stark told Byron to pull in to a free
parking space in front of the bank. Once parked, Byron looked
over at Stark, who was holding his hands tightly in his lap, as
though he were trying to wring the tension from them. After
several seconds, Stark took a deep breath and said, "Wait for me
here."

"No you don't," Byron said, getting out his side of the car. "I'm going with you."

Stark made no reply, but continued on his way across the sidewalk and into the revolving doors of the Coolidge Bank. He joined a line in front of one teller's window.

"What are you doing?" Byron, standing behind him, whispered. Then looking at Stark, he pulled out a handkerchief and said, "Here, clean up your face."

Stark ran the cloth around his mouth. "They screwed up my account," he said finally.

Byron thought Stark had lost control. They were wasting valuable time. He pulled at Stark's arm. "Come on, let's get out of here."

Stark stood his ground. "Don't ask questions."

Byron looked at him, worried. "About what?"

The teller said, "Next, please." Stark stepped forward. He had his temporary checks with him and laid them on the counter before her eyes. She had a pleasant, toothy smile. "Can you tell me my balance?" Stark asked.

She took his blank check and typed the account number on a computer terminal. No more than five seconds passed, and she reacted with a raised eyebrow. "It's $82,467. You should ask one of our officers about a savings plan."

"Not today," Stark said in the same flat tone of voice. He borrowed the teller's pen and wrote out a check for $60,000 even. "I'd like that in cash, please," he said.

"Well . . . I don't know." She laughed nervously. "I don't often handle sums this large. Excuse me for a minute," and she went to a file drawer to match the check against the signature card. When she returned, she said to Stark, "I'll have to ask one of our officers."

"Is Mr. Fulton in today?" Stark asked. "He handles my account."

The teller went out the gate onto the main banking floor. On the officers' platform, she whispered to Fulton, who looked in Stark's direction. Taking a Kleenex from a box, Fulton got up and came over. "Mr. Owens," he said to Stark and extended his hand. "It's nice to see you again."

Byron looked at Stark in disbelief. At last Byron was catching on.

"I mentioned making a substantial withdrawal," Stark said. He handed Fulton the check. "Can I get this in cash?"

Fulton examined the check, then asked the teller for his balance, which she confirmed. "Well . . . this will take some time, for cash, I mean." He looked at Stark. "It's dangerous to carry so large a sum, even for a few minutes."

Stark nodded agreement. "Is there a way I can get it now, right now?"

"Don't get me wrong, Mr. Owens," said Fulton. "Cash isn't a problem, but it will take time."

"I'm in something of a hurry."

"I can give you a cashier's check right away, if you want, with, say, five hundred in cash."

"That'll be fine."

While Fulton went to prepare the check, Byron pulled Stark aside. "What's going on, *Mr. Owens?*" he asked.

"We're robbing a bank, that's what. I needed money; we need money."

Byron whispered, "How did you do it?"

"Easy."

"That doesn't answer the question."

He told Byron about the fake name, the new account, the magnetic typewriter and the deposit slips. "The bank has an automatic sorter," he continued. "It passes the deposit slips with magnetic ink—automatically. No human eye sees them. Only the slips without the ink, the ones people write out when they get to the bank, are handled by the bank workers. So—"

"So this money is somebody else's. The sorter passed their deposits into your account?"

"Here we are," Fulton remarked, coming up to the pair and handing Stark a cashier's check and $500 in cash. "All in order."

Stark shook his hand and without lingering said, "You've been most helpful."

"Anytime, just call on me."

Back on the sidewalk, Byron said that he would walk the short distance to the Dunster lot where his Volkswagen was parked. Stark opened the door on the driver's side of McKinnon's borrowed Fairlane. Before he set off, Stark handed him a wad of bills without thinking why. A gesture perhaps, or a sign of their complicity. Each knew what had to be done alone now, so there was no need for words. Yet Byron said, "I'll be waiting for you at Dunster when I get back. Good luck."

2:45 P.M., *EDT: En route to Cape Cod, Massachusetts*

Except for a sprinkling of commercial traffic, the Southeast Expressway was clear of heavy traffic. In another twenty minutes or so, thought Stark, he would reach the approach to the Buzzard's Bay Bridge that would take him over the channel onto the Cape, and from there, perhaps another half hour if the traffic stayed like this, into Barnstable and Hyannis. Once there, he would drive through Hyannisport until he found the road to Squaw Island, which he knew was connected to the mainland. Squaw Island, he recalled, was a private reserve of the very wealthy. The Kennedys all had houses there. It made sense to him that Elliman also would choose that island.

Stark knew how Elliman had discovered the truth about the faked formula, but Stark did not understand how he had traced the fake to Douglas Thornton—not through Stark, in any case. Because Merrill's grandfather was connected to Stark, Elliman had killed him. For the same reason, Elliman had probably killed Merrill by now. Stark felt so utterly without hope that he wanted to cry. If Elliman had been so ready to kill a defenseless old man, surely he would have already carried out his threat against Merrill. If so, why should Stark continue? Why make this needless trip? Why send Byron off in the other direction?

Up ahead Stark spotted an off ramp. He took his foot off the accelerator. Feeling desolate in a way beyond anything he had known before, he braked the Fairlane and pulled into the Howard Johnson's lot. Inside the restaurant's foyer, he found a telephone. He had little hope. Lapham would still be tied up, and what use would it be? As the minutes passed and the phone in Lapham's office rang on without answer, Stark cared less and less if he ever reached his Pentagon protector. The worst damage was almost certainly already done.

He was about to hang up when there was a loud jangling on the other end of the line, as if the phone had been dropped. A moment later Ben Lapham himself came on the wire. "Yes, who is it?"

When Stark answered, Lapham shouted breathlessly: "Stark, where the hell are you?"

"Outside Boston, Ben," he replied. "Ben, they killed the old man. He had nothing to do with any of this, and Elliman killed him, just like that. I'm sorry, Ben, you must believe that. It was my fault. I told Elliman about the fake, and he found the old man. He has Merrill, too. Ben, I think he might have killed her. Please, Ben—" the words tumbled out in one phrase.

"Listen," Lapham said in a steady, controlled voice. "Calm yourself and listen. Merrill is okay. Army Intelligence found her at your apartment just a few minutes ago. She's with a man named Verdeen. He brought her to your apartment. Do you hear me?"

"She's alive?" After all the false starts, the hopes that had been destroyed, Stark was cautious. He could not allow himself to believe her alive and well, only to have that belief destroyed.

"You said you were outside Boston. Where are you going?"

"To Elliman's—"

"Don't! I've been trying to reach you for hours. It's not safe there. You must get out. Turn around and go back. Don't go to Elliman's. Do it right now. Stark, are you listening?"

"Yes, Ben, I heard you," Stark said, his voice coming to life.

"Drive to Logan International Airport—directly. A jet is there waiting to take you out. You and Merrill. Go to the private air terminal. Merrill is en route now."

"Is she all right, Ben?"

"Groggy as hell, they told me, but yes, this Verdeen guy got to her just in time. Forget about anything else and get there."

"Ben, there's a friend," Stark said, remembering Byron with alarm. "He's heading for Wellesley right now."

"You can't do anything about it," Lapham said. "We have people converging on Elliman's house. Your friend will be okay; believe me, don't worry about him. Get to the airport."

3:01 P.M., *EDT: Wellesley, Massachusetts*

Filled with grim curiosity, Byron navigated his Volkswagen at top speed along the turnpike. At the first exit for Wellesley he pulled off. Spotting an Arco station on the main road, he pulled in and went to the attendant, who was wiping his hands near the compression pumps. "Can I help you with anything?" he asked in a heavy Boston accent.

Byron handed him the piece of paper with the address on it. "Do you know where I can find this place?" The attendant scratched his head and looked up the road. "Half a mile. Mile at the most." He indicated with his arm. "Go on up in that direction to the light. Turn right, then third on your left. Pitkin Road. It's marked."

A half mile, Byron thought, sliding behind the wheel. He turned the ignition key and put the car in gear, heading off.

A few minutes later, having passed the light and coasted down a long, tree-lined grade, he saw the sign out of the corner of his eye. He pumped the brake and pulled up the Volkswagen short, then reversed. "Pitkin Road" was concealed partly behind the drooping foliage of an old elm. He drove slowly now past a high white fence—newly painted, he noticed. Beyond the fence, horses and cows grazed together on rolling pastureland. A hundred yards farther on, he stopped the car and got out. Between the trees, to the left of the pasture, he could see a three-story Colonial house with black shutters. It was set well back from the road, perhaps two hundred yards or more. Byron crouched to get a better view. He stood up, craning to see if a car was parked in the drive. Trees lining the driveway blocked a clear view.

Suspicious now, he returned to the car and edged slowly onto the road's surface. Another hundred yards, and he came on a sign, "Larking Hill," white with black lettering. The wooden gate was latched, he noticed, but not locked. Without hesitating, he got out and swung it back.

Oaks and elms lined the private gravel drive, and the trees, now almost in full summer foliage, still blocked his view of the house. Byron wondered if he should leave the car and walk, but he quickly abandoned the idea. He was not capable of stealth. He would be fooling himself. And the last thing he wanted was a physical confrontation. He had come to look, and that was all.

He put the Volkswagen in gear and crept up the driveway. Halfway up the drive, as he began to flip the wheel right and then left, trying to gauge how quickly he could turn the car around in the narrow space, the sound of an approaching motor startled him.

Almost at once, a maroon Cadillac limousine appeared around the slight curve and sped toward him. In a quick glance, Byron's mind registered the plate "LING" and a windshield of smoked glass that prevented him from seeing the passengers. Assuming the Cadillac would brake on the drive, he pulled close to the trees on the left and rolled down the window, waving his arm. To his astonishment, the big car increased its speed. It was now within twenty yards and closing fast.

Byron tried to get out of the way, spinning the wheel to the right and depressing the accelerator, chewing gravel and turf beneath the rear tires. "Jesus!" he yelled. "Stop!"

He stood on the brakes and set himself for a collision. The Volkswagen was broadside across the drive, making passage of the Cadillac impossible. Immediately as the larger car hit, its doors flew open. Byron was thrown below the window edge; he pulled the far-side handle and shoved hard against the frame, then spilled dead weight onto the gravel.

After the initial crump, there was barely a sound. Shaken but unhurt, Byron got to his feet. His first instinct was to run, and as he looked toward the gate, he heard heavy footsteps to his right. Just as he turned his head back, the flat of a rifle barrel slammed across his chest, knocking the wind from him.

"Wessel!" a voice yelled from behind the Cadillac. "Hurry up!"

The man lowered the rifle. With his free hand he twisted Byron's arm behind his back, pushing him around the Volkswagen.

Byron gasped for air, staring at a man in a neatly tailored suit standing by the Cadillac. Byron's eyes flicked from him to the car. It was just a glance, but he thought he saw a Japanese in the front passenger's seat, holding a rifle across his lap. And there! There in the rear beside the far door was a glint of blond hair!

"Merrill!" he yelled.

The well-dressed man advanced. "Who are you?" he demanded.

Lamely, Byron replied, "I got lost and was turning around."

Suddenly the man stepped back, staring over Byron's shoulder, his mouth agape. Byron heard the sound of a car approaching fast on the driveway. He turned, grimacing against the pain of Wessel's armlock and saw a black sedan slow in the gravel as its tires sought purchase, then race toward them. Twenty yards from where they stood, it braked hard, sending up a cloud of dust.

Four men burst from behind the doors, the driver yelling, "Hold it!" Then: "Army Intelligence! Freeze!!"

Wessel dropped Byron's arm, forcing him to the ground. He snaked beneath the frame of the Volkswagen and covered his head with his hands.

"Niigata, stop!"

Then Byron heard the explosions of rifle fire from near the far side of the Cadillac.

An explosive blast of return fire came from the sedan.

Byron slithered on his stomach toward the Cadillac. "Get down, Merrill!" he screamed. But his voice was drowned by the explosions. He heard the thuds of bullets piercing the soft metal of the Cadillac. He saw the feet of the men near the sedan, using the Volkswagen as a shield now and pouring bullets point-blank into the Cadillac.

Byron again screamed, "Merrill, get down!"

Then, as suddenly as it had begun, the fire fight ended.

Minutes passed without a sound. Byron opened his eyes and was staring down the barrel of a pistol. "Come out of there," Shimkus ordered.

"I know nothing about this," Byron said in an excited, nervous voice.

"Shut up! Lie down there; hands behind your head."

He ran his hands swiftly along Byron's sides. Satisfied, Shimkus sprinted back to the sedan, and Byron looked up. Three agents had been wounded, one appeared serious. The one who had frisked him checked their wounds and said, "Get those two into the back."

The Cadillac was riddled. Wessel was lying in a pool of blood near the rear tire, dead. The Japanese had escaped and was nowhere in sight. Elliman's body, torn and limp, sprawled grotesquely in the gravel. The exit points of the bullets had shredded his back into lumps of raw flesh.

"Merrill!" Byron yelled. When there was no response, he got to his feet and looked through the Cadillac window. The blonde was wedged between the door and the seat, her face a pulp.

Byron doubled over. Merrill was dead, he sobbed to himself, and just as surely as though he had pulled the trigger himself, he was the cause. If he had not stopped the Cadillac, she would be alive.

"Who are you?" Shimkus asked, coming over.

Byron straightened up and wiped his mouth on his sleeve, averting his eyes from the Cadillac's interior. "You killed her," he said angrily. "She had nothing to do with this, and you killed her!"

Shimkus searched the limousine, pulled out wallets found in the glove compartment and returned to his sedan.

Byron drew in a lungful of air, then, tentatively at first,

grasped the Cadillac's door handle and pressed. The door popped open, and Byron jumped back in horror. The blonde's grisly head slid limply down the edge of the seat. Byron forced himself to look. Tears streamed down his cheeks. She had been so joyful, so beautiful, a friend whom he loved. Without thinking, he kneeled down and wrapped her in his arms, gently rocking her back and forth. He brushed back her hair and pressed his face against her neck.

Then slowly at first, the thought dawned. Something was wrong. Despite her condition, something about this girl did not square. Then in that instant as he thought it over, more elements seemed out of place. He pushed her from him and stared at her neck. He laid her on the seat and frantically searched the floor of the Cadillac. Nothing there, as he suspected. Then he ran his hand over the soft fabric of the seat and into the crevice. Again, nothing!

Hope welled up. The necklace, the heavy gold chain with the double-eagle coin. She would never take it off, no matter what. And it was not there. It was a beginning, but it was not enough. Perhaps they had removed it at the hospital or at the police station. The dress, a black-and-white checked skirt. He had never seen it before on Merrill, and it reminded him of a fashion worn by an older, more sophisticated woman. He kneeled down beside her now and pushed up the hair above the nape of her neck. He could see clearly. The roots were dark. This woman's hair was dyed.

This was not Merrill.

Such was Byron's relief, he started to laugh nervously, till he couldn't stop. He felt sorry for the dead woman, whoever she was, but Merrill was alive somewhere.

Shimkus signaled him with a wave of his hand, and Byron, who was bent double, straightened up, then walked to his limousine. Shimkus had a remote microphone in his hand, and he was listening near the open window. He looked at Byron, and an instant's awareness flashed in his eyes. He looked at the wallet. He was about to ask a question when the radio crackled with static. Distracted, Shimkus put his head in the window to hear more clearly and said into the microphone, "Repeat that, please."

The radio crackled. "An ambulance is en route, ten minutes ETA."

Shimkus prodded Byron with the pistol barrel. "What's your name?" Again he glanced at the wallet. The President would have his balls for killing Elliman. The order specifically had been to take him courteously as a special arrest. Elliman was connected with the man in the Oval Office. "I said, what's your fucking name, sonny?" Fueled by fear of the consequences, his anger increased.

He looked at the wallet for the third time, as the thought dawned of shifting blame. Nobody was to be the wiser, and Church would back him. An accident would hide the truth. He would be in the clear. Army Intelligence would be clean. An accident, he thought, raising the pistol to Byron's head.

Byron was suddenly frightened beyond words, staring sideways at the bead of a pistol less than an inch from his head. His mouth turned dry, and he wondered what he could say that would not trigger the gun. He heard himself say "Stark." Yes, Stark could explain why he was there. Lapham, the phone number in his pocket. In a sharp voice he said, "Yeah . . ."

Before he said another word, the pistol exploded. Byron saw a spray of flashing bright colors, and in that fraction of an instant between life and death, there were a thousand images, like scenes on the mural: his mother and father, the wagon, the books and the classrooms, the dull brown banks of the Congo, the faces of students in their seats, laughter, a bright blue sky, and then as though somebody had erased the scenes, there was blackness.

Byron crumpled to the ground, the side of his head torn away.

SATURDAY, JUNE 20, 1987

"Certain persons in an organization must be given the cipher key. Like a key that locks up a bank vault, it should only be given to persons who can be trusted. The possibility is always present, however, of the key falling into the wrong hands or being misused."

JAMES MARTIN,
Communications Satellite Systems

11:00 A.M., *AT: Barbados, British West Indies*

The Sandy Ledge overlooked a glistening white beach; beyond, the emerald waters of the southern Caribbean shone brilliantly. On the inland side, lush gardens of bougainvillea, hibiscus, oleander and frangipani lined the trim lawns and the winding driveway from the road, while the music of whispering palms and birds filled the air. Sandy Ledge's privileged guests stayed in a low white stucco structure whose red tile roof seemed to ramble in all directions from its central court. The estate also included a separate pool house, a beach cabana and changing rooms near the tennis court.

Incongruous in this placid, tropical scene, a black Daimler-Benz with smoked windows had stopped at the gate near the road. The window rolled down, and the driver, leaning into an electronic speaker box, issued that day's passwords: "Blue Jacket." The gate swung open, allowing the limousine to enter, then, monitored by an electronic eye, quickly closed with the resounding clunk from its tempered steel bars. The car swept silently down the curved driveway and stopped at the entrance, where an island native in a servant's coat stood rigidly at attention.

The driver opened the rear door, and an Air Force colonel in military dress stepped out. Constricted by the uniform, his short, compact physique was all coiled energy. He surveyed the lawns near the house with determined gray eyes, then he said with a small, thin-lipped mouth, "You can get out." The statement was an order, only slightly more polite than what he would issue to troops in his command. He stood impatiently waiting for the passengers to obey.

Wearing white slacks and a green pullover, Merrill was the first to respond. She looked around, feeling disoriented, then glanced at the clear sky. "Where are we, Colonel?" she asked in a weakened voice.

Neither Merrill nor Stark were told their destination, for their own safety, the laconic colonel had explained during their flight from Logan International Airport. Their unmarked Gulfstream II-SP had landed thirty minutes before at the island's international airport a few miles to the west of a large town they had seen from the air on final approach. They were hustled by the colonel to the waiting limousine, which took roads skirting the town to the island's southern coast, the hotel strip down the beach, and finally to the government-owned "safe house" the Pentagon had named Sandy Ledge.

The colonel answered vaguely, "In the Caribbean, miss."

Merrill had never met anyone like the colonel before. During the flight he had kept strictly to himself, dour and sullen, a military man to the manly dimple on his chin. He had spent much of the flight in the cockpit behind a closed door. She guessed from his personality that he related better to airplane mechanics than to people, but that was all right with her, because she knew that he was there to help.

Stark joined them in the driveway. "Thanks for getting us here," he said to the colonel. "You've been a big help." Stark knew that they were in the hands of an expert, and if there were to be further trouble, the colonel would be a good ally.

They followed him into the house as the servant retrieved their bags with clothes that had been hastily collected for them by the colonel's subordinates. As they entered the foyer, Merrill asked, "What do we call you, Colonel?"

"Stone," he replied.

Perfect, thought Stark: no first name, strictly by the manual. According to Lapham, the colonel was there to protect them. He would not interfere as long as they obeyed his orders. Lapham had said that they were to remain on the island for days, maybe longer, depending on what Army Intelligence learned about the Japanese who had escaped, the Mr. Niigata whom Stark had met at Elliman's office the morning before, who was somehow involved in the shootout at Elliman's and the murder that was intended, apparently, for him, and had got Byron instead.

The details of Byron's death, as they were related to Stark over the jet's radio by Lapham, were still distant and unreal. He had listened to Lapham's report in the relative privacy of the cockpit with the objective quality of a scientific dissertation. While Stark understood that Byron had been killed, Stark's emotions still would not allow him to accept the fact. And yet, the surface guilt was already palpable. After all, he had sent Byron to Wellesley. Of anybody, Stark should have been caught in that crossfire—if that was indeed what happened. Lapham had seemed confused on that score, confused and worried.

Thank God for Lapham, thought Stark. Lapham had sounded so bewildered and upset, although he confessed relief in knowing that Stark and Merrill were safe. Quickly Lapham had described the tragedies—the deaths of Elliman, his wife, his company's chief of security in an exchange of gunfire with agents from Army Intelligence, the escape of Niigata, the death of Byron. Lapham sounded guarded about Byron's death, as if he did not trust the description given to him by Shimkus—something about "powder burns" on Byron's skull. Lapham had ended the communication by insisting, "You are to contact nobody, talk to nobody, answer no questions. Do you hear?" Stark could not read Lapham's mind, but he inferred more than Lapham had let on.

"Please come with me," a black servant said, showing them through a door and down a long breezeway.

Merrill was revived enough after the long, restful flight to appreciate their surroundings. What a room, she thought minutes later, as they entered the bedroom, her eyes falling on a king-sized bed, a dressing table, lounge chairs, a highboy, a filled bookcase, a television with a video cassette recorder and twenty or so cassettes, and last, a large adjoining bathroom with a sunken bathtub. She ran her fingers down the neck of a chilled bottle of champagne on the coffee table. This was not so much a safe house, like the colonel described, as a palace. The Pentagon had thought of everything.

The servant set down both their suitcases.

"Am I staying here, too?" Stark asked him.

Before he could answer, Merrill pointed to the champagne bottle and said, "Look here," and handed it to him to open.

Stark forgot the question and popped the cork, then remembering, asked, "You can't drink liquor, can you?"

Merrill shook her head and asked the servant to find her a glass of orange juice. "That shouldn't stop us from a little celebration," she said to Stark. "We deserve it, we really do."

Stark poured out the bubbly liquid and raised the glass to her, sipping. Looking into her drawn face, he realized again how much she had suffered for something he had done. While the Army doctor had administered to her at the airport, Stark had met the clumsy, country-style investigator named Verdeen and discovered from him just what Elliman had done to her. He had thanked Verdeen, even asked if he could fly with them to the safe house, but the colonel had forbidden it. Verdeen was to be debriefed by Army Intelligence in Washington.

With Merrill safe and recovering quickly, the important thing, thought Stark, was Elliman's death. Now no one on earth was in a position to exploit the formula. Erased from Thornton's data banks, the invalid combination resided in Stark's head alone —another reason, he guessed, why Lapham wanted him guarded, at least until the hunter-killer satellites were launched.

"Stark?" Merrill asked softly, seeing that he was lost in concerned thought. When he focused on her, she asked, "Have you told me everything that happened, *everything?*"

Stark averted his eyes. "Yes and no," he said, honestly. "I don't know everything yet, and Lapham will need a few days to untangle it. Mr. Verdeen should be able to help him." Stark had related to her about Douglas Elliman and the extortion; then when he had received the news about the shootout, he had described Elliman's death—carefully avoiding mention of Byron's death and that of her grandfather.

Stark recalled again what the Army physician had told him in private at the airport. Her spirits would recover fast, probably before they landed, as the drugs administered by Elliman's nurse wore off. But her body was a different matter. It had been punished severely and would require days before she returned to full health. "Don't be deceived by her attitude," the doctor had warned.

When could she be told about the deaths of her friend and grandfather?

Stark had no desire to hold the tragic news from her: She had more right than anyone else to know their horrible fates. Stark did not want to "protect" her from knowing. Merrill was her own woman, and, he knew, she would be justifiably furious with him if she learned that he had intentionally withheld bad news. The doctor, though, had advised him to bide his time until she was stronger, in a day, maybe two, maybe three. "Find the right moment," he had replied to Stark's question. For now, Stark would wait and watch.

Seemingly satisfied by his answer, Merrill now opened her suitcase on the bed, took out something and disappeared into the bathroom, while Stark went to the window and absorbed the beach view. He could not understand what had gone wrong at Elliman's house. He had warned Lapham about Byron and received his assurances that Army Intelligence would intercept him. His death did not make sense. He shrugged sadly, thinking that Lapham would find the answers eventually. For now, Stark and Merrill had a duty to themselves to try to enjoy normalcy.

"A penny for your thoughts," he heard her say behind him. He turned around, and the sight made him blush, a reaction that made Merrill smile. "You like it, I see," she said, then, "I want to lie in the sun."

Stark had trouble reacting normally to what he saw. From their first meeting he had admired the beauty of Merrill's hair, her face, the way she laughed and talked. But now, seeing her there in the bikini, she was also breathtaking in her sexiness. Clearing his throat, he said, "Sure."

She moved past him, touching him softly on the arm, then opened the sliding door.

"I'll meet you as soon as I've changed," he said, watching her walk to the shore, her hair blowing in the wind. Her body moved with exquisite grace—her back was straight and proud, square shoulders, thin, long legs and, he thought, hurrying to find his bathing suit, an ass that was desirable beyond his imagining.

When Stark joined her a few minutes later, Merrill purred, "Isn't it lovely here?" and stretched languidly on the beach towel.

"Perfect," he replied, watching her raise up on her elbows.

She smiled, flattered by his appreciative stare. He was so entirely natural, she thought. Once he overcame his initial shyness, he enjoyed what he wanted boldly. Most men would steal glances, but Stark obviously had not learned that deception, and she loved him for it, although now it was Merrill who was embarrassed under his stare. "Look," she said, pointing to the sea. Several hundred yards out, a sailing galleon swept past with a red mainsail emblazoned with a Maltese cross. Onboard and clamoring at the gunwales, hundreds of tourists laughed and shouted, their voices heard across the water.

Stark walked to the sea's edge, then looked back, shrugging. "Warm as a bathtub," he reported. "Come on, let's swim."

"You go ahead," Merrill said, lying flat on her back, her arm under her head. The midday sun soothed her skin. She watched Stark enter up to his knees, then dive in, swimming with strong strokes toward a raft anchored a distance offshore. Merrill raised her shoulders to the sun, thankful for an end to the terrible events of the last two days. The reward of this beach . . . the reward of Stark . . . she had earned them, she thought with a delightful, tingling sensation.

Merrill could not say that she loved Stark; it was too early for any certain emotions, and she was not one to rush a judgment that important. She admitted that he interested her, maybe more than that. He fascinated her. She wanted to search him out naturally, and if what she discovered was as good as what she already had found, then love might result. She tried to think of the future, but as she did, her eyes closed and she was fast asleep.

"Merrill," a whisper in her ear. Her arm was being stroked gently, a cool caress. "Are you asleep?"

She opened her eyes slowly to see Stark's face above hers,

blocking the sun, then touching his lips with hers. The tang of salt and the coolness of his wet skin excited her. She reached to embrace him, as he rolled on his hip, resting on his elbow. She wiggled closer, so that their noses almost touched.

"Do you know why we sleep?" he asked, a grin set on his face.

Merrill smiled not so much at the strange question as at the memory of his first words about pain. Then as now he kept her off balance, and she sensed that he always would. "Tell me," she replied softly.

His brow furrowed a little. "It might seem odd, you know, that an animal the size of an elephant needs almost no sleep at all . . . while humans need a minimum of three hours in every twenty-four. The explanation is adaptation. If an elephant sleeps, it will starve. It must graze. It can graze day and night because it has no natural enemies. We can get along by eating once or twice a day. We used to have lots of natural enemies." He paused to laugh. "We were particularly vulnerable at night, so we adapted. We learned to sleep at night during the periods of greatest danger, eating when it was light. Sleep was protection. . . ."

"Stark?"

"Um?"

"Kiss me again."

His lips pressed softly against hers, and he moved closer so their bodies touched. Her mouth opened slightly and he felt the tentative touch of her tongue. He responded by lowering his hand to her bare thigh. She murmured, almost a whisper. As their excitement increased, she pressed him against her, running her hand up the nape of his neck into his hair.

Wordlessly, he broke away and pulled himself up to his feet, then reached down for her hand. She got up and embraced him. They kissed again. Stark looked back, then led her anxiously up the beach toward the house. As a sign of their desire, they moved across the warm sand, locked arm in arm.

It seemed to Merrill as though she were in a dream. She wanted him more than she could remember ever wanting anything or anybody. She felt weak with expectation as she lay on the bed, reaching out as he lay down beside her. There were no words. She felt him reach behind her back. Helping him, she untied the bikini top, then sitting up for a moment, took down the bottom, lifting one knee as she settled back. Stark was out of his bathing suit and excited as he lowered himself onto her. She drew him against her, her mouth open at the feel of him against her. She reached down and softly touched him, moving her legs apart as she guided him into her. Her nipples hardened against his chest as his hips moved over her. Merrill cried out and held him tightly into her, arching her back. A time passed in the pleasure of touch, look and expression. And then with strokes that left Merrill gasping Stark came into her, shuddering with each release.

Their minds diffused, they again lay side by side, Merrill's leg around his hip, as they kissed, tasting each other, laughing at the raw sensitiveness of their bodies. They smiled with the joy of finding something neither ever wanted to lose again.

She whispered, "I've never felt happier."

"Two of us then," he said, kissing her eyes.

Merrill knew that she was falling in love. Her body had told her too. "Whatever," she said, "will you promise that this will be the first of a billion times?"

He laughed again. "A *billion?*"

"Maybe even more."

"A thousand million." He paused, pretending to calculate. "No, the limit of my promise is a billion, no more."

"I won't count if you don't."

"You got a deal."

Merrill swung her legs over the side of the bed and brushed back her hair. She went to the table, where she poured them champagne, then handed Stark the glass. Back on the bed, Stark made a solitary toast to the discovery of their love.

As he sipped, there was a knock on the door, which sent Merrill scurrying into the bathroom.

"What is it?" Stark asked, wrapping a towel around his middle.

The voice of the servant declared, "There'll be a light dinner served in fifteen minutes."

"Can you bring it to the room?" Stark asked.

"Certainly, sir."

Stark lay on the bed, listening to the sound of the shower and Merrill singing cheerfully. He got up and opened the door, peering through the steam coming from the shower stall. Slipping off the towel, he slid back the glass door, and with a laugh from Merrill, he joined her under the spray.

They dried each other off, laughing at their need to touch. Stark wanted to make love again and said so, leading her back into the bedroom. Merrill smelled of sandalwood and shampoo. He nuzzled her neck, then kissed her breasts, as another knock sounded at the door. Merrill dove under the covers, raising the sheet to her chin, and Stark slipped on a pair of shorts, slightly annoyed by the interruptions. He opened the door and the servant, who studiously kept his eyes on the trolley, laid a tray of cold lobster, crab, salad and wine on the table. Without a word he served the food and departed.

They drew up their chairs and ate hungrily, talking to each other with their eyes. Finishing his meal, Stark leaned over and looked toward the beach. Cream-puff clouds hung over the water, casting myriad shadows. A light wind ruffled the leaves, while the sound of water lapping on the shore underscored the peaceful beauty of the scene. Stark looked back at Merrill and said, "Let's take a walk."

Merrill readily agreed, dressing in a cotton shift, a shirt and espadrilles, and quickly brushing her hair, as Stark dressed in the clothes he had worn during the flight.

Merrill asked, "Should we tell him?"

"Him?" Stark replied. He'd almost forgotten about Colonel Stone. "Oh *him.* He's probably lifting weights or something by now."

"He said we weren't to leave the house, remember?"

"That doesn't mean we can't take a walk."

"There's no sense in angering him unnecessarily," Merrill said. "At least we shouldn't be *obvious* about it."

A few minutes later, they were ambling up the beach away from the water near where the palms shaded the hot sand. As they went, they began to hear the refrain of a steel band playing up the beach near hotel row. The sound, and then later, the sight of pastel Japanese lanterns swinging from wires between the palms, led them onward. A distance farther and they were stopped by the sight of a chain-link fence at the boundary of Sandy Ledge's property, a high barrier that ended twenty feet in the water.

"This is as far as we go," Merrill said, pressing her hand against the fence. "It's sort of like a prison, isn't it?"

A prison, even one for their own protection, was still a prison, Stark thought, impetuously pulling off his shirt and unbuckling his belt. The fence reminded him of what he had left behind in Boston and wanted desperately for them both to forget.

"Stark, what are you *doing?*" Merrill asked with a laugh of girlish embarrassment.

Naked, he replied to her question by balling up his clothes and tossing them over the fence. They landed on the other side. "I'm going for a swim," he said, running to the water's edge. "Come on, Merrill," he yelled back playfully. "Nobody will see you."

Merrill was hesitant, but she did not want to be separated from him. She watched as he paddled on his back in the water, exhorting her with, "What's the matter, don't Boston Brahminettes swim bare-assed?"

Merrill looked up and down the empty beach, then turning her back on Stark, she stepped out of her skirt and unbuttoned her shirt, now wearing only a brief pair of panties. She jumped in the air, throwing her clothes over the fence, then ran down to the water's edge. She waded in and sank to her knees, then sidestroked to where Stark was treading water. He dove down and came up behind her, wrapping his arms around her waist and pulling her close. She felt him and with a squeal of laughter, she pushed away, saying, "Imagine what the fish would think! Stark, you are impossible!"

A few minutes later, breathing hard from the exertions of swimming, they headed around the opposite side of the fence, toward the shore. They stayed in the water until it was too shallow, then got up and sat on the wet sand as the hot sun dried their bodies. In the distance they could still hear the steel band and the sounds of laughter.

"What is that up there?" Merrill asked.

"A hotel, I guess," Stark replied. "Should we check it out?"

Merrill looked in the direction of Sandy Ledge. "We'd better not. He'd kill us if he knew we'd gone even this far. We are escapees."

"Oh come on," Stark said, getting to his feet. "There's no sense escaping if we're just going to go back. What kind of a prisoner are you, anyway?"

"Not a very good one, I guess," she replied, joining him near their clothes.

Once they had dressed, they walked in the direction of the hotel, looking like urchins. Merrill's tangled, wet hair hung down her back. Stark rolled up the cuffs of his trousers, then pecked Merrill on the lips, taking her hand in his. Soon they came even with the hotel, an old Colonial structure with balustrades and terraces. Because of the sun's intensity, none of the guests was on the beach. Instead, they sat at tables drinking and eating under canvas awnings.

"What do you think?" Stark asked, looking toward the hotel.

"That we should head back."

Stark hesitated. "Look," he said, "they're dancing." He faced her, kissing her forehead. "One dance won't hurt."

Merrill followed him up to the hotel. As they reached the lights, they saw scores of vacationers on the veranda dance floor swaying to the steel band's version of "Jamaican Love Song." Stark took Merrill in his arms. "I guess we're in Jamaica," he said.

They whirled clumsily across the floor. Merrill laughed, throwing back her head. "Ouch!" she cried. "You got *both* feet that time." He spun her around dramatically, nearly losing his balance. Merrill whispered, "Do you mind if we continue this dance in the room . . . in bed?"

They went to one edge of the dance floor. "Let's get a drink before we go back, okay?" Stark asked. Merrill nodded as Stark waved down a waiter and ordered a Planters' Punch, and a ginger ale for Merrill. They found seats at a vacant table and watched the dancers. The waiter returned and set down the drinks, asking, "Your room number?"

"Ummmm," Stark thought, looking embarrassed.

"We don't have any money," Merrill exclaimed, giggling.

Stark reached in his back pocket, then laid the bank check on the table. "We have precisely $60,000." Then to the waiter, "Will that cover it?"

"They won't cash a thing like that," Merrill said, thinking that the check was a joke. "We're not even guests."

"We can always call the colonel," he teased.

"No! He'd be furious."

Stark looked at the waiter. "I'll get you the money in a minute." To Merrill he said, rising to his feet, "Come on. Maybe we can cash the check *and* have fun."

They went up a flight of stairs to a broad, concrete-banistered porch overlooking the dance floor, then through a portico that faced a door from which a party of guests emerged in animated conversation. Merrill noticed a brass plaque on the door: "Le Pirate."

"This could be the place," Stark remarked.

Merrill guessed what it was. "How could you tell?"

"Every hotel in the islands has to have a casino, doesn't it?"

She put her arm in his, and they swept through the door into a large, air-conditioned room. They stood close to the entrance, surveying the scene. There was a bamboo bar at the far end at which a few gamblers stood watching the tables. Roulette balls clicked on the wheels. Silent gamblers stood huddled in small, tight circles around the tables like ghoulish spectators, watching games of *chemin de fer,* blackjack and craps. The smell of suntan lotion, perfume and aftershave hung heavily in the room.

They passed the tables, occasionally stopping to admire the swift, sure movements of the croupiers. Dressed in fluorescent blue dinner jackets, they contrasted favorably with the casual dress of the patrons. One, an Arab in a linen Nehru jacket, played blackjack. A wall of chips separated him from the cards; his dealer seemed unconcerned by the high stakes. But a pit boss with oily skin swept the table with interested eyes. At another table a woman watched the roulette ball with glazed eyes and parted lips; seconds before it fell into the groove she licked her lips sensuously. At the far end of the room to the right of the bar, a man with a heavy gold bracelet sat in a cage counting bills. Stark went over and slid the cashier's check between the bars.

"This in mixed-denomination chips," he said in a voice that strained for authority.

The banker examined the draft, then lifted a telephone. A minute later a fat man in a vanilla suit entered the cage and cautiously introduced himself as the manager. He glanced at Stark's check, then said, "Well . . . ?"

"What's your percentage?" Stark asked.

Merrill looked at Stark. Another aspect of the unexpected.

"Forty."

"Thirty-five."

"Done! Lose it."

Merrill held Stark's arm as he scooped up the plaques with his other hand. He didn't bother to count under the manager's gaze. When they turned away, Merrill asked, "What in heavens was that *about?*"

"A simple, illegal transaction," he explained. He didn't say that he had studied probability during his undergraduate days. That had led, naturally, to gambling, which fascinated him. This scam, washing money, was done in countries with soft currencies. "We are expected to lose at least 35 percent of the $60,000—and he gives us the remainder in cash when we leave."

"We can't just *lose.* My God—"

"If we don't, he'll throw us out and . . . give back the check, or he'll take it off the top! It's the *game,* to win by losing, isn't it? Since we have to anyway?"

She saw how serious he was all of a sudden. "Well . . . let's *try.*"

"Right," he said, sliding onto a blackjack stool. The cards were dealt—two kings for Stark against a seven and a two for the dealer. Stark bet £5,000. The dealer concentrated and laid out the next run of cards, as others playing at the table lost interest in their own paltry bets. The young man was a fool, asking for another card with twenty. A complete fool. They couldn't believe when he tapped his finger. Even the dealer asked, "Are you certain, *monsieur?*"

"Card!"

An ace. Twenty-one.

The dealer had to stop at seventeen.

"Oh God, what poor luck," Stark moaned, rolling his eyes for the benefit of Merrill, who laughed.

The dealer thought him mad, and dutifully paid out £7,500 pounds. These two kids were downright goofy!

"Here," Stark said to Merrill, handing her a stack of chips, "see what you can do with roulette. It's easy to lose there." And he continued to gamble, losing one hand, then winning the next three—one with blackjack.

A quarter hour passed before Merrill came back, not certain whether she should frown or smile. She handed him back the chips. "I'm hopeless," she said. She had won a further £10,000.

Stark took his chips and slid off the stool. "This is not going as planned," he said.

Merrill looked around. "Maybe we should just give him the percentage. I think we should leave."

Stark looked at his watch. "It's early yet, and when I'm determined, I never fail. Let's try *chemin de fer.*"

"Have you ever played?"

"Of course not. All the better."

By now they had a gallery of followers who had gotten caught up in their game of trying to lose. One man in Bermuda shorts nudged Stark and said, "Try me. I haven't won in three days." He turned to the plump woman behind him. "Ask my wife."

"Here," Stark said, handing him a £1,000 plaque. "And *bad* luck."

"Thanks, buddy." His wife looked as though she could kill Stark.

Stark was having enormous fun. "Merrill, take the winnings and buy us a drink . . . more champagne, okay?"

On the third run of the cards, Stark finally began to lose, and he increased his bets with every loss, trying to calculate the 35 percent. The game bored him. It was slower than blackjack and more mannered, with a certain dignity that Stark did not appreciate. The time passed as he neared his quota. After one draw from the shoe, he turned in his chair, expecting to find Merrill at his back. She wasn't. He stretched his neck to see back to the bar, and she wasn't there either. Suddenly he began to worry. To the dealer he said, "I'm out," and he collected the chips in his arms. He passed the other tables quickly, but Merrill was not anywhere in sight.

At the cage he asked the manager, "Have you seen the girl I was with?"

The manager, counting the chips, replied, "The beauty? No. Maybe she went to powder her nose." The girl probably found a high roller, he thought; it happened all the time. He wondered, though—this kid looked panicked, not jilted.

Stark took his money, and, thanking the manager, ran out the door. He looked down from the balcony at the table where they had ordered the drinks, and she wasn't there either. What in hell have I done? he thought, as real panic filled his mind. He plunged down the steps and across the dance floor, down the beach to a line of palm trees. He looked both ways; there was nobody in sight. It did not make sense that the Japanese would follow them here. How could he know? The answer did not matter. Merrill was lost, he screamed to himself, running up the beach. Merrill had been taken, again, against every promise he had made to himself. He had acted foolishly, and now she was again paying the price.

Suddenly, violently, he was hit from behind by a heavy blow and pulled backward. An arm pressed into his thorax. He tried to see but was pushed forward brutally. He fell to the sand.

A knee pressed into his neck. He did not struggle now. He had given up. They had found him, and this was the end. Struggling would only drag out the pain, he thought, about to lose consciousness.

A harsh voice close to his ear said, "I'd kill you."

The pressure lessened. Miraculously . . .

Then the voice again, "If you ever do a stupid thing like that again. . . ."

Stark swiveled his head around. Towering over him was the colonel. Stone.

"What the hell do you think this is, a game, a vacation, a fucking college weekend?" Stone's voice was vicious, and his face was contorted in rage.

Stark choked. "What about Merrill?" The words caught in his throat.

The colonel straddled Stark. "Get up, you bloody fool."

1:00 P.M., *EDT: Washington, D.C.*

"For want of a nail the shoe was lost, for want of a shoe the horse was lost, for want of a horse . . . the kingdom. . . . I tell ya, friggin' Lucy ain't worth jackshit." First Lieutenant John Tolliver, U. S. Army, pulled back his foot and kicked the side of the computer with a loud crash. "Ouch," he yelled, hopping on one foot.

Another technician on duty that afternoon in the bowels of the Pentagon's Systems Command computer facility laughed at Tolliver. His love-hate relationship with "Lucy," the powerful CRAY-1 computer that interpreted warnings fed into it from satellite and radar sensors, was a long-standing joke that, they had discovered, reflected the tranquillity or turbulence in the relationship Tolliver had with his girlfriend, Barbara. When everything was smooth between them, Tolliver loved "Lucy."

Robert Denchley, a second lieutenant on the same shift as

Tolliver, took a sip from the styrofoam cup and said, "Maybe it's true, but she's the best there is and all we got."

Tolliver unbuttoned his tunic and pulled an envelope from the inner pocket. He threw it at Denchley. "Who got blamed when she burped last November? Who did they hang it on when she threw up twice in the winter? Look at that."

The letter was an official reprimand from Hedley Church, general in charge of Systems Command, for dereliction of duty. "Because of mitigating circumstances," the letter ended, "this reprimand will not be entered in your Fitness Report, but note of it verbally will be made at the Promotion Board's next consideration of your qualifications for captain."

"Ain't that sweet?" Tolliver said.

"You can't be blamed for the equipment," Denchley said. "Is a private responsible if his gun jams?"

"If some hard ass's got his number, yeah."

"But it was you, John, who straightened out the problem, all three times."

"And look what I got for it."

"Lucy hasn't even *sneezed* in months. You're just pissed at her now because Barbara shut you off."

"How did *you* know?" He laughed, trying to wipe the letter and the angered thoughts of Church from his mind.

"It'll blow over, believe me," Denchley said. "Let's see if our little family is healthy and happy."

They walked toward what they called the doctor's office, a Control Data STAR computer with slightly less power than CRAY-1. Nobody had ever thought to make a count of the hundreds of EDP machines in the Systems Command facility, but the cavernous basement room was considered to be the largest assembly of computers and tangential EDP equipment anywhere in the world, with the possible exception of the Kremlin. In fact, the machines were so numerous that the doctor's office was installed and programmed to maintain a constant watch on its brethren computers and inform technicians like Tolliver and Denchley the instant one failed to operate.

As they passed IBEX VII, the targeting computer, Tolliver said, "Surprised he didn't pin that on me, too."

The technical shifts were still laughing behind their hands about that one. General Church had embarrassed himself publicly with IBEX at a symposium in Boston, and as a result, "Dr. Rousseau" had become an instant hero. The facility personnel respected Church for his rank and his ability, but they did not like him. All the technicians were diligent to an obsessive degree; they loved their work and knew that they could earn much higher salaries on the outside. They stayed because their mission was important to the country.

They did not like General Church because he nagged at them constantly, was quick to reprimand and slow to praise. Burps and sneezes and throwups were not uncommon computer occurrences, but when one happened, Church blamed the technicians, never the machines. The general knew but he didn't seem to understand. If America were ever attacked by nuclear weapons, technicians in the facility would know even before the President. "Lucy," the Alert computer, picked up data from the satellites and radar, digested and analyzed the data within nanoseconds, then reported incoming ground- and submarine-based enemy missiles. Targeting computers like IBEX were triggered, the lids on Minutemen silos rolled back, SAC crews jatoed off strips from Maine to Hawaii, battle-control 747s were readied, and one based in Hawaii went into the air—all within one minute, twenty seconds.

"Can you go over Church's head?"

Tolliver stopped and looked at Denchley. "What are you asking dumb questions for?"

"Sorry," Denchley said. They reached the doctor's office a few seconds later. "What's the scoop?"

Tolliver scanned the three blank VDTs over a terminal and pushed the "test" button. The screens showed identical lines with the same word: "NEGATIVE."

"No patients—" Tolliver said, reflecting the data.

"And doctor's helpers can go fishin'."

"Chess?"

"How about backgammon?"

"You're on; fifty cents a point."

"Make it twenty-five."

Although they played strictly by the ancient rules of the game, theirs was not normal backgammon. Near the doctor's office, they set out their chairs and equipment, and Denchley, anxious to get started, was first to insert a "floppy" disk into his personal Apple minicomputer. Tolliver in time did the same, making the match a contest of programming skill. At each move, they consulted their Apples, which gave them the best options drawn from the programmed compilations of experts' theories of the game. Tolliver moved conservatively, and in six months of play he was ahead by $32. Denchley was more daring, preferring the wild assault to Tolliver's cautious back game. The thrill of unexpected maneuvers more than compensated Denchley for any temporary aberration that Tolliver called a win.

Between moves, Denchley asked, "Why did you kick Lucy?" Tolliver did not abuse the computer often. It was a sign that other problems weighed on his mind. Cooped up together in the facility for such long hours at a time, discussions of their personal lives were common and surprisingly candid.

Tolliver rolled the dice by keying "enter" on his Apple. A 6–1 combination move. "Barbara's fooling around with some upwardly mobile type at the House." His girlfriend worked as a typist in the White House secretarial pool. "She thinks programming is a dead end. 'Boring' is how she describes it . . . rather, describes *me.* She met this whiz-bang assistant to the assistant press secretary, and she thinks he's exciting. Anyway, he's trying to get in her pants." He shrugged. "Maybe he already gave her one."

"Do you care?"

Of course he cared. Barbara was not the prettiest woman, but he liked her all the same. He guessed because she was independent and did not make demands. "Sort of," he replied. "I care enough, anyway, to wonder why I'm working for the Army."

"What does that have to do with it?"

"We make squat, that's what. I think Barbara's fooling around because she doesn't think I'll go the distance. She wants to get married. How can I marry anyone on what I make?"

"And you got an offer . . . ?"

"From Honeywell."

"You going to take it?"

"After this letter," he said, glancing at his tunic lapel, "what choice is there?"

"It'll blow over; it always does. And that reprimand wasn't official, remember?"

"Yeah, but the poison'll spread. Next thing you know, I'll be the goat for everything that goes wrong around here, even on other shifts. It's no good, because if I stay, my reputation will get worse, and I may end up without any offers. I should strike now."

Denchley checked to see what his Apple advised, then said, "Double you."

Tolliver pursed his lips, examining his position on the board. "Let me consult the whiz," he said. "Well . . . I guess . . . maybe . . ."

At the braying, ear-splitting sound of klaxons sounding in every corner of the facility, they looked at one another, suddenly scared.

"What the hell?" Denchley shouted.

"Alert!"

"A test?"

"Check the doctor's office!"

Denchley jumped out of his chair, stretching his neck to peer into the three VDTs above the the doctor's office terminals. The same "negative" appeared that had been there a quarter hour ago. This was not a test. All equipment was 100 percent.

Denchley said, "We have an alert."

"You stay at the doctor's office," Tolliver said. "I'll check out Lucy."

Both men knew from hours of drill and instruction that a "no test" alert meant incoming enemy ICBMs. They had been drilled to expect impact within ten to twenty-five minutes from initial alert. The first two people in America to know of an imminent nuclear holocaust, their reaction would be the same as anyone else's, including the President's—gut fear and mild disbelief.

Tolliver raced down the aisle between the mainframes and ancillary equipment, finally reaching "Lucy," the control panel of which confirmed what the doctor's office already reported, that she was 100 percent healthy. As Tolliver scanned the board, the red telephone, a direct open line to the White House's Situation Room, rang insistently. He reached over and picked it up.

The voice on the other end said simply, "Verify the sensors!"

2:30 P.M., *AT: Barbados, B.W.I.*

Stark lay awake in the darkened room staring at the ceiling, anger pumping adrenalin into his blood. He had apologized—profusely, he thought—but the tight-lipped colonel had continued to hiss insults. Perhaps Stark had been out of line taking Merrill to the casino, but that was no reason for the colonel to treat him like an adolescent, a juvenile delinquent. The colonel did not have to scare him half to death like that, nor yell at him. Once back at Sandy Ledge, the colonel had ordered them not to leave the house again, not even for a stroll on the beach. Stark felt like a college student who had been grounded for taking an illegal overnight.

Stark understood the seriousness of their position, probably better than anyone. After all, *he* had seen the carnage at Thornton's house. If he still wanted to take risks, that was his concern. Niigata had not followed them to the island, which he knew now to be Barbados. So where was the danger, unless what Lapham implied about Byron's death being no accident was true.

Before she fell asleep, Merrill had been equally confused. The colonel had pulled her out of the casino with a terse command, then he had gone back for Stark. Merrill knew that the colonel wanted to make an example of the incident to impress on them the gravity of their position. She sympathized more with the colonel than Stark did. Stone had a job to do, and by what she had seen of him, he did not fail. Merrill had been theatrically contrite, but she was honestly ashamed. The colonel was hard on them only for their own safety, and they had made his task difficult.

Merrill stirred and snuggled closer to Stark in a relaxed half sleep. After the colonel finally finished his tirade, they had returned to the bedroom, undressed and turned in. With unspoken desire, each had wanted to make love again, but they suspected that Stone not only would know if they did, but also that he would take umbrage. They suspected that they were being spied on; everything they did now would be known instantly to him and they had no desire to make furtive love.

Stark responded to her closeness by placing his arm behind her so that her head nestled in the crook of his shoulder. "Merrill," he whispered softly, choosing this moment. Slowly and deliberately, holding her close, he told her of the deaths of Byron and her Grandfather Thornton. As he spoke, she lay perfectly still, almost with stiffness, he thought. He could not see her face and did not want to. The moment was personal and private. A tear moistened his shoulder, then another and another as she sobbed. He could feel her shudder lightly against his side, and he wanted to offer her succor, but by being with her in unspoken support, he was offering all he could. "Oh Stark," she said finally, "it's so horrible." Then she buried her face in his shoulder, letting loose the fullness of her sorrow.

"I know, my love," he said, using the word for the first time. "I know, I know." Minutes passed in silence, long minutes of deepest grief. Stark waited for her to ask how, but the question never came, as though she suspected and wanted to be spared that pain. "I'm sorry," he said, "so very deeply sorry, because, you see, it was my fault."

Merrill turned on her side and covered his mouth with her hand, then said fiercely, "Don't say that, never say that. Because it isn't true. Promise me you won't believe that."

Stark did not answer. He would always believe in his guilt

and be forced to live with the truth of it. He did not think that he alone could make up to her for such losses as Byron and Thornton, but he pledged to himself to do everything in his power to compensate Merrill for the dual tragedies.

Minutes passed. Merrill demanded again, "You must never blame yourself."

There was an insistent knock on the door. Before they had time to reply, it opened and the lights were turned on. Colonel Stone was standing there in full uniform, an expression on his face so different from what they had seen that they looked at him wordlessly, expectantly.

"Get up!" he shouted.

"What the—" Stark protested.

"I said, 'Get up!' "

Stark tightened his hold on Merrill and stayed where he was.

Colonel Stone marched to the bed and yanked back the blanket, then grabbed Stark by the arm and physically pulled him from the bed. "Two minutes ago precisely," he said in clipped, cold tones, "the Russians attacked the United States. Their missiles are en route."

"What did you say?" Stark asked.

Colonel Stone seemed not to hear. "Both of you. We are going back."

11:00 P.M., EDT: Washington, D.C.

Ten hours had passed since the alert. In *another* ten hours . . . Lord help us, thought the President, trying to rub away the persistent throbbing in his temples as the Crisis Committee watched his agonizing in silent sympathy. Crises were blind-siders by definition, he thought, yet the country had elected him to find peaceful remedies when such seemed impossible. He was the father of his country's people, and they were unruly children who sought shelter and comfort in him at times like these. He could handle almost anything with the powers at his command, from a nuclear plant disaster, a hostage situation, an embargo, a limited conventional war, to a flood and a fire. . . . But there were limits. If his advisers described the boundaries of a problem, resources could be found for a solution. When there was no clear focus, like now, consternation was the response. This emergency seemed random, yet all knew it was not. It seemed impossible, but the evidence could not be ignored. The President had seen it coming years ago, in his first term. The problem was complexity. A fear that he had carried everywhere, he knew at one juncture in the country's history, a problem would arise for which there would simply be no solution at all. He had hoped that his Presidency would escape such a fate, but now that hope was an illusion of the past.

The fabric of his country was unraveling. Although he knew why and how, he was immobilized. The sensors reported that the Soviets had *not* attacked; they had not even alerted their forces. The Alert computer had erred, but no fault could be found in the system. While appearing perfectly normal, it malfunctioned consistently. Not just the Alert computer either. All Systems Command computers in the Pentagon had . . . *rebelled,* he thought. That was clearly impossible: He and the other men in the Oval Office knew that computers did not rebel unless someone ordered them to. Compounding those malfunctions, reports were arriving hourly of other major failures without apparent causes—the Chicago Commodity Exchange, the Internal Revenue Service, General Motors, the General Accounting Office . . . the list went on. It seemed to the President that most important computer systems in the public and private sectors were in trouble—as though a huge tap were being turned off, as though the entire understructure of the American system were crumbling, senselessly.

Looking up again, he asked, "Is there a connection?"

Ben Lapham briefly reviewed the data he had received from the coordinated intelligence services. "We've blocked every exit, sir," he said.

As Lapham was about to continue, the President interrupted. "Obviously we haven't," he said. "We eliminated Elliman messily, but he never had the damned formula in the first place. Nobody but Dr. Rousseau has hold of it, unless I'm totally wrong."

"But we don't know if this *is* the formula, because it's not poisoning the systems as Rousseau described it would," Lapham said.

"Explain that, please."

"The satellites are at the core of Rousseau's theory."

"And from what you described earlier, all these systems" —he held up a sheet of paper on which the destroyed computer systems were listed—"use the satellites."

Lapham nodded. "That much *does* fit, sir. But the way the infection is contaminating the systems doesn't. It's random, single-shot. And as you recall, Rousseau's formula is supposed to hit all the systems using the satellites simultaneously. I repeat, at once. So far, sir, that has not happened."

"And pray for your life it doesn't. The difference, though, is merely one of timing. Whether it is the 'correct' application of the formula or not, the effect is the same, wouldn't you say?"

"Over time, I agree, sir. But look at what has not been hit, sir. At the top of the list, our strategic forces, the computers in the silos, aboard our fleets, the Strategic Air Command. These, sir, are secure. Add to that thousands of corporations and government agencies that depend for their existence on their computer systems. They are also on INTELSAT and are safe. No, sir, somebody is playing cat-and-mouse with us."

"Somebody," the President said emphatically. "We know the millions we can count *in,* as potential perpetrators. Who can we count *out* with any degree of certitude?"

"Only Elliman and Rousseau, and, of course, Thornton. Rousseau's been under constant surveillance, as you know, in Barbados." He checked his wristwatch. "In fact, he should arrive any minute."

"Who did you say?" General Church asked, electrified.

In that instant, with the single alarmed question, Lapham knew the truth. "Dr. Stark Rousseau," he said, explaining.

General Hedley Church turned pale and gripped the arms of his chair. He glanced at the clock on the President's desk, wondering if there was time to countermand the order and intercept the agent he had sent to Cape Canaveral. Rousseau alive? That could not be true. Now Lapham was describing a safe house in the Caribbean. Rousseau would walk into the Oval Office any minute?

What have I done? Church thought with alarm. He wanted only what was best for America. And himself. He had only hinted to Shimkus about Rousseau's elimination. True, with Rousseau and Elliman eliminated, so was the formula. There could be no real harm from what he had done to the new satellites waiting for launch at Cape Canaveral. It was LTW that would look bad: The company would be accused of negligence, a charge that could eventually be argued away, when the MX missile contract was finally reviewed. He had done nothing more than place a slight interference into the machinery of the satellites. But his action had always presupposed Rousseau dead.

Their timing had been so perfect: Now angry with himself, Church thought how brilliantly Hennessy had maneuvered. He had guessed that the exchanges would open on Monday, leaving the LTW investors a full weekend to make up their minds to sell. The exchanges' computers had started to function yesterday, but by the time they were thoroughly checked it was too late, and a decision was made to start business afresh on Monday morning. Hennessy would have his controlling stock, and Church his seat on the Board.

The President asked, "What about Niigata?" He addressed the question to Shimkus, head of Army Intelligence. Frowning, the President wanted to communicate his extreme displeasure. He would not mention the mismanagement of Elliman's arrest. If they resolved this crisis, he would ask the Pentagon to censure its own. He would have come down harder on Shimkus, he thought, if the Intelligence head had not partly redeemed himself. Shimkus and his agents had fanned out after Elliman's death, and they had found Niigata. They had followed him from Boston, and Niigata had led them to Washington.

"We're interrogating him now," Shimkus replied quietly, badly shaken by the news of Rousseau. Shimkus glanced at Church, who lowered his eyes. "The story he's given so far doesn't wash," he said to the President, trying to concentrate. "But . . . but eventually he'll talk."

"Eventually," the President almost shouted. "We don't have an eventually."

"I understand that, Mr. President. We're doing everything possible."

"We must assume that he works for the Russians," the President half asked, half stated.

The *Russians,* Church thought, alarm now freezing his mind. Why hadn't he been told? He looked at Lapham, who peered at him with the smallest hint of a grin. Lapham knew, Church thought, and he was waiting patiently for Church to hang himself. "Sir," Church blurted out, "Mr. President, did I hear you correctly? What did you say, 'the Russians'?"

Lapham answered in an even voice, looking at Church while he spoke. "Niigata was picked up outside the Soviet Embassy. Neither CIA nor Army Intelligence has background on him. But that affiliation is an assumption that we must make."

The Russians, Church thought again. He hated them with every fiber. Confused now, he asked, "But Niigata worked for Elliman—"

Lapham said, "We have not established a connection. Hopefully, Shimkus will be able to tell us something soon."

Church allowed the assumption. If Niigata had infiltrated Elliman's operation for the Russians, then he had the real formula. Hadn't the NSA's intercept reported the transmission of the formula from an unidentified terminal? "Has NSA determined anything yet about the intercept?" he asked, looking at Lapham with loathing. Church had been intentionally kept from valuable information that would have altered his decision to help Hennessy.

"It went from Thornton's house to Elliman's headquarters," Lapham said. "Stark told me that."

"So it *was* the real formula," Church said, realizing how fully he had betrayed his country.

Lapham shook his head. "Stark said he altered it. What was sent to Elliman can never be used against the country. Stark guaranteed me. He bluffed, hoping to get the girl back. And later, he erased the formula at Thornton's."

The President asked, "Ben, you briefed me this morning on this, but one thing isn't clear: Could this Niigata have received the real aspects of the formula from Thornton?"

Lapham shook his head. "Definitely not. The Japanese and Elliman could not have known that Stark used Douglas Thornton's terminal to transmit the faked formula. As far as they were concerned, Thornton had nothing whatsoever to do with the formula itself."

"Then what was the connection?" the President asked edgily.

"The girl, and I doubt if Elliman realized her grandfather was helping Stark."

"Why bother to kill him, then?"

Lapham answered, "We don't know, although we hope that Niigata will be able to tell us."

The President turned to Shimkus. "Work on him," he said, waving his hand in a gesture of dismissal. Then he turned to Ardy Sullivan, the White House press secretary. Sullivan had a bloated face that looked like it was about to explode, tiny features and a shining bald head. The President had asked him repeatedly to trim his weight for appearance sake. The President did not want the public to think that his press aide spent all his time stuffing his face in expensive restaurants, and Ardy had tried, but to no avail. "What are they saying in the press room?" the President asked.

Sullivan wiped an imaginary line of sweat from his neck. "They're taking it . . . well, in a confused manner," he said in a rich television-announcer baritone.

"Bullshit," the President retorted. "I can read."

"They're looking for somebody to hang the blame on, and this office is sort of their focus. They want to know why computers are so vulnerable."

"Were *allowed* to be so vulnerable."

"Yes, precisely."

"Well, by tomorrow their confusion will turn to anger. Bet on it. And when the press is afraid, we have wholesale panic. It's a progression we have to stop in the confusion stage. Tell them I'll talk for background at two tomorrow."

As the President outlined to Ardy what he should tell the press tonight, the door farthest from the President's desk opened. Accompanied by Colonel Stone, Stark entered the Oval Office. Trying not to be obtrusive, he took a seat against the wall and sat listening. The briefing he had received en route by radio from Lapham had put him in the picture.

The President glanced at Stark but did not acknowledge his presence. To himself the President thought: How young he is. The indirect cause of the crisis was a shiny-faced kid! In one sense that single fact pointed up why government and business leaders had been shortsighted about computer protection. Computers were the province of young men. They understood the machines, worked with them companionably, even liked them. The older generation, the leaders, felt just the opposite. They came to computers late, with apprehension and misunderstanding. Computer safety, the reason for this crisis, had fallen into a generation gap. "Before we go any farther," the President said now, "let's try to put this in perspective." He placed a cigar in his mouth and struck a match. "Milt, what about your bailiwick?"

Milton G. Cummings III headed the Council of Economic Advisers. Shrewd, experienced and rich, Cummings had been an investment banker at Lazard Frères before the President tapped him for the Council. Gray-faced, with bushy eyebrows, small, shy eyes and silver curly hair, Cummings looked weak and retiring. Yet any businessman who ever tried to act on that assumption was destroyed with devastating thoroughness.

"Mr. President . . ." Cummings paused, weighing his words.

"This thing's a snowball that's gaining velocity and volume. The Europeans and the Arabs are screaming their heads off. They think we *planned* this. The French are accusing us privately of *legerdemain.*" The French, he thought, could always be relied on in a crisis to act like schoolgirls. "Particularly in relation to the banks and the stock exchanges. They think we've blocked their funds, and they've implied—or I've inferred, at least—that if we get out of this bind, they'll move their capital; that's around $400 billion. Bluff, of course, but you will have to reassure them personally."

He would do that immediately after the meeting broke up, the President thought. "What about our own bind here at home?"

"I was getting to that," Cummings replied. "The snowball is rolling. Remember, two major banks and the New York Stock Exchange were out of service for three and a half days this week. After a half day's normality, things start going screwy. If we don't straighten this out by Monday morning, the country will be on the verge of psychological collapse. When that occurs, confidence will vanish. In this peculiar circumstance, the money will be there but access won't exist. Put simply, people can't give IOU's for gas, for food, for medicine, for everything they pay for with cash and credit cards, daily and hourly. Because of computers. The speed and access and facility of our economy rests on them. Without computers, we teeter and start to topple; at the very least, we can't cope. That, sir, is what's happening."

The President said, "Let's go back to where we—"

"Sir?" said a meek voice from the back of the room. The men, some who already had spoken and some who had not, turned. Lapham got to his feet, waving Stark to join their group, saying, "Please, this is Dr. Rousseau." No further introductions were made as Stark shyly crossed the carpet, all eyes riveted on him. There was not an extra chair around the President's desk, and one wasn't brought forward, so Stark remained standing. He folded his arms in front, wondering if he had been rude to interrupt the President.

The President leveled his eyes on Stark, again trying to get his measure. A genius, the President thought. Never trust genius because it could be as dangerous as it was beneficial. The President believed in persistence and hard work, attention to detail and an awareness of the whole. Genius was mercurial and could not be relied on. Geniuses were flaky, fuzzy people. When the going got tough, they raised their hands to heaven and blinked. They could not help what they were, the President thought, but that kind of brilliance was still a terrible affliction. "You were saying, Dr. Rousseau?" the President asked.

Stark put his hands in his pockets and fixed the President with a stare. "I have three succinct points. First, my formula is being used. Either through lack of hardware or intelligence, the people involved are not employing its full range of power. They are taking out individual systems. The formula was designed to destroy all those systems on line with the satellites *at once.* If my guess is right, they are testing, which explains its partial use. A further explanation centers on the timing of an eclipse. Tomorrow, precisely at noon, the summer solstice begins. The solstice provides a maximum eclipse of sixty-five minutes, during which all INTELSAT's transponders are inoperative. During that period of time the formula can be inserted, followed by a massive data burst. That will cause the infection of all systems on line with the satellites. The people with the formula are waiting for the eclipse, in my opinion."

The President and, indeed, all the Emergency Committee, listened intensely. The President spoke first: "You said 'hardware or intelligence.' Do these people have what it takes?"

"They know enough to experiment with it," Stark replied. "So the assumption must be that they have what it takes. Originally I predicted that no one could decipher the program, but regrettably I was wrong."

"What do you recommend, then?"

"My second point, sir. I may be able to locate the emanation point. I can't make any guarantees. If Lapham gives me permission to use those computers in the Pentagon that have not already been tainted, there is a remote chance of finding where they are. It is remote. I must stress that."

"A trace?" Lapham asked.

Stark nodded. "I managed something similar when I located the origin of the blackmail threat. The important difference now is the mode of communications. Elliman used land lines, and they were easier to identify and locate. These people now are obviously using INTELSAT. It may well be impossible, but I'll try."

"Any objections, Lapham?" the President asked.

Lapham shook his head. "The equipment is all his."

"Then I suggest you get started."

Stark stood where he was. "Sir, I have one further point. It may be nothing, and I hope it is nothing, but it should be mentioned. When I was researching the design of a filter for the new series of satellites, I ran across an item that may come into play now. The primary fire control of our Minuteman force, as you probably know, is communicated through land lines. So, too, is the secondary . . ."

"And the third backup . . ."

"INTELSAT."

The President turned to General Church, who had not yet spoken. "Can you confirm that?"

Church searched his memory. "The satellite link exists, sir," he said, finally. He passed the question back to Stark. "How that connects to the formula, I can't say."

Stark picked it up. "Neither can I, sir, because consideration of that element was not part of my original research. Perhaps we can never know."

"Until it happens."

Stark nodded, repeating, "Until it happens."

"What odds would you give?"

Stark thought for a moment, then replied, "Millions to one. You see, sir, when the burst goes through the satellites, there is a spillover effect. It will take out the systems on line, but in the instance of the fire-control systems, they are on *third* redundancy through INTELSAT. Most likely it will have no effect whatsoever."

"Even at millions to one, we can't take the risk," the President said without hesitation. He turned to General Church. "The hunter-killers are ready for launch. I suggest we put them up without delay. Even if our defensive posture is weakened for a matter of hours, we are safer than if we wait."

General Church began to perspire at the thought of what he had done. It was not supposed to happen like this. Hennessy had guaranteed him. It was not fair, he thought, starting to panic. It just was not fair that a simple solution to his personal problems should balloon into such a threat. Yet he had no real choice now but to admit to the truth. "Mr. President, there may not be time."

After he explained, the room erupted in chaos.

SUNDAY, JUNE 21, 1987

". . . the battle for technological supremacy ultimately in the eighties and nineties will be won by that nation, whether the Soviet Union or the United States, possessing the more sophisticated computer systems."

DR. K. S. G. ROVNO
The Lenin Institute
<u>Izvestiya</u>, *February 2, 1980*

2:30 A.M., *EDT: Washington, D.C.*

Niigata was naked, the bones of his hips jutting against the taut skin as he sucked in his abdomen and strained against the webbed straps around his waist and thighs. Wired for pain, raw copper leads were taped to his scrotal sac and his rhinal cavities. A third wire was inserted in his anus and rested against his prostate. With every metered jolt of electric current, he swam in a sea of agony, beneath the surface, somewhere between life and death. The single lucid thought in his mind was the desire for death, for release from this horrible pain. But he knew they would not provide him with that luxury, not unless he told them what they demanded to know.

The white tiled room had a powerful light overhead and smelled of sweat, fear and pain. Shimkus took a mint from his pocket and placed it on his tongue. This was textbook torture learned from the British with the IRA in Northern Ireland. Time and body weight were the only important considerations if the subject was not to be lost. The body weight determined the time of application and the force of electricity. Men's bodies and minds were remarkable, Shimkus thought. They had started on Niigata with small bursts of current, and the body had protected itself, requiring them to increase the time and the voltage. Shimkus knew the limit of what the Japanese could take and stay alive. Despite his small size, the man was a bull.

Eventually, even bulls broke.

"Again," Shimkus said to a technician in the room, who pressed a celluloid trigger, then concentrated on a voltometer. Detached, Shimkus watched as Niigata's body flailed against the straps in spastic jerks. His face contorted as his lips curled back against his teeth. "Hold him there," Shimkus said, counting the seconds on his watch. Five, twelve, eighteen, twenty. "Stop." Niigata's body fell against the surface of the table, and his lungs heaved.

Shimkus calculated. Niigata was barely alive now, and therefore ready. Shimkus placed his mouth close to the man's ear. The technician moved from the switch to a tape recorder, then he adjusted the microphone that hung on a wire above Niigata's head.

"Name!" Shimkus demanded.

Barely a second passed. "Niigata," he muttered.

"Rank!"

"Captain." Niigata's voice was soft and dreamy, that of a man talking in his sleep.

Shimkus had made the correct assumption. Now, he thought, let's find out what he does. "Directorate!"

"Third," came the reply.

Wet work, Shimkus thought, the unexplained killing of Douglas Thornton coming partly into focus. He pushed that thought from his mind. The old man's death was irrelevant to what they needed to know while Niigata lived. Shimkus was about to ask another question when he saw Niigata turn a muddy gray. "Cardiograph," Shimkus shouted to the technician. "Don't lose him."

"Flat. He's fibrillating."

Shimkus ran to the door and yelled. Instantly two doctors in green surgical gowns pushed in a crash cart. One of the doctors filled a syringe with 25 cc of adrenalin, then gripping its base hard in his fist he plunged it directly into Niigata's heart, depressed the valve and threw the needle to the floor. With both hands the second doctor pressed rapidly with his full weight on the man's chest.

"Give me a reading," the doctor said to the technician.

"Flat."

The pallor of Niigata's face deepened as the doctor continued the massage. Fifteen seconds passed. "Keep reporting," the doctor demanded. Then to Shimkus, "I think we've lost him."

"You can't!" Shimkus shouted.

As suddenly as his heart had stopped, it began again. "We've got him by a thread," the technician reported.

Shimkus knew that he had mere seconds, and he yelled into

Niigata's ear as though to sear the question on his brain: *"Who Is Your Control?"* He straightened up, placing a palm on Niigata's forehead.

The mouth of the Japanese began to work silently, then the words formed.

"Borznoi . . . Domintrin . . ."

Blood poured from a rupture in his nose and frothy pink bubbles foamed at his mouth.

"Scorched . . . earth."

"Reading?" the doctor asked.

"Flat."

The doctor said, "We won't get any more. He's dead."

7:30 A.M., *EDT: Washington, D.C.*

Artificial intelligence, the offshoot of computer science that by itself had created a new proof of a Euclidean theorem neater than Euclid's own, that identified faces, fingerprints and voiceprints, that competed in chess tournaments at a nineteen level, that taught other machines, drawing from volumes of data that were a partial sum of human knowledge—artificial intelligence was the key, and Stark sought its help here in this palace of digital equipment, the main facility in the Pentagon. Stark looked around him. The Labs' facility was a log cabin compared to this mansion, he thought. The machines were a computerized Olympic track on which he now had to race for solutions—ultimately, he hoped, to break through a barrier of theory that no man had ever approached alone. If Stark was ever to succeed, if there was ever a need, it was now, he thought, surveying the hardware, the beautiful hardware: the prototypes, the hybrids, the intertwined experimental-and-proven—all these hunks of metal and plastic linked together in the most powerful logic-machine anywhere in the world. With his brain and with artificial intelligence, he would create the software, the instructions that, he prayed, would make the machinery, all of it, talk. And what would it tell? The point of emanation of the formula. He was a hunter now. The time of the hunt would not be great; he had advised Lapham of that fact. Within several hours, Stark would either identify the source or . . .

After he entered this realm, he asked to be alone. Others, bystanders, advisers, consultants—they would only distract him. And now he had to squeeze every irrelevant thought from his mind, to focus with a clarity that even he had not attained, not even when he had formulated the damnable cause of what he now searched to reverse. Essentially, he thought, he had to find a precise electronic signature, but in this instance it was a location, not pure data—although the discovery route was similar.

He stepped into the horseshoe, a shallow U. To his right was a digital communications console for feeds of pertinent data; that console was connected miles distant with two of the largest parabolic reflectors anywhere. One was the Defense Systems Command's uplink to the Minutemen silos; the other was backup. He moved the chair and requested RAVEN, the artificial intelligence mode locked in the Labs' Honeywell. RAVEN had a voice-language function, which on remote could not be used. That was unfortunate, he thought, but not so bad; RAVEN would "advise" him on VDT.

Placing his fingers on the comm-order digits, he wrote: "KP 182 START. HELLO RAVEN." He heard a "clunk-cheep" from the console's small speaker and knew that RAVEN was waking up. Just as he relaxed his hands, the VDT above the center terminal lighted: "KP ZERO 44. HELLO. THIS IS RAVEN."

"PUT ON YOUR THINKING CAP, RAVEN; TRIGGER STORAGE FOR REVIEW."

Clunk-cheep. "KP SCAN O–INFINITE. WE CATCH THIS MORNING MORNING'S MINION."

"COMMENCE SCAN. FIRST THROUGH FIFTH SIDEBANDS, FREQUENCIES $(f_c + 5f_m)$ AND $(f_c - 5f_m)$." While RAVEN searched, he swiveled the chair from the comm module and concentrated to the left of the *U* on the function control of calibration. There were literally thousands of earth stations in CONUS (Continental United States); some of them were huge, like the Systems Command's, and some, primarily for corporate use, were no larger than a home movie screen. In order to connect with INTELSAT, a complex dish was required, nearly on the order of a radio-astronomical transceiver. He instructed the calibrator: "QUATERNARY PHASE SHIFT KEYING (QPSK)," then gave the approximate dimensions and ordered the parameters shifted to the computer. While that function searched, he faced straight ahead, toward the keyboard and VDT. The geographical coordinates were crucial: If instructed to spread wide, precious time would be lost; if too narrow, the scan would miss the emanation point. From memory he judged the exact shadow or "print" of INTELSAT's downlink transponders; the same area applied to uplink range. He typed on the keyboard, the largest of the three: "SET GEO SCAN 122 DEGREES 27 MIN LONGITUDE WEST INCL 71 DEGREES 8 MIN LONGITUDE EAST, CLOSED 37 DEGREES MIN LONGITUDE SOUTH INCL 51 DEGREES 19 MIN LONGITUDE NORTH. READY COMMENCE SCAN. STAND BY."

Clunk-cheep.

Stark looked right. "RAVEN, RECORD VDT," he wrote, "SUMMARY ONLY—STORE TOTAL IN CDC 9000 CALL INDICATOR 51 02 00 37/9."

RAVEN responded, "SEARCH COMPLETE, TEST *SPADE* 36 —MHzPSK." RAVEN had narrowed the bandwidth with astounding speed. If RAVEN had not missed signal candidates, Stark now had the crucial element: The uplink trajectory averaged and narrowed from the infested systems. RAVEN had found the invisible "wire" down which the computer could search within the geographical parameters. He typed, "NICE JOB, RAVEN—CONTINUE SEARCH TO CONFIRM AND REFINE BANDWIDTH."

Clunk-cheep. The comm VDT went blank.

Stark hastily rolled left. The calibration data blinked impatiently on the VDT.

$$\frac{E_b}{N_o} \le \frac{2(R/W) + 1}{R/W} \text{ MAX PHASE DEVIATION } \Delta_{\infty M}$$

The scans were in place. Now it was his turn to write the instructions for the scan to commence. Any *single* incorrect instruction would have a negative quantum effect on every previous and subsequent instruction. He lay his fingers lightly on the keys, half closing his eyes and breathing in deeply; as with ALPHA rhythms, he willed his heart to pump at a reduced rate, forcing *his* organic systems to focus internally. This was the moment when every minute of his life, every scrap of learning, every bridge of intelligence had to peak. He had to pour his total self into the instructions if the larger and faster digital brain were to function at *its* peak.

```
"GET EDIT (SECRET) (A(48)):
DO K+ 1 TO 48 BY 2;
I  =  INDEX  (ALPH,  SUBSTR  (SECRET,  K,
1));

J  =  INDEX  (ALPH,  SUBSTR  (SECRET,  K  +  1,
1));
SUBSTR  (SECR,  K,2)  =  ENCODE  (I,  J);
END;"
```

The CDC 9000 absorbed the instructions, searching for logic flaws.

"MORE," lighted up on the VDT.

Stark depressed the keys.

```
"UNSPEC (SECR) = UNSPEC(SECR)&REPEAT
('10111111'B,47);
M = 0;
DO 1 = 1 TO 10;
```

```
"IF ((SUBSTR(TEXT, J,1) = ' ')&M<80))
THEN DO;
M = M = 1;
SUBSTR (MESS, J, 1) — SUBSTR(SECR,M1);
END;"
```

Again he waited for the CDC 9000's logic scan. As he did, a sound, a human sound, registered in his mind. It was far in the distance, soft and unrecognizable. He turned his mind from it. A distraction, an irritant . . .

The CDC 9000 responded on the VDT, again, with "MORE."

This was the last, thought Stark—the final instruction before the hardware took over:

```
"GET EDIT (MESS) (A(48));
DO J = 1 TO 48;
Y = SUBSTR(MESS, J,1);
UNSPEC(Y)=UNSPEC(Y)CUT,'010000000'B; PUT
EDIT (Y) (A(1));
END;END."
```

Stark's breathing quickened now as he waited while the CDC 9000 examined, then bypassed millions of data bits, coordinating and collecting before following its instruction to transmit through the earth station to INTELSAT, where the transponders would provide a trace. They had no memory components, of course, but they could be shifted in line electronically, thereby producing a digital image, similar to the lifting from glass of fingerprints invisible to the unaided eye.

The sound was louder. Stark got out of his chair and walked around the banks of whirring disk drives. Near the door, Colonel Stone, who had stayed within sight of Stark every minute since their return from Barbados, was saying something under his breath to Peter Shimkus. Stone waved Stark aside. "I'll take care of this," he said, then opened the door. He blocked access to the facility with his body, then said, "He isn't to be disturbed. Now move it."

Shimkus ignored the order. But when he tried to move toward Stark, Colonel Stone grabbed his arm. "I have my orders," he said.

"And so do I," Shimkus said. He waved a manila folder in Stone's face. "There is something in here he must see."

Stone looked at Shimkus, then at Stark. Finally making his decision, Stone escorted Shimkus to Stark's side and watched the man from Army Intelligence with tense anticipation.

Shimkus pulled a photograph from the folder. "Do you recognize this face?" he asked Stark.

Stark examined the picture. The face was intelligent and sensitive, almost feminine, he thought, but it was totally unfamiliar to him. He handed it back. "Who is it?"

"The name's Domintrin, Vasily Domintrin. The KGB sent him from Moscow."

Stark's expression went blank. He had heard . . . no, read the name before. He tried to remember where, in what context. It had been a technical paper, of that much he was certain. Computers, definitely. Then it came to him. Domintrin, the developer of the Soviet Union's advanced EDP program. He was brilliant; a scientist of distinction. Stark felt a chill on his spine. If Domintrin had the formula in his control, he could cut through the theory and make it work. Domintrin was one of the "few" whom Stark had mentioned. He fit the category of brilliance and experience, probably better than anyone else in the Soviet Union. "I know his reputation," he said to Shimkus.

"And this one?" Shimkus asked, handing him another photograph.

Stark looked carefully. The photograph was out of date, taken perhaps five years ago, and the man was in military uniform, but the face was unmistakable. "Dr. McColough," he whispered, the awareness dawning. "Douglas Thornton's assistant."

"Alexi Borznoi," Shimkus said. "A colonel in the KGB, head of the North America Section."

"So that's how," Stark began to say, then he noticed that Shimkus did not understand. "This . . . Borznoi, you say, was working with Thornton on IUSUC projects. He was *in* his house." How foolish he had been. How easy he had made it for the Russians. Had Thornton known all along? No, Thornton was no traitor. He'd been duped, then killed once his usefulness was gone. "Thornton had nothing to do with the Russians," he said.

"That's irrelevant now, totally irrelevant," Shimkus remarked. "What pertains is the absolute fact that the Russians have the formula and the capacity to make it work."

Stark nodded solemnly. "Which leads us back to this," he said, turning in the direction of the computer terminals. "Unless this works for us, we have nothing left."

He had said it all, he guessed, watching Shimkus leave. Returning to the terminal, Stark checked his calculations mentally, wondering if he might have issued too many instructions, or too few. Had he made some small mistake in the trace program that had gone unnoticed, even by the superior logic of the CDC? It was impossible to tell. Where he was now, theory interfaced with the unknown.

Stark and the colonel continued their vigil over the machines as the logical components worked to discover the location. The computers were sorting millions of possibilities, narrowing and refining. Perhaps it couldn't be done. Even the Pentagon's EDP had limitations.

For something to say, something to take their minds off the consequences, Stark asked the colonel, "What will they do to Church?"

Colonel Stone shrugged. "Maybe a court-martial, but I doubt it. They'll drum him out certainly and see to it that he can't pick up the pieces."

"Why . . . why did he do it?" The sabotage of the new satellite series had sealed their fate. To check the large assemblies would take more time than they had. And if they were to send them up, they had to be certain of their destroying the old satellite series.

Stone did not want to talk about it. "Greed," he answered laconically. "He didn't think there was any harm."

"You don't believe that, certainly," Stark said.

"I guess I don't," Stone said, then, "Listen, sometimes you do things assuming there won't be consequences, and things get out of hand, sometimes so fast you can't prevent them. Church isn't a murderer, really, or a traitor. He wanted you dead to help the country, and there was a matter of greed. He wanted his own, too. And he got caught. A bad apple," Stone said, "it is as simple as that."

Stark was not as understanding. "Isn't there a chain of command, someone the agent could have confessed to?" Stark asked, wondering why anyone would have carried out Church's orders to sabotage the hunter-killers.

"You don't ask questions when a general gives an order. He was a major in Church's command. If he had appealed over his head, his career might have been destroyed. So he flew down to Florida and ripped into the hunter-killers. For all he knew, he was doing the patriotic thing. That's how we operate."

Suddenly the terminal hummed, starting up, about to reveal its answer.

"Here it comes," Stark said, excitement and anticipation in his voice. He and Stone bent over the VDT, waiting for it to light up.

The LED words announced their fate.

```
"DCL (S,R) FIXED BINARY (48):
NEGATIVE; NEGATIVE; NEGATIVE;
INSUF DATA; PARAM SCAN NEGATIVE;
END;END;"
```

9:00 A.M., *AT: Cap-Haïtien, Haiti*

In the Caribbean, the twentieth parallel slices an invisible line through Santiago de Cuba, Guantanamo and, across the narrow Windward Passage from Cuba, the quaint fishing village of Jean-Rebel on Haiti. From there it bisects the small uninhabited Île de la Tortue on one side and on the other, an ancient port. Centuries ago brigands lowered the Jolly Roger and anchored there, safe from those who would hunt them. And since that time, succeeding generations of the patois-speaking locals have tilled the soil and tended their goats and cattle decade after unchanging decade— with a slight variation in the summer of 1959, when the modern world visited the town, looked around and decided to stay. To the local residents' great curiosity, the Americans arrived in shiny Jeeps emblazoned with a word that they didn't understand: NASA. The Jeeps were followed by trucks from the capital and later by a ship that dropped anchor off the point.

Far from being outraged, the locals laughed when they saw what these strangers intended. The abandoned fort, such a familiar sight, commanded the heights of the outcrop that overlooked land and water for miles around. On the tallest parapet the Americans installed a gleaming white dish and pointed it toward the heavens. The strange totem neither made a sound nor moved; so within months, after the laughter had died down, it, too, was forgotten.

The Americans used the dish, they explained in simple terms to the mayor, to track the progress downrange of Redstone missiles that were said, according to the disbelieving mayor, to carry *humans.* During those first suborbital space shots, the locals looked intensely into the sky . . . and saw nothing.

When the NASA program ended, the tracking base was abandoned, but the dish remained and gleamed less and less with every year that passed.

By now the townspeople were accustomed to white-skinned strangers from the North. From time to time in the winter, tourists visited the fort and clambered over its crumbling parapets. They complained that the dish ruined the fort's ancient beauty, but the government did not listen and the dish stayed, protected by heavy canvas and a chain-link fence.

One white-skin who seemed to tolerate the dish was the old man who walked from his hacienda on the shore every afternoon to the fort, where he sat and read in the dish's round shadow. Then when the sun dropped to the west, he made his way home on foot. The locals hadn't seen much of the old man in recent years, but the hacienda, everybody in town knew, was kept ready at all times for his return.

The people of Cap-Haïtien humored the old man; he was kind to them and generous when their children were sick. The small hospital had been his donation. He rarely talked to anyone, unless you counted the bartender at the local bar, the Flore, which the old man visited every afternoon for a glass of orange juice and soda.

The old man had not returned for many months, but now, the whole town knew, something was about to happen. A small blue jet had landed yesterday at the asphalt strip near the police barracks just outside of town. The captain knew to call the hacienda and tell Jean Valois, the head caretaker, who had spread the news. The two men who had flown in the jet had told him: The old man was expected any day.

Valois had been watering the flowers in the beds in the front yard when the telephone rang. The captain said the two passengers needed a ride. Valois had turned off the water, then drove through town to the strip.

The guests were strange men, Valois thought. Not at all polite like the old man. They had sat silently in the back seat on the drive from the airport, then, halfway to the hacienda, had asked him to stop the car. One of them had opened the door. They were at the base of the old fort, and the man who had gotten out had looked up at the old dish, the white circle, and grunted. Why would he want to make a special stop to look at that thing? Valois had asked himself. It could be seen clearly enough from the hacienda! The guest had returned to the car. In a muffled voice, he had said something to his companion. On top of that—as if that weren't already strange enough—he had asked Valois to stop the car again, this time at the side of the old water tower. Finally, they had reached the hacienda.

A ruddy-complexioned, simple man, Valois took a proprietary interest in the hacienda. Beautiful and expansive, it had once been the vacation retreat of the country's former President, who had died more than a decade ago. The President had refurbished the old house, adding a wing of rooms, security fences and air conditioning. Then, when the old man bought it from the government, he added broad picture windows looking toward the Île de la Tortue, and on the land side, to the fort. But for all the house's grandeur, Valois had a special interest in the flower beds, which he cultivated with love. Normally, it would have been the duty of the kitchen maid to pick bouquets for the house, but Valois had put the beds off limits to everyone, except, of course, the old man, who rarely intruded.

Valois now clipped a final hyacinth bud and placed it in the overflowing basket. As he went around the house to the kitchen entrance he passed the large study window, the one with the view of the fort. They were in there, he noticed—the guests. And they were working! Valois shook his head. Americans did not know how to relax, he thought ruefully. They came to Haiti for the sun and the easy pace of life and yet they never enjoyed those things. The old man had even installed those machines, years ago, a tremendous number of them. At first, while they were being put in the room and connected, the machines caused great excitement among the hacienda's staff. Their use was a mystery, which the old man did nothing to explain, except to say that they were "computers."

C'est incroyable, vraiment incroyable, Valois mumbled to himself, entering via the kitchen screen door. They had barely slept since arriving, and yesterday, the thin man with the unfriendly face and the other guest, the refined, distinguished-looking one, had walked to the fort, Valois had thought at first, to enjoy its beauty. But even there, they didn't relax! They worked on the *dish,* climbing on it.

Americans, he fumed. An insane breed of people.

9:30 A.M., *EDT: Washington, D.C.*

Clunk-cheep.

Stark looked up, grimacing. In the hour of depressing inactivity since the CDC 9000 had delivered its verdict, he had forgotten to disengage RAVEN, which was dutifully carrying out Stark's instructions to narrow the frequency bandwidth. Without regarding the first console, he reached for the "off" toggle.

Clunk-cheep.

He grinned, admiring RAVEN's persistence, now pointless, a waste of artificial intelligence and time. Nothing remained but to wait for the shadow of the solstice to cross the satellite.

Clunk-cheep. Clunk-cheep.

Not persistence, he thought, lowering his arm, but insistence! RAVEN was trying to tell him something. He glanced at the VDT, then focused, stared . . . and shouted!

The VDT read:

"ERROR ON *SPADE;*
HOLD;HOLD;"

"What's it mean?" Stone asked. He came over and sat on the shelf beside the VDT.

"Having second thoughts, I hope." The minutes passed like hours as they waited, staring at the blank VDT. In the time since its last communication, RAVEN had searched and cross-referenced millions of frequency nuances, shadows, edges, interfacings—and in view of the sheer volume of data, a shift was probable. Stark balled his fists angrily. He should have considered that, planned on it, provided for it.

Clunk-cheep.

The VDT came to life.

"TEST ANVIL 36 MHZPSK;"

"ANVIL," Stark whispered to himself as he checked his own calculations; ANVIL's trajectory, its invisible wire, had an

extended range. The previous frequency undershot the accurate dimension, as a missile would skip aimlessly in the earth's atmosphere, its thrusters defying gravity, yet not permitting it to escape into deep space. He examined the pattern input called up on the VDT—the longitudes and latitudes. He expanded them by five degrees flat and entered them. He requested the same CDC 9000 search, using the identical program as before.

The center VDT hummed to life, and Stark pounded the shelf, instantly losing hope at the immediacy of the response. By his calculation the search would have to take the CDC a quarter hour, as before, or more. The timing was off! It had to be off, unless . . .

He wanted desperately to slap the hold-stop toggles, to do anything now that would tell the CDC to continue its search. The computer was giving up. He had miscalculated with RAVEN, the error being an assumption of time, that RAVEN would produce the correct frequency within minutes; and now he was assuming that the CDC would spend fifteen minutes in its search, while in fact only three had past.

The LED illuminated in green lines:

```
"DCL (S,R) FIXED BINARY (48);
19 DEGREES 59 MIN NORTH LAT;
HOLD;HOLD;"
```

Then:

```
"DCL (S,R) FIXED BINARY (48)
72 DEGREES 30 MIN WEST LONGITUDE;
END SEARCH; END SEARCH;"
```

Stark lunged for the phone. "Where is it?" he asked Lapham, giving the coordinates.

"It sure isn't the United States," Lapham replied off the top of his head. Then he went to the map in his office. Returning to the telephone, he mumbled, "Jesus—"

Stark looked at his watch. INTELSAT would enter the shadow's rim in little more than two hours. Yet they had some time, he exulted. They could still make it. "Where?" he demanded.

"Haiti."

9:15 A.M., EDT: Washington, D.C.

"Boy, I'll tell ya, young lady, ya sure *look* better," Harry said with a shy smile in Merrill's direction. "A little rest always does ya good."

They were together in a suite on the nineteenth floor of the Hay Adams hotel, not more than five hundred yards from the White House. Ever since her return from the island with Stark and the colonel, Merrill had been sequestered here, watched over by a solicitous Harry Verdeen, who, once he had completed his debriefing at the Pentagon, asked especially if he might take care of the girl. Lapham had liked the idea, agreeing readily. Even while Merrill was en route, Harry had been in the room, making a nuisance of himself with the staff by checking the security of the fashionable hotel.

Clutching the bathrobe around her, Merrill agreed mentally that she might feel as good as Harry said she looked if only Stark were with her now. They had been separated at Andrews Air Force Base, and she had not heard from him since.

Minutes ago, she had come into the living room of the suite after trying without success to sleep. Steady and predictable, Harry had ordered a pot of coffee from room service. Now, to pass the time, she joined him on the sofa and poured herself a cup, asking, "Are you sure the telephones are working?" The instant she asked, however, she realized. Soon after arriving here, she had used the telephone to call her parents in Millbrook, breaking the news to them of Grandfather Thornton's death.

Harry got her meaning, knowing how confused she must be. "Don't you worry none," he said soothingly. "He'll call when he has a minute. I gather they have him working pretty hard. They got a crisis on," he added, as if it were a television series.

The unfolding computer crisis, about which he had received scanty details, had little effect on Verdeen. During his debriefing, he had not been interested in anything but Wessel. Lapham had told him all he knew. Although Harry would never know for certain, in his mind he was convinced utterly that Wessel had killed Horace. Retribution, if only by accident, had been meted out. Wessel was dead; the score was even.

"Have they told you what's going on?" Merrill asked, certain that Harry was as much in the dark as she was.

Harry shrugged, "Not much, except they got a traitor over there in the Pentagon who sabotaged a satellite or something. Unless your boyfriend finds out where some people are trying to wreck our computers from, they all go flooey in a matter of hours, I guess." He turned around on the sofa to face her directly. "He's pretty smart, your boyfriend."

Merrill sighed and nodded. If Stark had not been so brilliant, none of this would be happening. Merrill sensed that Harry was thinking the same.

"Don't take this wrong, hear?" Harry asked. "But it looks like you've got some work cut out for yourself, as well. On him. You see, from what I know about people, sometimes smart folks are just flat-assed dumb. Sure, they can recite all of Shakespeare or figure out the most complicated problems, but all the same, they're dumb. The reason is, with all those smarts, there's no room for horse sense. They forget that everybody isn't as smart as they are, or smart in different ways—like those spies or whatever that are fooling with our computers. They probably can't hold a candle to your boyfriend, you know, in terms of IQ. But they were smart enough to get that formula from him. He didn't figure on that, and lookit the trouble it's caused. You got to teach him some horse sense, that's all."

Merrill understood his words all too well, but that did not

stop her feelings of love. She would work on Stark, subtly and with patience, she hoped. She opened her mouth to defend Stark as best she could, when the telephone on the table rang.

Harry picked it up on the first ring. "Yeah, hello," he said, glancing at Merrill and smiling. "It's him," he said, handing her the receiver.

"Stark, are you safe?" she exclaimed.

Stark's voice had an urgent edge in it. "Everything's going to be okay. I'm going over to the White House right now, and I may not be able to stop at the hotel. But you'll promise me to stay there with Harry?"

"Of course I will. But why can't you?"

Stark cut her off. "Merrill, please listen to me. Did your grandfather own a house in Haiti?"

"A hacienda," she replied without hesitation. "I haven't been there in years. Why?"

"There isn't time to explain. I want you to tell me everything you remember about the place. Everything."

Merrill thought for an instant. The painting over the mantel. It was a rambling old house on the beach in which he had invested large quantities of money. She described its location, the number of rooms, how it looked toward Cuba, the nearby fort. She couldn't remember much more and said so.

"Can you recall if it had a computer installation there?"

Computers were such a ubiquitous part of her grandfather's life, she had forgotten to mention it. "Don't ask me the details, but he installed, I think, most of the same machines he had in Boston. Even when he was on vacation, he got bored without them around. Is that important, Stark?"

"Very." He paused for a second to speak with Lapham, then continued, "I don't know what's going to happen, Merrill. Either Ben or I will be in touch as soon as we know something. In the meantime, promise not to let Harry out of your sight. I have to go now, Merrill," he said, about to hang up.

"Stark," she said in a worried voice, "I love you."

9:30 A.M., *PDT: Los Banos, California*

Neddie Vickers did not think he cared any longer about the consequences to his career. Saving his own pride now was worth infinitely more. And the humiliation he was suffering at the hands of Susie and Clinton Hennessy had become intolerable. He could not stand being under this roof, watching Susie flaunt herself around Hennessy. And their host, though pretending disinterest, acted differently behind Neddie's back. Neddie angrily jabbed his leg across the bed, feeling the coolness of the other side. Did they think him an utter fool?

Neddie had seen them together by the swimming pool and later, yesterday, playing tennis. When Hennessy spoke, she looked at him flatteringly. Sure enough, Hennessy had responded.

Last night at dinner, with all three sitting at the table, Hennessy had manipulated the conversation. Whenever Neddie had a thought to add, Susie would say, *"Listen* to Clint; he has much more experience. Neddie, your problem is you think you know everything." Why hadn't he slapped her across the face, as he had wanted?

Hennessy had been ecstatic since his return from Washington. The euphoria over the success of their plan had relaxed him enough to notice Susie. Neddie had done what Hennessy needed, and now that the acquisition of LTW was almost a fait accompli, he could throw him out. He did not have to play the country gentleman any longer.

Naturally, Neddie had retired early. He was exhausted, and he could not stand the two of them together for another minute. He left them giggling together in the living room, Susie curled up in front of the fire on the rug, and Hennessy lounging nearby on the sofa, a snifter of brandy in his hand. As he turned his back on them, Neddie thought: Tonight will be their night. He hoped only that Susie would spare him public indignity.

But she had not been that considerate. Susie had finally come to bed with him, but only for a short time, until she was satisfied that he was fast asleep. Then stealthily she had slipped from beneath the covers and left their room. All night long he had tossed and turned.

Now, as the morning light gleamed through the windows, Neddie took the pillow in his fist and threw it across the room. He swung his legs over the bed. Rubbing the stubble of his beard, he started for the bathroom. Suddenly there was a loud knock on the door. Before he could answer or put on a bathrobe, Hennessy burst in. Susie followed.

Neddie stared at them in disbelief. Susie's hair was disheveled, her makeup smeared. She looked whorish and silly. She made a sleepy yawn and one breast peeked from beneath a silk dressing gown. Hennessy had on pajama bottoms and stood breathing hard.

Neddie turned away from them in that instant, wagging his head sadly. "I'm not into threesomes," he said, as he went toward the bathroom.

"It's fallen out of bed," Hennessy said in a husky voice.

Neddie turned and laughed, pointing his chin at Susie. "You mean she has. I'm not surprised." He laughed again, this time a little louder and with more feeling. "What, did she meet somebody richer between your room and here?"

Hennessy looked around for the first time, and noticed Susie behind him. He gave her a disgusted look and pushed her back. "Get out of here," he said, then closed the door in her face.

Susie kicked the door open. Rage contorting her face, she yelled, "You fucker. You don't do that to me, ever." She stood there, her small hands clenched in fists.

Hennessy appealed to Vickers with his eyes. "Can you do anything about this?"

"It's all yours now, fella," Neddie replied, suddenly feeling better.

Susie spluttered and raged at Hennessy: "You don't take advantage of me like that, then treat me like a whore! Neddie, say something to him."

Hennessy had heard enough of her whining. He picked her up in his arms, carried her into the hallway and dumped her on the rug. He growled something at her, then came back into the bedroom, locking the door behind him.

"We've got trouble. That's what I was trying to say." He looked back at the door and said, "I'm sorry about that. For both our sakes."

The apology was not sufficient for Vickers. With a look of disgust he picked up his suitcase and set it on the bed. From the bureau he started to throw shirts and underclothes in the case.

In a severe tone, Hennessy said, "I'm telling you. The deal has fallen through." He could not understand why Vickers did not seem to care.

Neddie said, "Tough. But it's not my trouble, not anymore. I'm finished with you, Clint."

"You don't understand, General Church told the *President* about everything we've done. The SEC will be after me. I'll be out of business."

"And you didn't plan for that eventuality when you began?"

"Not the President."

"You'll be okay, Clint. You guys always come out smelling sweet." Then he thought about it for a minute and said, "And don't try to make me your dupe. If you try, I'll give the SEC details that Church couldn't even guess."

"I wouldn't do that," Hennessy said. "I need your help now, in covering this over." The telephone call from Church had come just a few minutes earlier; Church was in distress and Hennessy had not been able to hear the whole story. The general had told the President about the hunter-killers—but had Church mentioned Hennessy by name? Church did not remember; perhaps there was hope.

"We can say you were buying for somebody else," Hennessy said to Vickers in a pleading voice. "It's my word against Church's about the rumor. They can ruin me, Neddie, if they know I was the one buying the promissory contracts." He saw that Neddie was not listening. Neddie was the key, the only person who could make inevitable charges stick. "Please," Hennessy pleaded.

Neddie turned from the suitcase and looked at Hennessy for several long minutes as he formed a reply. He had Hennessy in a corner, and he could ask anything he wanted. Anything at all, if he only would lie to the SEC. There would be an investigation, and he would be asked to testify, under oath. What was the value of a lie? he wondered. He did not need Hennessy, and if he perjured himself on his behalf, his career could be finished. Hennessy had humiliated him by taking his woman. The big man, he thought sourly. The rich bachelor. He could have anything he wanted just by taking it. Except a lie.

Neddie breathed in deeply, then said, "Okay, Clint, I'm your man."

Their complicity again fully intact, Hennessy extended his hand to Vickers. After several seconds of silence between them, they threw back their heads in laughter—Vickers for a future that was assured, Hennessy for the enormous relief he felt.

10:15 A.M., *EDT: Washington, D.C.*

The President skidded the photographs across his desk. Taken fifteen minutes earlier with a high-resolution camera set inside a modified ATS-6 surveillance satellite that had hovered on station at twenty-two thousand miles above Cuba ever since the Soviet military buildup there in 1979, the prints showed Cap-Haïtien in minute detail, the fort and most clearly of all, the earth station, the round dish that almost seemed to sneer at the camera.

He had seen all he needed. His problem was now one of options. The advisers had gathered again in the Oval Office, and they had a dearth of viable ideas. And yet, the President thought, before another thirty minutes passed, he had to put a response in motion. The simple, direct solution, now, had been obviated by General Church. LTW and NASA technicians at Cape Canaveral were this minute working feverishly to make alterations in the satellites, but the general's interference had cost them as much as twelve hours. The hunter-killers still might be launched in time, but the President could not sit and wait for that eventuality. He had to act now.

What a joke "preparedness" was, he thought. Why, he wondered almost cynically, did America always seem incapable of responding with effectiveness and determination in a crisis? The fleets were *forever* steaming in circles thousands of miles from where they were needed that minute. Air strikes often took hours to mount, and the jets never seemed to have the necessary range. Helicopters failed. Transports crashed. Troops . . . *troops!* What a joke. Their commitment meant months, and by then the crisis was a memory.

"The hunter-killers," he said now. "I want to make absolutely certain of their launch, the minute they're ready to go."

The chairman of the Joint Chiefs of Staff, Admiral Dwight Hormer, a stolid, laconic career man in his early fifties, replied, "Those instructions have been transmitted, sir." His voice was clipped, almost a bark. Embarrassed by the failure of the military —General Church—he wanted everything the President needed to go exactly right. Nothing from here on in would fail. Hormer sounded more hopeful now as he outlined his option. "A F-4E Phantom can be over Cap-Haïtien in minutes, sir," he said. "Homestead Air Force Base is standing by."

The President asked the room, "Who heads the government down there now, anyway?"

The Secretary of State answered quickly: "Papa Doc's kid . . ." The Secretary briefed his leader quickly. "Baskethead, he's called . . . Jean-Claude—Jean-Claude Duvalier. His mother tells him what to do. Can't sneeze without her okay . . . stopped him from marrying a girlfriend a few years back . . . a real Mommy's boy. The kid's a joke, but in fairness, he's done some good. He took over when he was only a teen-ager, and he has partly revitalized tourism and the economy. That's something, anyway."

"Is he reasonable?" the President asked. He meant several

things at once: Could he be bought? Was he already in America's debt? What were his political alignments?

"Damned if I know," the Secretary of State replied. "His father wasn't cooperative, and I recall, the kid's less quick-witted. Reasonable, though . . . ? Haitians don't think so. The secret police, the Ton Ton Macoute, still thrives. We have cases tied up in our courts over the status of Haitian refugees—whether they deserve asylum."

"But will he listen to reason?"

"To *bomb* his country?" In different circumstances, the Secretary of State would have laughed. "Would *you*, Mr. President?"

The President scowled at the Secretary of State. "There *are* other options," he said.

"We can try him," the Secretary said.

Admiral Hormer interjected, "If he doesn't give us sanction, we'll have to act, anyway." He looked at the President, trying to reassure him with his eyes, if not with his words.

The President again drew the satellite photos in front. "It's in the middle of the town. Look . . ."

"One laser or TV-guided and it's gone." The admiral didn't need to see the photos.

"And if your pilot should miss, just for conversation's sake, Admiral?"

"Sir, we don't have a choice."

"We could drop commandos."

The Secretary of State said, "That may be very true, about not having much choice. But it's my duty to point out the pitfalls. Cuba is a few miles across the Windward Passage. If we bomb— or drop commandos—that close to Castro, the Soviets will raise hell. Diplomatically, this could blow up in our faces. . . ."

As the Secretary of State continued, the President leaned into the intercom and barked an order to the comm specialist in the White House basement—one of the Air Force majors who were on duty around the clock to reach anyone at the President's request at any time, in any part of the globe. "Let's see what the . . . what Duvalier has to say."

Stark sat on the sofa, speechless. This was the most important office in the most important country in the Western world, yet the conversation seemed to be going around in circles.

The President cupped the telephone and said, "Communications reports that Duvalier understands English, but he doesn't speak it," then: "Hello, Mr. President."

A translator in the basement interpreted the Haitian President's words of baffled greeting. Duvalier had never spoken to an American President. He hadn't even made an official visit to Washington. At first, when his aide told him that the President of the United States wanted him, Duvalier had thought it was a crank call. He had asked for confirmation, then ordered someone to bring his mother home—she was off touring a government hospital in Les Cayes.

Slowly and clearly, the President outlined the problem, punctuating his monologue from time to time with, "Do you understand?" He did not see the need to tell Duvalier the nature of the crisis in detail. There wasn't time, and he didn't want to confuse the Haitian leader with technical jargon. Finally, he asked the central question: Would Duvalier give America permission to bomb Cap-Haïtian?

The question was met by silence.

Finally, Duvalier spoke.

"You will?" the President exclaimed. "Mr. President, as a nation, we are grateful." He nodded "yes" to the men in the office. Relief spread on their faces.

Admiral Hormer stood up, preparing his return to the Pentagon, from where he would issue the order to the pilots at Homestead in Florida. The F-4E Phantom would be over the target in minutes; and without interference it could make a test run at the target before finally releasing the laser-guided ordnance.

The President listened to the translator, then gripped the receiver until his knuckles whitened. With his free hand he waved Hormer to stay. *"What?"* the President exclaimed. Then to the translator, "Did you get that right?" The President closed his eyes. "Well, how long will that take?" As Duvalier's reply was translated, the President said, "But I told you, we don't have days."

Duvalier repeated, "Désolé, Monsieur le Président! Je suis désolé, mais c'est comme ça! Je ne peut pas tuer mes enfants. Il faut que l'évacuer en avance. N'importe quoi."

The President continued, "But we can land commandos. Nobody but the people involved will be in jeopardy, I give you my word."

Duvalier gave his reply. It was no. Finally, he finished with, "Peut-être je peut vous donner un réponse plus positif quand . . ." He was going to say that he might answer more positively when his mother returned to Port-au-Prince, but he stopped at the last moment. ". . . quand j'ai parlé avec mon . . . mon Conseil d'État."

The President knew that he couldn't push the Haitian farther, so he thanked him rudely, then hung up. He looked at the room of expectant faces and said, "He's all for us bombing and dropping in commandos—but *after* Cap-Haïtien is evacuated, and that, he estimates, will take a full day. The most he'll do now is alert his militia in Cap-Haïtien." He looked at the Secretary of State. "He must have read your mind. If we go ahead without permission, he'll go to the Security Council and claim an act of aggression."

Especially now having been denied permission by Duvalier, any incursion would be an act of aggression. "We can talk our way out of it," the Secretary said to the President. "Our allies will understand, most surely, and nobody else, including the Russians, will get their feathers too ruffled."

"Intelligence," the President said, as though they should all understand. "Do we have time to insert a couple of people to find out what the Russians are doing there?"

The question had nagged at Stark, too. But he had said nothing. It would have made sense for Borznoi and Domintrin to seek safety directly in Cuba, except for one circumstance. Stark cleared his throat. When the President looked at him, he said, "Thornton had hardware in Cap-Haïtien. Once Domintrin sets up the equipment, they'll make a run for Cuba."

"That's what we have to find out." The President turned to

Admiral Hormer. "Do your personnel have the expertise to assess what they have down there?"

Hormer thought for a moment. "Someone could be found." But that, too, would take precious time.

Stark shook his head. Even if they could identify it, they could do nothing to dismantle the output components. There was nothing else to say but, "I'm the only person who can do that efficiently, sir."

The President looked at him, then got to his feet and jammed his fists in his coat pockets. When he spoke, he was finally decisive. "Admiral, I want our options in the air immediately. That means your F-4E, and I want a C-130 loaded with our Blue Light force. If and when, I'll give the order to go, and to hell with Duvalier and his *enfants.* But first, we have the time just to do this quietly and cleanly."

11:45 A.M., *EDT: At altitude, leaving the Continental United States*

Forty minutes after takeoff from Andrews Air Force Base, the two-seater F-15D screamed at Mach 2.2 through the thin air high above the Florida Keys. Forward of the broad delta wings in the front tandem pilot's seat, Colonel Stone worked out the coordinates for the Cap-Haïtien strip that DIA had just radioed—its length, estimated surface heat and wind direction. While helpful, the data were not about to guarantee anything.

Stark was belted into the systems operator's seat to the rear, nearly deafened by the whoosh of the fighter's two F100-PW-100 turbofans. He felt tense and slightly frightened. The environment of the shoulder-tight cockpit was alien, and he set his hands firmly in his lap, daring to touch nothing. He had given over total trust to the colonel whose helmet he could just see in front and below the ledge of the Perspex. The ground crewmen had strapped Stark in the seat and instructed him on the mechanics of the ejection system. That was all he needed to know. The colonel would handle everything else.

The jet, equipped with the most advanced avionics and Fast Pack auxiliary tanks, had been stripped to ferry weight for the flight. On takeoff, the colonel had snatched the gear only feet off the runway, then shot vertically to 36,090 feet before leveling at right angles and re-engaging the reheat to push the aircraft to its maximum Mach. Stark had been stunned to silence since then, and the colonel had said nothing yet to him on the intercom, although Stark could hear him talking to the ground. Minutes ago Andrews had communicated coordinates.

"Rousseau!"

Stark did not recognize his name at first.

"Wake up, Rousseau!" It was the colonel.

Stone had to gain Rousseau's confidence in the few minutes of idleness he now had available. The colonel was afraid his civilian would panic when they finally landed, and so, though he hated to waste his words like this, he tried to explain about the flameout of the F-15 and the final approach. "You ever see an elephant fuck a gnat?" He didn't wait for a reply. "If you haven't you will, in a few minutes. This rocket we're tied to has the glide profile of a brick. I'm going to flame out at four thousand with spoilers up and flaps down. If McDonnell Douglas didn't fuck up with a rivet or two, the airframe should hold. But it'll be real tight, okay?" Stark still didn't reply. "Just say something to let me know you're alive, huh?"

"I'm here," Stark said.

"All you're to do is hug yourself and unless I say otherwise, keep your hands off the ejector. Push that by mistake and you go down, get me? Not up. The pod you're in will be your coffin." The colonel gave a rasping laugh. "We'll come in like a flatiron. If we can't make the strip, I'll try like hell to reignite the turbofans."

Try as he may, Stark could not catch every word. ". . . Stopping," the colonel was saying. "That could be a bitch. I'll deploy a drogue, but we'll still tear all manner of shit out of the gear. We won't have use of reverse thrusters."

Stark had one question. "Is all this really necessary?" The approach and landing seemed a terrible risk, and to what end?

"The end of the strip is about three hundred yards from the dish, right? When the Russians hear the wail of the turbo fans they'll be warned, so we go in quietlike. There's no alternative." Without the element of surprise, they had nothing; with it, they still had little.

Fourteen minutes passed in silence. Below and to the right, the colonel saw the town of Baracoa on the northeastern tip of Cuba. As he reduced airspeed, the digital Machmeter became a blurred blue light. Seconds later, as they went subsonic, he reached down near his knee and depressed the air-brake controls and then pushed up the flap levers to "FULL." The jet's nose lifted slowly and the colonel felt the forward pressure of the safety belt and harness against his stomach and shoulders.

He looked over his shoulder at Stark. "We're at twelve thousand," he advised. "In five seconds I'll shut down the engines and we're going to drop. Cinch up your harnesses."

When he turned forward, he slid the throttles back, chopping the power. The F-15 hung aloft in eerie silence. Suddenly it shuddered. The colonel moved the control column, but the jet could no longer respond. Lights on the console flashed and a "stall" warning horn sounded. With amazing calm, he turned several electric switches for reserve hydraulic power.

The F-15 plummeted, first on its wing, then straight on its nose.

As their air speed built up, the heavy air beating against the extended flaps shook the fuselage violently. The sound of the vibration was thunderous. Stark grabbed the frame of the seat, grimacing as the harness cut into his shoulders. The fall seemed endless. . . .

Then, fixing his eyes on the instruments, the colonel hauled back on the control column. With his left hand he lowered the gear, which should have stabilized the jet but didn't. They were directly over the end of the strip at about a hundred feet, falling at the sink rate of a rock.

Colonel Stone felt beads of sweat roll down the furrows on

his forehead as he yanked back the control column, raising the F-15's nose, almost violently, then, in a back-and-forth motion, he pushed the control column full forward. The jet's rear wheels slammed onto the asphalt, and as the shock vibrations shot through the fuselage, his hands flew over the controls. He raised the air brakes on the wings and deployed the drogue, which gulped air and jerked him against the harness. He stood with all his weight against the rudder brakes: Behind the jet he heard an explosion: a bursting tire. The jet lurched to the right just as the nose wheel made contact. With every mechanical element except the thrusters engaged to stop the fighter, they were thrown forward in the cockpit. The colonel fixed his eyes on the end of the strip, which was closing on them fast, and he made an unconscious growling noise in his throat.

Twenty yards from the end, where the banana trees began, they skidded to a stop.

As the colonel grabbed at his harnesses, he said in the intercom, "Rousseau, unhook." Then he turned a small crank by his right foot, and the canopy opened a small crack with a whoosh of escaping pressurized air.

The colonel stepped in the footwells on the fuselage and jumped to the ground, waiting for Rousseau to follow. The colonel examined the F-15. It had rolled to a stop in loam in which the nose wheel was already sinking. He shrugged. Above them he heard the faint drone of engines, and he looked skyward. The F-4E was right on schedule, its contrails tracing a tight circle in blue. The pilot up there, he knew, was straining his eyes for the sight of a starburst signal from the ground and then he, too, would dive out of the sky, his electronic "back-seat" technician fixing on the white spot on his targeting screen.

A fleck of black to the west of the F-4E caught his eye. It was too far off to tell for certain, but the colonel guessed it was the C-130 with the men of Blue Light aboard.

The colonel hoped the force waiting on those wings would not be needed.

"Come on, Rousseau," he yelled again.

11:58 A.M., EDT: Washington, D.C.

Of this much the President was certain: What he had to do would be like accusing someone of a major crime when all the thief presumably knew was that he had stolen something very minor. If this was a procedure without much hope for success, it was nevertheless a step the President had to take. He was alert and as far as possible, confident as he walked briskly through the door of the Situation Room deep within the bowels of the White House.

The room itself was compact. Everything there had the single, immediate purpose to coordinate the defense of the country. The Pentagon had a much larger room, but this was the decision center, and therefore it was the most important area of square footage in America at times like this. It was bombproof, naturally, except for direct hits. While interior decorators made the White House itself into a historical showplace, they did not even see the Situation Room. Its walls were dull, eye-easing gray. The lighting was bright, so that shadows were cast off every piece of stationery equipment. The single "decoration," on the wall, was a display board, which, at the touch of a series of buttons, could schematically present the President with visual military options.

The best known item in the room was the Red Phone, the cumbersome telephonic transceiver fixed with a scrambling potential. The Red Phone connected the White House on a constant open and hourly tested line to the Kremlin. It was to the Red Phone that the President went now.

He nodded to the Army major who said, "He's waiting on the line now, sir."

The President pressed the telephone to his ear. He had decided the best approach was a direct one. There was neither time nor desire now for diplomatic courtesy. He introduced himself formally, then said: "You are endangering the health and security of both our countries, Mr. Premier, and I demand that you order your people to desist."

The Premier hesitated for several seconds, then in a voice

that seemed half serious, said, "Perhaps you will explain this . . . crisis."

"Your agents have acquired a formula intended to destroy the computer systems of America. What they do not know is that our Defense Systems Command network—our Minutemen—are on that same system. If they use the formula, the missiles might be launched. *Your* country, Mr. Premier, will be hit, but so, too, will ours."

In the Kremlin, the Premier took the telephone from his ear and spoke to advisers at his side. He knew about the various Scorched Earth plans—he and he alone had reviewed them—but nobody had said anything about missiles. Finally, after more than twenty minutes, he came back on the line, and his voice was changed. "Your fire control is land-line-based," he said softly.

So he knew about the satellites, and therefore about the formula, the President thought. "The tertiary backup for the fire control goes through the INTELSAT series. The data burst of the formula can spill over, and if it does, it can trigger the tertiary. Pray God it doesn't happen, but there is a chance it will unless you call off your people. We know where they are, and we are trying to stop them now, but we need your help. For both our countries' sakes."

Again, the Premier turned aside and conferred with his aides, of whom one was head of the KGB's First Directorate.

The President turned to a general at his side, the commander of the Situation Room. He had the responsibility to maintain the equipment and replace outmoded technology with new. "Can we display it for them?" he asked.

The general reached for a nearby telephone. "Put it through," he said. The line was connected to the Pentagon.

Lapham had had the foresight to know that the Kremlin would need proof, no matter how flimsy, and he had prepared the fire-control schematics for INTELSAT from the Pentagon's manuals for transmission. These detailed drawings and plans were now sent instantly the thousands of miles to the Kremlin's similar Situation Room.

The Premier came back on the line. "I do not need your evidence, Mr. President," he said. "My advisers here say what you claim to be possible, and that is all you allege, the possibility. Naturally, it is unacceptable."

"Then you will call off your agents. One is a scientist named Domintrin; the other"—he referred to a sheet of paper on a clipboard—"is Borznoi, of your First Directorate. As you know, they are now in Cap-Haïtien, Haiti."

"We know no such thing!" The Premier said, alarm ringing in his voice. Scorched Earth, as a designation, had no fail-safe. It was to be executed with no possibility of callback, and part of the operatives' mandate was to carry out the assignment without continually checking progress and moves through the KGB's chain of command. The Kremlin and the First Directorate not only were unaware of Borznoi's present location, they also had no means of reaching him.

12:33 P.M., *EDT: Deep space, above the Continental United States*

The apogee motor whined, but nobody heard; nobody for thousands of miles could hear, as an electronic signal streamed into the guidance "memory" and a small spray of hydrazine coursed from the storage tank along 3 feet of stainless tubing to the 5-pound thruster. The hydrazine squirted into space and moved the hunter-killer in a lateral orbit at the precise speed of 10.6 miles an hour. The hunter-killer floated for 8 seconds before a 1-pound thruster, on the satellite's "earth" side, further decelerated the 300-pound astral complex to less than 1 mile an hour. By now it was about to kiss the satellite's solar "sail," and with another quick squirt of hydrazine, it stopped dead—22,000 miles above the center of the continent.

Another signal reached the killer, and a small tongue of electronic flame licked a detonating cap embedded in 400 pounds of plastic explosive contained inside an oxygen-rich tank deep within the hunter-killer's gut.

No human heard and no human saw the bright orange flash as the hunter-killer exploded, tearing the first INTELSAT into particles of metal and plastic. The pressure of the blast sent both dismembered satellites, the hunter-killer and INTELSAT, speeding for an infinity of time into deep space.

The shadow of the eclipse, meanwhile, sped like light toward the remaining satellites in the INTELSAT series.

12:36 P.M., *AT: Cap-Haïtien, Haiti*

As they half ran, half walked through the center of the town, Colonel Stone reviewed his assignment. Under no circumstances was he to risk the safety of Rousseau and, by inference, himself; but he was to facilitate Rousseau's access to areas that Stark thought necessary. Rousseau was to check out the technology visually, and from that he would determine the Russians' potential. If what the colonel surmised turned out to be true, he would call in the F-4E and, if he judged them necessary, the Blue Light force riding the C-130. He adjusted the musette bag slung on his shoulder and turned to see that Rousseau followed.

At this hour the sun beat straight down on the town, and most of its inhabitants huddled sleepily in the shade of wood and rock-walled buildings. Stark looked in the eyes of several whom they passed. It was too hot even for mild curiosity. A scrawny dog emerged from the shade, sniffed the air and then retreated without a sound.

Duvalier had said that he would alert the militia in Cap-Haïtien, but the order, if given at all, had not yet been received, for there was no sign anywhere—even at the airstrip—of their presence. It was just as well, thought Stark. They would ask questions, and their interference would stir the interest of the townspeople.

Cap-Haïtien wasn't large enough to have an outskirts. But as they moved toward the beach now, the shops and markets were spaced at greater intervals. A few hundred feet farther and they passed beneath the big stilted water tank that they had used as a directional landmark from the airstrip. Before leaving Washington, Stark had examined the high-resolution satellite photographs of Cap-Haïtien, and he knew now, with the sighting of the tower, that they were within two hundred or three hundred yards of Thornton's hacienda.

He looked up at the tank and suddenly stopped. "Hold it," he said to the colonel, who turned back and gave him a questioning look.

The anomaly was almost breathtaking. Bracketed to the wood staves of the tank above the utility walk, a small microwave antenna peered, like a Cyclops' eye, into the distance. Haiti had telephonic communications, but surely the volume of calls could easily be handled by land lines. Unless the government had the foresight to get the jump on future growth, microwave transmission was an alarming waste of money and technology.

"I think we should do something about that," Stark said, pointing to the antenna.

The colonel checked his watch nervously. They had a quarter hour remaining before he had to decide whether to commit the F-4E, and he was far more anxious about the hacienda than this sideshow. He noticed that the metal ladder on the tank's stilts reached no more than a hundred feet to the utility catwalk. "I'm heading for the house," he said. "Do what you want here. Remember, it's the big dish on the fort we're worried about. But hurry!"

Stark watched him disappear, then swung up on the ladder's first rungs. As he climbed, he again questioned the existence of the transmitter. A microwave antenna worked on the principle of line of sight. It had to be aimed at a receiving antenna, and the accuracy of the aim was everything if a transmission was to work.

If the Haitian government had installed it, why hadn't they put up a warning sign for the locals, or at least removed the ladder? When activated, the antenna could be dangerous, and none of the local people could know that. It was incredibly careless, he thought.

Stark easily reached the utility catwalk. From that vantage, he looked back toward the airstrip. Five or so men in police uniforms circled the F-15. In the other direction, he saw that the colonel had neared the hacienda and was crouching near some banana trees off the edge of the dirt road leading up to the house. Last, Stark glanced toward the fort. When they had approached the airstrip in the F-15, he hadn't thought to look. But now he took a couple of seconds to inspect the big earth-station parabola, NASA's tracking dish, their main objective. The F-4E could not miss.

He edged along the catwalk, avoiding the front of the microwave antenna. He had to reach up to grab its smooth edge, then he pulled with all his strength against the brackets holding it to the water tank. It moved, first an inch, then two, then four. Those few inches, he reckoned, would throw the accuracy of transmission off target by as much as several hundred yards. Whatever its purpose had been, the microwave was now rendered useless.

As he climbed down the ladder, he tried to orient himself; he wondered why the microwave had been aimed to the northwest.

Colonel Stone surveyed the front of the hacienda from his hiding place in the clump of vegetation. He glanced over his shoulder toward the water tank. Rousseau was climbing up the catwalk. "Come on," Stone said impatiently to himself. That thing on the tank was a diversion, and he could not understand the professor's interest.

Stone rose from his crouch. There was nothing in the least unusual happening around the house. The colonel ran through a flower bed to the side of the hacienda. He squatted beneath a window on the landward side and peered in. A native was setting a long table in a dining room and behind him, a local woman in a bright red dress worked at a stove stirring a large pot with a wooden spoon. God, he thought. It was all so normal that he had to wonder if they had not made a tragic miscalculation. Perhaps this scene was only a decoy. Perhaps they had been set up by Borznoi, who was right now in Cuba.

Almost casually now, he unstrapped the musette bag and removed its contents. He extended the antenna of the compact but powerful transceiver, then tested the batteries by pushing the squelch button. It worked perfectly. He removed a foot-long tube. The starburst flare would serve to signal the pilot of the F-4E. But he doubted if any of this equipment was going to be necessary. As the seconds passed he became more and more convinced that they had been faked. Borznoi and Domintrin might have stopped here, but they had gone to Cuba.

"Fuck," he said to himself, starting to rise.

It happened so fast only the glint of sun off a metal surface crossed his vision. The hand holding the knife whipped over his shoulder and closed on his throat. A grunt of determination and surprise turned to a gurgle as the blade severed his windpipe, then his carotid. An arc of arterial blood drenched the musette bag and radio.

Reconnoitering the house, Stark came upon the copse of banana trees where he had last seen the colonel from the water tower. He knew that they were running close to time, but the responsibility was the colonel's, and Stark was confident the stoic Air Force man would do what was necessary for them both. Stark had not yet seen enough through the windows to draw conclusions about whether the Russians had the capability to insert the formula from here, but on the basis of the NASA earth-station dish alone, he guessed they could.

The colonel probably had moved in closer to the hacienda, Stark thought, emerging from behind the wide leaves of a stubby banana tree.

As he ran toward the side of the hacienda, Stark suddenly began to worry. There was no sign of Stone anywhere. He had expected a whistle or yell, or more likely, a sudden tap on the shoulder from behind. Instead, nothing.

At the window, Stark knelt on one knee. When he saw the musette bag, he suddenly froze. The blood was sticky and red-black, caked by the sun. Flies buzzed in a frenzy. All of a sudden, he felt terribly depressed; another dead person as a result of what he'd done. He reached down with his hand, but was revulsed by the blood. He couldn't touch the radio. It horrified him.

He closed his eyes and thought. Now it made more sense to run, to put as much distance between himself and whatever was happening inside the hacienda. What could he do on his own, anyway, but continue to foul things up?

As he was rising from his knee to leave, he heard the low groan of the F-4E, a speck circling high above him. At least he could do this one thing. He again reached for the radio, and he saw the stainless tube of the flare. He picked it up and examined it. There was a D ring with a safety cotter, like the pin on a hand grenade. A red tag was attached to it. He pulled at the tag, and the cotter slid easily out of the restraining holes. He planted the tube firmly in the soft earth, insuring that the open end was pointing skyward, then he yanked the D ring. The flare fizzled at first, rapidly building a burn for expulsion from the tube, and then with a loud report, it blasted in the air. Stark crouched and looked up. Several seconds passed, and he could see the exhaust trail forming an erratic pattern in the blue sky. The flare exploded in a brilliant white-phosphorous starburst and could be seen for miles.

Stark turned his eye from the flare. The jet broke its pattern, and Stark forced air from his lungs in a sigh.

The F-4E shot out of the sky, reheat afterburners howling, its delta wings bristling with armament. The jet spun once to form a line with the target, then at the apogee of its dive, it swung hard up. The flame of its turbofans glowed an angry orange. On its belly, an AGM-65 Maverick was released from the restraints. It seemed to hang in the air. The missile spurted to life, the laser sensor in its snub nose fixed on a light track to the white dish. Stark watched, fascinated, as the missile shifted trajectory, then locked in. It sped downward, then leveled.

An explosion on the fort's parapet demolished the base of

the white dish, which rose from its supports and scaled through the air for ten or fifteen feet, then crashed down the crumbled masonry of the fort's wall. The sound of the explosion and the disintegrating dish echoed off the hacienda wall. Seconds later, a servant dashed from the front door and stared at the fort. Shrugging, he went back inside.

When Stark saw the door close again, he sprang to his feet. Anyplace, he thought, it didn't matter where. He now had to run as far away as possible. Just as he began to take the first step, something smashed his skull behind his right ear. His mind swam as he crumpled to the ground. His only thought was that he was going to die.

1:45 P.M., EDT: Washington, D.C.

In the Situation Room, the President let out an uncharacteristic yell. None of the military brass by his side said a word, but to a man they smiled broadly. The pilot of the F-4E had just reported a successful mission.

"Okay, put me through now," the President ordered, his joy short-lived. He hoped to defuse Duvalier's inevitable anger by reaching the Haitian President before he knew about the bombing. The recipient of a fait accompli was often more inclined to be reasonable.

When Duvalier came on the line, his voice was loaded with suspicion and mistrust. "Qu'est-ce que vous voulez?" he asked without diplomatic preamble.

He sounded like a petulant child, thought the President. He explained, "We took every available precaution, including the landing of two technicians, who determined that the Russians indeed had the capability to destroy our computer systems. We had no real choice. We had to destroy that earth station for our own very critical security reasons." Without allowing the Haitian President to interject anything, he went on: "Of course there will be reparations, and our two governments will draw much closer together, if that is also your desire." The President thought he heard the young Haitian leader conferring with someone nearby. "I need to ask one more favor. Will you allow us to consolidate our operation by landing two platoons of commandos? They are standing by right now over your northern border in a C-130." It would be difficult for the Haitian to refuse. The President turned to the general in charge of the Situation Room and asked, his hand cuffed on the telephone, "Shouldn't we have heard from the colonel by now?"

The general nodded. "His instructions were to communicate with the F-4E, which would retransmit to us. Perhaps something happened to the radio." He realized an explanation was in order. "Remember, the *colonel* signaled the F-4E with the flare."

"Could something have gone wrong?"

The general shrugged. "I can only read it as a success, sir. They reconnoitered and called in the strike. With the dish gone, the Russians are dead in the water. I shouldn't worry."

Since coordination was still an unknown, there would be serious concern until the colonel or Rousseau made contact. The hunter-killers had not destroyed all the satellites in the INTELSAT chain, and the eclipse now bathed the remaining two in darkness. The President uncupped the receiver. "Yes, Mr. President," he said, over the Haitian's hysterical objections. "I understand, just as I hope you understand what our position is." This was getting neither of them anywhere. "Do you agree to my request?"

"NON," came the reply.

The President sighed. He would have to wait until the colonel communicated. If the Blue Light force was required, he would order them in, and damn Baby Doc.

3:46 P.M., AT: Cap-Haïtien, Haiti

"Get up!"

The voice sounded as if it had come from the farthest end of a long, dark tunnel. Stark felt the dull crack of a hand across his cheekbone.

" 'Get up!' I said."

Stark didn't want to wake up, let alone obey the command. There was peace in this sleep. It made no demands for decisions and softly walled off a fear he knew would prevail with the opening of his eyes. He dreamed that he was floating in water. The pleasing warmth of the sun made his skin tingle. There was no one and nothing in sight, and for that moment he basked in solitude. Then a girl appeared. Merrill! She was smiling and he saw through the shimmering blue of the water that she was naked. He said to her, "Let's never leave here. I want to stay forever." She smiled again, and he knew that she wanted that, too.

"Get up, damn you!"

Reluctantly, Stark opened his eyes, blinked. Without lifting his head from the floor, he took in everything. Even through the daze he knew that he and the colonel—all of them—had failed. He was inside a computer room. Domintrin was standing at a terminal. Borznoi, with his back turned, was looking out the window toward the fort. Back to the terminal: A yellow tape hung from the hasp. It was the formula. Ready for transmission. But that couldn't be! Stark thought. The earth station was destroyed. He had seen it happen. He had issued the order!

Why was all this equipment here? he wondered. It was a complete facility. Within their limit of time, the Russians could not have assembled it so fast. Then he remembered. This was Thornton's house, the hacienda he cared enough about to have its portrait hanging over the mantel in the house on Beacon Hill. He must have spent many months here, at one time.

The barrel of a pistol entered Stark's field of vision, inches from his face. He raised his eyes from its ugly stubbiness and was looking directly into the face of Alexi Borznoi, who put the barrel under his chin. Stark shivered at its coldness.

"Get on your feet," Borznoi said.

Unsteadily, Stark did as he was told. He wanted to beg Borznoi not to hurt him, but he knew it was too late for that. He said, "Nobody cares anymore. We've stopped you."

Borznoi laughed. "You don't give me much credit," he said.

"You can save yourselves," Stark said. "A strike force is landing any minute. They'll destroy this place."

An alarm on the wall sounded. On a black-faced clock the sweep second hand stopped at twelve. The time was exactly 3:47 P.M., and Stark had to think for an instant before he remembered its significance: The shadow of the eclipse had now enveloped the entire satellite chain. The transponders in the remaining satellites were grinding to a stop. The data-feed components were now at their most vulnerable.

Borznoi looked at the clock, then kneeled down beside Stark. He called to Domintrin and handed him the pistol. "If he moves, pull the trigger," he said in Russian.

Domintrin pulled back the hammer with his thumb and pressed the barrel against Stark's forehead. Stark noticed that the weapon shook in the scientist's hand. Borznoi bound Stark's hands behind him. Then, forcing him into a bowed position on his stomach, he strung the cord from his hands to his ankles. Why hadn't they seemed to hear him? It was as though they didn't know about the earth station. They must have heard the explosion, though.

"The dish is destroyed!" Stark shouted. "You're *helpless.* You can escape!"

Borznoi threw back his head and laughed. Then: "Is the tape ready?" he asked Domintrin, who nodded yes.

"Let's begin."

"You can't," Stark said. "It's useless."

"Please begin, Mr. Domintrin," Borznoi said serenely, then to Stark: "The dish, Dr. Rousseau, was a decoy. We did not expect the attack, of course, but we were prepared, anyway."

The tape started to feed through the hasp into the computer.

"I don't understand," Stark said.

Borznoi watched the tape for an instant and turned to Rousseau. "We needed these computers, according to Domintrin. But our transmission point is miles away—in Cuba, across the water. You don't think that America is the only country with earth stations? No, of course you don't."

Stark saw clearly now what they had done. Borznoi and Domintrin needed these computers. The Russians and certainly the Cubans had nothing as sophisticated. But the big white dish on the fort was a decoy, which meant that they were transmitting the formula from Haiti, where they were now, across the Windward Passage to Cuba. And Cubans did have the communications equipment to relay the formula to the satellites. The Russians had not gone directly to Cuba because they needed Thornton's computers. How clever Borznoi had been, Stark thought, almost admiringly. While Borznoi worked at Thornton's house, he learned about the hacienda and what equipment it contained. His curiosity had probably been raised by the sight of the painting over the mantel.

Stark had lost. They all had lost.

"Mr. Borznoi!" Domintrin yelled across the room as he pulled back from the VDT. "The computer reports an error in transmission!"

"Impossible," Borznoi said, bending over to see. He was not certain what the VDT indicated, but he had to trust Domintrin's word now. "Stop the tape," he ordered, then to Stark, "What have you done?"

In that instant as he pondered his answer to the question, Stark realized one possibility of escape. Nearly by accident he had created a means, and he still had a trump to play: He recalled how Domintrin's hand had shaken. Domintrin was a scientist, and he would understand. Stark forced a laugh, then said, "It was the microwave antenna, wasn't it?"

Borznoi came over to him, staring down viciously. "Tell me what you've done," he demanded again.

Stark had to convince Borznoi. And that meant he could not answer his question too willingly. "Tell me first, what is Scorched

Earth?" Borznoi bent closer, waving the gun in Stark's face. Stark goaded him with a smile.

"Please do not hurt him," Domintrin said, standing beside the computer console, his eyes wide with fear.

"Answer my question," Borznoi demanded.

"I thought that you could figure it out," Stark said. "I've already given you the answer." He looked across the room. "Haven't I, Mr. Domintrin?"

Domintrin replied to Borznoi, "He has altered the microwave antenna."

Borznoi looked at both men. He could trust neither of them now, but he needed them more than ever. They were under his ultimate control, and yet they possessed the power to make Scorched Earth fail. He returned his eyes to Stark.

Stark said, "The calibration. You are shooting off-target to Cuba. . . ."

Borznoi pushed him back, speaking hurriedly in Russian to Domintrin. It had come down to this, Stark thought. Domintrin had to remain in the computer room. Borznoi did not possess the technical expertise to do what was necessary. He had to adjust the antenna, following Domintrin's instructions. There was no choice. Saying something more to Domintrin in Russian, then grabbing a two-way portable radio, Borznoi ran from the computer room.

"He's recalibrating it," Domintrin offered, loosely waving the gun in Stark's direction.

"Mr. Domintrin, please cut these," Stark said, glancing at the bonds.

"I can't," he replied. "He'll kill us both." Domintrin wavered for an instant, lowering the pistol, then raising it again with renewed purpose. "Neither of us has a choice, Dr. Rousseau. Unless we do exactly what he asks, we are dead."

No words passed between the two men. Stark tried to assess Domintrin's purpose. He was an unwilling participant, he guessed, against whom his Russian masters must have applied tremendous pressure. He looked confused and frightened of the consequences of failure that probably would reverberate thousands of miles away. Domintrin had tried to conceal from Borznoi his certain awareness of the microwave antenna's alteration in an effort to buy time. If he had been a man of Borznoi's same mentality, he would see now what Stark planned. But Domintrin was benign. Killing, even to save his own life, was alien to his nature. Stark depended on the accuracy of that judgment. "I'll ask you again," Stark said calmly. "Please untie me."

Domintrin lowered the gun, thinking. Borznoi terrified him, not so much for his immediate and direct threats as for what he held in reserve. His deviousness terrified Domintrin; he could never know fully what Borznoi planned. Like now, he thought. Borznoi had stayed within eyesight of Domintrin since he had arrived from Moscow. To separate from him now by leaving the hacienda was inconsistent. And that suggested to Domintrin something fearful and unexpected. He thought for a moment longer, then, as he was about to move closer to Stark, the radio crackled.

"Come in, Domintrin," Borznoi said in Russian. "Give me the instructions."

Domintrin turned back to the communications console, lowering his eye into a simple beam-fixing camera. He pressed the "transmit" button on his walkie-talkie; then, thinking of a better approach, he went to the window, which commanded a clear view of the water tank. He saw Borznoi standing at the right rim of the microwave antenna.

"We will get your family out!" Stark said. "I promise you. Our government will not let them be harmed."

Domintrin turned and looked at Rousseau, sadly. "I'm afraid it's too late," he said softly.

"Think of what you are destroying," Stark said. "It's everything you worked to accomplish. We will all suffer. Please, you must . . ."

Domintrin looked at the beam fixer. He said into the walkie-talkie, "Gently move the dish three inches away from you, Mr. Borznoi. Gently, and put no downward pressure on it."

"We will get your family out," Stark pleaded, again. "I will use all my resources."

Domintrin held the gun on Stark. *"Please* don't make me kill you."

Borznoi did not understand how the microwave antenna worked, though he knew that the formula would run through the computer and into the coaxial cable that led from the computer to the microwave dish, which would transmit the formula across the Windward Passage to a receiving microwave dish in Cuba. From there it would be linked with a big earth station and transmitted up to the INTELSAT series. But he didn't understand the line-of-sight requirements of the microwave. Had they miscalculated, or had Domintrin plotted this very error?

Borznoi reached up and touched the edge of the dish, then ordered Domintrin to guide him.

Borznoi thought about the boat now. Thornton's forty-foot *Hatteras* had been fueled and now was standing ready at the Cap-Haïtien pier. He calculated that the trip to Cape Maisi in Cuba would take just over an hour. Then, and only then, he would be home free. Scorched Earth would be a success, and he, Alexi Borznoi, would be responsible for that success.

The dish moved slightly to the left under the pressure of his hands.

Stark watched Domintrin's gun hand waver as he turned from the window. He had softened Domintrin with other arguments, and now they had reached a critical point. Stark knew that Domintrin would listen. More than that, he knew that the Russian scientist would believe.

"If you go through with this your family will die, anyway," he said. "That is the truth."

Domintrin glanced out the window, then back at Stark. "What do you mean?" he asked.

The trump was played. "Our ICBM force could be triggered by what you are doing," he said. "The fire control is on line with the satellites." No further explanation was needed, Stark knew. Domintrin would understand.

Domintrin winced in reply, thinking suddenly of his multiple duties and responsibilities. Rousseau was talking of war and annihilation. Perhaps this was a bluff, but there was not time to discover the truth. What was he doing, anyway, he thought? Even if Rousseau was lying, what guarantee did he have? How long would he remain in favor before he again was perceived as an enemy of the state? If the formula succeeded and Scorched Earth became a fact, the Directorate—Dolowsky—would again demand of him more than he could produce. He would be pushed to achieve a technological parity with the Americans. And since that was impossible, again, he would be back where he started . . . how long ago was it? A month? On the missile range east of the Urals? He looked at Stark and asked, "And you are certain?"

Stark shook his head slowly. He would not exaggerate now. There was no need to embellish on the truth. "The odds are against it happening," he said. "But the possibility is very real. You must believe that. The choice is yours, Mr. Domintrin. Are you willing to risk the consequences?"

Domintrin did not hesitate. He dropped the pistol to the floor, then came over and bent down to untie Stark. "Do what you must," he said.

Free from the bonds, Stark said, "Tell him you can't find the correct calibration. Stall him." Stark went to the computer terminal and released the hasp, then reinserted the tape. "It doesn't matter now," he said, "just get him in front of the antenna. Position him in the beam channel. I'll do the rest."

Domintrin gasped, now understanding what Stark planned to do.

"It's the only way," Stark said. "Tell me when to start transmission."

Domintrin spoke Russian into the two-way radio. Ten seconds passed. Stark concentrated on the transmit switch. Domintrin watched the water tower, then again spoke into the radio.

"NOW!" he yelled.

As Stark hit the transmit switch, the tape streamed into the computer. He ran to the window and watched the water tower as though it were a gallows.

The high-energy impulses pinned Borznoi against the rail. A hole the diameter of a finger, then of a fist, burned into his chest. White smoke billowed up his back as his shirt caught fire. The data burst—the formula—was searing his flesh, consuming his lungs and heart.

Borznoi's arms flayed at the air as he tried in his last desperate seconds of life to move from the beam's path. Tearing at the air, his back arched grotesquely as he plummeted to the ground.

Stark ripped the tape from the hasp.

The formula was dead.

TUESDAY, JUNE 30, 1987

"The experts who say there is no totally effective way to stop computer [penetration] are wrong. One guaranteed method is to pull the plug . . ."

LEONARD KRAUSS *and*
AILEEN MACGAHAN,
Computer Fraud and
Countermeasures

4:15 P.M., *EDT: Marblehead, Massachusetts*

"I should be going now," Stark said.

"Oh, land's sake alive, stay a minute longer," Claudette said, waving at the air with her arm. "I haven't seen you in the longest time. And I still don't understand all this foolishness you've been telling me."

Claudette was propped up on her bed, against a mound of pillows. No longer flat on her back, she rarely reflected on the ceiling crack, choosing instead to take an interest in other patients, some of whom she visited in the new wheelchair that she could propel herself.

Claudette was really not so much interested in hearing her son's adventures one more time. That was an excuse, and she barely believed the story, anyway. But she was curious. She sensed a change in Stark—subtle and tentative for sure, but nevertheless a change. She had mixed feelings about it, but knew she had better adjust. Stark had been quite unabashed in describing his feelings toward the girl. Even if he had not been so forthright, she would have recognized a difference in his eyes, a shining that she knew to be love.

"A minute . . . then I must go," he said to her.

"Do you think . . . you might marry her?" she asked in a tentative voice.

Grinning widely, he said, "I really don't know yet. It's too soon to think about that."

"Stark, in some ways I hate to say this. But she seems good for you."

Stark was pleased by her unselfish reaction, and smiled. "There's so much for me to get straightened out right now," he said. "One thing I realize: Intelligence isn't everything."

"It couldn't have been helped," she said, not wanting him to shoulder all the blame. "You implied as much yourself."

"Mother, I was impetuous. I have to learn patience before

I shoulder anything as serious as marriage." Stark lapsed into silence for a minute. Then he continued, "Mother, I'm going to take some time off from the Labs."

"To do what?" she asked.

He shrugged. "I don't have the slightest idea." And then he laughed. "It's been too much of my life for too long. If I had some perspective I would have acted differently. Maybe if I get out and explore the way Byron did, I won't be so shortsighted. I don't really know any other world except the Labs, which was why I thought a formula or theory would never interest anybody, except maybe other mathematicians. Merrill and I have talked about taking a trip. We're going to start out this weekend, in fact—we're going to have a reunion in New York City with Harry Verdeen—you know, the fellow who saved Merrill. He's quite a guy, and who knows, maybe he can teach me some of his patience." Stark laughed. "We talked on the phone last night with him and he threatened to take us to every country-and-western place in the city—there're more in New York now than in Houston, to hear Harry speak."

Suddenly concerned for herself, Claudette asked, "But what about me?"

"You'll be fine, Mother," he replied. "We won't be gone long, and when we return, I'll have to think about finding you a place to stay."

"You mean I'll leave Wainwright?" Nobody had mentioned it to her.

"That's what Dr. DeAngelis says. You will never regain full use of your legs, but you can get around easily, he says, on crutches and a wheelchair."

She smoothed the sheet over her. "Won't that be wonderful," she remarked, a little afraid. Then, "I guess we all have little adjustments to make."

He got up to leave, saying, "Always. From now on, anyway." He bent to kiss her on the cheek, then smiling at her, he said good-bye and silently disappeared.

Claudette sighed at the thought of what she was losing.

RFTERWORD

In August 1980, IBM formally requested Congress to provide their computer technicians with statutory exemptions in the event of gas rationing. The corporation's rationale: Unless their computers are maintained, the country will rapidly grind to a halt.

ACKNOWLEDGMENTS

I must thank James Martin for the invaluable information in his books *Communications Satellite Systems, Security, Accuracy and Privacy in Computer Systems,* and *The Computerized Society* (with Adrian Norman). I was aided in my research by J. Mack Adams and Douglas H. Haden's *Social Effects of Computer Use and Misuse,* by *The Encyclopedia of Ignorance,* and by Leonard I. Krauss and Aileen Macgahan's *Computer Fraud and Countermeasures.*

In writing this novel, I borrowed liberally from these sources, using their research and scientific data for my own fictional purposes without regard to the authors' accuracy of scientific fact. As anyone with a knowledge of computers or satellites can immediately tell, I distorted descriptions of scientific hardware and its use for narrative purposes. No such program as Stark Rousseau's invalid combination exists. ECHO indeed writes computer poetry, but it did not create Merrill's poem. ELIZA, a truly interesting program, does not have the capacity to "search" an individual's personal background or psyche.

In addition to these authors, a large debt is owed to Larry and Nadia Collins for their enthusiasm and helpful criticism; to Lord and Lady St. Just, for their warm friendship and *cold* chauffeur's cottage. Last of all, more gratitude than I can express is due Paul DeAngelis, senior editor at E. P. Dutton, a friend with a wonderful imagination and playful mind who shepherded this book from initial idea over hill and dale to completion.